T0149576

KRONOS REVIVAL

KRONOS REVIVAL

RICHARD G. OSWALD

KRONOS REVIVAL

Copyright © 2016 Sharen Oswald.

All rights reserved. No part of this book may be used or reproduced by any means,
graphic, electronic, or mechanical, including photocopying, recording, taping or by
any information storage retrieval system without the written permission of the author
except in the case of brief quotations embodied in critical articles and reviews.

This is a work of fiction. All of the characters, names, incidents, organizations, and dialogue
in this novel are either the products of the author's imagination or are used fictitiously.

iUniverse books may be ordered through booksellers or by contacting:

iUniverse
1663 Liberty Drive
Bloomington, IN 47403
www.iuniverse.com
1-800-Authors (1-800-288-4677)

Because of the dynamic nature of the Internet, any web addresses or links contained in
this book may have changed since publication and may no longer be valid. The views
expressed in this work are solely those of the author and do not necessarily reflect the
views of the publisher, and the publisher hereby disclaims any responsibility for them.

Any people depicted in stock imagery provided by Thinkstock are models,
and such images are being used for illustrative purposes only.
Certain stock imagery © Thinkstock.

ISBN: 978-1-5320-1226-6 (sc)
ISBN: 978-1-5320-1227-3 (e)

Library of Congress Control Number: 2016919994

Print information available on the last page.

iUniverse rev. date: 12/09/2016

Dad and Mom at the museum in Gettysburg.

With his grandson at the Gettysburg Cyclorama.

"Life- like the time-space continuum is not a river, swift and strong, but rather a capricious maelstrom with thousands of eddies and violent storms. At the end is calm, every time."

-Dad

After my dad died, I opened up his first novel, *The Kronos Conspiracies*, and I found this quote on the inside cover of the copy he had given me years ago. The quote seems so fitting and omniscient. It truly makes me miss his calm strength and wisdom.

After my dad's unexpected passing this spring, my family has decided to publish his recently finished novel, the sequel to *The Kronos Conspriacies,* as he had originally intended. He enjoyed history and science fiction, and this novel is a combination of both. Just last year, I was on a bus trip to Gettysburg that my father hosted for our local school. His enthusiasm and knowledge of the history of Gettysburg is something that will always be a part of me and many others who encountered his wisdom. His love of Gettysburg and Pennsylvania history truly show in this book, and serve as an additional memory for those who experience it.

Kronos Revival is a tribute to my dad, a tribute to his love of history and storytelling. We love you and miss you, Dad.

FOREWORD

ANY TIME A reader picks up a book, he or she should be able to understand in a reasonable length of time what is happening with characters and plot. Unfortunately, when one starts out with the sequel to a previous work, it normally takes some time to catch up. In essence, this is the case with *The Kronos Revival* that proceeds from a former work, *The Kronos Conspiracies.*

Like its predecessor, *The Kronos Revival* is a story of time travel and the interactions of its characters, both real and fictional, from various periods of history through which the characters journey. In the original work, Kronos International Time Excursions, an organization composed of top scientists-- archaeologists, historians, engineers, computer programmers, and technicians—had developed a basic method of sending individuals back into the past and then retrieving them. The Kronos experiments had originally evolved from the discovery that one woman, Thelma Thayer, possessed natural time traveling powers, inherited through the generations of her ancestors from as long ago as anyone could trace. It was not surprising to Thelma when she eventually realized her granddaughter Lydia Thayer had inherited the same abilities as her grandmother.

It was the sincere hope at Kronos that they could not only use Thelma Thayer's ability to develop a computer model by which they could duplicate the time travel process themselves, but also improve on the efficiency and safety of those who might attempt time transfers. For example, scientists at Kronos were able to successfully program a surgically-implanted universal language interpretor and translator

(ULIT) in their group of selected finalists for their first time venture that was able to understand and replicate speech in any of thousands of languages. Another sector of Kronos, using combined technologies from a number of places, came up with a body armor, Komodo, that was not only extremely effective, but comfortable and virtually undetectable as well. These and other state-of-the-art twenty-first century improvements served the mission of Kronos quite well in safely maintaining a crew in the First Century.

The first Kronos team had been intensely trained in a secret underground facility in an isolated region in the mountains of West Virginia where the final squad of three had been pared from nearly two dozen well-qualified prospects. Bill Thayer, the son of Thelma Thayer and father of Lydia, was named the captain of the team. Bill, it was discovered, had not inherited the time travel abilities of Thelma or Lydia, much to the chagrin of the people at Kronos, but had somehow come to possess an almost eerie understanding of any known languages. That, along with his implanted ULIT device, proved extremely valuable to the mission. Mel Currier,adept in a wide variety of endeavors, was a former football player, selected in large part due to his valorous military record in Iraq and Afghanistan, as well as his physical stature and athleticism. Kathryn Spahr's expertise and dedication in her medical career and her practical experiences in that field, proved a deciding factor toward awarding her the last selection on the Kronos team.

Once transported into the first century, Thayer, Currier, and Spahr, disguised as foreign ambassadors, proceeded on the initial Kronos mission into Biblical Mid East to verify the reality of the Nativity of Christ. Incidentally they came to befriend some of the locals, in particular a tradesman landowner known to them as Ara.

The mission was soon complicated when Manning Jones, a former billionaire sponsor of the Kronos program, financed an intervention, corrupting former disillusioned Kronos candidates who had recently been cut from their training program. Jones' plan, it was discovered, was intended to affect radical changes in history that would eventually enhance his own power and wealth in the twenty-first century. Manning Jones ended up joining forces with the infamous (and quite insane)

King Herod in a plot to deform history by preventing the child Jesus from being born to enable events that might dramatically influence the development of mankind just to enhance his own ego and financial enrichment. Two of Jones' recruits, Olivia Pelser and Trinia Williams eventually defected back to the Kronos team once they figured out the billionaire's demented plans. Both of these women later proved significant figures in foiling Jones' warped plans.

Pelser and Williams, along with Mel Currier and Bill Thayer risk becoming stranded in the past, but hold out hope that they would eventually be rescued by Kronos extraction team. It turns out, some of the time travelers are able to return to the future but they spend nearly five years in the first century before Kronos, after a difficult search, can return for them.

Meanwhile, Thayer's wife and daughter, Cheryl and Lydia, themselves become whisked into Renaissance Italy inadvertently through Lydia's developing time travel powers where they have adventures of their own with some of the masters of the Renaissance including DaVinci and Michelangelo. Most of the major characters finally end up in Pompeii where their fate is decided where rescue teams from the twenty first century finally arrive.

PROLOGUE

I T WAS NEVER my intention to ever again return to the past.

The recent mission assigned to me by Anton Lueenhuik and Marge Paladin, directors at Kronos International Time Excursions, had almost killed me and my friends, or at the very least nearly left us hopelessly stranded, in the First Century Roman Empire at the time of Christ. The sense of adventure itself at first had lured me into it, but in the nearly five years I was marooned there, I eventually developed a more sane sense of personal maturity. Originally I had selfish reasons to participate in the time jump as well. My whole life had been rather aimless. I had been bequeathed a hefty inheritance from my parents, whom I was led to believe had been killed in an accident, but the money from the inheritance was actually set up to be distributed through a trust account for me and my family in increments as it was deemed as needed until I satisfied the requirements formulated by my parents. The only stipulation of their will was that I make something of myself. My parents knew what I was like, and in their absence, had designed a program for me that would force me to improve my self-image and sense of responsibility. I had tried for awhile, but, not having much motivation, never found anything that truly interested me. I was in the process of beginning to proceed with my lazy drift that would most likely not only have endangered my future with not only the loss of the inheritance, but the apparent resulting disintegration of the admiration of my wife and daughter for me as well. The Kronos opportunity came up at just the right time.

Don't get me wrong. Lots of good things came from the expedition. The friendships I developed with my co-time travelers are treasures in themselves. Kathryn Spahr and Mel Currier, the two other Kronos recruits, became extremely close to me, and even though I had never served in the military, I think I grew to understand the camaraderie military men engaged in war fostered among those on whom they could rely in any situation--to cover their back-- when things got tough. We were in many respects soldiers in that regard. Today, those two individuals hold prominent positions in our society, enhanced to some extent from their shared experiences with me in the time-space continuum. I believe my situation has improved in that regard as well.

There were other time travelers as well, in particular, the New Crew recruited by the billionaire Manning Jones, to thwart our operation. Two of them, Trinia Williams and Olivia Pelser came to realize the errors of trusting in Jones' cunning manipulations, and in the end, became valued allies to our cause. The struggles we all shared in that venture cemented an unbreakable bond between us that we could never forget. And just the happiness that came from a satisfactory conclusion to the project --the defeat of the malicious forces against us, the struggle for our very survival, and the understanding gained of some of the actual people who lived in that time--left us with a definite feeling of personal accomplishment.

The people at Kronos were hard-working, dedicated scientists, who for the most part, held the good of society as their unselfish, ultimate goal. Anton Lueenhuik and Marge Paladin were like the parents that had been lost to me since my youth. They had, along with my mother and dad, developed and experimented with time travel for years and had searched diligently all over the world for a staff who were talented and trustworthy and who held the same altruistic ideals as they did. Unfortunately, people in the world of science, though geniuses in their field, are seldom good judges of character, and some of their choices, nearly resulted in the demise of the whole program and many of the people in it.

John Dodsworth was, himself, a complete study in applied human psychology. A gifted computer genius, he was credited with single-handedly creating the only workable program that could run the Kronos time travel pods without the assistance of natural time jumpers. After John's paranoiac betrayal that allowed Manning Jones access to the Kronos time travel mission, he reconsidered his actions and reversed his allegiances back to Kronos and our mission, eventually redeeming himself by committing the ultimate personal sacrifice, transporting himself and Jones' malevolent army of societal dredges back somewhere into some vague, irretrievable past.

Another thing that happened, probably the most vital fact of all, was that I discovered my family had passed a special talent along through their genes from one generation to another--the ability to go back into time and return safely to the present. It was apparently only the females that were able to utilize the inherited trait even though the gene was passed through the males as well. My mother, Thelma Thayer, had developed this ability long before I was born, and after cooperating in experiments at Kronos, John Dodsworth, as previously mentioned, was able to develop a computer-aided transfer of his own designed from the electronic input of my mother's brain waves. When I unknowingly participated in the Kronos Mission, I was informed by Kronos of mom's prior value to the research before she had apparently mysteriously disappeared with my father in a time travel experiment. Later I actually came to find that my parents had not really died but were actually in hiding in order to avoid further misuse of my mother's abilities. Much more illuminating to me was that I eventually found that my daughter, Lydia, had inherited the time travel trait as her grandmother and had been secretly using it from the time she was around ten years old, and more shockingly, that she had accidentally transported her mother into Renaissance Italy and was unable to retrieve her!

Things eventually worked out, but because of Kronos and my friends, my whole life was changed immensely. The time travel adventure had been extremely challenging and emotionally draining and had soured me, at least temporarily, with the idea of pursuing time travel ever again.

1

AT THE EDGE of the swamp, a very large, scaled crocodile-like reptile had emerged like a gigantic beached log lying motionless staring with unblinking gold-slitted eyes at John Dodsworth. John seemed only casually impressed with the creature's enormity, and he examined it with a professional curiosity. The creature appeared to be all of thirty feet in length, its massive head taking in about six of those feet itself and sporting rows of bone-crushing teeth in its smiling jaws. Dodsworth balled up a Hershey bar wrapper he had just licked clean of warm, melted chocolate and indifferently tossed it at the unblinking animal.

From across the marsh, a cacophony of automatic weapon fire suddenly thundered and rattled breaking the solitude of Dodsworth's soliloquy with the reptile he had encountered at the water's edge. In seconds a rush of small flying creatures streamed madly over the open water before him.

"Sounds like a bit of trouble out there, Mr. Sarcosuchus Imperator," Dodsworth whispered softly as if to console the massive creature that had just blinked once at the sound of the gunfire. With a wry smile, John could visualize the trouble that might be befalling Manning Jones and his band of cutthroats across the bog.

"My guess is velociraptors," John continued. "In any event, they've finally met some carnivores, I suspect."

The giant Jurassic crocodile appeared unimpressed with the rhetoric of this strange being that appeared a short distance in front of him, apparently unafraid. That was the only thing that kept the man from being devoured instantly since this animal was seldom challenged as the undisputed ruler in this marshy jungle domain. Even the larger reptiles in this steamy region were wary near these waters where he often lay in ambush. The reptile's muscles now tensed, prepared to lunge at this insolent being and end any defiance to its authority. Just at the last moment, his prey was reprieved.

There were only a few hazy ripples against the green-fern backdrop, like a mirage of distorted heat waves one might see on the roadway on a hot summer day. Then two images began to form--two images much like the one that stood staunchly fearless before the great beast. The two helmeted man-figures materialized more solidly in a few short moments and stood with feet at shoulder width and wielding a short-snouted device that was carried as a man might hold a rifle and pointing it at the beast about to launch itself at John Dodsworth.

With a bright blue bolt of laser light and a resounding harsh snap, the crocodile creature left the earth, involuntarily twisting into a great U-shape in mid air, and then descending motionless with a dull thud onto the muddy shoreline of the swamp.

Dodsworth showed more emotion now than he had over the whole recent experience as he rushed to the side of the creature's body, and dropped to one knee near its quivering form.

"C! He's not dead is he? He's such a magnificent example of the sarcosuchus crocodiles found in this region of Jurassic Italy."

"Just stunned, John. You know I wouldn't hurt anyone or anything I didn't have to," answered the man who had materialized from the recent distorted waves that had mysteriously appeared near him. "These lasers developed by Higby are quite effective, you know."

"Yes, yes I know, C. I was somewhat instrumental in their development myself if you remember."

The other man-form accompanying the shooter, now advanced, touting a similar laser weapon identical to the one the other had just utilized to stun the great beast, and deftly slipped a glistening silver hockey-style helmet, over the silver-haired head of a woman who obviously displayed a serious and resolute demeanor.

"Are you all right, John?" the woman inquired firmly.

"I'm all right, Thelma. You guys did shave it a little close though. For a few seconds, I figured I might end up as this guy's supper."

"Have we ever let you down before, John?" chided the man good-naturedly.

"No, but I didn't want this to be the first time either!" John was still impressively distracted by the awesome animal that lay stunned by Cecil Thayer's laser wand. "You know, judging from the scale pattern on his tail, this one is a young one. There are probably some bigger specimens around here."

Again gunshots echoed through the forest breaking off the monotonous high drone of insect sounds, causing the two newcomers to start. This time, though, the number of shots, John calculated, was significantly diminished. As before, small flying creatures darted by in panic, but even this event was not so pronounced.

"That's Jones' men. I suspect they won't last too much longer," Dodsworth assured his saviors. "Good riddance to a bunch who have no redeeming social value."

"Let's get out of here. I know they're a bunch of criminals, but I'd rather not stand by idly and witness their demise, Cecil," said Thelma. "It was always my hope that Mr. Jones might actually be rehabilitated …"

"John, are you ready? There's no reason to hang around is there?" Cecil rolled his eyes at his wife's comments.

John Dodsworth had a faraway look in his eyes when he answered. "This is like Heaven to me, C. You know this was always my favorite era in the world's development. I think I like it because there aren't any people--at least until we got here that is. Did you get a chance to see the brachiosaurus Jones' men killed …?" John casually pointed with his thumb over his shoulder toward the underbrush about a hundred yards away.

"Well I don't know about you, but you say this croc over here is just a baby. I don't want to be here when his daddy or mommy comes looking for him. My laser was on full stun for him. I don't think we have the inclination for a tour of Jurassic life right now," rasped Cecil Thayer as he scanned the nearby rippling surface of the bog.

Thelma tried to look sympathetic to Dodsworth's cause, but her eyes danced nervously as she spoke. "Don't worry, John. I promise you, if you really want to, we'll arrange for you to visit this era again sometime later after we get things settled, of course."

John looked at the just-reviving giant crocodile sorrowfully and joined his rescuers on the rise of land at the island's center, linked hands, placed his head together with theirs, and at once melted back to the future with them.

2

THE SURF RUMBLED in and washed softly ashore along the sandy beach while gulls dipped aimlessly from the bright azure skies. The green, transparent waters of the remote lagoon lipped and splashed gently along the dark ring of the coral reef on its perimeter. This private resort on Cat Lick Island was a treasured retreat away from interruption for those who could afford its special isolation.

Cheryl Thayer casually wiggled her sand-coated toes, lazily surveying the rolling swells of the Caribbean through her half-closed eyes. Sweet coconut oil scents wafted on the salty breezes drifting in from the ocean. Cheryl loved the mindlessness of these secluded beaches where her unlabored thoughts could drift along on their own without fear of any outside expectation. This afternoon as loose wisps of her tightly-curled blond hair whipped disobediently from under the floppy brim of her straw bonnet, protesting the sudden change in sea breezes, she sat forward on her beach towel, her lithe, bronzed arms tightly cradling her upraised knees.

"Angels," Cheryl whispered.

"Huh?"

I was lying on the blanket beside Cheryl, propping my head on a rolled up towel against a small green cooler containing two cold Coronas. My wife assumed I was napping. A paperback, an unfinished copy of *The Tell*, sat carelessly like a miniature A-frame, on my lap, my fingers intertwined in the black loops of my chest hair, but from behind my chromed Polaroid lenses, my eyes furtively drank in my wife's soft body lines perfectly enhancing the tiny white bikini I had insisted she purchase for herself at Freeport two days previously.

"The clouds look like angels today, Bill."

"Oh, yeah, right, just like angels."

Cheryl was a bit younger than I was, having met me as a freshman at Garnet University shortly after I had just entered the graduate program there. Our friends said we were opposites, and of course, opposites are said to attract, and we were resultantly engaged and married within a year. She was the pretty, perky blond girl that talked incessantly often without much direction, and yet everyone seemed to take to her upon first meeting. I had always referred to her as "my Gracie Allen" the oft dim-witted sidekick of George Burns on the reruns of the old George Burns Comedy Show. The truth was, she not only looked a lot like Gracie, but acted like her as well. I, on the other hand, was always more serious and had a difficult time with first impressions. Once people got to know me, though, I believe their friendships with me usually became solid. I was more academic--loved history and was extraordinarily gifted with languages. This gift was enhanced greatly by the ULIT translator I had implanted at Kronos. My daughter Lydia was like that too. She was extraordinary with picking up virtually any language she heard. That, along with her own special ability that will be developed later, made for a very special young lady. My wife Cheryl, had none of those gifts and yet passed successfully through her collegiate experience, but most people suspected her grades were a result of her bubbly personality combined with a sufficient dose of my help rather than her own intellect.

I felt I had finally become satisfied with my life. Most of my forty years had been spent searching for the elusive man inside. Despite being eminently qualified for many positions and careers, I had elected to hop from job to job, searching for the perfect niche in my life, a task I had found formidable indeed. It was not until my recent association with Kronos International that I took the steps to discover who I really was and to finally develop a better relationship with my wife and daughter, Lydia.

"Bill, you awake?" Cheryl sighed as she watched high, puffy marshmallow clouds slowly scuttle by.

"Of course, Dear," I answered reluctantly, raising my sunglasses. I had actually slightly resented the interruption of my voyeuristic journey. "Just what is it that you want?"

"It's your daughter, Lydia, Bill."

"Yes, Lydia my *only* daughter, Cheryl," I returned somewhat sarcastically.

"Do you suppose she might--you know--think of doing something--something which we might not approve of, I mean?"

"She's going to make her own decisions now, Dear. I hope after what we taught her about morals, she would make the right decisions about men and all …"

"Oh--that too!" Cheryl cut in excitedly. "But I wasn't meaning that stuff. I was talking about her-- her abilities. The time travel stuff she's gotten into."

I was a bit relieved at the realization of Cheryl's inference, but knew the topic of time travel was at least as serious as the one I had assumed was concerning sexual matters. I had given the thought much personal consideration recently now that the excitement from our recent escapades had somewhat dimmed.

"Lydia has given me assurances that she would not be assisting the people at Kronos with their time ventures--at least not until she is given our explicit approval. I've been looking into the records there. As we've spoken previously, neither of us feels Kronos has any evil intentions, but we're not so sure how secure their work is from those who might deal with time travel more selfishly. You remember Manning Jones and how he manipulated things just a few months ago?"

"Oh Bill, I don't think Lyd would violate that trust. She understands the implications of letting bad people get control of her powers. I'm talking about her desire to use her own time travel capabilities without involving outside influences."

I had considered this idea my personal scrutiny for some time, but still struggled with the reality of the answer. For the most part I had attempted to convince myself Lydia would never resume doing this dangerous thing. I was pretty much surprised when I answered the way I did.

"Lydia's been time jumping for years, Cheryl--since her early teens, at least. Most of those jumps were not of her own volition then, and she didn't realize it when she was going to do it." Bill paused for a breath, as though he had just come to a personal realization, but the truth was--he knew the real answer.

"Cheryl, we have to come to the understanding that, even if she intends to comply with our wishes, our daughter is likely to at least return to her personal in-born wanderings in time. I think it would be extremely difficult for her to give them up particularly since she has greatly benefitted from the improved methods and technologies she's had developed for her with Kronos--the language translators, inoculations, the body armor, and such--- that would certainly enhance her own natural talents. I think, just as we have faith in her making her own moral decisions which we just referred to, we must also hope she makes wise decisions in this area as well and doesn't go off gallivanting somewhere through time by herself and maybe getting in serious trouble."

Cheryl wasn't looking at Bill as he spoke and maintained her eyes on the horizon.

"Of course, as always, Bill, you're probably right."

3

IN THE YELLOW half-light of late afternoon, the slight, scruffy-bearded man, a Civil War tintype himself, paused at his massive dark oak desk. Professor Carson Hardwick, head of the Department of Field Studies of Applied Archaeology and a professor of advanced studies in American history at Chicago's Metro University at first gave little attention to the petition he had from a young lady to meet with him for what she had referred to as an urgent situation. Hardwick had often heard these urgent requests made and was rather leery when they were requested by women. Not that the vaunted professor of archaeology had anything against females in general. He had had his share of them throughout most of his life, and in his youth was considered pretty much of a lady's man. Rumors often circulated around him about alleged affairs and clandestine rendezvous--rumors that were difficult to prove, but were, nevertheless, knowing Hardwick's reputation, likely valid. Now, as a more mature gentleman and head of the applied archaeology department in a prestigious institution like Metro University, he could take no chances with his reputation. He made it a point to never be alone in his office with women, or even men for that matter, without the presence of his personal secretary and hidden cameras to verify his innocence in the event of any allegations against his character.

It would have been a simple matter to pass on this appointment, but the magnitude of this particular meeting was intensified when he received a long distance European conference call from two former associates, Anton Lueenhuik and Marge Paladin, that this matter did deserve his immediate attention.

"Miss Thayer is a very special young lady," Lueenhuik remarked firmly. "It is not my place to divulge the contents of her circumstance with you. That will be up to her. But I can only say the information she has is rather remarkable."

"You won't be sorry you listened to her, Carson," added Marge. "I would surmise that your chances of believing her at first will be difficult, but it is to your significant advantage to hear her out."

Hardwick was now more curious about Lydia Thayer than anything else. His past association with Lueenhuik and Paladin in the field during several important digs would normally have been sufficient enough to convince him to follow through with the requested audience with this young lady, in any event, just as a courtesy to his two long time friends. When he hung up, he immediately buzzed, Nancy Yang, his personal secretary and set up a meeting for that afternoon.

About an hour later, Dr. Hardwick's intercom crackled.

"Miss Thayer is here for her appointment with you, Doctor," Nancy pronounced melodically.

"Bring her right in, Miss Yang," he answered.

That was quick thought Hardwick. *She must have been waiting by the phone for my call.*

Certainly Lydia Thayer exuded a rather different presence than any of the female guests with whom he normally scheduled appointments. Hardwick usually found that his women visitors were either elderly, frumpy-looking professors in baggy pant suits and MU blazers with theories to offer or with university problems for him to solve, or else they were very young ladies who thought they might influence the professor with their diverse charms. These women often wore short skirts, low cut blouses, and high heels and always appeared to struggle with the position of their long legs as they sat in the chair in front of his desk. The professor, as most men would, enjoyed their titillating show, but it never affected the outcome of any decision he had to make.

Lydia Thayer briefly stood in the doorway of the Metro University Archaeology Office, her mane of dark brunette curls lying unevenly over her shoulders contrasted against a halo of light in the doorway of Yang's outer office. As Lydia approached the desk of the Archaeology

Department head, he was aware of the stern gaze of her large brown watery eyes set in her deep nutmeg tan. The young girl was dressed as many of the other students at the school, wearing a burgundy Metro U. sweat shirt, loosely-fitted blue jeans, and a well-worn pair of silver-gray Michael Jordan Nike Air women's sneakers.

The archaeology professor had perched himself at his oversized oak desk, itself a contrast of the antique among the tangle of the most recent technology of wires, computers, and other electronic equipment that shared his diverse world. Hardwick studied the youthful figure before him and quickly reassured himself Lydia Thayer certainly fit none of his characterizations of other female visitors to his office.

"Please sit down, make yourself comfortable, Miss Thayer …"

"Just *Lydia*, Professor."

"All right--Lydia--what is it that brings you here? It seems you've turned some mighty important heads to get your way," he kidded lightheartedly.

Lydia's demeanor remained serious, but she smiled politely at his comment.

"It's the … " Here Lydia Thayer pulled out a palm-sized note from which she read slowly and with an attempt at accuracy. " … It's the MU201WP-144 site, Doctor."

Without hesitation, Hardwick instinctively tapped the corresponding keys on his desk top keyboard, and a data-filled screen popped into view.

"Yes, that's the site of the Amerind subculture identification number Z1623 excavation. The one in the western area of Pennsylvania a few miles from the Ohio border, I see. That's the one we've slated for abandonment I understand."

"Yes, yes, that's the one. And that's the problem--you can't abandon that site, sir. It's just too important. We've gotten so much valuable information from that dig. I've been deeply involved personally through this university."

Hardwick scrolled down to a list of names on the screen. "H-mm, yes here's your name on the list of archaeologists--*Lydia Thayer*-- quite impressive. It says here you are the site coordinator--quite a feat for someone so young. Amazing--a freshman! This is normally a position reserved for someone of deeper experience."

"Professor, I'm here to request you change your plan to scrap the project at this site," said Lydia firmly as she stared intently into the older man's eyes.

"Impossible, child, if you are what you claim to be, you have to be aware that this site has been compromised." Hardwick proceeded, reading from the file on his computer screen in a firm, emotionless voice. "Specifically--at exactly 17.4 feet at a depth corresponding with level of the subculture SC835 previously mentioned, we encountered a Code 5580. This refers to some extraneous piece of evidence, an anachronism, obviously planted at a more recent date that does not fit into the era from which it was intended."

Lydia's determined expression had not changed as the professor expounded on the information on the file and simultaneously brought up a color image of the offending material recovered at the site.

"It's a toothpaste tube, Doctor," Lydia rasped. "It's a plastic, partially-depleted tube of Aquafresh Triple Protection toothpaste."

"Precisely! And you realize that that tube of toothpaste had to have been planted by someone--someone who had broken the seal of the dig and deliberately placed that and likely other things into the site at an earlier time. The site has become contaminated, irreversibly violated. No one could any longer ever believe in the authenticity of any data obtained from the dig. Anything we have found up to now must also be invalidated."

"If your premise is accurate, Professor Hardwick, we must assume the 5580 material noted in the report--the toothpaste tube in question, must have been planted there in a period at the present or very-near past. Am I correct?"

"Absolutely, my dear. My point exactly."

"Well, then, there's the rub! You see Professor, that tube of toothpaste was placed there during the time of the existence of the Amerind subculture you have indicated."

Carson Hardwick usually took little joy in maintaining a condescending attitude toward others, even though he often met those to whom he might easily belittle. At this point, though, he was completely overcome with the audacity of this girl who had entered his office and greeted him with a preposterous story about a toothpaste tube being deposited into a site during prehistoric times-- a story which she expected would likely convince him to restore one of her own pet projects. Out of respect for his former archaeologist friends who had somehow been duped with her tale, he attempted to maintain a degree of dignity in his voice as he cast an all-knowing glance over Lydia's shoulder at a smirking Nancy Yang who had been witnessing the discussion unfolding in the office.

"Miss Thayer," he said through clenched teeth, "you expect me to believe this absurd revelation that a twenty-first century tube of toothpaste was actually placed there at this prehistoric Pennsylvania site years before Columbus landed on San Salvador. What could possibly convince me that this could ever happen?"

Lydia Thayer had now stood before Hardwick's desk with the same firm expression she had maintained through the entire visit. Placing both palms on the desk top she leaned forward.

"Professor Hardwick, I tell you this fact as truth. I know it to be true. The toothpaste tube was indeed placed there in the year the Europeans numbered as 1250 AD. And I would know-- because it was actually *I* who was there at that particular time-- and left it there --myself!"

4

Doctor Carson Hardwick had been standing quietly for some time with his back to his young guest who sat for what seemed an eternity at his massive oak desk cluttered with much of his life's memorabilia. He had realized the impact of the forthcoming revelation and then hastily dismissed his secretary, Nancy Yang, and now stared absently out the window down on the sprawling oak-lined campus green below. Professor Hardwick could not think of anything for the moment except that he very much desired a cigarette. It had been three years since he had given them up, and, until now, had never given tobacco another thought.

"Professor," Lydia Thayer spoke, interrupting Hardwick's thoughts, "I know it is difficult for you to accept such an abstract theory like time travel, but I am prepared to offer you definitive proof of its existence."

Carson Hardwick turned toward Lydia but did not look her in the eyes. Instead, he chose to study the small crack in the plaster above the chair where the girl sat. He often chose the same crack when he needed to contemplate some difficult concept.

"Miss Thayer, the theory of time travel is not one that is completely new to me. In fact, Anton Lueenhuik apprised me of his work in that field back in '85 about utilizing a woman he had discovered who natural abilities in what he had referred to as "time jumps." He claimed then to be on the verge of sending an individual back to a previous time using newly-developed technology, and then be able to retrieve that person unharmed. I must admit, even though the idea excited me then because of its implications in the field of archaeology, I gave guarded credence to the success of the project at the time, and Anton never reiterated the information to me again through all these years. I figured one of two things--either the whole concept was disproven, the project stopped, and he was too embarrassed to call me, or it was successful and Anton was unable to share information with the rest of the world, including me, until he was given the go-ahead by his fellows."

Lydia smiled weakly at Hardwick. "Well, sir, the project was successful--at least on a limited basis. I mean, it's still being developed. It has a few hitches that need worked out …"

"And you must be the woman who was the subject of his work … " Suddenly Hardwick reddened as he looked over at Lydia. "But no--I'm sorry. It couldn't be you. I mean you're obviously much too young."

"You're right of course. That was my grandmother, Thelma Thayer. She's … gone now … I mean."

"I understand. Passed on," said the professor softly.

"Well, yes, you might say it that way. Passed on." Lydia did not wish to divulge the information entrusted to her by Thelma and Cecil about how they had actually intentionally disappeared only to hide out somewhere in the past. "The Lueenhuik people later found out I had inherited the same time travel genes that my grandmother had. The gene had been passed down for--well, for centuries. Who knows how far back? The scientists at Kronos …"

"Kronos. Yes that's what Anton called it."

"The scientists there were developing a computer program that mimicked my brain waves during time jumps, much as they had earlier from Thelma but without the aid of recent advances," Lydia went on. "For a while, they were really making progress until one of the men named John Dodsworth …"

Hardwick suddenly brightened. "Dodsworth! The computer whiz! Class of '79. I knew him well. An unusual fellow to say the least."

"As I was saying, Dodsworth was working on the project and then suddenly disappeared. As it turns out, he was instrumental-- I should say-- indispensable-- to the computer programming aspect of the mission. When he disappeared, everything ground to a standstill."

"So then, Miss Thayer, that made you the indispensable one, right?"

"That's what Kronos would have preferred--to use me for their experiments. They involved me extensively for quite awhile until my father returned from the past and refused to let them continue with their research on me."

"Your father--he was a time jumper then as well!"

"No, no, not Dad. Not naturally anyway. He carried the gene, but only women in the family seemed to turn up with the ability. No. Bill, my father, was sent back in time using the Kronos' computer program developed by John Dodsworth. He got lost, then ... Oh that's another story--very complicated. Sometime you can read of the details in the Kronos Mission Report."

"All right then. I'm somewhat anxious to find out more about you and how you got into this situation with the western Pennsylvania Amerind site. From what I surmise, you say you actually traveled back to that time and witnessed their culture firsthand?"

Lydia bobbed her head in assent.

"Impressive. And the contamination. You left the toothpaste tube there by mistake?"

Lydia Thayer twisted a bit in her chair, showing some emotion at Hardwick's question. "Let me explain," she smiled wryly. "This may take more than one session together."

5

OVER THE NEXT few days, Lydia Thayer met Professor Hardwick in his office. What had originally been, for Hardwick, to be a short get-together to satisfy his old loyalties to a former friend, turned into an amazing saga of which he could not seem to satisfy his inquisitiveness. Each day began with a steaming urn of coffee and iced fruit-filled breakfast rolls that Nancy Yang brought in on a dessert-sized, doily-covered cut glass platter from the famous Darrel's Coffee Shoppe in Center City.

"After my involvement at Kronos," explained Lydia the first day, "both my parents advised me against using my abilities for the benefit of the company despite Kronos' stated good intentions. They explained to me that a great deal of trouble came soon after power hungry people became aware of the first development of travel in the time-space continuum, and, that what had seemed a plan to help the world, had rapidly deteriorated into a real mess. My grandmother, Thelma Thayer, as I had mentioned, had started in the program when Kronos scientists discovered she had carried the genes--the same ones that had later been passed on to me. She and my grandfather, Cecil, realized what was happening and covertly plotted to leave, and at the first chance they got, left the program by faking their own demise, hoping the whole thing would collapse without them. Of course, I understood the problem Mom and Dad related to me, having been immersed in it myself, so I finally agreed to their suggestions."

"I take it then that the Kronos program did survive despite your grandparent's hopes otherwise?" Hardwick slurped black coffee between each sentence.

"Unfortunately it moved on with its research due mostly to the computer files gathered from what they had gleaned from all the experiments with Thelma up until that time and also those they gathered from me in the short time they had me there. I mentioned the expertise of John Dodsworth. He was able to build a computer program that somewhat emulated Thelma's time travel skills by duplicating her brain waves and converting them to electronic readouts. The whole thing was a bit primitive, but it actually worked."

Hardwick slurped his coffee again and raised both eyebrows in furry gray arcs when he spoke. "If that's the case, then why did they need you?"

"Professor, there have been so many advances in computer technology alone. That's not even considering the monumental changes in the medical industry and what they can do to read the workings of the human mind."

"Of course, you're right, Lydia."

"And you remember too that when Dodsworth disappeared, no one could interpret the program. Likely key parts were deleted. I think John was believing the same thing as my grandparents did about the danger of having corrupt individuals tamper with time travel."

Carson Hardwick slurped his coffee again. "I'm surprised, given those parameters, that Kronos didn't dump the whole thing right there."

"Well they didn't," said Lydia. "There are a number of dedicated and hard-working, but perhaps a bit naive, people at Kronos who simply figured they could work things out and eventually move on. Some of them were expecting Dodsworth to show up again, I think. The different departments continued working on various things such as the body armor they had developed, laser weapons, and language translators so they would be ready with the most advanced equipment and know-how once everything started back again."

"I see now why they looked on you as the savior of Kronos!"

"Right, and they've continually been after Dad to change his mind about letting them continue their experiments on me. Dad and Mom have been traveling all over the place I think to just to get away from them. Right now they're on a Caribbean cruise."

"So you don't see them much?"

Lydia shrugged. "Oh I guess I get to see them fairly often. They've just made it hard for Kronos to figure out where they are at any given time. You know--keeping them off balance and all. Besides, I've been pretty busy with my work at the University at the Western PA native American site."

Hardwick had taken one of the larger breakfast rolls and, using his silver butter knife, manipulated it around on the dessert plate with a grating sound before slicing it neatly in two nearly perfect halves.

"You do enjoy archaeology, my dear? What I mean is, how is it you like these old sites so much when you've experienced them for real? Isn't it a letdown then?"

"Oh no, Professor, not at all. You see when I was young--well younger than I am now I mean--these things like historical places--museums, old homes, forts--whatever. Those were the catalysts for my early jumps. It seems the more I thought about them, the more likely it would be for me to just dissolve away into that era. It's the excitement of the mind that made me jump back then. Eventually I came to control my abilities."

Lydia watched Hardwick greedily stuff half of the strawberry-filled breakfast roll into his mouth as he listened, enraptured with her story.

"But now that I've gone through Kronos' experiments, I've refined my time travel skills and I can control them quite precisely. I can come and go through time much as I please without the intensity of the excitement of thoughts about the period. But I still love these historical places. I can see the people moving around them just as though they had just been there. The truth is that's sometimes actually the case. There are a number of times when I would arrive at a dig early in the morning before anyone got there, travel back into the time of our study experiencing the materials, individuals, and artifacts we were finding about the previous day, visit with the people there, and return minutes later and see an object buried in the sand that I could imagine someone had been handling only moments before."

Carson Hardwick had stopped eating and his grayish eyes were slightly glazed as he listened. A small red smear of strawberry jelly hung suspended on his chin as he waited.

"Of course, of course, Lydia. I understand the feeling. I only wish I could do these things myself. Actually I'm quite jealous of you, you know. I'm still waiting to hear the part that explains how the tube of toothpaste got left back in that time."

Lydia shook her head and lowered her gaze. "You'd never believe it unless I told you, Professor."

6

As I HAD mentioned to Cheryl, I figured Lydia was likely using her time jumping abilities as she had for years. I truly understood what it meant to be able to move about in the parameters of time and experience the adventures through which I had gone. Secretly, I missed the camaraderie and adventure of my recent trip to the past. Technically I was still under contract with Kronos and usually went in to the local lab near Pittsburgh each week and was sent by helicopter for a few weekends at the Kronos facility in West Virginia, often renewing my friendship there with Mel Courier and Kaye Spahr who were also easily convinced by Kronos officials their term of employment had not yet run its course.

We were all reminded each time we came to the training center that it was best we not know the exact location of the facility, to keep as few people who knew the place where Kronos did their research and mission preparations as a secret. Originally we were not quite sure where it was, but had each made educated guesses while training together in the center. We had suspected either West Virginia or the western mountains of Virginia, judging from our departure point in Bethesda and the length of the trip by windowless van that had clandestinely transported us. Now the journey by helicopter verified our calculations as we passed over the snow-covered mountainous terrain west of Charlottesville. A half hour or so later, we set down and were ushered to a waiting silver Escalade that transferred us effortlessly up a winding blacktop road and along the ragged ridge of the mountain we came to affectionately refer to as "Ol Sawtooth". Suffice it to say the site was certainly remote enough. I doubt anyone lived naturally within at least ten miles even though the facility's planned cover as an elite ski resort would necessarily demand at least a limited population in order to achieve some sense of believability. The locale by now was no mystery when we approached the facility disguised as a private ski resort. Its clientele, we were informed, consisted of various former members of the CIA, many retired or injured while working, who were sworn to not divulge anything they observed at the Kronos center.

Those elderly couples that had always hung around on the front veranda of the outer building maintained the masquerade well as I mounted the flagstone steps to the main entrance. I certainly believe they had to be aware of the ruse of which they were a part as they smiled to me distantly and bobbed their heads as if in assent to my admittance. The fact was, these people likely knew nothing other than that something unusual was going on somewhere in the area, and their job was to dutifully maintain the perception to any casual hikers or other visitors that the place was nothing more than what they presented it to be.

The massive dark mahogany door swished behind me as I entered the lobby where dusky flickering faux candles burned faintly through antique opaque lenses of lantern-like wall fixtures placed evenly along the corridor. The rough-hewn pine plank walls and beams supported the whole ski-lodge ruse with a hodgepodge of antique skis, wolf traps, snow shoes, and other impressive ski mountain-themed debris secured randomly about the walls of the main hall where another cadre of sham vacationers lounged in leather chairs reading newspapers or casually drawing on pipes as they stared solemnly into the smudged empty fireplaces along the outer walls. To me it was almost humorous since there wasn't anyone else here except me and maybe the other Kronos trainees who knew what was going on just as well as I did.

James, the sham bellboy, was still there, just as in all my previous visits. He too, like the others, smiled blandly and with a slight bow and gesture directing me into the lobby.

"Your accommodations are as always, Mr. Thayer. Thank you for returning to the lodge, sir. Your business is always appreciated." James led me to the elevator as he had done before. "Your bags will be in your room, Mr. Thayer."

Of course they will James. Along with all the other stuff Kronos wants to show me to entice me or Lydia back into the past. I thought as James continued his masquerade.

"Going up," James would recite dryly as the chrome doors of the lift swished softly behind us. Once the elevator door clicked shut, James immediately let his bellboy charade drop and immediately extended his hand to me.

"Welcome back Captain Thayer," he grinned. "Hang on, sir. As before, we'll be going down."

With that, James slid a hidden panel behind the main console back revealing an alternate set of controls. In a quick move he slapped his palm onto one red button, and it immediately felt like the floor dropped out as we descended giddily into the depths of the top secret Kronos International Training Facility.

In the background, there was a rush like the sound of air being released, a pause, and then the elevator door let out a final gasp as it re-opened to the brilliant lights of the underground city.

"Bill Thayer! You're a sight for sore eyes!"

Before I could even react with a smile, Melvin Currier had slammed his massive torso into mine, knocking me somewhat off balance, and had buried me with a tremendous bear hug. Even though I had spoken with him several times over the phone, we had not seen each other since the Kronos rescue mission had finally extracted us from our original mission at Pompeii. Mel, it seemed had followed a career that utilized his degree in divinity and was active on the preaching circuit in Louisiana when I had last heard. Despite our separation, our team had previously grown together through our time travel experiences, had suffered through desperate situations, and had survived attributed mainly to a great deal, on our interdependence.

"Mel, I didn't expect you to be here," I gasped, finally extricating myself from his bear-hug embrace. "I thought they just wanted to see me for an ongoing debriefing. Now that I see you here, I'm not so sure there isn't something else going on."

"My own thoughts precisely, my man—but things have been in a state of upheaval here, and someone figured our combined astuteness and experience gained from our recent excursion might be more effective if utilized together. Kaye's here too. She's in the dining hall renewing some old acquaintances."

Of course Kaye Spahr would be here. By all indications she had led most everyone to believe she would be perfectly content with her work in the medical field and leave Kronos in her past. By all accounts, she had made an international name for herself in the field of women's medicine. Anyone else would have been satisfied with those accomplishments, but we all knew Kaye could never stay away if she thought she was missing anything.

When the door to the briefing room swung open, the sudden glare of fluorescents was nearly blinding, taking me several seconds to quickly adjust to the brightness. On this particular occasion, standing amid the modern hospital sterility of Kronos International, my two associate-friends, past co-directors of Kronos, Anton Lueenhuik and Marge Paladin greeted me with wide smiles. Nearby were two men I did not recognize.

"The last I heard you two were in the digs at Pompeii," I laughed shaking their hands and giving Marge a belated hug.

"Yes, yes, we were in fact in Pompeii as recent as last week," sighed Lueenhuik. "But just as for you, duty calls, and we must meet our obligations, you know."

"Don't worry, Bill," interrupted Marge Paladin, "as soon as we can, we'll be back there sifting through volcanic dust and bricks for any little historic tidbit we can discover. It's great therapy!"

"By the way, I'd like you to meet the two directors that have been appointed to take our position here at Kronos," said Anton. "Mr. Kenneth Deane …"

Mr. Deane stretched out a limp arm and shook my hand weakly. "How do you do, Mr. Thayer. I've heard much about you and your adventures."

"Hope they were favorable stories, I smiled.

"Mostly, Mr. Thayer, mostly I guess," answered Deane firmly without much expression.

"Our other director is Anthony Perry. Mr. Perry ..."

I immediately recognized Mr. Perry from the time I was given my interview to get into Kronos. Then I had mentally referred to him as 'Mr. Green Bean' because of his slim profile and choice of colors for his suit.

"Mr. Thayer," answered Mr. Perry without the traditional handshake. "And these other people I assume are Currier and Spahr, your fellow fortune hunters?"

For the first time since I had come to Kronos, I felt an unwelcome coldness. I was rather curious as to what these gentlemen's agenda might include and how that might affect future expeditions. I had the distinct feeling these two newcomers were not exactly going to be cooperative in the way I had become accustomed. To my relief, Deane and Perry turned and moved down the corridor leaving me with Anton and Marge and an opportunity to make some inquiries.

"What's with those guys?" I gasped.

"Those're the ones supposedly taking our place," said Marge exhaling loudly.

"Yes, and they always have had a chip on their shoulders, so to speak," returned Anton shaking his head. "Neither of them knows much about the program, but they both think they should be offering advice and their acidic opinions any time they can. They're always questioning the technicians and even Higby and Graffey."

"Must not be too much to pick from, I guess," smiled Marge as she shrugged.

"Suppose there aren't too many people out there we can trust with information."

"They are always questioning the financing of the program," grinned Lueenhuik. "They have no idea how we maintain an ever-increasing funding." Looking from some to side, he added, "And I'm not about to let them in on it. Suffice to say, they should be happy they don't have to go out and do fundraising!"

"This is the main reason we come back. We hope we might influence the new appointees to let things move along naturally. Also, as long as we keep a presence here, they have to hold back on any attempted takeover." Marge was a bit glassy-eyed by now. "We plan on returning and helping out here as much as we can. Maybe things will improve."

Their dedication was one of the reasons I had decided to return to Kronos in the first place. Anton Lueenhuik and Marge Paladin had persuaded me in mission debriefing that my five year contract was now only a year old despite the fact that I had spent at least four and a half years in the Mediterranean on our first mission.

"It may have been nearly five years for you, but here in the twenty-first century, less than a year passed," Lueenhuik had argued. "Our present time must necessarily take precedence since your contract was signed in this time."

"You've served admirably, Bill," broke in Marge Paladin. "If you really wish to get out of the contract, we can have it arranged, but you have become a valuable member of Kronos, and even if you never wish to go on another mission, we can pick your brain for vital and greatly important information from your veteran experiences."

In essence, I did indeed feel I was a part of Kronos and was easily convinced they were correct in their expectations. Besides, it was fun to get away, reminisce with old friends, and to be the point of admiration for a couple dozen fawning computer geeks around the facility, all of whom either secretly or outwardly wished they were able to go on a mission themselves. I had originally been granted the rank of captain on the initial mission, and now, after my return, I was considered one of the senior officials on the project, and, as a result was conferred top level clearances wherever I went in the complex.

In the meantime, I was able to periodically meet with my old friends Norton Higby, one of Kronos' top technicians, and Dr. John Graffey, both experts in body armor, stun guns, and other useful devices of practical experience, to discuss and update more recent technology and hear the most current developments on which Kronos had been working.

"So where are we Norton?" I asked Higby as we sat around the lounge with hot coffee balanced on our laps. "I mean, how far has

Kronos come in duplicating artificial time travel compared to the time travel of natural jumpers such as Lydia and my mother Thelma?"

"Time travel that has been developed by the labs at Kronos can be a little ticklish--as you are certainly aware, Bill. There are inherent dangers you realize. We can't forget the first directive of Kronos toward time travelers not to interfere with anything that might directly influence our future. We refer to that as the "Back to the Future" rule. Another theory, supported by both Einstein and Hawking is one to which you should be aware of, Bill, especially if you would ever go on another jump. It is the immediate danger of you, or anyone else, with coming into contact with a copy of yourself as you might have appeared in that time. I mean, you can never touch or perhaps come into close proximity of your original person. The result would be immediate disintegration of both entities!"

I let out a deep breath. "Do you mean …"

"Yes, Bill. We've known about this complication since the outset of the program and had been quite sensitive to it when working with your mother, Thelma Thayer. Some around here feel many time jumpers have likely met this fate in the past—perhaps Thelma and her husband as well."

I was sure that statement by Norton about Thelma and Cecil was not accurate since I had seen both of them on a recent foray, but I was bound to secrecy over their plan to keep their disappearance quiet. I did not doubt the veracity of the theory though. It seemed to make perfect sense.

"There is another situation involving time travel to which Kronos has been working. When natural time jumpers, like Thelma Thayer and your daughter Lydia, move about in the time-space continuum, somehow there is a natural safety net that protects them when they arrive at their destinations in the past. What I mean is there is no record of any of them ever materializing inside a stone wall or falling over a cliff unexpectedly. They seem to have developed some sort of natural protection, or instinct, in that regard. Well, anyway that safety net has not existed for our computer-fabricated time jumps. In one of our very early experiments, we met with worse disaster. We tried to transport more than a dozen crewmen aboard a ship at sea. Well, to make matters short, the ship moved -- as ships have a tendency to do--and some of the men were inadvertently transported to solid areas inside the ship's structure itself. A disaster of monumental proportions! We had a difficult time quieting that one down.

I'm sure you recall the more recent fiasco when Manning Jones' New Crew launched its initial time jump into the First Century. On their opening venture, they were scattered all along the eastern coast of the Mediterranean and Judea. One of them actually was unceremoniously crushed to death against the sea cliffs near the ancient city of Sidon."

"Yes, that's right," I agreed. "Mel and I found him there the day after our own arrival. That was O'Connor. He was almost unrecognizable!"

"Unfortunate of course," Higby went on, "but certainly a graphic example of what I was attempting to explain."

"And the others--Trinia Williams, Olivia Pelser, Kris Benson, and Verma Rashid--they were spread everywhere along the coast of ancient Asia Minor. It took them a week or so to get back together with Jones. They were fortunate there weren't other mishaps as well."

"Yes, and we believe the problem of their separation resulted from a simple error in the initial manipulation of one traveler's time launch. It was a minute fraction-of-a-second difference in reaction time."

"And now this problem is corrected?" I asked.

"Well--no," Higby drawled out slowly. "We were on the verge of great things in this area when John Dodsworth mysteriously disappeared. Apparently he used his latest developments in his final jump where he disappeared with Jones and his motley crew. As it turns out, he held the key to everything. He not only was the solitary person who fully understood the computer program to run the Kronos operation, he had worked with a method to overcome the very problem we've just discussed. In his quarterly report, he referred to his solution as Automatic Hazard Avoidance. John shortened it with the acronym *AHA*. John was big on the use of clever acronyms."

"So what you're saying then is you're at an impasse without Dodsworth."

"More or less. We haven't given up mind you, and we believe we've made some progress. The people here at Kronos International Time

Excursions are intelligent and industrious, but we need something to have a breakthrough."

I knew where Higby was heading. For the past year, he had been attempting to get my approval to continue Lydia's testing. She had previously been subjected to a battery of tests that were intended to convert her brain wave patterns during time transfers into electronic computer data. That process necessitated having my daughter initiate time travel and then return to the present again. My experiences with Kronos had convinced me that it was too simple for her or anyone else to get into serious trouble messing with this phenomenon. Lydia, of course, was no longer a minor and was perfectly capable of making her own decisions in this regard. The point is that the people at Kronos respected my opinion, and Lydia had agreed to go along with my wishes as well. My problem was that I knew the unscrupulous people who would stop at nothing to gain the power of time travel for their own unselfish gains.

"Your daughter--Lydia," he started.

"Yes, Lydia, my *only* daughter," I interrupted. "I'm not going to have her come down here as a Kronos guinea pig. Time travel can be a bit dangerous you know."

"But she would be well-compensated, Bill. Kronos has extensive funds!"

"Our family is well enough off. None of us need any of the Kronos money."

"But Bill, you're one of the important captains here. You made a huge commitment to the program yourself. How can you deny that same experience for Lydia?"

By this time I was rising to leave. "It's no use Norton. I would never recommend these experiments to her, and besides, I figure she had her belly full of time travel with her recent misadventures. Lydia would likely never wish to time travel again. For my part, I feel obligated to the Company. Perhaps it's a bit of ego …"

In my heart, just as I had indicated to Cheryl, I believed Lydia's lack of desire to time jump to be an exaggeration, but it was to no advantage to our family's well-being to share our knowledge of Lydia's personal recent dabblings in time travel with the people at Kronos.

7

SHORTLY AFTER ONE of her time travel returns in mid-July, Lydia Thayer had materialized behind the back porch, the spot she often chose because of its location hidden by the lush lilac bushes where she might arrive unseen by the eyes of those who might not understand how she might magically appear out of nowhere in a blur of distorted transfer waves. As she began to re-establish a sense of feel under her own weight, she suddenly became aware of someone sitting in the shadows on the porch swing, casually observing her arrival. The slight creaking of the rusty chains rubbing against metal sent a sudden sense of urgency through Lydia.

"Who's there?" she whispered hoarsely.

A shadow form stood and emerged from the evening grayness. The figure, a middle-aged woman possessing familiar tightly-curled blond hair and stunning blue eyes emerged into the diminishing light. The voice that emerged was firm, but somewhat icy. "It's your mother, dear. Were you supposed to meet someone else here?"

Lydia often had a difficult time translating the tense, tight smile constantly competing with the posed friendliness of her mother's azure eyes.

"Mom! I wasn't expecting you."

"I'm sure you weren't, Lyd. So where have you been? Or should I say *when*?"

Lydia had expected to be discovered sometime, but this confrontation with her mother was still a shock, and she was trembling as she answered. "Oh Mom, you knew I had to jump again. I know you and Dad think it's dangerous, but I've been doing it ever since I've been about seven years old. Time travel is intoxicating. I can't leave it. I'm a powerless addict when it comes to this. It's in my blood! Besides, it helps me with my work in school. Metro University is so impressed with what I know that they've named me student captain at the dig over in Ohiovue. That's aid money too."

"Lyd, we don't need the aid. Your father has a fantastic income due to the inheritance."

"But Mom, I … " Lydia did her best to look ashamed, but she didn't do a very good job at it even though she stared at the ground, shuffled her feet in feigned nervousness, and made sad faces for her mother's benefit.

"It's all right, Hon, actually I understand. I've noticed you leaving and arriving on your forays all spring and summer long. I only wish we could have worked this out where you weren't sneaking away like some sort of thief."

"You're not mad then?"

"No, I was a little at first, but then I realized I was actually a little envious. I kept thinking about our adventures in Renaissance Italy last year, and then how we ended up saving your father in Pompeii."

"Mom, we didn't save him. It was actually Thelma and Cecil-- and they saved us too!"

"Whatever! It was an adventure I'll never forget. We got to see those famous people and all. I see what you mean when you say it's addicting. I kept dreaming of the time when I could go back somewhere again and see Leo."

"Mother, why didn't you say something?"

Now Cheryl Thayer was the one looking a little guilty. "You know. It's Bill. Didn't we all agree not to time travel again?"

Lydia paused and then answered thoughtfully. "Do you ever remember my agreeing to not time travel at all? Actually all I agreed to was to not cooperate in any way with Kronos or go on any more of *their* time jumps without his approval. There was never any mention by Dad of continuing using my own abilities to go back." Here Lydia paused for effect. "I actually think he never really expected me to stop going back in time. It's always been a family tradition you know. And I know Dad never got any such promise about using time travel from you."

"Ok, ok, you've convinced me. Now tell me where you've been going all summer. I've been so darned curious for months. What time in history is it?"

Cheryl and Lydia stepped back and sat on the porch swing and enjoyed the coming coolness of the evening as they talked.

"Lately I've been limited to places locally--places in western Pennsylvania and the immediate surrounding area. You realize that my powers limit me to leaving here and arriving in the same spot I leave from in the past, give or take a few feet to avoid obstructions and such. The *when* has been mostly frontier times and more recently visitations to the early American natives who lived around here. They refer to themselves as Ka-tee-a. That translates into something like *nomad*. Those trips have corresponded with my position at the University at the archaeological digs.

What's interesting in the past year or so is I've followed my ancestry back one jump at a time until I got to the 1600's. So far I haven't been able to trace our lineage any further. In each time period I've found someone in the family who has the time jumping genes that Thelma and I have. I've gotten to meet and talk with them."

"You've met these ancestors?"

"I've not only met them, I've lived with them and gotten to know them. It started with Grandma Thelma's family before she was married to Cecil. Her mother Eleanor Bartram was also a jumper. Her grandfather Russell Bartram carried the gene but not the ability to jump. His mother Genevieve, a Brandt, had some abilities, but she hadn't developed them much. Before her, I hopped back to the nineteenth century and met the rest of the Brandt's. Louise Brandt related stories to me of some of her adventures into the founding of the city of Pittsburgh and later of events during the Civil War. Then I traced our roots to the early 1800's and Lionel Freed. He also carried the gene but his mother Charlene was the next time traveler. Once again I was able to follow the line back through the Pearson's and their mother, Winifred Sweed, the next traveler I located. The most distant connection I could find so far was

Elizabeth Sauers who lived in this area near Darlington in around the mid- 1700's. I've spent considerable time with Elizabeth whom I found had been considerably confused by her abilities until I arrived. It seems her church elders had convinced her she was somehow possessed, and she had begun to believe it because she had no other explanation."

"I can understand that," sighed Cheryl. "I once considered contacting Father Joseph to have an exorcism for you!" Cheryl suddenly noticed the stunned and growing hurt look on her daughter's face.

"That's before I found out about your gift I mean," she snapped defensively.

"Well, anyway," answered Lydia rebounding from her mother's insensitive statement,

"I found Elizabeth Sauers was an orphan who came through Philadelphia. She had no idea where she came from before that, and so far I haven't found any records indicating her origins. Given some time, I'll be able to walk through her past simply by personally backtracking."

"Looks like you've been a busy girl."

Lydia grinned and shrugged. "It's been fun."

"So when can I go along with you, Lyd?"

"You're serious? I mean after that fiasco last summer when you were stranded in Renaissance Florence?"

"I never had so much fun! Now I'm a veteran of time travel."

"All right, Mom." Lydia smiled broadly, the pressure of secrecy now lifted. She was actually glad to have someone she knew share her adventures. "My next scheduled jump is tomorrow morning from the dig in Ohioview. Be ready at six sharp, and I'll have some appropriate things here for you to wear."

Cheryl Thayer jumped up and clapped her hands. "I'll pack a few things myself and be here tomorrow when you drive over to the site."

8

"A NICE STORY about the relationship you have with your mother and how you were able to bond, Lydia," Professor Hardwick acknowledged a little tired. "But what relevance does it have to the situation?"

"Bear with me, Professor. I think it's to our advantage to introduce how my mother got involved with the dig." Lydia Thayer sipped the sugary and heavily-creamed liquid from the coffee cup on the desk. She wasn't much of a coffee drinker, but somehow sharing this habit with Carson Hardwick seemed to create a link of understanding between them. "The point is that you need to not only know how she got involved with this particular time jump, but also a little about her personality. And I don't want you to get the wrong idea or anything like that. I truly love my mother and enjoy doing things, even time journeys, with her, but the fact remains, she is one of those people who seems to say or do the wrong things in vital situations. The funny thing is it seldom backfires on her and things work out in the end."

"I still don't understand," said Hardwick as he leaned back in his leather swivel chair.

"You will," answered Lydia firmly.

Lydia took another small sip of the tepid coffee she held in her hand. "You need to know a few things about our former adventures. Mom really didn't know much about the history of the time, but when she was stranded alone in the Renaissance, she not only survived, even without a working knowledge of Italian, but she met and influenced some great men of the time. Would you believe Leonardo Da Vinci and Michelangelo?"

"You're kidding, of course."

"Not at all. When I finally arrived there with the Kronos rescue unit, poor Leonardo looked as though he was so relieved when she said her good-byes. Mom told me stories of some of the conversations between them. She spilled the beans, so to speak, about time travel and let Leonardo know about many modern inventions of our time. I truly think he got many of his futuristic ideas from her. I could go on and on, but you get the idea."

"It sounds almost funny," smiled Hardwick. "But I could see where she could cause some real trouble."

"Yes, and now you're beginning to understand."

"OK, go on, Lydia."

"Mom was in on the rescue team to get the other time travelers back from ancient Rome, but she messed that up too and nearly got us all killed in the eruption of Vesuvius at Pompeii as well. We were saved by … shall I say, by other means--something I'm not supposed to mention."

Once again Lydia had almost accidentally let the Professor know of Thelma Thayer's clandestine intervention.

"So I assume then your mother was the one responsible for contaminating the Pennsylvania site?

"Let me finish the story, Professor. You be the judge."

9

LYDIA NEVER REALLY expected her mother to appear the next morning on time, exactly at six, as Lydia had mandated to her the previous evening on the back porch. She was actually pleasantly surprised when Cheryl's silver Buick Skylark, its power steering protesting angrily in a shrill squeal as it turned at the end Lydia's driveway, whined to a stop near her doorstep only a few minutes late. The power window on the passenger side whirred open.

"I'm ready!" she screeched at her daughter sitting calmly on the porch step.

"Mother, what in God's name is that thing on your head?"

"When I got home last night, I got excited and went on the Internet and looked up Indian women's clothes. I saw all sorts of things, but I saw a get-up that I thought would be appropriate for me. It looked like some things I had stored away in the attic."

Cheryl snapped the door open and stood displaying her self-designed costume in all its grandeur. On her head was a headpiece that would likely challenge the most hideous ones Lydia might imagine utilized by fashionable women from the 1930's, with waving brown pheasant feathers sprouting randomly in all directions from its multi-tiered base and bordered from under with frazzles of Cheryl's own golden locks. On her shoulders was thrown the old brightly-colored wool blanket Lydia had remembered her mother purchasing from a Navajo woman in Arizona when they had vacationed there when she was in seventh grade.

"What picture was that from?" gasped Lydia. "That doesn't look like anything any early American native would ever wear."

"It's from a photo of Sack-a-Jew-we-a," Cheryl announced disdainfully, her chin raised proudly.

"That's pronounced Sac a-ja-*wee*-a, Mom. And they didn't have cameras back in her time. It couldn't possibly be a photo. Likely it's an artist's rendition of how he thought she might have looked."

"Whatever. I think it looks rather impressive with this doeskin skirt I found in the closet."

"Isn't that from your old suede suit?" Cheryl asked.

"Well, yes, but it looks like doeskin, don't you think? And these fur mukluks are perfect for me to wear too."

"Aren't the pants a bit tight?" Lydia eyed the back of the skin-tight stretch slacks her mother had somehow squeezed into.

"I wore them a few years ago. Maybe they shrank or something. They'll be OK."

Lydia had dug out some less conspicuous apparel for their use, real buckskin suits and native-style moccasins specially tailored for them by a Seneca woman who lived near Tionesta. In past jumps into this period of time, she had fared well, wearing similar things and low-keying her presence among the natives. She had no idea what they might think of this gaudy rig her mother had adopted. Lydia also knew it would be useless to try to use logic with Cheryl once she had convinced herself this was the correct costume to use.

"I'm bringing my bag of cosmetics and hair stuff too. I remember how difficult it was to find stuff in Italy the last time. I think this might even be harder with the Indians and all," Cheryl reasoned.

Lydia looked at her mother's small handbag and rolled her eyes. She was afraid to imagine what she had deemed necessary.

"Mom, one thing, make sure there's nothing in that bag that will get into the hands of the people there. Keep everything away from them. Anything modern would mostly likely scare them silly. Anyway I doubt we'll be there very long as it is. I think we won't plan on being there much more than an hour or so."

The two slipped into Lydia's orange Cherokee, made a right at the bottom of the driveway, and headed for the Ohioview site about forty-five minutes west following the Ohio River along 68. Since it was

Sunday, no one was at the dig when they arrived. They pulled back through a narrow lane guarded by a cyclone fence gate that swung slowly open to Lydia's touch on the Jeep's dashboard device. The lane turned and ended near a low outcropping of shale and sandstone where various equipment--screening boxes, brushes, pails, and other items used in the delicate work at the site-was set randomly in strategic spots in readiness for the new day's work.

"This is the way I like it," said Lydia to her mother. "I'd rather not have anyone here when we leap. This is still my secret, and it's best we keep it that way."

"So where do we go to start the jump?" inquired Cheryl, her tassel of feathers springing as she turned her head from side to side.

"We don't need to go anywhere. We'll leave right from this spot here in the car. Ready?"

"Yep!"

"Lean this way," ordered Lydia. "Be ready for a slight drop."

The two women touched heads and immediately Cheryl felt a little dizzy and momentarily closed her eyes. When she opened them again, they were abruptly seated unceremoniously in a swirl of soft grass in a clearing near the woods where several men were just emerging from the pines. Cheryl rubbed her eyes to clear her sight. It looked like a scene from Paradise. The lush, emerald forest bordered the multi-colored meadow all along its perimeter and a meandering clear brook gurgled among a stand of cat tails and reeds. Near an outcropping of dark brown sandstone along the stream, a small band of men and women squatted in the clearing as they lazily chipped stone near a smoldering campfire. The sight of the two women at once caught the attention of two men and they stood and faced them stiffly.

"Lydia! Those men! They aren't wearing any clothes! Close your eyes right now."

"Mother, they're wearing breech cloths. That's all they wore in the summer weather."

"Well, *I* don't care for this sort of thing you know!"

"Do you want to go back--right now?" Lydia was not ready for her mother's prudishness at this time.

Cheryl wrinkled her nose "I hope they don't expect us to remove our clothing!"

"Don't worry, Mom, as you can observe, the women kept more fully clothed. I'm not exactly sure why, but I suppose if they were naked it might be more distracting for the men."

"Well, I don't know about you, but this is a bit distracting to me--you know."

"Just don't look. You'll get used to it. These are men I know--it's Wolf Howling and his brother Red Coot. Just relax when they come up. They're quite friendly you know."

The sun-darkened men plodded up the path toward Cheryl and Lydia. They each carried a short spear about four feet in length in one hand and another three-foot long device in the other that Lydia knew from her studies and first-hand experiences they used to throw their flint-tipped missiles.

"An atlatl," Lydia said in an aside to Cheryl.

"A latte? They had them back then? I love the spice pumpkin at Starbuck's …"

"No, Mom, an atlatl's a spear thrower."

"So why didn't you just say that in the first place?"

When the men came nearer to the women, they stopped sharply and stared wide-eyed ahead at them. One of them motioned to Lydia and made a few short gestures and fearfully beckoned for Lydia to come to them.

"Wait here, Mother. Let me speak with these people."

Lydia stepped down and walked the short distance to the men who were nearly bent at the waist with their eyes raised slightly.

"What is it, Wolf Howling? Why do you hesitate to come forward to greet me? That is very unlike you." Lydia's implanted translation device developed by Kronos had served her well in this time.

The taller man raised his eyes and held his cupped hand up to them as if shielding light from the sun. "It is not you, Mourning Dove, but the pale feathered creature who has accompanied you. Neither of us has ever seen any man or woman of this fashion."

"Oh Wolf, it is my friend-- Woman-With-A-Bird's Head--," Lydia smiled as she looked at her confused mother, "one who has come with me from the mists--just as you have seen me come here many times before. She means you no harm. Come and greet her."

Both men stood shakily and then cautiously approached Cheryl as she waited. There is a great deal of controversy in Lydia's mind here as to whom was more frightened of the other. It was easy to see why the men had misgivings about her mother. The feathered hat, the form-fitting tan suede suit, symbol-covered Navajo blanket, and fur mukluks she had worn were as foreign looking as anything they could possibly conjure up. Add to that, Cheryl's milky pale complexion, compared to the men and even to Lydia whose work in the sun left her as browned as any of the people of the woodlands, likely gave them the impression of a ghost or spirit of some sort, and her golden strands of curls streaming from under her feathered headpiece were things of which they had never experienced or even heard.

"What are they saying, Lydia? I can't understand a single word of their gibberish," Cheryl rattled on. "How did you learn this language? I know you're good with learning them, but this ..."

"Relax, relax. Do you remember our associations with Kronos, Mom?"

"Of course I do, but ..."

"Well listen then. Before our final time jump, they fitted me with an implanted ULIT device that made translating and interpreting thousands of languages a snap. Even these local tribal tongues, though not known to the modern world, were easily synthesized by the device in a very short time. In effect, I can speak and understand almost anything they throw at me. I also picked up some of the rudimentary sign language they use among other tribes they often encounter."

"Oh maybe I could pick up a few words. I understood Italian fairly well."

Lydia winced at this suggestion. She remembered clearly how her mother had butchered the language while previously on tour in Florence. Lydia turned to the two men and took their hands and dragged them forward.

"This is Woman-With-A-Bird's-Head," she whispered softly in their language.

Wolf Howling and Red Coot stepped nervously and lowered their gazes.

"This is Wolf and Coot," she said to Cheryl in English. She shortened their names, knowing it was unlikely her mother would remember them anyway.

Cheryl offered her hand to them, and immediately they recoiled and dropped to the ground and began mumbling. Lydia gasped when she looked at Cheryl's extended hand--on it was a silver, glittering rhinestone-covered opera glove she had fished out of her leather travel bag while her daughter had held the attention of the tribesmen.

"As we have decided, she is indeed a goddess, Mourning Dove. Look at her hands. These hands that glitter like sunlight on the morning waters are not the hands of our simple woodland people. Surely she is sent by the Great Spirit." The two dropped back a short distance as other people, now drawn to the distraction in the clearing, began to show up from the rocks and hemlocks nearby.

"We must have the elders sent for," said Red Coot slithering respectfully backward down the path as he talked. "They must come here to witness this visitation by the goddess, no doubt the goddess of fertility," Red Coot said as he eyed her flesh-colored pants.

"What is it Lyd? What are these strange people doing?" she began to shriek.

"They're going to bring the elders to see you, Mom. They think you're some kind of strange goddess of fertility."

"Fertility! Now there's one for you! I guess I should take it as a compliment I suppose. I'd better spruce myself up a little if we're going to have the big chiefs come up here." With that, she dumped the contents of her bag on the ground and began to sort out various combs, brushes, cosmetics, and whatever Cheryl thought she needed to make herself presentable. The throng of gathering people had formed a tight semi circle at a short but respectable distance and watched with bugged eyes.

"I'll need this," she shouted as she grabbed her toothbrush and carelessly squeezed a gob of multi-colored striped toothpaste onto it. Almost as a reaction she brushed feverishly as the tribe of people stared in amazement of the gyrations and manipulations of the divine creature, who in her divine journey, had chosen to appear before them that day.

"Lyd--Lyd! Some water to rinse," she garbled almost in desperation with toothpaste foam oozing sloppily over her chin.

"Look," shouted one. "Her mouth oozes the foam of a mad dog and she calls out incantations! We have angered her and we will all be punished."

A low moan went up as one voice, and the people began to scatter into the forest, leaving Lydia and Cheryl by themselves in the clearing.

"Now!" Lydia screamed. "We're leaving now."

In one motion she was at Cheryl's side, her forehead glanced sharply against her mother's, and they were immediately back in the twenty-first century dig at Ohioview.

10

"**S**O THERE YOU have it, Professor," sighed Lydia as she took the final swig of her cold coffee. "In a short fifteen minute visit, my mother single-handedly disrupted and traumatized a village of prehistoric native Americans to the point that I could never bring myself to return to them to continue any more of the first-hand research that I felt was becoming one of the most essential studies developed of these early American cultures to-date."

"No doubt you're correct in that assumption. Too bad about that." Hardwick took another bite of his pastry before continuing. "And," he continued, "I'm sure that explains how the toothpaste tube got into the site?"

"I have no question about that, sir. We can only speculate what exactly happened from there. Probably the other items Mom dropped on the ground were later held as sacred icons and probably placed in special pottery containers or shared among the people all over the region. Who knows where everything went? So far we can only account for the toothpaste tube. What happened to the combs, brushes, cosmetics, and whatever else Mom dropped on the ground when she emptied her bag?"

"Yes, yes, quite so," said Hardwick sorrowfully. "We'll never know when something else from your mother's bag will turn up and potentially contaminate another site!"

"And what about my Pennsylvania site--the MU201WP? Can you get it reinstated?"

Carson Hardwick stood and gazed out the window for a short time before he answered. "I'll do my best for you, Lydia. I know, of course, that the site may have been contaminated, theoretically of course, but, as you had originally pointed out, the contamination took place in prehistoric Pennsylvania, and the items were not planted there, but rather likely placed there by the native people themselves. Probably the best thing is to let the site alone for a year or so, and then bring it back. Hopefully I can use my influence to get the charges dropped and you can continue your work there. It might be a good idea as well to have someone in there who knows about your abilities and what happened and can keep your secret--just in case anything else turns up at the site."

"Thanks Professor," said Lydia rising and offering her handshake. Lydia realized Hardwick was likely volunteering to be that person who might speak out at the hearing. It was then she realized Hardwick's sheepish smile.

"What is it?" she asked.

"I was just wondering. Well, you see, Lydia, I've always had this interest in a particular period of history. You describe how simple of a matter it was to take your mother back. Could you maybe ... you know, take me there for a few minutes or so? It's the period right after the Civil War here in Chicago--1867--when my grandfather worked right here in this very building when the university opened that year. I'd just like to take a quick peek."

Lydia had never had anyone other than her mother ever ask her to take them back in time. This was a first. It all of a sudden legitimized the time travel process to have someone of Hardwick's renown to request this service from her. She was flattered.

"Of course, Professor," she said proudly. "It would be my honor. Is there anything--a robe or something we could throw on over our modern stuff so we wouldn't stand out?"

"I've just the perfect get-ups here in the closet. The ceremonial graduation robes we use here at the University. These were commonly worn on a daily basis by the instructors on campus back then!" Hardwick swung open an expansive cedar-lined wardrobe and revealed a line of brightly colored robes utilized by the faculty on special occasions. "There are some that would fit you too. Here try on one."

Lydia snatched a light blue one and held it up to herself while Hardwick wiggled into his traditional white history robes.

"Looks perfect," Lydia offered as she looked at herself in a floor length mirror. "I'll slip it on over my stuff."

The two were ready in a few moments.

"Put your head in contact with mine, Professor."

"Sounds simple." Hardwick leaned over and touched his head lightly against Lydia's. "Now what?"

Carson Hardwick felt something out of place. The room was not quite the same.

"We're here," Lydia announced softly. "It's your office--or rather your grandfather's right now, I would guess. We're in the year 1867."

"Amazing, this place looks almost the same as my office in our own time. I realize now there's no computer or intercom system, or even a telephone for that matter. Yes, yes, the more I look around ..."

Hardwick's observations were interrupted as the outer door swished open and he and Lydia turned wide-eyed. In the dim light, the silhouette of a tall man stood in the doorway.

"Oh sorry, Doctor. I thought you'd gone home. Stayin' kinda late aint ya?" An elderly man, a gaunt Negro with a wrinkled, downcast face started to back through the entrance from which he had just come.

"No, no, my good man, come in. You can work around us. We were just getting ready to ... to inspect the grounds," answered the Professor a bit nervously. "Me and Doctor Thayer here, that is."

"Dr. Thayer? Don't think I've had the pleasure, sir. Is she new on the staff? A bit pecu-liar for women, specially this young ...," The night janitor looked puzzled.

"Yes, new, quite new indeed. And you know me of course?"

"Oh everyone knows you, sir. Don't you be joshin' with me now. You're Professor Russell Hardwick."

Hardwick leaned toward Lydia whispering, "He thinks I'm my grandfather. There must be enough resemblance to confuse him in this poor light."

"And your name, my good man?" called Hardwick.

"Oh Professor, you're testing me again. Bertie. That's me. Bertie Layman. Just a poor nigra that minds his own business and is thankful for this employment and the opportunity to do some book learnin' on the side."

"Well keep at it, Bertie. And be sure you make your children keep their noses to the grindstone. Someday they'll be making a name for themselves. Make them mind, do you hear?"

"Yessir, I do. I'll do just that!"

"That's Jeremy Layman's great grandfather," Hardwick hissed under his breath to Lydia. "He's going to end up head of the philosophy department at the college in 2009."

"Wow!" gasped Lydia. "I guess Bertie's going to be taking your advice seriously."

"Let's take a little stroll outside, Lydia. I'm curious about the campus."

It was still late summer, August, by Lydia's estimation. The recent brick work on the newly-constructed Beall Building gave the impression of cleanliness and new starts. The great oaks along the perimeter of the school's inner green were not so large now. Rather some of the young trees lining the walkways might even be described as saplings. This would be a peaceful time in Chicago--the great Civil War was finished, and many young people were here in this growing Midwestern city, starting over. The campus was otherwise very much as they had left it before their transition to 1867, and the people of this period lounged and strolled about the grounds much as those who would follow them about a hundred and fifty years in the future. Now, however, the conservative dress--men in suit coats and women with hats and long ankle length skirts--indicated the obvious aberration in time.

As Lydia and Carson made their way along the shadows near Beall Hall, they stepped onto a bricked pathway and were unexpectedly met face-to-face with a man in the blue uniform of the Union army. Lydia was aware immediately that the man's left sleeve hung empty by his side. The man had turned fully to her now and wore a stunned expression.

"Lydia! Is it really you? You're alive! But how?"

Even before Lydia could react to the stunned soldier's clipped remarks, Carson Hardwick had frantically seized her by the shoulder and dragged her back into the open hallway of the newly constructed Wyatt Building in one motion. Initially Lydia had somehow connected this action to the sudden confrontation of the man on the sidewalk, but she quickly found the real reason.

"Coming up the sidewalk--it's my grandfather! We must not let him see us!" The Professor's voice cracked slightly as he spoke.

In those few seconds, Lydia made the decision. She had often been forced to make many of these snap judgments during her various time travel ventures in the past. She had found that a moment's hesitation could be costly, and the best choice was always to make the jump and think it over later in the security of her own time. Her head bumped Hardwick's lightly, and they were now standing safely along the now vine-covered wall of twenty-first century Wyatt. The low background murmur of those moving about campus and the occasional laughter of a pickup Frisbee tournament in the main courtyard seemed surreal to the two breathless time jumpers.

"That was close!" wheezed Hardwick. "Just as you turned to face that young gentleman, I saw Russell emerge from the doorway on the porch. I know he has a weak heart. In fact that's how he eventually passes away. For my part, I didn't want to be the one who hurried his end prematurely."

Carson Hardwick sat on the weathered capstones of the brickwork on the veranda of Wyatt Hall, exhausted from his short jaunt into the past. "Oh, by the way, who was that gentleman on the walkway? You've met before?"

Lydia shrugged her shoulders. "I've never seen him. At least I haven't *experienced* him yet. I'm sure he's somewhere in my past, and I'll find out more later. Right now, I haven't a clue."

"I can tell you this since my hobby is military regalia of all sorts. The man is a lieutenant and a veteran of the 8th Illinois Cavalry."

"You saw that in the brief time that flashed by?"

"Yes, that's right. I have a pretty quick recognition of those things. Even if I didn't have much time, my mind seems to take a visual snapshot and my recall kicks in later. Actually I own an old Civil War uniform from that unit. You'll have to visit my little museum on the east end of campus. Lots of memorabilia from that period."

"From my point-of-view, I noticed his arm was missing--his left arm, I believe."

"Yes, yes. Quite common in that time for soldiers. Surgical skills were quite primitive you know. It was often more expedient to remove an arm or leg than to risk something more complex in a poorly-equipped and undermanned field hospital."

"Perhaps then," suggested Lydia, "we could find out a little more of his unit's history. He's gotten me more than a little curious."

Hardwick was unbuttoning his robes as he spoke. "Give me the afternoon and I'll get you some info. I have regimental records in the archives on all the American units from Chicago. I don't know how much, but there's surely something there."

The two shook hands briefly, nodded and parted company, both determined to find out something about the mysterious man they had met in Chicago's past.

11

"HIS NAME IS Hunter Mathews—a lieutenant in the Third Indiana Cavalry." Hardwick was leafing through a dozen or so photocopied pages that he laid one at a time at a spot he had cleared on the desk. "And it says here he served honorably in several main battles of the Civil War and was decorated appropriately. Some of those larger campaigns along with a number of smaller skirmishes were—First Bull Run, Antietam, and Gettysburg. And that's where his military career ended. It seems Lieutenant Mathews was, according to the records rather seriously wounded during that campaign. Somehow he recovered rather unexpectedly. He was locally hospitalized until shortly after the battle when the Confederate army made its retreat, and then he was taken to a military hospital near Philadelphia where he, not only recovered, but served as a physician's aide until the end of the war. Then he returned here to the city in '66."

"So," said Lydia, "Gettysburg. I've been there several times—in modern times though and years ago--when I was still a kid. It was one of Dad's favorite places. So I have a little knowledge of the town, and Gettysburg is closer than the other Civil War battle sites mentioned in your report."

"I also have quite an archive of old tintypes from that battle as well as others. I particularly feel we might be interested in these ones ... " Professor Hardwick stood and slid open a drawer of a massive oak file cabinet, drawing a dark-papered expanding portfolio held together by a scraggly yellowed ribbon.

"Yes, take a look at these. These are photocopies of the originals-- about a dozen or so pictures of field hospitals during the battle," he said, spreading them out in a fan. "Perhaps, if we are fortunate, we might even spot our Hunter Mathews among some of the wounded."

Lydia was promptly on her feet and at Hardwick's side, systematically tracing the faces of the soldiers in each photo as she flipped through the material presented to her.

"None of these look much like our man," sighed Lydia. "Yet some of the faces are not very sharp either. It would be possible to miss him."

"And there were thousands of wounded men who never were recorded. Thousands … on both sides. It's not surprising." Hardwick shrugged. " I just thought we might be lucky."

"These pictures are still very interesting. Look here at these … " Lydia had pulled a few aside on the desk in front of her. "They're women, all standing in line with the men in front of the hospital tents."

"Likely volunteers from town. They recruited anyone they could to help out with the massive toll of injured and dying soldiers."

"This woman here … looks familiar," said Lydia suddenly pointing at one woman. "I've met her somewhere I think. Do you have a reading glass?"

Moments later both of them were studying the face of the figure Lydia had pointed out.

"She looks very much like one of Dad's friends who was on the Kronos time travel team. Kaye … Kaye something … I can't quite recall her last name, but she was instrumental in their final rescue when they had been stranded in time … but no, that would be too coincidental. As I recall, Kaye came back after that and retired from time travel--went into medicine … No this couldn't be her."

"I'm sure, if you look at different visages throughout these pictures," Hardwick explained casually, "you could *see* other people you know as well. The mind is a wonderful thing, but easily convinced."

"Yes, yes, you're right, of course. As I look through the other pictures I see other people too. This one," Lydia laughed, "kind of looks like Mom. Most of the faces are blurred and the cameras then were not capable of taking good pictures if there was any movement at all by the subject.

Anyway, if our mystery man, Lieutenant Mathews, ended up in Gettysburg during the battle, we can likely pinpoint an approximate time where I might be able to meet him simply by checking historic records of unit movements."

"You're planning on meeting him there? Going back in time? That could prove a mite dangerous. You know, with the war and all."

"Professor, I wouldn't miss this one for the world! I'm jumping around all over history without much direction, often landing in places that are dangerous. So far I'm unscathed."

Hardwick stared seriously at Lydia Thayer. "Yes—so far anyway. Aren't you afraid of a stray bullet or something, particularly on a chaotic Civil War battlefield?"

"Well sir, it seems I have several advantages," Lydia answered succinctly. "To begin with, I know from historical records the times and places to avoid in any given jump, particularly this campaign where I either know or can obtain easily, detailed accounts of the actions. Secondly, something you might like to know about, thanks to Kronos and your friend Anton Lueenhuik. Their Kronos technology has provided me with their latest komodo body armor."

"Komodo? You mean like the dragon?"

"Yes, right. That's what it's named after. The nearly impenetrable scales of that giant reptile. This stuff," bragged Lydia as she lifted her sweat shirt and ran her hand over her tanned stomach, "is virtually undetectable and is said to be able to safely stop a bullet shot from a high-powered rifle from as close as twenty-five yards. This stuff is absolutely the latest thing. Hardly anyone knows of its existence."

"You're wearing it now?" Hardwick wanted to touch the komodo skin but suddenly drew back, recalling it might not be appropriate to be touching this young lady. As an afterthought, he reached back and ran his hand along Lydia's proffered body armor. After all, what could be more personal than what they had just experienced in the time jump?

"Yes, and it's made of a material that conforms to the body like my own skin. It covers my upper and lower torso, upper legs and arms to the elbow. It's porous, flexible, and feels perfectly natural."

"I'm impressed! But you still aren't completely invulnerable I should think," argued Hardwick.

"No, of course not, Professor. There are some obvious weak spots, such as head protection, but then I don't rely completely on the advantage of body armor. You've witnessed a most effective natural protection I have at my disposal during our recent time jump. At the first sign of any danger, I can just instantaneously leap back safely to our own time. That has always been the single most effective defense upon which I've relied through the years of time travel."

Hardwick took a deep breath. He wanted to argue against the idea but knew Lydia Thayer had made up her mind. Besides, he was positive he would have been certain to make the same choice for himself given the opportunity.

Hardwick's mind was now racing forward in anticipation of his potential involvement with the proposed time jump.

"Well let me help at least, Lydia," the professor sighed. "I can give you as much info as my resources can permit. It might also be a good idea to have a liaison resource at the location of your time jump in case you need support on your return and to supply you with period costumes. I have an extensive Civil War wardrobe and other regalia for that period. I'd be happy to oblige in that situation."

Lydia didn't answer as she rose. "Thanks Professor Hardwick …"

"Carson, Lydia—just Carson, my dear"

She hardly heard Hardwick as she left. Her mind was already swimming with her own plans for the upcoming adventure.

Professor Carson Hardwick obviously was more than excited about the prospect of maybe visiting a Civil War battlefield. He had suggested to Lydia that he would act in a support role yet he secretly toyed with the prospect of a deeper involvement.

If things go well there, Miss Thayer surely would give a man, especially an aficionado an opportunity to live his lifelong dream.

12

THELMA THAYER WAS fully aware of what to expect when she decided on this jump. After all, she had just recently visited a dinosaur-infested Jurassic jungle with her husband Cecil.

"It's too dangerous," Cecil protested. "Everywhere you look—monsters!"

"John Dodsworth had no trouble with those creatures. The fact was he loved them."

"I'm not just referring to the dinosaurs, Thelma. It's the real monsters I'm afraid of—Jones and his men."

Thelma Thayer smiled—one of those smiles some people wore when they had already made up their mind. She had given it considerable thought. She knew Manning Jones, being not only one of the most malevolent people on Earth, but one of its most intelligent as well, would do her no harm simply because he would necessarily recognize her as his only ticket out of his hell. Thelma saw this as a challenge. Seldom could Cecil get away with telling his wife that one particular task or another was impossible. In fact, that was one way to get her to take on some messy project she would never have done otherwise.

"It's impossible," Cecil would tell her, his impish eyes flitting sideways. Thelma would likely already have that stubborn little half smile of hers. And then Cecil knew she had taken the bait.

This time, the *impossible* word had backfired.

"To rehabilitate Jones and his men would be like reforming Satan and his Fallen Angels," Cecil announced a bit matter-of-factly after returning from their recent extraction of John Dodsworth. "It would be, in my mind, an *impossibility* …"

No sooner had he let loose of the word when he realized his mistake.

There was no real way to stop her other than knocking her on the head and somehow keeping her unconscious. Of course Cecil would never have resorted to violence.

"I'm doing it Ceece,"she said, her face set harshly. "You can't really stop me, you know."

"Mind sharing your plan with me, Dear?" he asked in resignation. "How, in God's name do you plan to change these brutes?"

"That's it … exactly," whispered Thelma softly.

Before those words had any chance to be processed by her husband, she had dissolved away.

This idea had not been a hasty decision by Thelma Thayer, and her plan, rehearsed over and over in her mind, was rather simple. Over the years, she and Cecil had developed a well-oiled machine for various time travel venues and now Thelma planned to use the machinery for her solo venture. She had followed this procedure before numerous times, almost all of them with her husband Cecil sharing the jump and tagging along with her. She proceeded to the site of one of her safe houses nearby, and then slipped back a decade or so to pre-911 years—a time she and Cecil had opted for when air travel, was almost completely unimpeded by lengthy searches and delays at the airports. It was a short drive to the airport from there, and one of the passports she carried had been conveniently set up for that period of time as well, and additionally, was extremely economical since her travel credentials never would expire. The airport at Pittsburgh International was usually busy in those years—lots of flights, before security cameras were in vogue-- plenty of cover for a clandestine adventure. It was a simple matter to book a flight to Rome using funds she and her husband had deposited at the bank there at the airport, and then take the People Mover connector to Airside Terminal C. In those days Delta flew directly into Rome.

About seven interminable hours in flight (Thelma was used to moving much faster), and the plane landed at Da Vinci, she rented a red

Fiat convertible and drove south through Naples to the ancient site of the ruins of Pompeii. Using her Garmin GPS she punched in a nearby preset destination just to the northeast in the direction of the dormant Vesuvius. That was another good thing about this era. There were still enough satellites available to gain a sufficient signal for her electronics.

"Right about here," Thelma smiled after a short drive. "Now I estimate I should launch about a quarter mile from here," Thelma said aloud, "just to eliminate the chance of an encounter with the nasty creature I faced on our previous trip."

In modern times, it was a much more stress-free walk than it was in the Jurassic times into which she would be arriving. It was warm that day in southern Italy, but Thelma knew she had to be prepared for something a bit more extreme than those temperatures. She had dressed lightly—khaki shorts, cotton short-sleeve shirt, and a suave-looking wide-brimmed Aussie style brush hat, looking very much like a female big game hunter.. Thelma wasn't much for weapons but knew the chance of a happenstance meeting with one of the denizens of the period might be likely, so she reluctantly carried a powerful stun gun adapted and upgraded by Cecil from ones developed by John Graffey at Kronos.

13

Less than two hours after Lydia had returned to her apartment near the Museum of Science and Industry on Lake Shore, a white Jimmy van bearing a faded red and blue Metro U logo, its tires squealing noisily through the parking area, swung to the right, and adeptly backed smartly into an open space at the end of their walk.

"Lydia! Lydia!" Hardwick squalled excitedly. "I'm here. Come on out and see what I have for our trip."

The Metro University history professor had the right-side sliding doors open before Lydia or her mother had recovered enough to step onto their porch. Hardwick had raced to his home, not more than fifteen minutes from the university, rolled open the spacious walk-in closet where he had stored his vast collection of Civil War accoutrements he had mentioned to Lydia after their aborted time travel escapade, and proceeded to selectively pull down a number of items he thought might be needed. Breathlessly he threw as many things as he could over his shoulder and transferred them to the van he had borrowed from the University. After several trips between the building and the van, Hardwick sat in the van breathlessly, his heart racing.

The Chicago temperatures had changed rapidly from that afternoon. Residents often said of the weather there: "If you don't like the weather right now, just wait around fifteen minutes." Now, the temperatures had dropped and there were flurries, dancing dandelion fluffs, flitting about playfully around the van.

"Professor," called Lydia as she and her mother came up to his open vehicle, "I didn't quite expect to see you so soon."

"Lydia, my dear, you've got to see what I've brought you. Lots of period clothes you can pick from. And some other useful things as well."

Lydia cocked her head to the side to peer around the open van door and was immediately aware of the smell of moth balls and a familiar musty odor she readily associated with *old*.

"There sure are lots of things you've got here. I doubt I'll need all of these items."

"Never can tell, my dear," said Hardwick. "Made sure there was a variety of sizes for you to pick from."

"What about these uniforms, Professor?" asked Lydia taking the braided sleeve of one jacket. "They look like men's clothes."

"Oh, I just wanted to show off my collection, Lydia. You know how I am."

"I see you have several swords hanging there. Are they officer's?"

Cheryl Thayer had been hanging back. It had been a bit unusual that she could be quiet so long.

"Ahem," she interrupted, clearing her throat.

"Oh Professor, I'm sorry. You've never met my mother," apologized Lydia. "Mom, this is Professor Hardwick. Professor, this is my Mom, Cheryl Thayer."

"Carson, Mrs. Thayer, just Carson," smiled Hardwick graciously taking Cheryl's hand and lightly kissing it in a manner reminiscent of ante bellum society.

"How gallant, Professor—I mean –Carson," squeaked Cheryl.

"I take it you will be accompanying your daughter and me on this exciting sojourn," whispered Hardwick.

"Oh I don't know about that, Carson, but I'm going to go with you two to Gettysburg, I understand. Maybe we can go to that other place later?"

Carson Hardwick paused for several seconds. "Whatever you wish, Mrs. Thayer," he sighed.

"Wow! You sure have lots of junk in the back of your truck, Carson. Looks like a yard sale, I'd say. Could I look through your stuff?"

Hardwick smiled, bowed and gestured to the open van door.

Inside the van was a long chrome bar extending the length of the cargo compartment. On it were perhaps a dozen items of clothing hanging there. As Lydia had mentioned, there were a number of blue Union uniforms slid to the back beyond a neat row of dresses, ranging from rather plain-looking to a bit more elegant both in style and color. On the near side of the compartment was an open gray, metal storage trunk about five feet in length. Hanging on hooks beside it were two swords and a holstered pistol in a black leather belt.

"You'll need money," Hardwick grinned gesturing toward the open metal box. "As much as you'll ever need, I'm sure." At that, he produced a thick wad of bills and slapped it down on the driver's seat.. "US money mostly, in smaller denominations. There're some Confederate bills as well but not as much."

"So where did you get all this Civil War cash? This stuff has to be rare, especially in this condition," said Lydia leafing through the crisp currency Hardwick had plopped down in front of them.

Carson Hardwick smiled impishly. "The best that my Hewlitt Packard laser printer could produce," he laughed.

"You mean it's counterfeit, Professor?"

"And likely a better quality than the money they had then. These color laser copies will pass all but the most intense examination!"

"How about these dresses?" asked Lydia as she ran her hands along the fabric of one skirt. "They're counterfeit too, I assume?"

"I'm afraid the originals wouldn't be in very good shape to wear, my dear, but these outfits are made to the exact specs of museum pieces of which I have had access. I've gone to great lengths to have expert seamstresses spend untold hours in the process of duplication. Quite an expensive proposition, I might add."

"The uniforms too?"

"Of course. I've wasted no money or effort in their production. They are perfectly replicated as well."

"Love these feathered hats," said Cheryl emerging from among the clothes. She had chosen a rather gaudy wide-brimmed hat with a white ostrich feather duster plume that curled downward around her neck.

"Those hats were used formally by the women then," interjected Hardwick. "Very stylish and popular at the time."

Cheryl turned sideways trying to see herself in the side mirrors of the van. "It will be just perfect for me when I go back with Lyd!"

"Mother! I thought that wasn't decided yet. This was still a discussion, I believe."

"Oh Lyd, you know you wouldn't deny me this chance. Look at the good time we had the last time you took me along."

There was a prolonged hesitation. Lydia stared glassy-eyed into the space just above her mother's head. A knowing sidelong glance at Hardwick summed up her recollections of the jump to prehistoric Pennsylvania.

Lydia sighed. "Yes, Mother, I remember that adventure quite well."

"Well," interrupted Hardwick smiling, "perhaps we all should take a look at these costumes I've brought."

Lydia always knew she would inevitably surrender to her mother's wishes and had prepared herself to deal with them as best as she could. For some reason Professor Hardwick had pushed into the picture as well. Her intuition had suspected that he would somehow get entangled when he had showed with all the uniforms and other regalia --it just confirmed her suspicions. In one way, she welcomed Hardwick's expertise in this area of history, realizing he would likely be invaluable in providing information she would need to find the mysterious Hunter Mathews whom she had recently met in post Civil War Chicago.

The rest of the afternoon and into the evening, the trio spent time carting various items of clothing that interested them into Lydia's apartment, each trying them on, and parading around the living room for the review and approval of the others.

Cheryl Thayer, after several trips between the van and the apartment and untold changes, had finally settled on her costume. With her final decision, Cheryl emerged from the bedroom sporting an azure full length skirt with a matching jacket with a white puffy-sleeved blouse, that surprisingly fit her perfectly. The whole getup was set off with black leather mid-calf length riding boots, and a rather smart-looking off-white floppy-brimmed hat that was accented by her loose blond wisps that contrasted her deep sapphire eyes and full, pouty lips.

The effect of Cheryl's trim figure was not lost on Carson Hardwick. The Professor had shifted uneasily in his chair as Cheryl had entered the room.

Adjusting his spectacles, he exhaled loudly. "Cheryl Thayer! You look rather handsome, indeed. I had no idea those old things could look so impressive on anyone."

Lydia, on the other hand, had made her selection quickly with little fanfare. She had chosen a light-weight full length charcoal summer skirt and a white blouse with frilly lace at her throat. As an afterthought, she slipped on a yellow buttercup-print vest that Hardwick had convinced her was fashionable for a young lady of the time. In addition, she found a well-fitted pair of button-hooked ankle boots that proved quite comfortable. The Professor suggested Lydia choose some sort of headwear.

"I'm really not a hat person," Lydia protested lightly. "Too much hair."

Relenting, just to be on the trendy side, she grudgingly settled on a loose-fitting beige bonnet with a thin gray ribbon that fit charmingly under her chin.

"That should suffice to attract any of the eligible bachelors in the area," smirked Hardwick, lifting one approving eyebrow.

Hardwick took almost as much time to decide on his own attire as Cheryl had.

"I believe I should take on the identity of a Union officer. I'm sure I can bring it off," boasted Hardwick. "I believe my being an officer would certainly enhance our position and allow us access in areas perhaps not attainable otherwise."

Carson Hardwick finally returned from the bedroom sporting a trim uniform that had obviously been tailored perfectly for him. The standard navy- jacket exhibited a set of gold epaulets along with several campaign buttons apparently earned from earlier battles or campaigns from the Mexican War and an Indian operation.

"These campaign buttons would represent minor conflicts, vague enough that anyone, without a chance to research them, would easily appear valid," beamed the Professor.

The hat he had chosen was a buff Stetson with a dark brown braided cord tied neatly above the brim. Hardwick strutted stiffly across the living room revealing his glossy black, calf length officer's boots.

"Aren't you a little worried you might attract undue attention in that get-up, Professor?" suggested Lydia. "I would be worried someone might look into my background if I were you."

"Not to worry, Lydia. I have documents, here in this leather document pouch, signed by some of the highest officials in the US government. Actually photocopies, you understand. Of course that technology is completely foreign to anyone at that time and certainly above suspicion. Besides that, I doubt anyone could ever keep track of the merry-go-round of changes going on in the military at the time. George Meade had just been appointed commander of the Army of the Potomac a few days before Gettysburg. History confirms he didn't last too long after that either." Carson Hardwick was smiling broadly. " Maybe I better be careful I don't get promoted myself."

"So if you're some fancy military man, what am I?" asked Cheryl.

"No problem at all, dear. You see there were lots of women who were – should I say—attached to the armies. Camp followers in a way."

"Camp followers?" squeaked Cheryl. "What do they do?"

"They're women of the night, Mom," snapped Lydia. "You know …"

"They only come out at night …?"

"No Mom, let me put it more direct. They were there for the pleasure of the soldiers!"

"Ohh, that sounds like it might be fun …"

"No, Mom! You don't understand. Trust me." Turning and glaring at Hardwick, Lydia firmly announced, "Professor, be careful not to assume too much in this venture. You are on the verge of being left out altogether.

"Oh I was just kidding around, ladies! Of course, Cheryl would do well as my personal secretary. And you, Lydia …"

"Secretary! I should think not, Carson," protested Cheryl. "I never was much good at typing. Besides, I'd like something a bit more impressive—like the thing you're doing."

"Hmm," pondered Hardwick, "I think I have the perfect thing for you. I need to get a few more items ready that I'll need to set up your new persona. I'll show you those when we get to Gettysburg. I'm sure you'll like my idea. And are you all right with your characterization, Lydia? I can get something else for you if you wish."

"Don't you be worrying any about me, Professor. I'll be operating independently from both of you. I can take care of myself."

14

A s she had expected, the heat and humidity she had jumped into was just as oppressive as it had been when she and Cecil had come to rescue Dodsworth. When she re-materialized in the Jurassic swampy jungles of southern Italy, Thelma was at the ready position, her stun gun leveled and her eyes peeled for any eventuality. This gun had been designed by John Graffey and the Kronos labs. It had been a simple matter for her to materialize there inside the complex, help herself, and then disappear. This weapon was designed, using a rheostat, to adjust he charge to various levels. It was meant to be a stun gun, but could be set to eliminate an enemy. Certainly there were the obvious dangers of meetings with reptilian creatures, oversized insects, leeches, quicksand, and a variety of other lethal menaces she might encounter, but the real threat would likely come from Manning Jones and any remnants of his swarthy crew.

They're near here thought Thelma. *I remember clearly, this raised area where Jones and his men were making their stand. Cecil and I heard their shouts and gunfire.*

Suddenly there was the sound of something thrashing, like a wounded animal, through the underbrush towards her. Instinctively, Thelma wheeled around, her stun gun ready for the imminent peril bearing down on her.

There before her was a bedraggled, muddy, wide-eyed man on all fours whose shirt hung in shreds on his emaciated torso . For the longest time, he made no sound but stared blankly at the casually-dressed woman posing resolutely above him with an unfamiliar, but menacing, weapon of some sort.

"Who ... who *are* you?" he gurgled weakly.

"To you, I am your saving angel, Mr. Rashid—come perhaps, to rescue you, if things go right," Thelma firmly indicated to the man on the ground before her.

"What do I have to do? Anything! This place is beyond my worst nightmare. Everywhere we turned—nothing but nasty creatures of all sorts, each time they got bigger and nastier. They've eaten us all—all except me and Manning Jones ..."

"Jones! He's still alive then. Good." Thelma Thayer was surveying the scene for the object of her search—Manning Jones."

'Where is he, Verma?"

"How do you know me, lady? Where in God's name did you come from?"

"Jones—where is he, man?" demanded Thelma sharply.

"Back there a bit. He climbed a tree to get away from some big lizard. We emptied our guns—used our last bullets on that one—but he was still alive. Just got away in time. Then, I ... I saw you here."

"Hell-o!,Hell-o! Jones, Manning Jones!" Thelma's hail echoed through the swamp toward the mangrove-like trees in which she suspected Jones had taken refuge.

"Here! Over here! Save me!" came a whining reply from the shaking fronds of a palmlike tree.

Suddenly a gigantic beast, a great dinosaur of some sort, broke through the underbrush, screeching in a high-pitched sound like a passing jet, and lunged angrily at the prone, squalling and defenseless Verma Rashid who could now only cover his eyes with both shaking hands. In a brief moment, a flash of blue spark cracked through the air, and the enraged monster instantly froze in its tracks as if hit by lightning and rolled slowly over like a giant cement truck, all four of its legs frozen stiffly to the side.

"You got him lady," babbled Rashid. "He's finally dead—good shot."

"Not dead—stunned, "Thelma corrected him. "He'll probably be out for about fifteen minutes or so. After that, he'll be as good as new." Thelma was talking calmly. "By then, we could be out of here. Or—if you insist, you can always stay as this guy's guest."

"What do you want? Anything. You name it. Jones is really rich. He can give you anything you want," rambled Rashid.

"Jones or you don't have anything I want for myself. It might be difficult for either of you to comprehend," whispered Thelma staring at the pathetic figure before her, "but I would like to do something for *you*. You just have to want it." Thelma pointed in the direction of Jones' last voice. "Let's get Mr. Jones off his perch in the tree first. Then I'll explain the deal in more detail to both of you."

Shortly after Thelma had coaxed Manning Jones from the refuge of his tree, Jones and Rashid sat warily watching the edge of the swamp. Their recent encounters with the prehistoric menagerie had left them a trembling bundle of nerves.

"They just kept coming-one after the other," muttered Jones. "We had enough firepower to knock out an army, but that was ridiculous. One of my men had a bazooka, but he was killed in the first attack! And our armored vehicle went down in the swamp along with some of our other guys. They're all dead now. Food for those nasty creatures! What a nightmare."

"I can only say," smirked Thelma, "that crime never pays."

Jones was still too stunned to comprehend the implications of Thelma's sarcastic statement. By now, he was only attempting to assess what had happened to him since jumping with Dodsworth from the twenty-first century, who this woman was who had appeared out of nowhere and saved Verma Rashid and him from certain annihilation, and, more importantly, what was going to happen from here.

"My dear woman," Jones began, sweat trickling down his right cheek, finally gaining a sense of the false flattery that had been largely responsible in his modern world rise to power. "Could I possibly have a name for the angel of mercy who has saved us?"

"Thelma, that's all that is necessary, Jones."

"OK then, Thelma it is. So where'd you come from? That awesome weapon you've got there," he said referring to Thelma's stun gun. "Where can I get one like it?"

"That thing's remarkable," shouted Rashid. "Zap! Pow! A big blue thunderbolt and that critter was down!"

"Don't get any ideas, either of you. This thing can only be used by one person—that's me. In your hands it's just a piece of high tech plastic."

Jones just smiled.

"Next question—if you don't mind, Thelma. Quite a lot has been happening and my mind has been spinning. How did you get here? Why bother saving us? I don't even know where—or when we are …"

"That's more than one question, my, sir. But here's what you need to know. First, I am a time traveler—a solo one—naturally …"

"Not with Kronos then?"

"No, not exactly," she answered. "I know Kronos well, but am not with them. As I said, I'm working solo. My powers to move through time are considerable, and I can, if I wish, take you and your friend here, with me. And why I'm saving you—well, I'm still not sure that's going to happen. That will be up to you. I'll be giving you a proposal to consider."

Jones shrugged. "Go on, then if you will. What's the proposal?"

"As I mentioned to Rashid, I want nothing from you—nothing like money or anything like that anyway. What I want is for you to see a sort of therapist—one that is sure to change your ways."

"A shrink?"

"No, not exactly. Rather, I want you to visit with the one person I think can turn you from being the most untrustworthy scoundrel in history, to an acceptable human being."

Jones looked sideways at Thelma, his eyes narrowed. "And who might that person be, my dear?"

"It's a no brainer, Jones." Here she paused for effect. "That person is—Jesus Christ."

15

As I STEPPED outside the Kronos facility, I was handed a satchel containing my belongings that had been collected when I had come in. Things like electronics—cameras, cell phones ... were simply not permitted for security reasons.. The first thing I did when I opened the bag was attempt to call Cheryl to check in. Unfortunately, the reception in this part of West Virginia has always been problematic. There was no connection. I tried with Lydia with the same results.

They're always busy anyway I reasoned *Cheryl's likely getting early Christmas shopping in and Lydia's so darn dedicated to her studies at Metro. I'll have to try later I suppose.*

It was a short, but brisk walk to the parking lot where my transfer was waiting, the chauffeur stoically posted in his heavy military overcoat by the open passenger door.

"A message, sir," said the driver of the Escalade, handing it to me as I approached.

"Where did you ..." I stopped in mid-sentence knowing full well the driver likely had no idea who had sent it, and even if he did, would be ethically bound to keep it to himself. My name was scrawled on the envelope in a familiar handwriting that just did not register at first.

Bill. I need to meet with you in a matter of great importance. I will be at the airport when you get back. Meet me at the Taveras Lounge at B terminal. I have also left a message similar to this with some of your friends whom I believe might be of assistance. Dad

Dad and Mom, as a rule, kept a very low profile. In fact, as I had previously mentioned, the two of them almost certainly reposed somewhere safely in another time period, utilizing Mom's time travel powers, and they would seldom make an appearance in the present. Receiving this letter from Dad was a great shock for me. This was completely out of character for either of my parents. It had me trying to comprehend why this new venture of his was so important, and, why would he involve some of my "friends" in it. Who were these friends? I could hardly wait till I could make my transfers into Charlottesville and fly into Pittsburgh.

The copter flight into Charlottesville seemed about three times longer than usual and the fifteen minute connector with US Airways was late arriving and delayed for about half an hour. When the flight finally landed at Pittsburgh, my nerves were on end and was nearly running through the terminal to the Taveras Lounge. Dad noticed me right away and stood up at the long table and gesturing for me to come on over. The three others at the table were facing away as I approached.

"What took you so long, Captain?" laughed Mel Currier turning to meet me.

"What the …" I was speechless. I had just left the Kronos facility and I had left Currier lounging in the facility cafeteria with Kate Spahr.

"Right, Bill. You must be getting slow in your old age," cracked a smiling Kate Spahr.

"What is this?" I gasped. "How did you all get here ahead of me?"

"Some of my old military connections, my man. Nothing like direct flights. Kate and I hopped a Blackhawk heading into the 911th Airlift. Forty-five minutes and here we are. We've been sitting here having a drink or two for about an hour now."

"So you're the friends Dad was referring too then? Dad what's up with all this secrecy. And where's Mom?"

Cecil Thayer cleared his throat nervously. "I got the message to these two right after you left. Also contacted another acquaintance of yours."

I was already in enough of a state of shock with these rapid fire emotional bombshells being tossed at me, but the final friend blew me away! Spinning around on the bar stool, was none other than the Black Medusa herself, Trinia Williams.

It didn't take long to get comfortable with my former associates. After all we had shared a great deal including life and death situations—things that inevitably bonded people together much like soldiers who fought and sometimes died together on the battlefield. Those friendships became indelible. That was much the way it was between Mel Currier, Kate Spahr, and Trinia Williams and me. But as much as I wanted to sit and reminisce, I was aware of the fact that my father had brought us altogether for a more essential reason. My friends seemed to be in as much of a quandary as to why Dad had asked them to be here at this meeting place.

After a brief confab at one end of the table, they all agreed to sit back and let me handle the inquiry.

"Never really got to meet your father, Bill. Heard lots about him though," Mel confessed. "Actually heard he had been killed, but I guess I was wrong. You can imagine my surprise when I got the call."

Kaye blurted, " Same with me. I just knew it had to be important."

"Like they both said," replied Trinia, "I knew it was important and out of respect for you, Bill, there was no hesitation."

"Right," added Mel, "and we're just as anxious to hear what's going on as you are. We've been on pins and needles since we got here."

"Dad, what's going on?" I turned and asked him pointedly.

"A mission. A very important mission." Dad looked at us as seriously as I've ever seen him. " Do you remember when your mother and I came to your assistance and pulled you out of volcanic Pompeii?"

I raised my eyebrows and nodded in quiet assent.

"Well, this is a lot like that. In a sense, now your mother needs rescuing. She thinks she is all right, but I know any time she lets her emotions get the better of her, I begin to worry. She's off in time somewhere and put herself in an extremely dangerous situation, and I'm afraid that danger might have far-reaching implications that she is not foreseeing."

"Really?" I answered. I knew from what Lydia had told me that any time traveler who wishes to suddenly move or disappear could do this with ease and flaunt any attempts at being stopped. "If it involves time travel, how in the world are we ever going to attempt any rescue?" I reminded Dad." None of us are capable that of that skill on our own from the last I've heard."

"Not any of us, Bill," Cecil agreed. "But let's not forget our ties at Kronos. All we have to do is get one of their techs to let us use their systems, and I'm positive we can make a time jump without any of the girls. The other choice would be to use Lydia, and I, like you would rather keep her away from Kronos."

"I'm a bit puzzled about this plan and Kronos. First, everyone there thinks you and Mom were lost in an airplane crash and perished years ago. Of course, we know that was a cover up just to get Mom away from the program, but the fact is, they at Kronos think you're gone, and I seriously doubt you want to renew those ties."

"Right and wrong," interrupted Cecil appearing a bit serious in his tone. "You are correct in assuming that neither your mother nor I want to recommence our business relationship with Kronos." Here Cecil paused as if carefully preparing his response. "There is, however, a way to gain access to their program without tipping them off about our ruse. Just let it be understood that I do have a way to overcome that problem, and I ask you to trust me there without asking too many questions about it. Let it suffice to say, I have that covered."

"All right," I answered, still a little unnerved about the nebulous plan Dad was revealing to us. "But here is yet another problem—perhaps the most difficult of all for us to surmount. To begin with, how do we know where and when to find Mom? The needle in the haystack is a bit of an oversimplification. Before we can even begin to look for the needle, we have to pick the right haystack out of millions of possibilities! And then, once discovering this undisclosed location, how do we approach her and convince her to give up her quest? It would be the simplest thing for her to just dissolve away given any sort of challenge."

"It's true," Dad said. "When your mother is determined to do something—something she has methodically reasoned through—it would be extremely problematic to even get a chance to say anything to her at all. Like you said, she would just dissolve away somewhere else in time and we would have another million haystacks to look through. The solution I have decided is to get someone with whom she has a deep respect to talk to her--someone whom she would accept and be convinced by that person to give up on her plan."

"This is so mysterious, Dad. You're expecting us to trust in a plan in which you cannot share the details. You have someone from Kronos to help us?"

"Yes, I do, Bill."

"And you know where Mom went?"

"Vaguely, Son, but close enough. I am fairly certain of her plan though. That in the end is the most important thing. It might interest you to know that one of the keys to this venture is to renew another old acquaintance of yours, actually two of them if you count her husband. Of course you know those persons would be Olivia and Dierk."

"And you also have some mysterious person who will intervene and convince Mom to abandon her mission? I doubt that would be either of those two."

"Without question. I have that person in mind, and I know where I can find him. Olivia and Dierk will be part of making that contact."

"Dad, I'm obviously uneasy about any plan of which I know so little. But—I cannot help but to trust you in this regard. You know I'm in. I can't speak for Mel, Kaye, and Trinia though."

All three of my former time travel crew had been listening intensely, drinking in every word of the conversation between the two of us. There was a prolonged silence before anyone responded.

Mel Currier was the man closest to me on our recent escapade. He had proven to be a man of tremendous physical strength and bravery, a former professional football recruit, and a member of for the Army Rangers who had served valiantly in the mountains of Afghanistan, and of course, was involved in several hand-to hand skirmishes with a bevy of pirates, bandits, gladiators, and Roman soldiers during our Kronos mission. Yet with all that background, Mel considered himself a man of peace, bearing a degree in divinity and serving as a minister in a small town in Louisiana. I knew personally that no one could be as prepared for a mission of this nature better than Mel who was at maximum mental and physical condition due to his continued training at Kronos.

Mel Currier raised his glass in a salute. "Here's to the mission. Mr. Thayer—Bill—I'm at your disposal."

Kaye Spahr was smiling too. Obviously she was in assent and indicated it with a thumbs up. Kaye, like Mel, was in great shape. She had been the only female on our mission, but she never slowed us down or was ever considered a burden by any of us. Basically, she had been appointed by Kronos as our chief medical officer, very skilled in traumatic wounds and their care, but in the real world, she had become renowned in women's medicine throughout the world. We all remembered the professionalism she rendered on our recent mission in that field!

"Wouldn't miss it."

Trinia Williams was lounging back in her chair now, both feet propped comfortably on the chair beside her. She had taken this particular time to drain the remaining beer from her glass and clanged it down noisily of the table in front of her. Trinia had not been part of the original team. In fact, she had been in opposition to it. She had been a part of Manning Jones' crew that had been bent on destroying the Kronos mission. It wasn't until Trinia came to the realization of the malevolent and devious character of her leader, that she switched allegiance and became an invaluable asset to the project. During her time in the First Century, Trinia had also become somewhat of a folk hero, becoming the "Black Medusa," an armored, dreadlocked horsewoman, adept at swordplay and, having garnered skills from her Olympic javelin experiences, was capable of accurately launching a long range lance into targets at incredible distance. Trinia Williams had concluded her operations in the past as a gladiatorial hero and eventually maintained a similar persona in the present time, posing as a well-known women's tag team wrestler.

"You can count on me, Bill. I've actually wanted to get back to see how they're doing without me."

16

Lydia, Cheryl, and Carson Hardwick drove through the night, all of them eager to get on with their time travel foray at Gettysburg, each for different reasons. As they climbed through the Allegheny Highlands along the Pennsylvania Turnpike, the flurries turned into squalls. When the highway whitened, things turned a bit tricky for a while, but by the time they had reached the Blue Mountain tunnels, the squalls had returned to short spells of slushy snow, and when they had exited the Turnpike and onto Route 30, it was all a mixture of icy sleet and cold rain.

Early that morning, the three travelers checked into the two rooms they had reserved at the Quality Inn just outside town. After checking in, Lydia announced her plans.

"I will be going back, a few days before the battle to check out the place and reserve a secure room in an inn I have picked out that is much the same in the present as it was back then. If things seem safe enough, I will arrange to hire a horse and buggy at the local livery."

"When will you be back for us?" whined Cheryl. "We can hardly wait you know."

"I realize that," returned Lydia. "I will be back fairly quickly. I'll walk up to the square and call you on my phone. You come as fast as possible because the weather today isn't very conducive to my waiting around in it. If everything is all right then, we can make plans for all of us to jump back into the room at the inn I rent."

The plan seemed to be a practical one, and Cheryl and Hardwick nodded in assent.

"Let's scout out the modern town and be sure of that pickup point," said Lydia.

"Reconnoiter," growled Hardwick. "That's the military word."

The short drive into town found them in the central square. They all unanimously opted not to get out as they witnessed the late November snows starting to whistle and whip outside the van.

"This is where we'll meet when I jump back," pronounced Lydia. "Tomorrow, after I get some rest, I'll make the jump."

Tomorrow for Cheryl and the Professor was a torturous wait. Both spent time anxiously trying on various combinations of dresses and uniforms.

Cheryl suddenly stopped and stared at Hardwick.

"Carson, I can hardly wait for the surprise you told me about. I mean, what am I going to be on this trip. Remember, I'm no secretary!"

"Thanks for reminding me. I almost forgot," grinned Hardwick sheepishly. "Let me show you what I've arranged for you." The Professor snapped open a leather valise he had kept close to himself the whole trip and pulled out a packet of papers. "Take a look at these, Dear."

Cheryl cautiously took the papers from the professor and tentatively leafed through them. "Looks like a program of some sort, Carson. What's this have to do with me?"

"It is replica of an old program, Cheryl. Did you happen to read the names of the actors? Look at the star on the outer page."

"It says here … oh my God, it's me! It says *Cheryl Thayer* right here playing the part of Florence Trenchard. Why, I have the lead part. Goodness, how could that be?"

"That's a program I had made up from historical records. That is a replica program from The Old Drury Theater in Pittsburgh, and I took the liberty with Photo Shop and made you the female star of the show. I thought you might like to be a famous actress from that era. That would be an excellent cover for you. I couldn't find what was actually playing at the time, so I came up with an interesting idea. The play I have is *Our American Cousin*, a rather famous production one might agree!"

"At least it *will be* famous," Lydia responded testily.

Cheryl was all flushed. For a while she could hardly speak and that was extremely unusual for her. Then she rose, she patted her new hairdo and batted her eyelashes seductively. "My dear, I think this might be appropriate for me indeed."

When morning arrived, the two had posted themselves, with all their latest costume and equipment choices, in the motel lobby having coffee at the breakfast buffet when Lydia finally emerged from her room. Anywhere else, the scene of people dressed in such Civil War regalia may have seemed unusual and attracted undo attention, but not here in this town. Lydia had chosen the simple outfit, the gray skirt and buttercup vest that Hardwick had suggested at her Chicago apartment.

"Take me down the road a bit—somewhere a bit remote so no one will see me leave or arrive," suggested Lydia.

After a short drive, Hardwick turned into a farm lane while Lydia, clad in her finest summer apparel, stepped out into the cold. The weather had no time to affect her. Seconds later she had vaporized into thin air.

Lydia at times had felt the familiar whirling sensation she had often experienced with the onset of former time transfers, but this time she was suddenly overwhelmed with a powerful feeling of near-suffocation and almost unbearable heat, an effect of the stark contrast between the extremely cold winter jump from her own time to this one in late June. At once she dropped to one knee, briefly stunned and a bit dizzy as she struggled to gain her breath and adjust to her new environment. In the distance Lydia could hear the distant grumble of thunder off to the west.

When Lydia had regained her composure, she rose unsteadily to her feet. She had experienced humidity and high temperatures like this before, but now, the jump from frigid mid-winter weather into the summer's heat and humidity, had caught her unprepared for these extremes. Lydia turned slowly, shielding her unprotected eyes and instinctively straightening the folds of the lightweight gray skirt and cotton long-sleeved blouse with frilled lace neckline Hardwick had selected for her. As her vision adjusted to the light, Lydia was able to appreciate the beautiful farmland panorama in which she had arrived.

She had transferred into the edge of a vast golden acreage of wind swept wheat. About a hundred yards away, just about where Pennsylvania Route 30 would be in her future time, a dusty road, not much more than a farm lane, ran east in one direction over low rolling hills, its gently dipping swells undulating about a mile or so toward a hazy village that was certainly 1863 Gettysburg. Far off to the west were the misty blue-gray hills that appeared generally as the same Pennsylvania ridges she had left behind in the twenty-first century. As she turned right and left behind her, she realized the farmlands of this time over two hundred years in the past would not likely be all that changed from those she had recently left.

Lydia winced in the bright sunlight and strained her eyes for any signs of life from the town off to her left and shuddered at her thoughts. In the distance, Lydia thought she could hear the low rumble of thunder.

Peaceful. Very peaceful. No one would ever predict the terrible carnage that's going to happen here in these serene fields.

Lifting the hem of her dress to her knees and exhibiting her brown leather over-the-ankle women's boots, Lydia eagerly waded through the field of thick waist high grass and onto the rutted roadway, only then allowing her dress to fall back naturally to her ankles.

"Yo there! You on the road!" a throaty voice growled from the trees.

From among the low-hanging branches across the lane, a tall dark-bearded man, carrying a single-bit axe in one hand and a light-colored short-brimmed hat in the other, stepped out into the sun light. To Lydia, she could only envision how Abe Lincoln himself might have appeared there in his rail splitting days.

"Oh, hello there," Lydia responded appropriately timidly.

"Taint very safe for young ladies to be cavortin' around. Specially one lookin' so fresh on a hot summer day." The man glanced up and down the road as though expecting someone. "Nope, not with all these soldier boys."

"Soldier boys?" Lydia had not expected to hear about either army to be around--not just yet anyway. Had she mis-timed her jump?

"You've been livin' under a basket or something, lass? We've seen both Rebs and Yanks scoutin' and spyin' and whatever they might be doin', runnin' their damned wagons and horses through our fields. It's been mighty hard to keep the peace so to speak. Most of our time is used hidin' our valuables and gettin' our folks out of the way. Who knows where their infernal skirmishes will develop. And if they find a pretty thing like yourself, there might be some trouble--if you know what I mean."

"Say, Mr …"

"Forney. John Forney."

"Mr. Forney, could you tell me the exact date. I think maybe I misplaced my calendar."

"It's the 26th, dear. And you never said who you were?"

"My name is Lydia Thayer, Mr. Forney. I live near Pittsburgh." Here Lydia hesitated to make sure she had the proper name Hardwick had given her. "I'm visiting … the Swigerts." Hardwick had researched the name and discovered the Swigerts had briefly lived near town and had moved away shortly after the battle--a perfect cover for Lydia. "They're cousins of mine you know. Oh is it still June then?"

John Forney raised his dark eyebrows and absently mopped the sweat on his forehead. "Yes, yes it's June, Miss Thayer. You must have lost touch with time, I'd say."

"I thought for certain I did, sir, but, as it turns out, it's exactly when I figured it was. June 26--1863."

The lanky woodcutter nodded with a tight-lipped smirk.

"Just as I had thought. Thank you very much for verifying it for me though," smiled Lydia intentionally flashing her eyes blankly. "And I'm on my way to town right now."

"Well I have to get on with my work, Miss. I have about a hundred fence rails to split."

Lydia smiled.

John Forney looked back to Lydia. "You're not afraid of the soldiers?"

"No sir, I think I can take care of myself."

John Forney turned away and rolled his eyes. "Yes, Miss, I'll bet you can."

Lydia turned and proceeded eastward toward town. It was nearly forty-five minutes before she approached a few brick homes on the outskirts of Gettysburg. As she walked, Lydia had some time to think through the plan. If things worked out, Lydia would quickly check out the town, making sure it was safe from any unexpected dangers, make arrangements using the money Hardwick had provided for her to rent a suite of rooms in a local hotel, and rent some sort of transportation for them to move about the area, and then, return to the present, walk up to the town square, and then contact her mother and Hardwick to come into town and retrieve her at the prearranged place. She knew her mother would be impatiently waiting for her chance to join her in the time jump, and she was certain Hardwick, too, would welcome any prospect of experiencing Civil War Gettysburg.

Lydia had misjudged the distance to town and the energy she expend for the walk. Recent storms had generated a steamy, junglelike quality to the air. The roadway was now a curious mixture of muddy ruts and a soft, treacherous rapidly drying putty-like texture that required developed skills one might utilize on a military obstacle course. Town had seemed much closer when Hardwick had driven Mother and her to the square, just to get her bearings. It was cold then too. Today the mounting heat and humidity of late June began to take a toll on her despite the fact she considered herself fairly fit with her work in the digs at Ohioview. When she finally came up to the first buildings on the edge of town, her cotton blouse had become dreadfully saturated in perspiration, her throat was parched raw, and a sticky layer of chalky dust grime covered her heat-flushed face.

"My dear." a strong high-pitched voice called out, "you look absolutely horrendous! Please come over and get refreshed."

A rather gaunt, sharp-faced woman was beckoning Lydia from a shaded alleyway between two red-bricked storefronts. "C'mon young lady, don't stand out in the sun. You might be melting."

Lydia stepped onto the covered porch where the woman stood.

"Singleton--Wilma Singleton." The woman handed Lydia a paper fan with her left hand, while fanning herself with another fan in her right. "Looks like you've been out in the sun already--kind of burnt?"

Wilma Singleton looked over Lydia curiously.

"My name's Lydia Thayer--cousin of the Swigerts--the Swigerts out toward Cashtown. Oh, and I'll take you up on some water if you would."

"Water's on the table. Use one of those cups," Wilma said pointing to a wooden bucket and several metal cups. "Help yourself."

Lydia dipped water from the pail, filled a cup and drank it down without a breath. The water was tepid but it did not matter.

"My, my, but aren't you the dainty one, Miss Thayer?" she said with a bit of sarcasm. "Want another?"

Lydia dipped out another cup, but this time drank more leisurely.

"A bit curious, dear," said Wilma closing one eye as she spoke. "You come down this road here, all sweated up, dragged out, and burnt almost as brown as one of the darkies. Your clothes indicate you aren't a working girl, but any of the town lasses round here has skin as pale as sweet cream." Wilma eyed Lydia cattily. "You might not be considered bad looking if it weren't for your dark-burnt skin."

"Oh Ma'm," returned Lydia between sips, "I'm from out west--near Pittsburgh. It's not fashionable there to be so white complexioned in the summer. We see the burnt look as healthy."

Wilma Singleton raised her eyebrows and fanned herself.

"Mighty hot for June. So what would a young Pittsburgh girl be doing in this lazy town?"

"Well for one thing, I'm trying to get to know the town a little. Like the livery. Could you tell me where to hire out a horse and buggy--you know--just for local travel? I need it for a man--a military man who wants to see the town and the area around it."

"Sweeney's Stable," she said casually gesturing up the street. "Harvey has just the rig for your military man. And a nice gentle harness horse to go with it. Was Doctor McGee's, but now he's off to war."

"Thank you, Ma'am, that will help a lot. And what about a room--a nice clean room--for this same man?"

"Easy. Next door … Hartsfield House. Nice place, has food and drink-- breezy rooms with lots of ventilation."

"That sounds great. Thanks for your help Mrs. Singleton. I'll go over and check that out."

Lydia took the last of her water in one gulp, then headed for the inn next door. There lounging back on a wicker chair on a wide, shady, balustraded porch, sat a gentleman wearing a navy blue suit with gray vest and scarlet cravat and sporting a short, dark beard, his white floppy-brimmed hat pulled partially down over his face, and a tall glass of what appeared to be lemonade about half full on a table beside him.

"Sir?" said Lydia softly.

At once the man sat straight, catching his hat at the last second.

"Ma'm? Could I be of service?"

"Yes sir … a room. Preferably on the upper level--away from things you know," smiled Lydia.

"David Hartsfield here. Yes of course, but that would be one of our more expensive rooms--$1.50 a night--a bit steep I know … It seems there are lots of travelers recently that might pay that price though. Would you like me to pour you a glass of my mother's lemonade?"

"That room's perfect, Mr. Hartsfield. And yes, that lemonade looks mighty inviting on a hot day like this." Lydia opened the black velvet purse she had picked from Hardwick's costume trove. "Here's $15," Lydia handed Mr. Hartsfield three fives Hardwick had copied on his printer. "--For ten days. If we wish to stay longer, I'll give you the rest ahead of time of course. When could you show me the room?" Lydia was certain their visit would be much shorter than the ten days she was bargaining for. The battle was only less than a week away and she planned on herself, the Professor and her mother being long gone before the action would commence.

As far as Lydia was concerned, the room at Hartsfield House was perfect. It was situated at the top of the stairs conveniently above the main lobby and dining area of the inn, and, already knowing from previously scouting out the town with her mother and Hardwick, Lydia was aware this very inn was still existent in twenty-first century Gettysburg, and as far as she could tell, was much the same in appearance then as now. This secluded room would be the perfect launching and return points for her time jumps once she returned to the future, and the same exact space would be rented in the future.

A few minutes later, Lydia had ascended the stairs, entered the room and let herself slip into her time travel trance.

The cool, slow November days, chosen by Lydia and Hardwick, provided for a handful of the more hardy tourists the chance to take advantage of the hospitality of the town's popular Gettysburg ghost walks. This particularly bitter day encouraged a few of the fans of the fashionable haunted history tours to remain indoors near the warm, inviting, blazing fireplace of one of the more notoriously haunted inns in town. A portly round-faced female guide in a lacy, beige period costume had gathered her small, but attentive, group in front of her gesturing emphatically as she spoke in a raspy, hushed tone.

"Ladies and Gentlemen, in this old tavern, the ghost of one Mary O'Brien who was said to have been killed here in this very room by Rebel grapeshot on the final day of the battle has often been known to frequent this place and be witnessed by many a visitor to this inn."

One man in the background stood with his arms folded. "Dear, I love these old houses and all their Civil War era things, but I'm afraid I find all this ghost stuff a bit ridiculous." The man, likely in his early thirties, had, that day, already endured a half dozen of these talks by "expert ghost hunters" along with his wife, who was obviously much more excited about the ghost walks than her husband.

"Mark ...," the woman hissed, "don't make a scene again."

The man had ceased complaining, knowing, in the end, he would endure as much as his wife would want him to put up with. In silent protest, Mark turned his back on the lecture by the tour guide, riveting his attention on the nineteenth century roof framing and the ornate Victorian style balcony stretching elegantly along the inn's west wall that was presently adorned with an interesting array of Civil War accoutrements and artifacts from the local battlefield.

In the next few seconds, the man's face had abruptly become drained of all color and his mouth and eyes widened. Where once there had been nothing, now in one startling moment, the shape of a young woman dressed in Civil War era costume, had begun to take shape out of thin air.

"My God, Taffy, look there--up on the balcony!" the husband gasped.

When Lydia had made her transfer from 1863 Gettysburg, the upper level from which she had departed had been a closed-in room, but now, upon arriving back in the twenty-first century, she came to the uneasy realization the outer wall had been razed in a recent renovation sometime in the interim and was now an open balcony. Lydia had materialized in plain sight of several gawking people!

"It's the ghost of Mary O'Brien," gasped Taffy in wide-eyed astonishment.

By now, all in the room were frozen, watching the wispy apparition still slowly coming together in front of them. The tour guide had dropped and scattered a clipboard of loose papers, and sharply clattering fork, the only sound in the room, was sent rattling along the oak floor of the dining room. A thoroughly electrified waitress stared awe-stricken up at Lydia, who was just now regaining her own bearings.

Grim-lipped, Lydia smiled and waved weakly to the crowd; then, after a few long seconds, she regained the power she needed to make an emergency leap. Moments later, the vaporous figure standing on the balcony had disappeared.

On this attempt Lydia had again reappeared on the very balcony in the same inn where she had accidentally appeared before a number of tourists, but now, it was several hours later and the place was deserted. As she cautiously descended the creaky steps from the balcony, she noticed the wayward fork, dropped by the waitress on Lydia's recent return jump, still lay glittering near the base of the wainscoting. The antique clock in the vestibule was chiming the hour, but Lydia did not count them off. In the shadows of the Victorian parlor, Lydia shuffled around among the folds of her dress and drew out the cell phone she had slipped into the lining that morning and nimbly punched in her mother's number on speed dial.

"Mom, it's Lyd. Could you and the Professor meet me in the square?"

"My goodness, girl, we were starting to worry. We figured you'd come right back. What happened? We were ready to send out a search party. You know it's after midnight."

"I'll explain after you pick me up. It was interesting."

Lydia pressed *End* and checked her messages. There was still no response from her dad.

Lydia was able to unlock the front door of the tavern and slip outside unseen onto the dimly-lighted front porch where a short time before (over a hundred fifty years before), Lydia had shared a lemonade with David Hartsfield. It was a short, brisk walk to the predetermined spot at the town square, but the contrast in temperatures from the balmy eighties of 1863 July to this winter's twenties, left Lydia shivering uncontrollably in the few minutes she waited for Hardwick's Jimmy to wind around the block to retrieve her.

"What took you so long? I'm frozen!" yowled Lydia as she rolled the sliding door shut. "Turn up the heat!"

"So what happened? Is everything OK?" Cheryl fired at her daughter.

"Yes, my dear, tell us everything. We're so excited," said Carson Hardwick firmly.

"Everything's fine," returned Lydia rubbing her hands for warmth. "Just be ready for a bit of temperature change when we arrive."

"Then you've agreed to take us back?" Hardwick's expression had at once become more jovial.

"Sure, I see no problem. Just as long as we're out of there before the first when the battle begins. I don't want to get you guys involved in anything dangerous."

"When can we leave?" Cheryl shouted. "I have to get all my stuff ready. Do you want to see what I'm going to wear? Just some basics mind you. How many days will we stay? I'm so excited!"

"Easy, Mom, first we have to take care of a few details around here like renting the room in the inn in town, the same room I rented in 1863, a place where we can return secretly. You'll have to hear my story about that! Also we have to go over the details of what we can and cannot do. We have to keep a low profile, so to speak. Let's be sure the identity cover we've discussed is perfect." Lydia took a deep breath. "But before we do anything, let's get some rest and get a good meal under our belts. You never know how long we have to go without sleep or food."

Professor Hardwick was smiling broadly. "Agreed!"

"Right," added Cheryl clapping her hands excitedly.

Carson Hardwick had returned to his own room fifteen minutes after leaving the two women and sat alone facing himself smiling into the reflection in the full-length mirror common in most motel rooms nowadays. Hardwick nodded self- approval as he draped a carefully-pressed, buff military jacket with scarlet trim over his shoulders. The uniform was not the traditional blue coat one might expect of a soldier in the Union Army and bore epaulets and other markings foreign to the those otherwise uninformed in military regalia. Those experts in Civil War trappings would most likely instantly have recognized the uniform of one of the lower echelon officers of the Inspector General of the Union Army.

"And these papers," Hardwick said aloud drawing several documents from one of his canvas file cases, "they will be the coup de gras in convincing any naysayers about my legitimacy as a prominent Union officer." The professor examined the signatures carefully, as he had done on several occasions before, just to convince himself once again of the infallibility of his ruse. "Randolph Macy, Inspector General of the United States Army—yes, yes—perfect. Macy was certainly in charge of that department, but there had been a lot of confusion during this period of transitions in the army of the North. George Meade himself had just been unexpectedly appointed Commander-in-Chief by President Lincoln. No one will question my status. All I need to do is present these papers to anyone and they will get me anywhere on the battlefield I want to go. Perhaps I can witness some history in the making." Hardwick looked around him suspiciously as though someone might actually overhear him.

"If things go as planned," he whispered, "I might even get to witness part of the battle.

At last," the history professor sighed, "a dream come true."

17

THELMA THAYER HAD never planned to take any of Jones' men straight back to the first century without implementing her carefully-considered, detailed plan. There would necessarily be a need for costuming and even more importantly, a briefing as to what her expectations of behavior and performance might be for them. Add to that, would be the difficulty in the logistics involved with transporting any of her prospective candidates for rehabilitation from southern Italy to the Middle East without the use of modern transportation. Any attempt to do this in a period other than a somewhat recent period would result in a lengthy and demanding voyage across a large section of inhospitable Mediterranean waters. Thelma was certainly aware of the inherent dangers with bringing either Rashid or Jones into an era where either or both could attempt escape and take their chances in a time where they would have foreknowledge of events—an unfair cognizance of history that they would definitely use to their personal advantage. No matter what period of time Thelma would utilize she would have to deal with that possibility. She knew the only weapons available to her were her Kronos stun gun and the threat the men faced that they would never return to the modern world without her assistance.

"Are you gentlemen prepared to make your time jump?" snapped Thelma to Verma Rashid and Manning Jones who squatted unceremoniously on a mud paddy near the reviving lizard-creature Thelma had recently dazed with her shock weapon. "I'll need your promise," she reminded them, "that you will comply with my terms."

"Yes, yes, anything," croaked Rashid, his eyes darting toward the awakening creature.

Manning Jones, attempting to regain some degree of control, stood slowly with both palms extended toward Thelma. "Could you give us some idea of the terms?"

"Sure, Mr. Jones. Simple and concise—in the name of efficiency. First, no escape attempts."

"OK agreed," said Jones calmly.

Rashid could only nod his head.

"And," continued Thelma, "you have to speak with my contact— Jesus of Nazareth—and give him the opportunity to help you."

"Sounds reasonable," smiled Jones." You realize of course, Ma'm that I've never been much for religion though."

"And you must understand that I do not follow Christian ways myself." Verma Rashid briefly had thoughts of resistance to the idea. "Of course, of course, let's go! " gurgled Rashid as he saw the lizard's great scaled tail shudder slightly. When he saw the sudden flash of the giant reptile's unmoving golden eye, he had scrambled onto his feet beside Jones in an instant. "I've often thought about becoming Christian you know. Let's get the hell out of here, Jones!"

"Sounds like we're both in agreement, Mrs. Thayer," said Jones softly, pretending to ignore the rhythmic breathing of the monster that was emerging from the swamp behind him.

"Put your heads together, men. When I touch yours with mine, we'll be on our way."

Rashid had immediately touched his head with Jones. Neither of them felt the delicate scalp contact from their deliverer.

Moments later the two men were sprawling in a stand of soft meadow grass a half mile from the present day ruins of ancient Pompeii, but Thelma was standing steadily over them with her stun gun poised and aimed at them.

"Sorry about this, guys, but unfortunately your past record indicates you can't be trusted. I just can't take any chances. Don't worry-- you won't feel a thing."

Instead of the expected blue bolt used effectively on the Jurassic denizen they had just left in the comfort of his own jungle marshlands, there was instead, a slight crackling sound like cellophane being crinkled. Rashid's eyes flashed open like a storefront manikin and froze that way. Manning Jones smiled, his eyelids fluttering slightly as he lost consciousness.

Thelma Thayer's well-thought-out plan was in motion. It was a short walk to her car which she drove up through the field to the site where the three of them had just beamed back. There she propped them up against the side of the car, and with a bit of urging, both rose, groggily and, zombie-like, took an uneasy seat in Thelma's Fiat. From there, she drove them to a safe house she had maintained for some time, slipped the teetering men into hospital gowns and proceeded, after an injection to each of them, to DaVinci Airport. There, dressed in medical attire, instructed the nurse-attendants at the airport to assist her in getting her patients aboard and fitted in their strait jackets to maintain their security on their journey to Israel for much-needed mental therapy.

"All the papers and passports are in order," she said handing them a stack of professionally forged documents. "Yes, that is I—Doctor Thelma Davis. Here are my papers, passport--anything needed."

Four hours later, the plane transporting "two mentally deranged men" and their world renowned doctor landed at Ben Gurion Airport in Tel Aviv. There a dusty, cream-colored Econoline van was waiting at a prearranged spot. The two "deranged" men shuffled into the vehicle and were driven off by their staid female doctor who sternly urged the men along. Despite the threat of recent guerilla activity in the vicinity, Thelma drove resolutely to the town of Galilee where she and her passengers backed the van into the rear parking lot of El Ba'arta's Hardware, and after being cut out of their strait jacket prisons, the men were led unsteadily along the south shore and took refuge in a large crevice between two outcroppings of rock along the sea, a place secretly Thelma had selected months ago. There, on schedule, Jones and Rashid began to sluggishly recover from their induced mental incapacitation.

"Gentlemen, as soon as you have sufficiently come to your senses, we will prepare for the final leg of the journey," Thelma announced. "I have assembled the proper attire for you so you might fit in a bit. Jones, as I recall, you have the benefit of a Universal Language Interpreter and Translator implanted, a ULIT as they say at Kronos. You should have no trouble with Latin or the local dialects. Unfortunately, Verma, you were not so fortunate to have the implant. As I recall, you were once instructed by Mr. Jones to keep quiet so as not to give away your lack of knowledge in local languages. I think that might be wise to maintain that same aspect now."

"You—you aren't going to zap us again are you, Ma'm?" squalled Verma Rashid cowering near the base of the cliff.

"No, Rashid, there won't be any need for that. Once you have come back with me, there is no chance of escape without my assistance, and I'm not about to do that without the proper assurances that the two of you are completely transformed."

"Where—where are you taking us?"

"The *where* is right near here. It's the *when* you'll find a bit interesting."

Jones was smiling. "Fantastic job, Mrs. Thayer. I couldn't have planned it any better myself."

"Enough talk," snapped Thelma. "Get some rest and something to eat. You may be needing your strength."

18

THE TEAM OF Cecil Thayer, and the former Kronos representatives--Mel Currier, Kaye Spahr, Trinia Williams, and I, flew into Rome at Leonardo da Vinci-Fuimicino, rented a beat- up Fiat minivan, and drove south along the Tiber about fifteen miles, yet taking nearly an hour in traffic on the traffic-clogged highway. Finally, we came to the second century ruins near the coast. When we passed the unchained gate outside the Ostian digs, Trinia and I were both saddened at the crumbling desolation there, having previously witnessed Ostia at its thriving pinnacle during our previous First Century adventure. As I recall, we had both come ashore at the bustling commercial wharves in Ostia in Roman times with our friend Ara while searching for Mel and Olivia, and we were immediately impressed then as to the industriousness--the constant movement of men and material-- around the ancient port as well as the variety of the structures about the city. These buildings were quite unlike those in other Roman cities or towns, being constructed mostly of kiln-fired brick as opposed to the imposing marble and granite of the typical larger Italian cities of the time. It seems to me that the building material reflected the attitude of the city—more worklike rather than extravagant. Disappointed, we saw those magnificent Ostian buildings were now in shambled heaps of brick and granite, now overgrown debris.

"Where're the harbor and the docks we arrived at originally?" asked Trinia her eyes roaming left and right. "This doesn't look much like the city we visited on our first trip."

Cecil turned to her and reminded her of the changes that had occurred over time. "The silt from the river has filled this area in over the centuries, Trinia. The sea is now nearly a quarter mile out from here." He pointed to the west and indicated a glittering silvery reflection of water in the distance. "You can see the Mediterranean there beyond those willows."

Mel Currier had been quiet, perhaps in awe of his surroundings. "So this is where Olivia ended up--in this city," he pondered," I guess Kaye and I are the only ones on the team that never got to come here. It seems I was waylaid at the arena in Pompeii until I was rescued by Kronos."

"Dad," I asked Cecil, "why here? Wouldn't it be more likely to find Olivia and Dierk living in their magnificent Pompeii estate with their family?"

"Trust me, son. Both of them will be here, and I also chose this place and this exact time for a reason. To begin with, Olivia established herself in this city at a place here on the outskirts called Salt Marsh nearly a year with her first Roman husband Octavio Quartio a year or so before his death, and she consequently inherited considerable properties here as well as in Pompeii. It might interest you to know Olivia was actually present in this place when you and Trinia came searching for your friends. You missed her by a mere whisker. There are a few more surprises I have in store for the team--pleasant surprises I think you'll agree."

I had been so excited about the prospect of revisiting with Olivia and her husband, that I hadn't considered any other possibilities. That reunion by itself had been enough to occupy all my thoughts at the present time, but now I began to weigh Dad's new comments and began to think of some of the other possibilities as to why we would come here at this precise time and place. I was certainly interested in how Olivia had adapted to life in first century Rome. I recalled as though it were yesterday of her recruitment, first at Kronos and later by Manning Jones, and then finally her return to our team when she realized the evil of Jones mission. Her decision to remain in Roman times came as a shock until we realized how much she had come to love her husband-to-be and also that she was pregnant with his child. I was quite anxious to see the child she would have had by this time.

"Right now--surprise number one, Bill! Look who's here."

As I turned, the sight of the man sauntering across the grassy courtyard toward us took my breath away. The last time I had seen him was just before our Kronos team had been launched into the First Century. Since then, I had only heard of his meteoric involvement and final intervention on our behalf.

"John! John Dodsworth! It's you," I called, my voice cracking. "You're back. We all thought you were gone for good."

Dodsworth smiled as he reached for my extended handshake. "Without the help of Cecil and Thelma I think my demise would have been certain. They not only brought me back from my self-inflicted banishment, but they gave me a secure place, tucked neatly in an obscure niche in time, to hide as well."

I had always suspected Dad and Mom were still living at the house--the very house where my family had lived from day to day--as well as the one they had lived in for decades. Several times the two of them had mysteriously appeared in the house and I was sure they hadn't come through the door--at least not in the present. And now it's verified. They and likely Dodsworth as well, were there all the time--probably dwelling secretly in the years just before my birth or perhaps just beyond my recollection of them.

"I was concerned how we were going to pull this time jump off without Mom's assistance," I sighed. "At least we have the best non-natural time travel expert available."

Cecil grinned weakly at this comment, a bit defensively I felt.

"The best *available,* Son. That's true. I'd feel more comfortable with Thelma or even your Lydia, but the two of them have apparently gone off somewhere in time, perhaps together. But we've worked with John here and feel he's confident in the success of his next phase in computer-aided time travel."

"That's right, C," Dodsworth offered. "And there're some advantages over what we're going to do rather than go *au naturale* so to speak. For instance I've developed a technique to safely arrive at our destination. I call it AHA--Automatic Hazard Avoidance …"

"Higby mentioned that to me earlier," I said.

"Yes, right. Norton's waiting for me to finish it for him. I plan to covertly insert the finished product into some file that he'll *suddenly discover*." Dodsworth paused out of breath after what for him was an exciting and lengthy revelation. "And that's not all. I have at my disposal, a new type of capsulation that will enable us to jump together and actually take some necessary items with us when we go."

"Wouldn't that new stuff be a bit dangerous? I mean, what if it interferes with the natural progression of history?" I asked.

"Not at all, Bill. It's actually been tested! Of course, we should still be careful to not introduce anything anachronistic from our time."

Cecil raised his eyebrows. "John, I know what happened in your test case with Jones, but do you want to share that with everyone here?"

"If we can't trust our friends, who can we trust?"

"Sure," Cecil came back, "but I figured the fewer who knew, the better."

"Perhaps you're right, my friend," answered Dodsworth nodding to Cecil "Maybe we'd best leave it at that and let it suffice that the system is, in fact, battle-tested."

Mel, Trinia, Kaye, and I exchanged puzzled glances and Mel shrugged his massive shoulders.

"We'll take your word for it, John. Let's do it."

"Come with me then, and I'll show you my operations center. Leave your bags. I'll have Orson bring them up and you can retrieve anything from them later."

John Dodsworth led us along a narrow grass path that wound through the former streets and markets of the ancient city and finally to the outskirts along an extensive low stretch of coarse wild sea oats on the perimeter of the crumbling ruins of what appeared once to have been an elaborate Roman estate.

"This looks strangely familiar, like I've been here before," whispered Trinia.

"You should," agreed Dodsworth. "As I understand, you've been to Salt Marsh in the past."

"The Quartio Estate!" I gasped.

"That's it," snapped Trinia. "It was just a short visit, but I remember the stonework along the eastern boundary clearly. This was a beautiful place then."

"And you'll get to see this magnificent Roman manor again--in all its glory," interjected Dodsworth. "The manor at Salt Marsh is the place where we launch. We can show up in this secluded spot, now and in the past, and no one will see us arrive."

"You're sure?" I asked doubtfully.

"Yes, our contact there has prepared this site and made sure it was off limits to anyone."

With that, Dodsworth led us cautiously down a path of loose white gravel to a large shed with bright white clapboards and a doorway adorned with ornate, oversized black iron hinges, looking very much out of place amid the crumbling brick masonry of ancient Ostia, perched by itself near the center of a meadow of wispy grasses. An open brass Yale padlock hung cockeyed from the loop of a small chrome hasp. John deftly slipped the padlock into his pocket as the door creaked open.

We all stood in a tight arc behind John as he swung the doors open. Dodsworth snapped a light switch revealing the cavernous interior of what appeared to be a bare concrete-floored storage room. The only semblance of any higher technology was a simple glossy black computer desk and office chair with an Apple desktop and a few other loosely-wired devices resembling the switch panel I that evoked memories of a prison death chamber scene from some old prison movie--all set back into an approximately six foot square recess along the rear wall, divided from the outer room by a wire screen. For the most part, the rest of the space in the shed was open, as though someone forgot to put the car away.

"So where're the time travel capsules?" I asked, painfully remembering the cramped torpedo-shaped devices that had originally sent our first team back into time.

"Yeah, we thought everything would be set up by now," commented Mel Currier. I could see the disappointment.

Dodsworth laughed aloud.

"This is it, my friends. Actually a major improvement over those original transfer pods. Too much chance for error, what with everyone operating his own send signals. That's what caused so much trouble before."

Dodsworth walked inside the shed and pointed out a few details unnoticed previously.

"Look up here. Around the perimeter along the walls, floor, and ceiling is a myriad of wiring, transistors, and other technical junk that makes this shed the actual transfer pod. A tremendous improvement, you must admit."

"You mean this old shed is the transfer pod?" demanded Kaye Spahr.

"That's correct."

Without direction of any kind we all entered the time capsule shed and gawked admiringly at the wiring and electronics pointed out by Dodsworth.

"And this will work?" I asked John.

"Absolutely. It's been tried. In fact, I've been on a very important excursion of my own."

Our newly-formed team poked around Dodsworth's equipment for half an hour or so before he led us to one of the ruined buildings nearby.

"This place is still in pretty good shape," Dodsworth explained. " I've been using it as a temporary residence thanks to the friends I know from the Ostian Aggettivo Associazione. As I understand it, this building was the Quartio servant's quarters during the halcyon years of Ostia. Of course we've modernized it a bit--electricity, plumbing,-- whatever we felt we needed. Actually it's rather comfortable and has plenty of room."

"Amazing," sighed Kaye Spahr as she pushed through the metal door of the apartment assigned to her. "Servant's quarters you say?"

"Yes, in fact this place was once the residence for Dierk, the husband of Olivia Pelser," said John.

"Of course--Dierk--I met him at the rescue. I believe his status as a slave has changed considerably."

"An understatement to say the least," laughed Dodsworth. "Very soon after he found he was the legal son of Octavius Quartio, he claimed his father's senatorial position in Rome and inherited Salt Marsh Manor in addition to many other properties, including the place in Pompeii."

"Pompeii!" shouted Trinia Williams, her eyes fluttering. "My debut as a gladiator!"

"And mine as well," echoed Mel Currier. "We've all got dark memories of that place."

These commentaries certainly brought back a flood of my own memories and also reminded me to call back home to see if I could contact Cheryl and Lydia again about our upcoming trip. I figured they should be home by now, wherever they had gone.

Once outside, I clicked on and swiped the Samsung S4 Cheryl had insisted I get and punched *Cheryl* under Favorites and hit Send.

After a short wait, an automated voice mechanically informed me that Cheryl Thayer was not available and instructed me to leave a voice message, which I did. I left a single clue word for her: OSTIA. I had spoken a number of times about our adventures there and was fairly certain, at least with Lydia's help, that they could figure out where I was going. When I tried Lydia's cell, I got the same message as on Cheryl's phone and left the same voice mail there as well.

I didn't like the feeling of this--not knowing where they were. Where could they be where neither of their phones would work? It felt like deja vu. The sudden intuitive realization hit me--they had to be somewhere together in time! All I could think of was their infamous debacle in Renaissance Italy.

When I went back inside, the team members had settled into quarters chosen for each of them, and John directed me to a cubicle of my own at the near end of the dark corridor. Each of the apartments was about the size of a room we might have booked at Holiday Inn. Except for the ambience of the cracked flagstone flooring and crumbling antique brick walls, we might easily have convinced ourselves we were in a modern hotel if we had awakened during the night. Whoever had done the wiring had taken little care in hiding the wires as I noticed several outlets dangling awkwardly from some crudely-cut openings in the masonry. Unquestioningly, the room was still in the process of modern restoration. The bed was surprisingly comfortable and I would have fallen asleep almost immediately except for the gnawing concern over my inability to contact Cheryl and Lydia. I consoled myself with the argument that I could be back in a moment of real time even though I might possibly spend years in the past. What could possibly happen in that time? Yeah, right. Eventually I drifted off in a fitful sleep filled with nightmares of the two of them being pursued by cavemen and prehistoric creatures.

19

Norton Higby and John Graffey often spent late mornings over a cup of coffee contemplating their successes and failures at Kronos. This morning was a bit different in that they were joined by the new directors, Anthony Perry and Kenneth Deane.

"Gentlemen," began Deane sporting a sour lemon face, "we have deep concerns over the future of this facility. I mean, it appears we are not moving forward at the expected pace. We also have the distinct impression that certain things are being held back from us."

"Like funding," interjected Anthony Perry. "We have no idea how much or from what source our money comes. I think our former full time directors, Lueenhuik and Paladin, are fully aware but play dumb when asked about it. They say the source is unknown to all but a few people here, and that it is not important at this time to divulge the anonymous source without jeopardizing future funding. They never indicated who the 'few' were, but I'm sure they're part of the in crowd."

"Yes, they say the fewer people that know about it, the safer it is," growled Deane. "There were rumors the money came in large part from billionaire, Manning Jones. They say, too, he was attempting some sort of takeover. Then Jones suddenly disappeared in a shroud of mystery. You don't suppose Kronos had anything to do with that, do you?"

Higby and Graffey knew as much as anyone as to where the money came from. It had been a windfall of sorts from investments made in the past that were a result of inside trading, so to speak. Knowing what investments would skyrocket and jumping back to the past to take advantage of them resulted in a huge profit for the company and would prove to be enough to sustain it through the past twenty or so years. Both Higby and Graffey had been sworn to secrecy over the issue and their loyalty to the program and the original directors was unbending. Both of them were well aware of what happened with Jones during the first time jump by the Kronos team and his return under secret arrest. What happened to him after that was anyone's guess.

Both men shrugged their shoulders as Deane and Perry froze their stares at them.

"Neither of you knows the source either?" hissed Deane. "Well someone around here does, and I plan to find out who it is."

"We've checked the financial records and have had our accountants trace all transactions as far back as they could." Anthony Perry paused here and stared at the two men again. "Of course everything was a dead end."

"Sorry," apologized Higby in his best Sergeant Schultz imitation, "but I know nothing."

"Right," agreed Graffey, "we just work here and take orders."

"On the other issue, the one about progress," continued Perry, "we see there have been no time excursions, or even attempts, in the last two years—not since a team was taken to Pompeii to rescue our first travelers."

"Safety is the main issue," said John Graffey. "We are working overtime on various software issues. In the meantime, we have perfected improved support and equipment such as the universal language interpreter and translator, enhanced the quality of time capsules, upgraded the stun weapons ..."

"Look, we don't care about these trivial matters," snapped Deane, his eyes flashing. "If there's not progress soon, I mean scheduled jumps into the past, we plan on taking matters into our own hands."

The two exasperated directors glared one final time at the two men before they stood and steamed from the room.

Graffey calmly took a sip from his coffee and looked casually at his partner. "Are you going to text Anton and Marge, or do you want me to do it?"

2 0

A SHORT TIME after renting the twentieth century version of the same Hartsfield Inn room Lydia had rented in 1863, the trio of Carson Hardwick, Cheryl and Lydia Thayer had arrived, touched heads, and materialized clandestinely in the room Lydia had used for her previous departure. The room was designed and furnished in Victorian style with blue flower-patterned wallpaper, two crystal shaded kerosene lamps and a collection of ornately carved wood and over-stuffed chairs accompanied by a footed dark mahogany table.

"How quaint," Cheryl remarked pointing to a kerosene lamp. "That lamp certainly does something for the décor."

"Mom, don't forget—that's not just décor. That's what they use to light the room—that and some candles."

"I'm all pumped up about actually being here in Gettysburg during the Civil War," interrupted Hardwick. "We can look at all the décor later. I'd like to go out on the street and see the town right now."

The three made a quick inspection of each other just to be sure nothing was out of place and then made their way from their room down the narrow set of stairs leading to the lobby where they were dazzled by an array of elegant furnishings, chandeliers, polished oak tables, and a variety of upholstered chairs and sofas.

"Ahh, Miss Thayer," shouted David Hartsfield suddenly appearing from behind a counter, "I see you've risen early. And these people must be your friends."

"Why yes they are, Mr. Hartsfield. This is my mother, Cheryl Thayer. And this gentleman is Professor …"

"Major General," interjected Hardwick.

"Yes, yes of course—*Major General* Carson Hardwick. He's here on Army business of course," agreed Lydia grudgingly.

"What else?" smiled Hartsfield. "And this lovely lady—you say she is your mother?"

Lydia returned the hotel owner's smile.

Turning to Hardwick with raised eyebrows, Mr. Hartsfield asked pleasantly, "I'm sure Major General that you will be meeting with the other military personnel who arrived last evening? They failed to indicate you would be here, but then—why should they let me know what is happening? I'm sure with the past few week's activity around here ... I'm only a simple innkeeper and should not be asking such important questions I suppose." Hartsfield grinned a bit sheepishly. "They've taken the liberty to pitch tents a short distance in the back of the inn. Should I send someone back to announce your rising?"

Carson Hardwick took this moment to have a brief coughing spell while he regained his composure. "Yes, of course, Mr. Hartsfield. Did you mention what unit they are from? I mean, there are so many units in the area ..."

"A cavalry regiment. I believe from Indiana. I believe they are attached to one of our Pennsylvania Brigades. I heard one of them say they were out looking for the Reb Army. Sure hope they keep them away from us! There have been reports of their movement in the area. And you're correct about all those other units. Seems we've had an influx of military people from both sides in the past few weeks. There was even a bit of a battle—more like a short skirmish though—to the north— around the college I understand. Even got a brief glimpse of Jeb Stuart gallivanting on north of town on his way east."

"*The* Jeb Stuart, you mean?" gasped Hardwick.

"Are there any other Stuart's? Sure hope not—one's plenty."

"Just wasn't aware Stuart came to Gettysburg for this battle, at least not yet anyway."

"Battle? No, Stuart wasn't here for that one. Not much of a battle anyway. More of a massacre, I'd say. Just a bunch of local college youngsters and untrained folks who thought they could defend the

Commonwealth. Didn't really stand a chance against those seasoned Rebs who came up. All scattered, killed or captured with hardly a fight."

Lydia stared at Hardwick as Hartsfield described the encounter that had taken place earlier in the month.

"Professor," Lydia whispered hoarsely, "I thought you said there was no action before the first of July and we were safe?"

"Lydia, my dear, I was just referring to the main battle. But never mind these little skirmishes. There's really little danger."

"One bullet is a danger, sir. I'm not so concerned for myself, but for my mother, I fear for her safety, and even yours, sir."

"But Lydia, my dear, I understood your main goal was to find this Hunter Mathews fellow we've met in Chicago. Surely you had to be aware the presence of soldiers in the region if you ever hoped to find him. We know his unit was here in Gettysburg a few days before the battle, so here we are."

The logic of Hardwick's reasoning was still being absorbed by Lydia when they were suddenly interrupted by a harsh clack of heels on the polished hardwood of the lobby.

"Sir!" A dark- mustached Union officer, himself wearing the epaulets of major-general, snapped stiffly at attention. Two stern-looking aides stood stiffly, the men on either side like two soldier bookends. "Sir, I was not made aware of your presence, Sir! If I had known, I would have had orderlies up at first light to attend …"

"At ease, General," said Hardwick as he was becoming more comfortable with his new starring role in the military limelight. "No one here knew I was coming. As you can readily see, I am ordered from the Inspector-General himself. Of course I have the authority to view the preparedness of our army from the top to the bottom. The War Department feels it is much more efficient to arrive unannounced, you understand."

"I understand, Sir. Could I have your name, Sir?"

"Hardwick," the professor answered briskly, "Major General Carson Hardwick. Here are my documents." Hardwick passed his sham identity papers to the soldier.

"Thank you, General. Is there anything I can get for you?"

By now Hardwick was beginning to sense the power one gains from positions of great authority. "Sir, if you could, please obtain some reliable maps of this town and its surroundings and have them dropped off as soon as possible. I would like to assess the area in case we would have to fight the Confederates here. Oh, and General, I do not believe I caught your name."

"Doubleday, Sir, Major General Abner Doubleday. At your service, Sir. And if it would not be too much to ask, General, are we expecting a battle soon?"

"I think, General, it would be wise to have your cavalry reconnoiter to the west. I have heard from civilian sources that the main Confederate army is not far off." With that, Doubleday saluted smartly, turned with his orderlies, and quick-stepped across the porch and disappeared around the building.

"Do you know who that Doubleday guy was, ladies?"

"Doubleday!" said Cheryl, "Doesn't he write books?"

"No, no, not that Doubleday," laughed Hardwick.

"Wasn't he the one that supposedly invented baseball?" asked Lydia.

"I believe that is the man, ladies."

"Well I never could understand the game," sighed Cheryl. "Probably that Doubleday fellow should think more about his publishing than playing with a ball."

Lydia stared through the window, hoping her mother would not notice the look she could not hold back.

Just then, more footsteps thumped up the front steps and onto the porch, and a young lieutenant, impeccably uniformed, appeared and stiffly offered Carson Hardwick an oilskin packet stamped "U.S." in black lettering.

"Sir, from the General."

"Thank you Lieutenant," Hardwick responded as he turned to greet the courier.

There was something familiar to the man's voice and when Lydia turned to face him, she could not hold back a reactive response.

"Hunter Mathews! It's you."

"Ma'am?"

The handsome, young cavalry officer was puzzled, perhaps a bit shaken, by Lydia's recognition of him. The man had no recollection of ever having met this perky young woman who most certainly he had met him on some other occasion. It was not like him to forget such a pretty face and was embarrassed by his apparent loss of memory. In one motion, he had removed his hat and let it hang stiffly in front of him.

"Oh, I'm sorry," stuttered Lydia." I mean—of course—I have access to information about you from the general here. You see--- I mean—I'm his personal secretary ... I noticed your name on some papers."

"How nice," whispered Carson Hardwick to Lydia.

Lydia rolled her eyes upward.

"I'm flattered that you would remember me—just from reviewing old files," remarked Hunter Mathews while offering Hardwick the oilskin packet. "General, I have the charts you requested."

"Thank you lieutenant. You're dismissed."

With a gallant bow towards Lydia, Mathews stepped backwards, saluted Hardwick, pivoted smartly on his left foot, and disappeared through the doorway from which he had entered.

"That was him, Professor—Hunter Mathews," gasped Lydia. "Why did you send him away?"

"Don't worry. We'll see him any time you want, Lyd," replied Hardwick. "Thought I might ask to have him assigned to our party. You know—just in case you wanted to get acquainted or something."

"Professor, it's not like that!"

"Of course it isn't, dear. That's why you made all these arrangements to come here in the first place, isn't it?"

Carson Hardwick hid a cat-that-ate-the-canary expression as he turned his back. As Lydia's stare followed Hardwick stroll through the outer parlor, she quickly made a reassessment of herself. Down deep she realized there was some degree of truth to what the professor had said. In her heart she knew there might possibly be something there other than curiosity, a physical attraction of the handsome Hunter Mathews she could not deny, but she knew too that any developed relationship she might imagine with this shadowy man from the past would be a bit bizarre. Still, Lydia felt the desire to somehow come to know the man better, if just to satisfy her own inquisitiveness.

Hardwick was not the only one who reveled in newfound renown. In the brief time after she had come to 1863 Gettysburg, Cheryl Thayer had actually become Cheryl Thayer, the famous actress. She had wasted no time expertly spreading gossipy information among a few of the more vocal waitresses in the dining room about her elaborate, but sham, career as an actress from Pittsburgh, and of course, Cheryl was sure to "accidentally" leave one of Hardwick's bogus programs on an outdoor tabletop as she sat mindlessly perusing a smudged copy of the *Gettysburg Times* while sitting under a frilly umbrella along the inn's expansive eastern veranda. She leisurely swished an oversized fan consisting of half dozen gaudy oversized white ostrich feathers near her right cheek. David Hartsfield, the owner and innkeeper, was quick to notice the theatrical program Cheryl had left for bait, and had snatched it up, just as Cheryl had planned for him to do.

"Mrs. Thayer, I had no idea you were so renowned," Hartsfield gushed. "You honor my establishment with your presence."

"Oh dear," said Cheryl with a wave of one gloved hand. "Did I forget to put that silly material away? I meant to throw it in the trash. It's really nothing much you know."

"Not at all, dear, do you mind if I keep this treasure?" answered a vibrant Hartsfield as he deftly folded the program and stuck it inside his vest pocket. "But what brings you to our little town? The closest thing we have in theater is a little play given annually over at the Seminary. Just wait until the ladies here find out about you—they'll be so thrilled. Can you tell me a little about this play you've done. It says here it's called *Our American Cousin.*"

"Oh Mr. Hartsfield, I wouldn't want to bore you with too many details ..."

"No, no, not at all, Mrs. Thayer. Are you planning on going on tour? Where will your next performance be held?"

"Hmm." Cheryl paused for some time in thought and then smiled broadly at Hartsfield. "Philadelphia or Harrisburg, I think." Then, remembering part of the briefing Hardwick had given her about the play, she added, "We plan to have the show in Washington sometime in a year or so. I think when the war's done. We understand it's one of the President's favorites, you know."

"Lincoln's favorite? You don't say," David Hartsfield gasped as he reached and touched Cheryl's wrist. "Couldn't you tell me a little about it?"

"Oh Mr. Hartsfield, I wouldn't want to spoil it for you," said Cheryl sheepishly. "Maybe you would like to come sometime and see for yourself. I'm sure we can find a few comps!"

Lydia had returned to the upper room above the parlor and was sitting on the edge of one of the overstuffed featherbeds furnished specially for her mother and her by the management when Cheryl entered, still swishing her ostrich feather fan furtively in front of her face. For several minutes, Cheryl stood silently, now and then batting her eyelashes in her daughter's direction.

"OK, Mom, what's up," Lydia finally said.

"What makes you think something's up, Lyd?"

"Just tell me what you've been doing. I hope you haven't done anything to mess up our mission here, have you?"

"Oh no, Lyd, I've just been enhancing my position around here as an actress. You know-- the role you and Carson made up for me."

"Tell me, Mom. What did you say? Whom did you talk to?"

"Nothing much. I told Mr. Hartsfield a bit about the play in the program. He wants me to be his guest at a tea this afternoon—with some of the women in town. I guess a few of them are real devotees of theater and want to meet one of the stars of the entertainment industry. That's me, you know, Lyd."

This was one of the worries Lydia had about her mother's participation in this project. Her past track record spoke for itself— Florence, Pompeii, prehistoric America. All she could think of was the misinformation her mother had probably yielded only an hour before when she had spoken with the innkeeper about the plot of the play that she admittedly had a difficult time understanding. Lydia knew right then she had better take charge of this afternoon tea if she did not want things getting out of hand.

"Mom, I better be there with you, if you don't mind. You might need some help with some of the questions they could ask."

"You don't trust me …?" Cheryl began. When she saw the penetrating gaze she was getting from her daughter, she suddenly conceded. "Well, Lyd, maybe that would be a good suggestion after all. You always seem to know what to say in these situations."

Meanwhile Lydia had been determined to make doubly sure Professor Hardwick would not slip up on his promise to include Lieutenant Hunter Mathews in their touring party. She could plainly see that both Hardwick and her mother had at present gotten intricately involved in the Gettysburg mission despite their stated intentions otherwise, and she was already getting a bad feeling. Somehow she was losing control of the situation. None of this was supposed to happen this way. Her mother was now a famous actress, hosting an afternoon tea and awkwardly fielding questions about herself that she had virtually no ability to handle. It would be only a matter of time before her mother exposed the whole theater stunt or perhaps be thrown into the nearest insane asylum over some wild claim about traveling through time. And despite Lydia's wishes to the contrary, Professor Carson Hardwick, not only had made himself an important major-general in the Union Army, she had unwillingly been cast into becoming his personal secretary. From the beginning, when the Professor had arrived at her apartment in Chicago with a van full of stuff, she strongly suspected he savored the opportunity to be involved. It would have been much simpler for her if she had driven to Gettysburg herself, slipped back to 1863, met, and resolved her curiosity about Hunter Mathews, and then returned to her own time.

About mid-morning, accompanied by a preening Cheryl the star actress, appearing much more the peacock than the feathered fan she carried, we rounded the inn and proceeded along the creek bank for about a quarter mile and, there, easily found the mounted encampment bivouacked in the grassy meadow. An area roped off behind the tents held perhaps a hundred or more, curried, well-fed, silky, dark-colored horses, as shirtless, sweating men actively forked generous rations of hay for some animals, while some men adjusted gray canvas feedbags on the snouts of others. As they came up to the military tent community bearing the regimental colors of the Third Indiana Cavalry, they were greeted with spirited fanfare by the men posted there.

"Hello there ladies," called one soldier, attempting to imitate Cheryl's swaying gait.

There were other noisy comments, laughter and hoots from the men.

"You're making rounds a bit early in the day, aren't you?" taunted another.

Lydia was aware that throughout history, armies always maintained their camp followers—women of all ages who tended to the whims and desires of the soldiers—for a price of course. She had seen other military men in various times before, and was not surprised or particularly upset by the soldier's crude responses to her sudden appearance.

"Attention men!" A growling order reverberated from the entrance to one of the more prominent tents. "Stand down!"

The men looked a bit confused, but grudgingly reacted to the officer's order to stand down. As they retreated to their former duties, a few still wore knowing, lewd glances.

"Miss Thayer," shouted Lieutenant Mathews, "what brings you to this place? I apologize for the men, Ma'am."

"No need, Lieutenant," laughed Lydia. "Don't be angry with them. I'm sure they misunderstood."

"So what can I do for you, Miss Thayer?" smiled Mathews. The lieutenant had seen Cheryl before but had not been introduced.

Lydia looked back at her mother. "This is my mother, Lieutenant—Cheryl Thayer."

With a wry smile, Hunter Mathews tipped his hat to Cheryl. "Nice to meet you, Ma'am."

This was the first time Lydia had been able to get a real good look at Hunter Mathews. Certainly the post-Civil War meeting in Chicago had been a fleeting one. She had just now and this morning, gotten enough of a look that she had remembered the man's dark curled hair, blue eyes, and handsome, rugged appearance.

"Lydia," tittered Cheryl as she pulled her daughter aside, "It's that Errol Flint guy—you know—the old movie star. I just watched him the other night in the motel—a story starring him and President Reagan when he was in the movies, where he was this dashing cavalry commander."

"Oh you mean Flynn—Errol Flynn," agreed Lydia whispering. "Yes he certainly does look a lot like him. And a dashing cavalry commander—so appropriate!"

This time when she met Mathews, of course, much to Lydia's delight, the lieutenant still was in possession of both arms, rather than having an empty left shirt sleeve.. By the time Lydia and Mathews had taken a few steps toward each other, Hunter Mathews had doffed his cavalryman's Stetson and stood before her as if at inspection. His uniform was well-pressed and immaculate, with several emblems, bars, and battle ribbons adorning his dark blue polished brass-buttoned Union jacket. The lieutenant presented himself quite impressively in Lydia's eyes.

"First time I've been in a cavalry camp, lieutenant," said Lydia smiling broadly. "Rather impressive, I might add." She took in as much view as she could of the camp—and of course, the lieutenant, without being obvious about it.

"Like a tour?" offered Mathews pleasantly. "We're mighty proud of the condition of our Morgans."

"Sure," squealed Cheryl like a teenager at a rock concert, "what's a Morgan?"

"That's our horses, Ma'am. The best in the country!" he answered uncomfortably.

"Actually, I came around back here to see if I could obtain your services," Lydia responded, attempting to divert Mathews' attention toward her. "But I'm very impressed with your whole operation here, Lieutenant."

"And how could I be of service, Ma'am?"

"The general" began Lydia, "and I, as well, would like to avail upon your knowledge and expertise to give us a short tour of the upcoming battlegrounds here near Gettysburg …"

"Oh I doubt there will ever be a battle here, Miss Thayer—the Rebs are mostly well over the ridges. If they start this way, we'll meet them somewhere to the west or maybe north. I think they're planning on Philadelphia or maybe even Harrisburg."

"Oh, but what about the Battle of …" started Cheryl mindlessly.

"Anyway, Lieutenant," snapped Lydia as loud as he could to cut off her mother's statement. "Washington has ordered the general to check this area out, just in case of course."

"Of course. I will definitely be at the general's service," snapped Mathews in a military fashion. And then he added more softly, "And yours as well, Miss Thayer."

"Please, Lieutenant—just, Lydia," she twinkled.

That afternoon, there rose an incessant cackling of conversation and bustle coming from the parlor of the Hartsfield Inn as more than a dozen women from the town gathered to meet the famous personality of the by-now-almost-legendary thespian, Mrs. Cheryl Thayer of Pittsburgh. David Hartsfield had efficiently spread the rumor of the personality housed in his inn and made the appropriate invitations to some of the more prominent people in town as well as a few ladies who he knew would both spread and enhance the meeting being held there today. When Cheryl entered wearing a black lace-trimmed, full length scarlet gown adorned with a realistic faux glass diamond necklace and a matching wide-brimmed hat, she carried a frilly parasol in her right hand and several of her fake programs under her left arm.

"Ladies, Mrs. Cheryl Thayer, star actress from Old Drury Theater in Pittsburgh!" announced Hartsfield proudly as she entered the room.

One of the women rushed up, curtsied appropriately, and handed Cheryl a bunch of long-stemmed red roses.

"Oh thank you all. This isn't really necessary." Cheryl Thayer virtually glowed with the exhilaration of the moment.

One of the women called out pointing to Lydia, "Who is this young lady with you?"

"Oh just my daughter, Lydia," she sighed. "She sometimes comes to these things, just to see what it's like being on the top so to speak. Sometimes I let her field questions. I have to save my voice, you know."

The women applauded and nodded assent. David Hartsfield announced that Cheryl had agreed to answer questions and perhaps talk on certain topics of interest about acting. Those present were instructed to state their names, say what they would like, and then be seated.

Some of them mostly asked things about costumes, the plot of the play, scenery, travel, and other things. Anytime Cheryl started saying anything inappropriate or anachronistic, Lydia, who had as thoroughly as possible, studied everything she could about the play in the hour before the tea, would intervene and patch things up.

"Hello, my name is Sarah Broadhead, and my question is—what kind of a relationship could you have with your husband when you are away like this?"

"Oh no problem," answered Cheryl nonchalantly, "he's always away doing something of his own, usually flying to West Virginia ..."

"When she says *flying* she doesn't mean it literally," interrupted Lydia. "And West Virginia—that's the name of the new state that recently separated from Virginia."

"My name is Liberty Hollinger," called out another lady. "Where do you get all the fabulous wardrobes like the one you're wearing today? Where does the money come from to pay for them?"

"That's easy. Of course money is no problem. Not in my profession, especially someone who has reached the heights of popularity I have. And I get everything from Carson ..."

"That's Carson *Smith*, right Mother?" said Lydia cutting her off in mid-sentence. She knew Hardwick had no desire to have his military persona become associated with the theater. "He's the stage designer attached to our acting company. Anything we want, he either buys or has someone make it."

"Smith? No, Lyd ..."

"Yes, Mother, *Smith* is his name. *Right?*" Lydia punctuated the last word hard while sharply bumping her mother's arm with her elbow.

Cheryl brightened a bit, finally understanding. "Oh, yes, that's right, dear—Smith it is."

Another older woman, Jenny McCreary, wanted to know how we had traveled here from Pittsburgh, and if we had seen any of the Johnny Rebs along the way.

"We rode in Carson's SUV on the turnpike," said Cheryl again without thinking. "And we didn't see much anything during the night of course, especially with so much snow and all."

Lydia laughed out loud. "Mother, you must not let your imagination run away from reality! " Turning to a tableful of women, she explained, "All you ladies must realize sometimes Mother plays with you a bit, attempting to use her theatrical imagination to demonstrate how creative she must be to be effective as an actress. You all know there's no snow in July, right Mother?"

"That's right, Lyd. I'm just messing with all of you. It's like you said—no snow—no SUV either—it's all something to get you all to realize how I'm so creative in my mind, you know."

Everyone there applauded politely.

Other than a few incidents that Lydia capably defused, the afternoon went well. As the satisfied and highly entertained audience departed, they filed by, making complimentary remarks, requesting information on upcoming performances, and even asking for Cheryl's autograph. One young lady with dark eyes and tightly-braided auburn hair was particularly enthusiastic and obviously interested in the performing arts.

"I've been in this town all my life. I love it here. I love the people here as well and hope someday we can attract more performers like you to Gettysburg. I would be highly honored if you would autograph something for me. I hope someday to give it to my children."

"You're married then?" asked Cheryl.

"No, Mrs. Thayer, not yet. My fiancé, his name is Johnston Skelley, is off to war somewhere in Virginia I believe."

"Why not sign one of your programs for her, Mother. That might prove interesting later, I believe," suggested Lydia devilshly. "And, say ... Miss ..."

"Wade—Jennie Wade," she answered.

There was an extended pause before Lydia proceeded. "Yes, Miss Wade, what I was about to say—I believe that in a reasonably short time there will be no shortage of actors and actresses circulating in this town." Lydia was envisioning a future filled with reenactors on every street corner of Gettysburg early in July each year

With a deal of fanfare, Cheryl autographed one of the copies of the Old Drury program she had laid out on the table and gave it to the girl. Everyone applauded and slowly began to leave, completely taken up in conversations of their experience that day. Lydia had a serious expression on her face, and when she turned to Cheryl, a tear glistened in one eye.

"Why so sad, Lyd. Everything went well. Didn't you have a good time?"

"Mom, it sometimes makes me sad when I meet characters in history who have tragedy in their futures."

"Oh? And who might we be talking about, dear?"

Lydia raised her eyebrows. "You didn't catch that girl's name? Jennie Wade? Do you remember the last trip our family took to Gettysburg about ten years ago? Do you remember the *Jenny Wade* House?"

Cheryl's eyes roamed back and forth momentarily-- a light seemed to, all at once, brighten her face, and then she blurted out, "Oh yeah, I remember. She was baking a cake or something …"

"Bread, Mom."

"Right, now wasn't that the house where the girl was killed by … Oh my God! That was the girl—that was Jennie *Wade*!."

"They said she was killed by a sniper," added Lydia sadly.

"My God, that's terrible, Lyd!" Then Cheryl leaned closer to her daughter and whispered, "What's a sniper, dear?"

"A sharpshooter, Mom—someone—a good shot—who just sits somewhere hidden and picks off people of importance.

Cheryl stared hard at Jenny Wade, tears now welling up in her own eyes. "Oh, Lyd, what are we going to do? Let's tell her to hide in the basement or something"

"Mom, we can't interfere with what is going to happen. Kronos has a general warning issued for all of their time travelers never to intervene in anything that might change the course of events. It seems to make perfect sense. Don't you remember what happened back in Ohioview? I always remember the *Back to the Future* movies where the meddling of some of the characters almost had disastrous results for their future. Also, I've discovered in my own time journeys, even when I've tried to step in and alter something, it has never changed anyway. It always seems to end up the same in the end. I think it's useless to even try."

"Oh, but Lyd, I feel so bad. Jennie is such a nice girl. And she's supposed to get married and all. I feel sorry for her boyfriend, John, too."

"If it's any consolation, Mom, I vaguely remember from what our guide that day in Gettysburg said that her fiancé dies a short time later in some battle and never finds out about the tragedy here with Jennie."

"Oh how terrible, and I was having such a great time till now."

"I understand, Mom. But now you may realize this time travel thing isn't all fun and games. It often leaves us with, not only bad memories, but a terrible burden—there are so many things that we could do that, if successful, could create a far different world than the one we came from—and probably changes we may end up not much liking. Can you imagine anything that might be changed if we happened to save Jennie?"

For a few moments, Cheryl was silent, pondering the question her daughter had asked.

"Lydia! I just thought of one thing. How could we have visited the battlefield and the Jenny Wade House with Bill when you were a kid and she had not been shot? There would have been no reason to go there." Cheryl held her hands to her temples. "This is so confusing."

"That's right, Mom, and for the sake of our own sanity, no matter how much we want to interfere, we have to keep our hands off."

21

A THICK, GRAY fog had drifted in from the harbor and enshrouded our encampment the next morning, hopefully not a dismal portent for the expedition we had planned for that day. I re-checked my phone for messages and there was still no answer from either of the girls. I was beginning to wonder if this upcoming excursion might be a bad idea. I held an uneasy mood—a feeling I had felt before on our past time travel escapade when I had found out Lydia and Cheryl had gone off into time and were almost lost. In the end, the assurances of John Dodsworth convinced me we would soon be returning safely, and he would work with me later that day using the powerful search capabilities of his equipment to locate Cheryl and Lydia.

We had all gathered back at Dodsworth's garage-sized time capsule shortly after breakfast, anxiously waiting for John to let us in. We had been directed to remove our watches, so we had no idea exactly how early we were. I was certain, though, knowing Dodsworth's penchant for punctuality that everything would be on schedule. After what seemed an interminable wait, Dodsworth arrived with a shrewd half smile. When the door finally creaked open and the light flashed on, we were overwhelmed by the hodgepodge of equipment laid out on the concrete floor. John Dodsworth carefully proceeded to go over each piece of equipment.

"These items will be taken back with you to the year 17 AD. First, notice the stun guns developed at Kronos by Norton Higby. They like everything else here are retrograded-- disguised to appear as items from that time. The stun guns, as you see, are made to appear as common items you might experience such as these walking staves, the kind regularly utilized by travelers for protection against thieves and other culprits. Of course, your staves pack a little more wallop than those of early Roman travelers. Be reminded, all stuns are to be set as mildly as needed. No one should be very badly injured."

"As per our Kronos directive to not seriously injure anyone," agreed Mel Currier.

"That's right," I agreed. "No one was ever very sure what impact the death of people in history might have on the future."

"Just like Marty McFly in the *Back to the Future* films," Kate reminded us.

Dodsworth went on demonstrating." "Here are small leather bags of gold Roman coins familiar at the time. These are similar to the ones Kronos provided on your last jump—high quality gold—quite pure. Each of you also has a short sword with high tech steel blade that will be able to cut through almost anything—also thanks to Kronos technology."

"It'll feel good to have one of these in my hands again," sighed Trinia as she tested the air with a few sweeping swings of her blade.

"You may recognize the costumes I have selected for each of you," continued John. As much as possible, I have reproduced the same getup that each of you used in your previous travels here. Bill … Mel … Kaye … the same robes and regalia that previously identified you as ambassadors from the legendary Atlantis. Trinia … the warrior's armor and lances that made you famous in the arena at Pompeii. I'm certain you will be quite readily recognized by much of the populace even though this is several years after your gladiatorial episode there. Olivia has pointed out that your legendary feats have lived on--flourished in fact--even been enhanced a bit. They called you Medusa, because of your dreadlocks, if I remember from the log--the Black Medusa. You were quite a hit. And Cecil, you will be dressed as a noble patrician if that's acceptable."

"That's fine with me, John," Cecil Thayer jovially assented. "Thelma and I have often posed as upper class Romans in our past ventures. I have a few costumes of my own similar to this one. Unfortunately that costume of clothes and equipment is unavailable at this time without Thelma."

"And of course, you're all equipped with komodo armor and ULIT translators?" interrupted Dodsworth, attempting to avoid further thoughts about Cecil's prodigal wife.

We all nodded in agreement. Even Trinia Williams had been given a minimal boost to her language powers, and recently had been outfitted with the latest komodo skin.

"Good. Then there are a number of other small pieces of equipment that need no explanation--things like lighters and mini flashlights-- and such. Things similar to the Kronos stuff you had with you before. Gather your gear together and get dressed. If you have any further questions that I did not cover, let me know. The sooner you're ready, the sooner we can get started."

As we broke away to make final preparations, I took Dad firmly by the elbow. "All right, Dad," I hissed in his ear, "This has gone far enough. It's time you let me know what's going on with Mom. Where is she?"

Cecil sighed. After a long pause he answered me. "Son, do you remember the discussion we had after the first Kronos mission? I mean the one about your mother's predilection with the life of Christ?"

"Yes, I remember it well. We spoke of the need to refrain from interference in historical events--to be certain we did nothing to change events in history that might affect the future."

"That's right, Son. But this power she has--the time travel thing that she's inherited--it sometimes gives her the feeling that she can do anything she wants--and get away with it. She's constantly, as long as I've traveled through time with her, toyed with the idea that small unnoticed things she could do might have a positive impact on the beliefs of our time."

"So she's off somewhere in time trying to make positive changes in the past? Well I'm sure she's going to do the responsible thing when it comes time to make decisions."

"I would hope so, Bill, but I'm not so sure this time."

"So why are you worried now?"

Cecil raised his eyebrows as he turned to face me. "You've asked the question yourself. Why aren't we together now? Why is it she didn't take me with her on her most recent time foray? I've always been a steadying influence on her decisions—a conscience you might say. She jokingly referred to me as her own Jiminy Cricket. I've always previously talked her out of interfering in ways that might be harmful on time excursions, and she's unquestioningly accepted my reasoning in nearly every situation particularly when visiting the time of Jesus Christ and doing things that would impact Christianity and religion generally. I think she basically just wants to be able to witness every important event in Jesus Christ's ministry on Earth."

The expression in Dad's eyes reminded of the time in high school when I had come home and decided I thought it might be best if I would drop out of school. He had that same look now—an outwardly, steely determined stare, but with just a deeper hint of uncertainty.

"Son, I'm afraid your mother has decided to do this one on her own without my interference, but I'm not going to let her do it."

I was a bit confused, but I was interested in hearing Dad's plan on stopping Mom's interference in the time-space continuum.. "Dad, how can you possibly stop her?"

"I understand your concern, Dad," I sighed, shaking my head, "but I don't see what you can do. She could be anywhere in that thirty or so year period of Jesus of Nazareth's existence. And if she sees you—or any of us for that matter—coming her way, she can jump away to--who knows? It's the proverbial needle in the haystack, but the needle keeps moving to unlimited haystacks!"

"Seems impossible doesn't it? That's the problem with you, Bill. You could never think out of the box."

I was more confused than ever.

"Well then, Dad, if this campaign to stop her is so important, why aren't we somewhere in Judea--perhaps during the early preaching of Christ …"

"Just another haystack, son. We don't have the concentrated technological ability with these Kronos capsules of Dodsworth's to jump around indiscriminately looking here and there. We'd burn out all of his machine's circuits after about half a dozen jumps!"

"So then, where--or when--do you suggest we try?"

Cecil packed his equipment without a word. It seemed like an eternity before he answered.

"Bill, the *where* is right here--in Ostia. The *when* is the exact month and year where Dodsworth's time contraption is going to take us-- 19 AD."

According to my quick calculations, realizing the birth of Christ actually was likely 4 BC, that would make Jesus about fifteen years old. It made no sense to me that Mom would be here in Ostia in 19 AD before he had actually begun his ministry.

It was as if Dad was reading my thoughts.

"No, Bill, your mother will not very likely be here when we jump back."

I held out both arms, shrugging in submission.

"There is no real need to find the needle. Sooner or later our needle will come home if there is nothing for it to mend," smiled Dad.

The electric lights all at once began to flicker, and then a blue spark zapped over the network grid above us. A few electronic crackles came from the wall-mounted control panel partially blocked by the darkened silhouette of its operator.

"Everyone ready?" shouted a wild-eyed John Dodsworth over the low drone of our nervous conversation.

All five of us looked around at each other and nodded a cautious assent. The blue spark had done nothing to alleviate our gnawing concern over John's gerry-rigged time capsule. From my past experience, I had never known any of the Kronos time travel equipment to emit any sound or sparks at all. In one moment, we observed a devilishly-grinning Dodsworth cackling like a mad scientist and crazily flipping an oversized manual lever like the one an electric chair executioner might throw in an old movie. Later, I came to realize this was all for effect. John eventually came to admit all the showmanship that morning was for fun. John had always enjoyed a practical joke.

Before any of us could react, I felt a brief light-headedness …

Dodsworth's time capsule-garage had changed little--the same brick walls, stone floor, electronic gadgetry. ... it was much the same as when we had left. Yet we all knew the truth-- we had experienced it all before—according to the digital readout on the capsule dashboard we had arrived at our destination—the year 19 Anno Dominum.

At once there was a pounding from outside, and Mel Currier who had taken a position nearest the heavy door simply leaned forward and easily shoved it open.

"Trinia! My God, I thought I'd never see you again!" A pretty blond middle-aged woman wearing a red, satiny full length gown had rushed wildly through the door at Trinia Williams and wrapped her in a tight embrace.

Both Trinia and the woman were giggling like two school girls. "Olivia, honey, it's so nice to see you again. We've got lots to catch up on!"

Trinia Williams and Olivia Pelser stood face-to-face just staring at each other and grinning. The two had originally been a part of the Manning Jones team that intended to wreck the original Kronos project, but in the five years in the First Century, they had not only become best friends, but switched allegiances after learning of the evil intentions of their leader and became staunch allies of our Kronos group that included Mel Currier, Kaye Spahr and of course myself. Olivia had later been kidnapped and spirited away to the city of Pompeii where she became involved with the wealthy senator, Octavio Quartio and later his lost half son Dierk who had fought as a gladiator in the Pompeian arena. In the end, Olivia fell in love with Dierk and elected to stay in the past with her husband when Kronos finally returned to rescue the time travelers.

"What's in those big cardboard boxes by the wall?" inquired Olivia pointing at three cartons stacked almost to the ceiling of the time capsule.

"Some equipment we might use. A surprise," smiled John turning to Olivia. "You mentioned the only thing you really missed about the twenty-first century was going to the movies. I'll have one of the men open those carton this morning when we come back ..."

"Do you mean you brought movies?" squealed Olivia as if she were reliving her teenage years. How can possibly you manage that miracle without electricity?"

"Simple, my Lady Olivia," John smiled even wider. "One large screen Samsung TV, capable of 3D; a 10 HP John Deere quiet-running generator with a generous supply of gasoline; and a DVD collection of every major movie I could gather, emphasizing those with Oscar awards."

"Oh my God," cooed Olivia as she hugged John. "How can I thank you?"

"Just keep your showings private, Olivia," Dodsworth reminded her. "It certainly wouldn't do to let the neighbors over for the evening. That wouldn't help our Kronos directive policy now would it?"

"Don't worry, John. I can hardly wait to let Dierk witness some of these windows into the future from Hollywood."

"By the way, where's your husband, Olivia?" asked Kaye.

"His schedule often takes him away—this time to the Senate. He's due here sometime today," added Olivia.

"Does he still perform in the arena?" asked Trinia.

"Not at all," smiled Olivia. "He's satisfied with his new role as husband and father. You know he is virtually the governor here in Ostia. Not officially, but in reality he demands a great deal of respect both locally and in Rome."

For about half an hour, we all exchanged our feelings and reminisced about old times during our Kronos mission. We were interrupted by Cecil's abrupt interruption.

"It's time! According to mine and John's calculations, there are some important guests arriving any time at the harbor."

By this time, everyone was unofficially accepting John Dodsworth as our captain. No one said a word but rose and followed him in a duckling-like parade winding through the narrow red clay paths of the vibrant Salt Marsh Estates floral gardens. Dad and I brought up the rear of the procession. When the group emerged from the grounds onto a limestone-paved roadway, we were almost immediately the center of attention of the residents who at once began to follow behind at a respectable distance or else work their way along the curb parallel to the time travelers' route. It started as just a few stragglers but soon grew to over a dozen towns people. As might be expected, any unusual commotion that would occur at the Manor was most certainly going to draw the attention of the city folk who viewed the proprietors of the estate in the same vein as we hold entertainers and sports personalities in our time.

"Lady Olivia!" shouted one arms-waving woman. "We love you!"

"Look there," gasped one man pointing at the dreadlocked Trinia Williams. "Am I mistaken or isn't that the Black Medusa?"

"You're right. She's back."

"The others must be of importance as well. Look at their clothes."

"Did you notice a few of them wore the medallions of diplomats?" added another.

The entourage, as it moved along, had now elected to move in a tight swarm rather than the single-file formation it had necessarily adopted in the gardens, perhaps from an unconscious response to the threat from its well-intentioned but inquisitive admirers.

"Oh, the price of fame and glory," smiled Kaye Spahr.

In short order, our Dodsworth group had reached the brow of the hill formed by the dunes along the sea. There the panorama of Ostia's harbor, one of ancient Rome's busiest seaports and the one that served the capital city itself, spread itself before them. The turmoil of sounds and sights was sensory-consuming. Everywhere men were laden with bundles or trundled larger crates on sturdy two-wheeled wooden barrows from the ships docked there next to the wharf that were crammed with every possible commodity one could imagine in these times, shipped from places like North Africa, Egypt, Greece, Britain, Spain and wherever else Roman ships might dare venture. Freight bound in heavy netting was being was swung over to the dock with winches manipulated expertly by wiry young men who climbed like monkeys in the rigging of the ships over to the wharf and the waiting dockworkers. Via Agua, the main street by the harbor front was jammed with creaking drays of all sizes and parked at various angles, its quarreling waggoneers vying for the most preferred loading positions near the dock's walkways. Teams of shirtless, sweat-glistened men heaved, pulled, and shoved cargoes onto the wagons at the persistent badgering of the overseers who often perched themselves atop their wagon loads carping at the workers for a more compact fit that might somehow permit a more efficient utilization of every possible bit of space. The dock workers mainly consisted of the lower class plebeians from Rome whose labors were basically considered slave work. Of course, there were actual slaves—men who had likely been taken in war by the Romans —or had even been born into servitude, maybe several generations previously.

"Rufus!" shouted Mel Currier. Mel, without any warning, leapt forward from our group and sprinted headlong down the hillside to one of the loading wagons.

"Master Mel, "grinned one man hopping down from his place on the wagon tailgate. "I thought I might never lay eyes on you again."

"Last I saw you," Mel said while roughly embracing Rufus "was in the arena in Pompeii."

"And thanks to you, I got out of that terrible place. All the men there owe you a debt of gratitude for what you did for them. Until then, being a gladiator was pretty much of a dead end."

Suddenly, Rufus's scowling overseer stood spread-legged next to the slave, wielding a short piece of leather with several lead-tipped thongs.

"You there, slave, get back up here," he shrieked. "We have no time for this dalliance." With those words, the overseer raised his whip as if to administer a lash or two on his slave, Rufus.

Mel's reactions were automatic. In a lightning-quick move, he caught the man's downward movement, firmly grasping his wrist.

"You ... you big, black b ..., let go of me or I'll have you flogged to an inch of your life!" squealed the red-faced foreman.

Mel was a composed man. He had been through much—pirates, thieves, storms at sea, crazy millionaires, theology classes, and much more—and he was able to maintain that developed composure. That did little to assuage the egos of the three burly men who came up at once behind Mel furtively brandishing heavy wooden cudgels. Mel was a composed man, but he was also a highly-trained soldier who had served in the special forces of the American military. He had seen more than his share of combat in the wastelands of Afghanistan, especially in hand-to-hand fighting of which he was expertly skilled. Other men may not have sensed the intruders in time, but Mel's self-preservation skills had automatically kicked in. With a quick twist of the foreman's arm, Mel turned and deftly swung the screaming man, like a human scythe, into the knees of the approaching men, taking them down to the ground in a humiliating heap of flailing arms and legs. Before any of them could recover, Mel had calmly grabbed a piece of cargo netting that had been hanging on a nearby wagon and looped it over the struggling men who just made their entangled and quite embarrassing predicament more pronounced.

By this time a large excitable group had appeared, encircling the adventurous skirmish scene.

"Okay, everyone." Olivia Pelser Quartio, Lady Olivia, as she was referred to by the locals, stood in the forefront of several toga-draped figures and one black leather-clad, woman with Medusa dreadlocks who had expeditiously made their way down the hill to the scene of the dockside fray.

"It would be to everyone's great advantage as well as their health to back off as quickly as possible." Turning to the assembled mob who had now turned silent, their attention riveted on the beautiful governess, Olivia announced in a piercing, authoritative voice, "This man, a personal friend, not only is an important diplomat from Atlantia, a land firmly allied with Rome, he is a trained combatant. As you can readily see, these bullies stood little chance against his skills. I hope you never have to see Mr. Currier when he's angry."

When the crowd had heard Olivia's assessment, they turned only to see Mel casually freeing his attackers, carefully extricating them from the web of rope that had temporarily imprisoned them.

"Sorry, Mr. Currier," one of them offered. "I had no idea who you were."

"No problem, guy. Just doing your duty." Mel took the man's hand and helped him up.

"Can't keep from getting yourself in trouble, can you, big man?" smirked Kaye with an impish grin, her arms crossed over her chest like a first grade teacher.

Mel just smiled as he assisted the other men from their hemp entrapment.

"Haloo there," a familiar-sounding voice blared from the wharf's ramp. "What's all the commotion?"

Turning to the voice, the Dodsworth group recognized the man they had all come to know well on their previous mission to Judea. Ara was accompanied by one of the numerous acrobatic "monkeys" I had recognized in the ship's rigging.

"Ara! I'm so happy to see you again," I laughed aloud.

The man I was seeing was the first person we had met when we had jumped from the future to the first century. As it turned out, Ara had developed a small fleet of ships and was cultivating a vigorous trade in the Mediterranean. Later, the young entrepreneur was invaluable in helping, risking great danger to his own welfare, to spirit the Holy Family from Judea to Egypt. Without his aid, history, and religion, may have been changed.

"I'll never forget our adventure," I smiled, adding lightheartedly. "I hope someone appreciates what we did for mankind."

"I, for one, deeply appreciate it Mr. Thayer," commented the ship's rigging monkey at Ara's side. The boy, somewhere in his early teens, much like the other young men of his profession, appeared fit and as lithe as a gymnast with a darkly-tanned torso. When I looked at the lad's sunburned face, I knew at once to whom I was speaking. The warm, penetrating expression in his eyes I had experienced those years previously immediately gave him away.

After all the adventures I have had in the Kronos missions assigned to me, I had thought I was prepared for most anything, but I must say I was so dumbfounded I could not utter a syllable at the young man's unexpected appearance. I had previously met the boy both as an infant and a five year old in Judea and each time I had been impressed then with his coping skills and incredible maturity. Even as an infant, his eyes, kind and contemplating, were the same. I had the extreme fortune to be permitted by his parents to actually cradle him in my arms, and at that time, I, Mel, and Kaye, agreed we had experienced unnatural warmth that seemed to radiate from the child's body.

All of us eventually had experiences that, while we underwent them, had attributed them possibly to luck—such as storms at sea being instantly quelled, great dust storms stopping a small, pursuing army, birds flying up from what seemed to be made of plain clay—these and more things that happened in Judea. We all brushed them off at the time as natural happenings, but later when we compared notes we came to the realization that neither luck nor nature could define what had happened there.

In later discussions, we had felt we had done something to assist the boy and his family to escape the persecutions of various madmen. After further contemplation on the subject, we grudgingly agreed that our efforts had been miniscule and that there had to have been some other greater intervention. Now after due consideration in the year or so after returning to the future and given much time to envision and appreciate my association with the child, I had come to the shocking realization that I was in the presence of as being revered by billions of mankind over two thousand years from his death.

At this time, I could not decide whether it was proper to embrace, shake hands, bow, genuflect, or whatever before the lad. Fortunately, I was saved from thorough embarrassment by my father's intervention.

"Jesus—Jesus of Nazareth, how good it is to see you again!" he shouted as he approached him, grasped his shoulder with his right hand and took him by the other arm with his left. As it was, this had been the traditional Hebrew greeting among friends at the time. Apparently Cecil had assimilated this procedure on many of the time jumps with Thelma.

"How is your mother, Issa? Has she been well?" asked Cecil cordially, using the familiar name Jesus had used as a child.

"Yes, Mr. Thayer, she is quite well. In fact, she, as you might suspect, has accompanied us here and is below decks on our frigate," replied Jesus.

"And Ara, my good man," Cecil continued turning to the man who had first addressed us. "I assume your shipping ventures have been profitable? This nice ship you have docked here, it's quite remarkable. I'll bet you've been all over with it."

"Yes, Cecil, we've done quite well with this vessel—Arachne we've named it – just fresh from Britain. We're carrying a cargo of tin from the Welsh coastal mines. I've built a rather profitable business from tin. Used for making bronze you understand—weapons and armor for the Roman army of course. Commands a good price."

Ara's eyes were warily watching the assembling crowd behind me as we spoke. Most of a smattering of the original dozen or so followers had swollen to more than fifty people and began to form a ragged arc of humanity, babbling and pointing at our renowned repertoire, especially Trinia and Mel who had previously gained a degree of notoriety from their exploits in the local arena.

"I suggest we take refuge on the Arachne," said Ara. "I doubt we wish to share our conversation with the general populace."

Without a word we followed Ara and Issa a short way to the gangplank set at a steep angle upward to the deck of his ship. A few moments later and we had all nimbly ascended up and onto the open deck of the vessel. A few of the townspeople had started to follow us on the dock, but when we made our way onto the Arachne, those few melted back to the waterfront. On the deck were crates, netting and several heavy coils of thick hemp rope stacked and set in neat rows or storage crannies along the bulwarks.

"Stephon! A table for my guests," he shouted in the air to some unseen worker.

Before we could gain our bearings, a small army of men had scrambled up bearing small kegs, a folded sail, and two rough-sawn planks about eight or so feet in length. In less than about ten seconds they had thrown the boards over some of the kegs and spread the sailcloth over the boards.

"My best tablecloth, friends," laughed Ara.

The few remaining kegs were placed at the table for seating, and as we sat, a platter of cheeses and various seasonal fruits were placed in front of us.

I was now regaining my faculties and my sense of curiosity was getting the best of me. "A question, Ara—I don't really understand why young Jesus of Nazareth is accompanying you on these forays." I reached for a small bunch of grapes. "I mean, shouldn't he be somewhere else like in Galilee or Nazareth?

"Long story, Bill. Let it suffice to say for now—and you've seen some of this yourself—Jesus is not always welcomed by everyone. His intellect is so far advanced—it appears anything he sees, hears or reads, he remembers. This makes many folks uneasy, especially those in authority when he illuminates any controversy with his instant understanding. He gives some the impression he is challenging them and their ideas." Ara paused here and raised both eyebrows. "Perhaps he is challenging them. But then maybe some of their antiquated perceptions need to be confronted."

"But the unnatural things he has done—the …" I hesitated a bit here attempting to find another word for *miracle.*

"Those things are precisely what cause the trouble," Ara returned. "Can you imagine a young child speaking to those in authority like he was their teacher? It doesn't matter whether his ideas make sense. He is challenging the egos of those who have developed a dictatorial relationship for ages. Now a kid comes in to upset the whole structure of the hierarchy. Then these little things happen about which you speak. Well those in authority are very defensive and quick to ascribe his powers to a more malevolent source. The boy's formal schooling has been rather problematic as well. It has been very difficult for Jesus to stay long in one community even though he has many who side with him rather than the leaders. Likely those supporters are afraid to come forward against the establishment."

"So things are going better now?"

"Mostly. Jesus is learning a bit about shipping. He seems to love the sea—nature in general. He would make a good sailor I suppose, but

I doubt he will stick with it. His interests are elsewhere." Ara sighed diffidently.

"Yes," answered Jesus softly, "I love the great serenity of the ocean waters to the west of Gaul especially. It is much easier to understand the fish and birds than the fickleness of the people. Yet, I long mostly for my native land. I do not know exactly why, but something is drawing me there. I feel there is something I need to finish before I die."

"Bill," a soft and familiar female voice interrupted, "some wine?"

When I turned, I was greeted by Mary, the woman I had come to know as the young mother of Jesus, who now tilted a large long-necked wine carafe in both arms as she offered to fill our cups. Previously I had seen the sixteen-year old mother in this same capacity when she clandestinely posed as a waitress at an inn. Silver goblets were being placed on the tables before the visitors as she spoke, and without my answer, filled my vessel with a quick, practiced twist of the shoulders, and then proceeded to the others.

It had been a bit over twelve years since I had seen her near Galilee. Jesus was then about five, but then as now, her face still maintained the freshness of youth and failed to confirm the unusual trials she must certainly have endured in rearing her son.

As Mary finished her serving tasks she looked at me closely. "So what brings you and your friends here in this harbor?"

Cecil raised his hand and raised himself partway as if needing recognized in a classroom. "It's not so much Bill as me. You see, I have a personal favor to ask of your son."

"You all remember my wife, Thelma?"

"We do," confirmed Ara, raising his goblet in a salute.

"The woman who disappears!" added Issa. "Perhaps a miracle then?"

"It's no miracle, Issa," I said respectfully, " at least not in the sense of some of the things you've shown us—like the time you made the clay birds you created on the Sabbath, and how you made them fly when challenged by some of the authorities. How could anyone explain that?"

Issa had taken a seat beside me and gazed in my face. "It is only a matter of time. You should understand that, Bill. It's in your family."

22

THELMA USED HER time alone for a peaceful stroll along the Sea of Galilee. Her senses were suddenly overcome with the ever-present pungent whiff of fish and the casual crackling and shrill calls of the coastal birds commonly associated with seaside villages of any era. Off on the distant glassy surface of the waters, small boats with triangular sails dipped and bobbed lazily basking in the morning sunlight. This serene setting helped Thelma focus on her plans. She had been here in this particular time before and she knew it was dangerous. That was one of the things of which both she and Cecil had been made aware. It would be absolutely mandatory that they did not stumble on one of the many Thelma's or Cecil's, their avatars as Higby had called them, that had resulted from the recurrent time jumps they had previously made into the time of Christ.

"In no way," preached Norton Higby at Kronos Labs during briefings, "should you ever touch or even take the chance of coming into near proximity with these avatars. To do so would likely cause instant disintegration. Perhaps the meeting might cause more of an implosion than that. No one knows for sure because there are no survivors of any of those instances."

"Just out of curiosity, how do we know about this phenomenon?" inquired Thelma.

"It's all theory of course," returned Higby. "But if we can believe the likes of Albert Einstein and Stephen Hawking, they both agree that if this chance meeting would happen, it would be instant and catastrophic destruction."

The people at Kronos had resorted to referring to these beings as *avatars*, but by strict definition, not a perfectly accurate description. An avatar, Thelma discovered after very little research, was a body that was taken over or adopted by another, either temporarily or forever. It was common for many of the young people in the twenty-first century to use avatars when playing games on the computer or game players. They could temporarily *become* another identity for as long as they wished. Thelma's avatars were quite different. The time travel avatars were actually exact presences of the traveler himself or herself— when it actually existed in that time of a past time occurrence.

Now, after time traveling so many times into her favorite spots, like the time of Christ, Thelma had unfortunately established a high-level danger zone where she had to be extremely careful about meeting one of her avatars. She had recently resorted to taking notes, indicating the exact times and places where she had been on past trips. Even now, she wrote a few lines mapping her recent steps along the Sea. Since she had visited this time and place at least six times, she knew she must inevitably watch for the six avatars she had created.

By the time Thelma had navigated along the lower arc of the shore and nearly retraced her steps to its beginning, she had formulated her plan. *Those two can't get back, not without my help anyway* thought Thelma as her feet choffed through the grainy sand near the rock overhang she had chosen as her temporary headquarters. A low acid smoke hung along the entrance to the shelter as Thelma ducked under the low entrance and then stood erect. Verma Rashid and Manning Jones sat a few feet apart along the granite wall, a rather large fire of driftwood ablaze in front of them. Rashid held a long-handled metal basket over the flames that licked hungrily around the basket that contained darkened remnants of something they apparently had chosen to cook.

"Boys," Thelma called, "how's your breakfast coming?"

Jones was attempting to ignore the question but could not hide his disgust.

"Not bad," said Rashid, "I'm starting to get the hang of this open-fire cooking, I think."

"Not bad if you like deep charcoaled fish, I guess," said Jones sarcastically. "Can't you get us something else but fish and hard bread?"

"It's what everyone else around here eats. Why should you be any different?" returned Thelma. "Besides, that's what I got when I bounced back and bought the food. What did you expect? Steak and potatoes?"

"Anyway the food suits the restaurant motif," growled Jones. "Just love how cozy it is here."

"Hey it's better than the prehistoric denizen scene we came from before Mrs. Thayer saved us," Rashid reminded Jones.

"Anyway, here's my proposition for you guys," interrupted Thelma. "Here's your chance to get some good food and a change in your venue." Thelma circled around the fire that had begun to die a bit. "How would you like to go to a wedding feast?"

"You mean food, dancing, booze …?" sighed Rashid rolling his eyes in ecstacy.

Jones leveled a spacey stare at his captor. "And the catch?"

"No catch. Just go, enjoy yourself, and most of all, observe what happens. I'm going to quiz you on your return."

"You're not coming I take it? You're going to trust us. I mean we can just take off and not come back."

"You could," agreed Thelma, "but then you might have to eat a lot more of that deep-charcoaled fish you like so much. And then you better remember, I'm your only ticket to the future. You get away from me and you're here for the duration."

Neither man said anything but their body language and knowing expressions indicated a clear-cut understanding and acceptance of Thelma's premise.

"When you're finished eating, we'll get ready to go." Thelma took the pen knife Cecil had given her previously and slit open a cardboard carton she had forced the two to bring along with them. "Here are some clean robes—the same you might be expected to wear at such a festivity. You'll be a big hit at Canaan."

Jones' choice of colors was a bit bland—a color about a shade of butterscotch pudding. Verma Rashid liked the more flamboyant effervescent orange that reminded Thelma of the same hue that might be assigned to prison inmates.

"Don't we need a wedding gift or something?" asked Jones.

"We didn't even get an invitation," protested Verma Rashid. "Won't they think we're crashers?"

Thelma shook her head. "Don't worry about an invitation. This wedding is quite large and they have relatives they have never seen. You'll fit right in. And the gift? Well these coins will suffice, I believe. You will be considered rather generous with these silver coins." Thelma shoved a jingling coin purse into each of the men's hands.

"Let's get a move on it, boys. It's about a thirty mile trip and we need to be there by midafternoon."

A five minute walk back to Ba'arta's Hardware parking lot found them packing themselves into the van. With a few grinding gears the Econoline spun from the gravel lot and whined deliberately along the seashore road for several miles before turning right sharply and climbing unhurriedly into the Naphian Hills. The van finally pulled off the main road and was swung around into a sandy area behind a grove of date palms.

"Your instructions gentlemen," said Thelma firmly turning off the ignition. "After we jump back into the appropriate time I have selected, you will be walking the remaining way to the wedding feast in the village. It's about three miles or so ..."

"Walk!" protested Rashid. "Why can't you drive us? That's a long way. We'll be all sweaty and dusty."

"Like everyone else," Thelma agreed. "You'll fit right in. They all had to walk for miles and they'll be just as dirty as you will be. It will help you appear more realistic."

"Why aren't you coming with us Mrs. Thayer? Wouldn't this be much easier if you were along to instruct us?"

"No Mr. Jones, I will not be coming. I have my reasons but do not wish to share them at this time. Anyway, here is what you must do for me. First, present yourselves as guests. Mr. Jones-- they all speak Aramaic which you can easily translate with your implanted ULIT translator. Mr. Rashid, of course, not having a ULIT, will be unable to communicate without translation through you. Second, I want you both to enjoy yourselves as any wedding guest of the time might enjoy himself."

"Easy!" smiled Rashid. "It's been a long time since I've had good food. I'm tired of grilled fish."

"And finally," Thelma proceeded, "you must sample any of the wine being offered. This is most important. I will expect you to report to me what you think of each sample."

"Ah, just my area of expertise," smiled Jones. "I take great pride in my training as a wine sommelier. I have grown to appreciate the nectar of the gods."

"Excellent then. You are well-suited to the task before you. Do you have any questions?"

"None, madam. I am elated that you are trusting us with this mission."

The two men slipped from the van and met Thelma Thayer as she came around the front of the vehicle. Without a word, she simultaneously touched her forehead against the temples of Manning Jones and Verma Rashid. When they looked around, the paved highway had disappeared and was replaced by a narrow, dusty cart path.

"Meet me back here tonight," said Thelma. "I'll be waiting."

Thelma was right. The two men fit in perfectly. Upon arriving they blended in with the other guests where Manning Jones exchanged a few orchestrated pleasantries with some of the people. Rashid was explained away as one of his foreign servants who did not speak a word of their local language. Both soon found their way to the wine decanters served by waiters and tables of fruits and local produce of which they helped themselves.

"There is nothing particularly remarkable about this wine," whispered Jones to his partner. "Judging from its aroma, I'd say it's an ordinary blend of muscat, likely aged for less than a year."

"Tastes good to me, Manning. Reminds me a bit of Mad Dog, I think," smiled Rashid as he drained the remainder of a hefty cup of the red wine the waiter had poured for him.

"I think I would rather have water than this foul stuff," grunted Jones. "Sir," he said turning to the steward who had provided the wine to them, "our journey has been long, and I believe a large draught of water would better suit me at this time than this horrific libation."

"Of course, sir. I have some cool water recently drawn and placed in these earthen vessels. I will have a pitcher brought to you at once."

"Appreciated, my good man."

Jones and Rashid had, as anticipated by Thelma Thayer, been accepted without question at the wedding celebration. As Thelma had mentioned, the place was crowded, jammed to capacity. There were isolated groups of guests who were familiar with each other, but it appeared the assemblage comprised scattered collections mostly of relatives and individuals with whom those in the crowd were barely recognized by most guests.

Both men headed to the food tables that were stacked with a variety of breads, figs, dates, grapes, and meats which they snatched and greedily began to consume as inconspicuously as possible. Verma Rashid had stuffed bread under his robes in large sewn in storage pouches.

"Hey," muttered Rashid between gulps of the cheap wine Jones had rejected, "I thought Mrs. Thayer wasn't coming here with us."

There, standing beside the table was Thelma Thayer accompanied by an elderly gentleman that neither of them recognized.

"Perhaps something is amiss," suggested Jones. "Let's hang around over there and I'm sure she'll get us the message if she needs something."

The men sidled toward the couple, attempting to remain as unobserved as possible, and were finally less than six feet from them. When Thelma did not acknowledge their presence at first, Jones decided to be sure they were seen.

"Ahem," he coughed.

Neither Thelma nor her friend noticed him at first. That was until he *accidentally* bumped the table and spilled a wine cup. Rashid immediately leapt forward and began desperately mopping up the mess.

"Sorry, sorry," apologized Rashid.

"Isn't that Manning Jones, the billionaire?" gasped the astonished man under his breath. "How would he ever get here?"

"It certainly is, Cecil! We've certainly seen enough of him to make a positive identification."

"Mrs. Thayer," whispered Jones as he approached the couple, "is there a problem? Have we done something wrong?"

"Pardon?" replied Thelma. "Have we met?"

"Oh …," replied Jones in a low throaty voice, "don't worry, there's no one close enough to hear us." Jones glanced right and left again just to make sure. "Is there a change of plans?"

There was a period of silence. Finally, after a knowing glance to her partner, Thelma responded.

"No change, Mr. Jones. Why do you ask?"

"Oh no reason. I just thought it strange you said you were going to remain on the hill outside town until we got back. Well—here you are, and here we are."

"Oh don't worry, Mr. Jones. You just keep doing what—I—said to do. Don't worry about us."

"So who's your friend?" Verma Rashid had just guzzled his third cup of wine.

"This is my husband, Cecil. He usually accompanies me on my little trips."

Cecil Thayer bowed uncertainly. "Pleased, I'm sure."

"All right then, it's back to our wine-tasting mission then," smiled Jones

"Wine-tasting …?"

"Yes, but I'm afraid there's nothing here but that rather wishy-washy stuff they're dipping from those big crocks."

"Pardon me, Mr. Jones, but I forget exactly what I said to you—back there on the hill. I mean did I give you any information as to where you are or anything like who would be here?"

"Oh no Ma'am, you're kidding me of course," answered Jones somewhat sarcastically. "Did you forget to tell me something?"

"Just look around sir. Does any of this seem at all familiar? This village is Canaan. This is the wedding feast at Canaan."

"Means nothing to me, Mrs. Thayer. I think you did mention the name of the place, but that was all."

"Do you remember the Bible story? I mean one of the guests is Jesus of Nazareth and another is his mother."

"Jesus! Of course I remember him. He was a little kid when I met him—just a fleeting moment you know. That was years ago. As far as the Bible is concerned, I'm not much for religion. I do know this Jesus of Nazareth holds a big position with modern churchgoers. Some of my executives actually wanted to say some sort of invocation mentioning the man. Of course I have no time for that mumbo-jumbo. And if I'm not mistaken, I believe you mentioned you wanted me to talk with him about something. You didn't say what yet."

"Perhaps we should step back and let Mr. Jones complete his work, dear," suggested Cecil Thayer as he pulled gently on his wife's elbow. "Thank you gentlemen, for checking in with us."

"No problem. See you later on, right?"

Cecil nodded toward the two men. "That's right, my good man. Later on we'll meet. Right where we said we would."

As Jones and Rashid departed they talked casually.

"I wonder where the other wines are that they want me to test," said Jones. "They absolutely have to be better than the first."

As the men walked away, Cecil and Thelma secluded themselves near the corner.

"You are aware," whispered Cecil, "that this means another Thelma is somewhere near here—an avatar, as they say at Kronos. You must be extremely careful, my dear."

"You're right. But then, I'm positive the other Thelma avatar is keeping her distance as well."

"I wonder if there's another Cecil around as well," smiled her husband.

As Manning Jones and his companion worked their ways through the gathering of wedding guests, they were becoming more aware of the presence of one of the guests—a man, accompanied by a handsome middle-aged woman.

"This man is rather obviously Jesus of Nazareth, Verma." Jones gestured toward a bearded man likely somewhere in his thirties. "You see he seems to have an aura—a personality. Everyone in the room seems to know him, and their attentions are drawn to him like a magnet. I have no doubt this is the man about whom the Thayer's have told us."

"This is our chance to meet him, Mr. Jones." Between wolfing down a fistful of figs and a crust of bread he had torn from one of his concealed loaves, Rashid had downed another cup of wine. Before anyone could stop him, Verma Rashid sauntered up to Jesus and his mother.

"Hi there," he blathered in English. "My name's Verma, but I'm not a Christian. I'm Hindu. At least my parents were. I'm still pleased to meet you though."

"Please excuse my idiot friend, Mr. Jesus," interrupted Jones now speaking in Aramaic. "As you can hear, he doesn't make much sense. He even has his own nonsense language."

Jesus had turned toward them and was smiling.

"I believe I have met both of you previously in our life travels, my friend. As far as your fellow wanderer is concerned, his voice may be thought more straightforward than some others speaking more boldly."

"Oh we have not met before. I mean--how could you remember?" Jones' voiced trailed off briefly in thought. "You were still a child ..."

"It would not be very strange for me to remember, sir. After all, would it be so difficult for one who has aged so gracefully as you after all these years to comprehend? Could one explain your presence any easier than it would be to have a man recall some of his more traumatic childhood nightmares and devils?"

"Anyway, sometime when you're not so busy, I think I need to talk with you. Not now, mind you. We have an assignment, you know."

By this time Verma Rashid, quite a bit inebriated, finished off his fifth cup of wine in less than half an hour. He was still babbling in English, a language few in the room could comprehend.

"This wine's pretty good, sir. Those big containers are about empty though. Gonna have to fill 'em back up, I guess. Might even have to send someone over to the wine store."

Verma was not the only one who had become aware of the impending wine catastrophe. Several kitchen stewards and servants had been in state of extreme anguish over the rapidly diminishing reserves of wine.

The number of guests had been severely underestimated, and after a long day, the wine stock was indeed running dangerously low. Various discussions and remedies were desperately relayed throughout the hall among those responsible for the feast. At one end of the great hall there was a low mumbling of the crowd as many had gathered there near the earthen jars from which water had recently been drawn. Jones could see some of the servants busily extracting water from the containers and bringing it out to the main dining area.

"This is the best wine I've had. I can't remember anything so fine," remarked one guest as he drank wine poured for him from the water pitcher.

"Why, they're drinking water and thinking it's wine," laughed Jones. "They must be pretty drunk. I just had water taken from that cask."

"I'll try some of that stuff," said Rashid extending his cup to the man with the pitcher. The servant expertly dribbled the remainder of the decanter's contents into Rashid's unsteady cup, careful not to spill a drop.

"Mmmm, not bad!"

"Rashid, you're just drinking water! That's the same container from which they just poured my pitcher of water ten minutes ago."

"No, no, Manning. It's wine. Good stuff," Verma gurgled, turning carelessly and splashing red liquid on Jones' sleeve.

"Let me see that!" demanded the incredulous Jones snatching the cup from Verma..

Manning Jones looked at the contents of the container, surprised to see something other than the clear water he had expected. Taking the cup in both hands he swirled it around and then smelled it. After a momentary pause, he raised the cup to his lips and sloshed the ruby liquid around in his mouth.

"Chateau Margaux, '09."

Manning Jones, upon announcing this appraisal to Verma, was at once aware that this wine could not possibly be the particular vintage he had declared, but its identification was certainly as close as he could come to anything he had ever experienced in his own era. It was easily comparable to the extremely fine vintage he had consumed to that which had sold recently in the twenty-first century for more than five thousand dollars a bottle!

"That steward is mighty crafty," he sighed knowingly. "After just about everyone has had his fill with whatever rot gut wine he can drink, the man brings out the good stuff. It'll leave everyone with a good taste in his mouth and the steward has made a handy profit. Smart man!

After a festive evening at the wedding celebration in the town of Canaan after most of the guests had filtered away through the town, Jones and his partner, Verma Rashid, had scrambled back up the dirt path to the prearranged meeting spot atop the hills above the village. Rashid had been happily humming some of the tunes he had picked up from the festivities, but Jones was his unaffected, staid self.

"You say the wine you tasted was, if not the very best, one of the finest you have ever tasted?" Thelma Thayer wore a knowing grin as she spoke to Manning .

"I tell you Mrs., Thayer, it was without doubt something similar to the best Chateaux Margaux I have ever had. I'm not exactly sure how he did it, but that steward somehow made the switch. It was a water container no more than ten or fifteen minutes previously, but when he drew the liquid out for general consumption, it was this fabulous tasting vintage I have described to you." Jones had lowered his eyes a bit as he observed Thelma. "But you and a man named Cecil were there tonight. Did you not observe what happened?"

"Mr. Jones," snapped Thelma, ignoring the question, "do you happen to know the Bible story about the wedding feast at Canaan—the one where Jesus was purported to have changed the water into wine?"

"Vaguely. I believe you explained it to me earlier. Don't you recall?"

"You are aware, then, that Jesus of Nazareth was present this evening?"

"Yes, we spoke very briefly, It was a bit uncomfortable, you know. I don't feel I could ever be completely relaxed while talking with that man."

"Do you suppose then, there could be any truth to the Bible story?"

"Only if you had a tendency to accept that crap," sneered Jones. "Personally, I feel it could be explained away logically. A quick change by a few servants, and there you have it -- wine in the place of water."

"And the vintage to which you referred?"

"Can't really explain that, Mrs. Thayer. As I understand from the history of wine in this area, no wines or even domestic grapes have survived from Biblical time due to their destruction by the nineteenth century Moslems who pretty much successfully rid the region of forbidden alcohol. Who is to say what kind of fabulous wines they may have produced in those times? Like that great variety they somehow came up with at the feast."

"Like Chateaux Margaux?"

"Yes, I suppose it, or something close to it, isn't completely out of the realm of possibilities."

Thelma had known Manning Jones would be difficult, if not impossible, to convince, but convincing him was not necessarily her goal. For many years of time trips into first century Middle East, she had been gathering information to personally support her own religious beliefs. It had been difficult, matching the precise times and places with the Biblical events, but as she had mentioned to her husband Cecil, they had all the time they would need. The dangers of meeting one of the avatars of herself, as demonstrated by Jones' and Rashid's casual meeting of one of them at the wedding feast, was becoming more and more pronounced with each of her time journeys to this area. Thelma knew she would have to become more efficient in her travels.

"Well Mr. Jones—Mr. Rashid, let's go back to our base of operation, and I'll structure the next leg of our mission. Come here and we'll return."

Verma Rashid staggered forward obediently, and Jones, after a momentary few seconds of indecision, reluctantly came up and, with Rashid, simultaneously lightly brushed his temple against Thelma's forehead. They had both adapted quickly to Thelma's technique.

In the same moment, the trio had appeared in front of Thelma's Econoline van parked on the hill above the ancient town but now in the time from which they had been previously.

23

SIMMERING MISTY HEAT had already begun rising along the backdrop of the trees materializing like unsettled spirits over the ridge by the Lutheran Seminary. The town seemed to be awakening along with the activity of the cavalry unit that had taken up residence there. Villagers strolled by the busy inn on the Cashtown Road and gawked and tittered at the horse soldiers as they busily clattered by in the streets. All around, orders were being shouted out amid the nickering of horses and the squeaking of leather mingled with the ever present aroma of fresh manure and damp grass.

Lydia, Cheryl, and Carson Hardwick had risen early for breakfast and had made an appearance in the dining room amid a short bit of fanfare from David Hartsfield and the kitchen staff, mainly directed at Cheryl. They were promptly directed like royalty to a special table near the dais on the veranda normally reserved for just the most special guests. Cheryl had adopted a pompous outfit—a canary yellow full dress with wide ruffled pleating. She also sported a white wide-brimmed hat adorned with multi-colored plastic spring flowers she had bought at Dollar Tree. Lydia was simply dressed. If it were possible, she would have worn the jeans and short-sleeved shirts she had customarily adopted working at the Ohioview digs, but now she had forced herself to slip into another plain summer dress similar to the one she had worn on the previous day. Hats were fashionable for young women but Lydia usually ended up removing them and carrying them rather than attempt hanging onto them to maintain their place on her head. Hardwick had come to the realization that simpler was better and toned down the gaudiness of his uniform—it was now sparsely adorned with a few small medals and battle ribbons. Under his left arm Professor Hardwick carried the oilskin map case that had been brought for him from Doubleday.

This morning, the others were excited about their upcoming Civil War experience, but Lydia was quiet as she leisurely sampled the array of fresh bakery items brought to them. Lydia had a faintly dizzying feeling—an unsettling feeling she had experienced previously—right before something critical was about to happen

"Sir! Ladies!" snapped Hunter Mathews smartly. He and a troop of cavalrymen had been standing unnoticed at attention in the lawn beside the portico. "I have several men to accompany us, Sir. And I'm having a first-rate horse brought up for you--and the ladies' carriage for Mrs. Thayer …" and with a slight turn and pleasant tip of the hat toward Lydia …"and her lovely daughter."

Carson Hardwick had not thought much about the prospect of riding a horse during his time here. He had ridden a bit in Hyde Park as a teenager. One young lady in particularly of whom Carson had taken special notice had been an accomplished equestrian and he saw this as the way to impress her. He had begun to be rather proficient in horsemanship before he had lost interest in the girl and moved onto more fertile fields. But now, after years of absence from riding, the unexpected thought of mounting a horse without making a complete fool of himself was a bit unsettling.

"Lieutenant," grinned Hardwick sheepishly as the three time travelers rose from their breakfast and moved out to meet the soldiers, "perhaps Mrs. Thayer might need assistance with driving her rig …"

"Oh not at all, Professor—I mean *general*—I won't have any trouble at all. I've seen lots of people doing it, and I'm sure I can get the hang of it quite easily," she giggled.

"But, but, Dear …"

"It's settled, Carson. I'll drive the buggy and you can show off your horsey skills to everyone. I know you'll be good at it—you know, being a soldier and all."

142

Before he could protest any further or come up with any better excuses, three cavalrymen rattled up the alley from behind the inn, leading a handsome russet quarter horse. All the men pulled up abruptly and dismounted in a single, gliding motion. One of them, an orderly, steadied the prancing russet with one hand resting on the military saddle and with the other, offered Hardwick the reins.

"Sir, your horse!"

Something kicked in. Hardwick grabbed the proffered reins, and without an organized thought, slipped his left foot in the near stirrup and lithely swung his right leg over the waiting mount. After all the years since last riding, the instincts he had developed in his youth had become automatic.

"Yes!" he shouted, pumping his fist in the air.

Hardwick looked at the soldiers' surprised looks.

"I mean, yes, this is the greatest animal I have ridden in years," he smiled, somewhat embarrassed at the stunned cavalrymen. Sitting stiffly erect in the saddle, he gave the horse a gentle nudge with his heels and then made a short, cautious circle in the street.

"Well, men. Are we going for a ride or not?"

In the brief time it took to bring up the doctor's rig Lydia had rented earlier, the troopers had taken positions to the front and rear of the procession as it passed the market square, turned right and proceeded south along the Taneytown Road.

"Oh how cute he is, Lyd. What's the horse's name?" demanded Cheryl as she sat straight-backed lightly snapping the reins.

"It's Bo, Mam," offered a nearby trooper

"That's a cool name for a horse. Get along there, Bo!"

As they made their way through the town, many, especially the children and a chattering flock of women Cheryl had impressed at the hotel the day before, shouted and cheered their passage. The market square, situated in the center of town was the hub of many roads that radiated like spokes in all directions from the central traffic circle. Rose bushes of various colors and scarlet geraniums were being watered by an elderly caretaker who never looked up as they passed. For the most part, the main body of townsfolk, like the caretaker, just quietly minded its daily business.

"You handle this carriage rather well, Mom. I never would have thought you would be able to do it," gasped Lydia.

"Much easier than the time I tried Pittsburgh traffic during rush hour," she returned.

Lydia had recalled that nightmare. Her mother had insisted on driving, and when she got into the inevitable traffic jams, no maneuver, even though illegal, she would make did she consider wrong, including driving through red lights or making unexpected lefts amid a cacophony of angry horns and nasty gestures.

"You're right about that," agreed Lydia.

"The cemetery," interrupted Hardwick pointing to the graves and stone walls to the right of the byway, "it'll make a good defensive position above town." Hardwick immediately became aware of his pronouncements. "That is, of course, *if* a battle would happen here. Lieutenant, could you have one of the men take notes?"

"Of course, Sir."

"Yes, all along this road along the brow of the hill would be good places to set up cannons and take defensive positions. I believe they call this area of high ground Cemetery Hill."

"Don't know, Sir, but it makes perfect sense to call it that with all the graves and such," smiled the sergeant mildly derisively. "And then there's a big monument about a quarter mile along that would support that idea as well."

"Oh look how pretty this is," gushed Cheryl excitedly. "Horses and cows all over the place right here on the edge of town. How peaceful. It's so green and lovely."

Lydia sat beside her mother on the leather seats of the carriage despondently taking in the tour. All Lydia could think of was the pain, death, and destruction that would very soon engulf the peaceful countryside and an overpowering sense of sadness came over her.

These people around here and a whole lot of military men are going to have their whole lives overturned Lydia thought. *Things are going to get interesting around here in short order.*

In a half mile or so, Hardwick raised his hand signaling a halt like the cavalry officers he had seen in the movies. The fields had opened up to the right. Lydia particularly remembered this extensive area well on her teenage visits to the battlefield. It was probably the most infamous spot of the conflict—the site of the disastrous Pickett's Charge.

"Limber the cannons over here to the left—by the monument," Hardwick pointed here and there and tried to use terms he had remembered from some of his military manuals "That would assure the artillery would cover this whole field when the Rebs attack up this grade."

"General, do you think anyone in his right mind would try to charge across an open unprotected area like this?" asked Mathews.

"Who knows, Lieutenant, anything could happen in battle. We should prepare for any eventuality."

"This road is really dusty," chimed in Cheryl. "My dress is already covered. And the dirt is starting to stick to me too. I'm really sweat … I mean *perspiring* … Cheryl flashed her eyelids seductively to the horse soldiers. "It's really getting a bit hot out of here."

"Not many paved roads out here, I'm afraid, Ma'am," grinned one soldier.

"Carson, when are we going to start back? I need to freshen up you know."

"Dear, we just got here. I have some very important military work to accomplish."

"Oh, whatever. Anyway hurry it up. I'm getting hungry too. You didn't happen to bring some sandwiches and drinks?"

"Would you like some water, Ma'am?" A sergeant offered Cheryl a canteen.

"Thank you."

Cheryl grabbed the water bottle, twisted the cap, and took several long swallows.

"A piece of hardtack?" another man asked opening a white cloth and producing a dozen or so dark-colored dough balls the men had fried in bacon grease that morning.

"Mmmm, doughnut holes," beamed Cheryl as she grabbed two of the fatter pieces and greedily stuffed both chunks into her mouth, popping her cheeks like a gluttonous acorn-fed chipmunk..

"Augh!" she gagged, "Poison! Water, I need more water!" Cheryl was spewing her mouthful of hardtack biscuit in wet chunks without concern for anyone's space. The uniform of the man who had offered her the biscuit was plastered with the remnants of Cheryl's unfortunate introduction to Civil War army field rations.

In a few moments, Cheryl had taken a long draught from a canteen she had yanked from the saddlebag of one trooper's horse.

"Augh! Augh! That's so awful. What's in it?" protested Cheryl as she disgustingly gushed the liquid out over the ground.

"Sorry Ma'am," apologized the corporal who had quickly retrieved his personal canteen.

"Whiskey," gasped Cheryl. "That's whiskey! I can't stand this. Let's go back to the hotel. I have to have some decent food and drink,"

"We've only been out here a half hour," Hardwick said.

"Seems a lot longer," whined Cheryl as she finally realized she was making an awkward and embarrassing scene for both Lydia and Hardwick. Lowering her eyes demurely, she surrendered. "But I guess I can put up with this a bit longer if it's that important."

"Just a bit longer, Mrs. Thayer," sighed the history professor who had hoped to establish his time travel-enhanced expertise in battlefield engineering to anyone who might listen to him. "There are just a few places we need to see."

Their little party gathered things together and proceeded along Taneytown with the "General" pointing out important strategic planning and tactics for some supposed and to the soldiers, a rather ludicrous future battle—a battle of which the time travelers knew all too well was a bit more than conjecture.

"Those hills up there—Little and Big Round Top they call them. Be sure they are defended well. They cover the whole left flank of any army posted along Cemetery Ridge," said Hardwick firmly.

"I'm impressed," said Mathews. "You actually know the names of the obscure landmarks around here.

"Oh they're not so obscure, sir," interrupted Cheryl. "They're on all the tours of …"

"Mother," said Lydia cutting off her mother's imminent divulgence of information she had picked up in the future. "Perhaps it might be a good idea in getting along. We could maybe go back if you wish."

Cheryl had come back to her senses for the moment. "Oh Lyd, I'm sorry I'm being such a wet blanket. I know you have other plans." Cheryl winked at her daughter and flicked her eyes at the dashing Lieutenant Hunter Mathews. "I think I can find my way back. This buggy is kind of fun to drive, and I think I'll like it lots more if those horses escorting us weren't kicking up so much dirt in my face."

"You're sure, Mom? Do you think you will be all right?"

"Oh, I'll be okay. And you might be able to ride double behind one of the soldiers." Cheryl once again flicked her eyes sideways at Lieutenant Mathews.

"It's pretty much of a straight shot back to town," said the sergeant. "Don't make any turns and it will take you right back into the square. You can find your way from there, Ma'am?"

"Sure, no problem."

"Mom, don't be getting into any trouble. I mean, mum's the word. You know what I mean?"

"Don't worry," shouted Cheryl, and in her anxiousness to be rid of her situation and not realizing the narrowness of Taneytown Road that was not much more than a farm lane in width, wheeled her buggy around sharply and bounced roughly over a small ridge of grass and rock on the road's berm and disappeared briefly down the steep grade. In a flash, Cheryl and her rig had sprung easily back onto the road, Bo's eyes wide with the excitement at Cheryl's startling and unexpected off road adventure, and was headed post haste north toward town.

"I think I'll see the ladies and have some homemade lemonade on the veranda."

"That's what I'm worried about," whispered Lydia to Hardwick as she watched her mother still holding desperately to her hat with one hand, disappearing down the road in a cloud of billowing, golden dust.

"Can you hear what she yelling?" asked a breathless Hardwick.

"No," answered Lydia, "but it doesn't really matter much."

For the remainder of the morning, the Hardwick tour proceeded around the battlefield-to-be with the professor getting bolder and louder in his battle tactics proclamations as they moved from one place to the other. The corporal, who had been assigned to take notes, could hardly keep up as his supply of writing material had begun to run low. Lydia, who had taken her mother's advice, had taken a seat behind Hunter Mathews, her arm comfortably around the handsome cavalryman's waist. Neither seemed to mind much.

Just before noon, after a circuitous route around the orchards and wheat fields of the Gettysburg farmlands, the small troop headed back to town. The men assigned to Hardwick had become silent, unsure as whether to be impressed over the general's boisterous revelations, or rather to see him as a pompous, obnoxious Washington-appointed lackey. In the days to follow the battle of Gettysburg, these men would come to respectfully remember the battle prophecies and military suggestions proposed by the garish but notable officer.

The dusty riders pulled up in front of the Hartsfield Hotel shortly after noon. Lydia threw her leg over the rump of the horse and gracefully slid to the ground.

"Thanks for the ride, Lieutenant Mathews."

"Enjoyed it, Miss Thayer. And you can call me Hunter if you'd like, ma'am."

"Only if you drop that Ma'am and Miss Thayer bit and call me Lyd."

Hunter Mathews tipped the brim of his Stetson and bobbed his head in smiling assent.

"Could you join us at lunch, gentlemen?" offered Hardwick. "I hear they make some delicious ham barbecues."

Soldiers at war seldom had the chance to enjoy the food or restaurant service associated with civilian life and were off their horses even before their officer had accepted.

"I suppose this means we accept. I mean if it's all right with you—Lyd?"

Lydia had looped her arm under Mathews' arm after he dismounted and pulled him gently along the flagstone path to the veranda. David

Hartsfield, the inn's proprietor had seen them arrive and was there for a personal greeting.

"Hello, Miss Thayer. Welcome—you and your friends. Do you wish to visit our dining room?"

"Of course, and could you see that my mother is informed of our arrival? I am sure she would like to join us."

"Yes, yes, of course. But was Mrs. Thayer not with your party?"

"Oh yes she was. But she left us and came here about two hours ago."

Hartsfield looked perplexed. "I'm sorry, Miss Thayer, but your mother never came back to the inn."

"Oh, maybe she went straight to her room then."

Hartsfield shook his head. "No, I'm afraid that would be impossible. I've been right here in the lobby or veranda all morning. Her rig has never returned from this morning. Mrs. Thayer has not come back here any time today."

24

THE UNEXPLAINED DISAPPEARANCE of Cheryl Thayer had put the town of Gettysburg and the Union cavalry encampment there in turmoil. Lieutenant Mathews felt responsible for her being lost. He had made the statement that it was a straight shot back to town and virtually impossible to lose one's way. But Hunter Mathews did not know Cheryl Thayer well.

The townspeople, too, who had developed a particular liking for the famous actress who had graced their little hamlet with a personal appearance, meticulously searched every corner of their community, utilizing every possible available citizen to bring even the slightest bit of evidence that might lead to her recovery. Everyone was looking for the beautiful actress in the bright yellow dress. In the end, the only evidence came from a single source.

"I seen a lady this morning ridin' round the square two, maybe three times or so and then suddenly take off north on the Carlisle Road!" shouted a lad who finally came forward. "Don't know for sure if it were her or not, but she wore a fancy yellow dress like you was talkin' about."

Everyone agreed this had to be Cheryl, but no one could figure out why she had turned north through town or for that matter, turned around and headed south, east, or west. Lydia knew her mother and realized how poor her sense of direction actually was. Lydia had no misgivings that her mother might indeed take the wrong turn at the square. She had remembered an experience back home with Cheryl driving on one of the many roundabouts that were common in small towns in eastern Ohio. For several minutes she had driven around the town circle, unable to decide how or when to leave it.

"The streets are all the same, Lyd," she called out desperately, "Which one should I take?"

Lydia knew Cheryl had taken the wrong road and was likely in any direction. North was the most likely choice for a search based on the boy's report, and she immediately set off to the cavalry encampment to meet with Hunter Mathews to inform him of her thoughts. The young lieutenant decided to dispatch a squad of troopers to ride north on the Carlisle Pike.

"I'd like to go along if you don't mind," said Lydia.

"I want you to stay here, Lyd," instructed Mathews. "There have been scattered reports of the movement of Southern cavalry to the north. Likely there's nothing to the reports, but one can never be too sure about these things. She probably couldn't get too far without realizing she was going the wrong way. My men will likely find her a few miles out. If you must do anything, check some of the side roads south of town. They should be safer. Your mother could have easily doubled back and ended up there if what you say about her sense of direction is true, and it might be a good idea to locate her before nightfall."

For her part, Lydia knew she had to jump back and try to communicate with her father. She had promised after hers and her mother's past escapade into Renaissance Italy that she would always let him know if anything unusual came up. That sense of impending trouble, maybe as strong a sensory skill as her time travel ability, was once again asserting itself. After her meeting with Mathews, she went immediately to her room, locked the door, and, without any delay, returned to twenty first century Gettysburg. From her room, she sent a text to her father.

Dad! Need help. Mom is in danger somewhere in 1863 Gettysburg. Call me ASAP. Bring Grandma Thelma if possible.

25

A MID ALL THE hubbub of the day in Ostia—the meetings with Ara and Jesus and Mary, the renewal of old friendships and stories by Mel Currier, Kaye Spahr, and Trinia Williams and their adulation from the town's populace—I was still concerned over the lack of communications from Cheryl or Lydia. It turns out Cecil had the same misgivings about Thelma.

That afternoon, soon after we had all returned to Salt Marsh, we approached John Dodsworth about a managing a brief return to our own time to check our phones and laptops for any messages that might have come to us. Dodsworth of course willingly accommodated our wishes, taking us to the time transfer capsule, and with little fanfare, sending us back to our time.

Dad was disappointed in not finding anything from his wife, but from the expression on his face, it seemed he was not expecting any response.

For my part, I was more fortunate to find a message from Lydia on my phone—a simple text. I was both shocked and relieved. The message indicated Cheryl had somehow come up missing during a time jump into Civil War Gettysburg. I'm not sure why Lydia would ever attempt such a dangerous jump, especially with her mother. When Lydia asked for help, I knew I had to do something, but it was not immediately apparent what I could do. Dodsworth's time travel capsule would be pretty much useless in its current location here in Ostia. If we were to go back to 1863 from this location, we would be there in the right time, but with the Atlantic Ocean between us. Of course there would be no air travel available then and a ship might take a month or more to get to

Philadelphia or Baltimore. From there it would be a long and dangerous journey through an active war zone. Our only real hope would be from my mother, whose time travel capabilities, combined with modern transportation, could easily transport any of us to within a few miles of our target. The big problem—how were we going to find Thelma?

Cecil decided this was the time to reveal his complete plan.

"Nothing's changed, son," he answered quietly. "My original plan is still in place. That's why we're here at Ostia in the first place."

I was still a bit confused with Cecil's plan.

"Come with me, Bill," he answered. "As soon as we get back to ancient Ostia, we can take care of business."

Jesus, Mary, and Ara had already been invited to stay at Salt Marsh by Olivia. When we returned to the manor, the three of them were sitting near one of the many ponds in the gardens waiting as though they had expected our arrival. The interior grotto, with its flowers, ferns, fish, and bubbling, fountain-fed waterways was like an Amazon jungle scene

Ara, as always, was the spokesman. "We've made ourselves quite at home as you can see. It seems Olivia and Dierk have somehow developed a soft spot for Jesus and his mother. Olivia claims she was somehow changed years ago when she participated in the rescue of the family of Joseph, and now she's even convinced her Roman husband Dierk that there was something special about Jesus."

"Yes, yes, I must say that all of us who were there have become stronger in our beliefs. All of us, especially Trinia Williams, Kaye Spahr and Mel Currier, feel we were a smaller part of a much larger picture."

"I've been made aware you and your father are in need our services," said Ara changing the subject abruptly.

"Who? How would you know that?" I sputtered, a bit confused.

"It matters little," interrupted Mary, "provided the response to your needs is satisfied."

It should not have surprised me after all the experiences I had undergone in the past with Jesus of Nazareth. It would be of little consequence that he would know what we had in mind even perhaps before we had actually planned it.

"Your request, my friends?" Jesus said.

Jesus at this time was a mere teenager. I could not help but view him as the boy, Issa, who would come to be the central figure of Christianity. Any other youngster who might have been confronted with problems of this nature likely would not have handled it as well as young Jesus would have, or for that matter would not have even been taken seriously.

"It's my wife Thelma …," Cecil started.

"Your constant companion on your various extraordinary journeys," smiled Jesus.

"Yes, I need your help getting her back to me. She's gone off on her own and she's vitally needed by me and even more by her family. The only way is to have you tell her to come back."

"I understand. Do you think I could convince her to return to you?" The lad was skipping flat stones in the pond as he listened,

"You're the only one who might do it, Jesus. You understand she presently is on one of her extraordinary journeys of which you speak. Sometime in the years to come, you will see her, perhaps accompanied by a couple of men whom she is trying to rehabilitate."

"A noble venture I am sure, Mr. Thayer." Jesus lifted his eyebrows a bit and smiled.

"Yes, but unfortunately, likely fruitless. I know Manning Jones all too well. I have never known him for anything except evil. Your mother could tell you a thing or two about Jones and his friends."

"The years ahead where this intervention is to take place," asked Mary, "would that not then be too late to send her back to you?"

I looked at her, realizing I would be unable to tell her the complete truth and a bit embarrassed to attempt an explanation of time travel. Even Jesus, I suspect, probably did not exactly comprehend what was happening with time travel, but had faith things would happen simply as they unfolded.

Ara had been made aware during previous time jumps that things happened he could not possibly grasp. He had long ago accepted both who and what we were.

Young Jesus opened his arms, palms forward as he spoke.

"Yes, Mr. Thayer, I believe I can help you with your prodigal wife."

2 6

CHERYL THAYER FELT as free as the wind. The doctor's rig had probably never been driven as it was being driven late that morning. In the fifteen minutes it would take her to reach town, she had decided to let everything go and just have some fun before she had to get down to business again. She had been getting terribly fatigued with this time travel business even though she would never let her daughter know. In the past few days, she had been pressed hard to uphold the arduous façade of being a famous actress from Pittsburgh, a role that at first intrigued her, but she soon found carried an almost unbearable burden of maintaining accuracy. As Lydia referred to it—"anachronistically precise." Cheryl knew she had perhaps made a minor mistake or two in past excursions with her daughter, but she felt there had been no need to make such a big deal about it. The incident with the toothpaste tube and the Indians was unfortunate, but that could have happened to anyone. Cheryl did not believe the futuristic information she had given to Leonardo DaVinci in Renaissance Italy had been terribly significant either.

"Some of these things you do or say while traveling in the past might possibly change history, Mother," Lydia would remind her. "You can't let people know how we got here, and you can't tell them things that would distort the future if they would act on them."

Cheryl wasn't always sure exactly what those things were that she couldn't say or do, and that was the problem. Weighing every act and word—not knowing whether they might invoke discord with Lydia—wore heavily on her.

I'll show them all thought Cheryl as she clattered recklessly down Taneytown Road past Cemetery Hill toward Gettysburg. *I'll get some rest at the inn, have a good meal, and I'll be all ready to finish this act. There will be no anachronis … no whatever they are called. I'll show Lydia that I'm perfectly capable of sharing her jaunts into history.*

Cheryl might possibly have sped into the town pretty much out of control except for the experienced Bo who had either become exhausted or else just simply had the sense to instinctively decelerate by the time they had approached the central market square. There Cheryl's slowing rig entered the roundabout, the old harness horse automatically circling to the right as it had been accustomed.

Straight. Straight. Lieutenant Mathews said. It's easy. Just go straight and you'll come to the inn he said. But we're going in a circle. Let's see. I think we turn off at the ice cream store. But where's there an ice cream store? Let's see. Let's see.

Cheryl Thayer drove around the square four times, each time getting more confused. In her defense, many of the landmarks she mixed up were from entirely different time periods and it was difficult for her mind to separate them. Ones in the twenty-first century had significantly changed from those in the nineteenth century and many of the modern structures and landmarks were the ones she remembered. Even if she had not been forced to deal with the difference of years, it still would have been an intriguing enigma for her.

I'll just pick a road and see where it goes. Eeeney meanie minie mo … Oh I'll just take this one. It looks kind of familiar.

Cheryl pulled hard on the right rein and the carriage wheeled sharply to the right heading north on Carlisle. The wayward cart had not advanced fifty feet before the Bo stopped abruptly, turning, his ears twitching and briefly eyeing Cheryl curiously.

"What's wrong you silly horse?" Cheryl reached for the buggy whip and snapped it lightly in the air. "I hope someone around here listens to reason."

It was about an hour or about fifteen miles north when she finally brought the buggy to a halt adjacent to sprawling pastures and wheatfields that typically made up most of central Pennsylvania in the mid 1800's..

"Well Bo, it's getting pretty hot this afternoon. I suppose you might be needing some water?"

Cheryl swung her skirts out of the buggy and, staring helplessly from the raised road, looked at the small stream that bubbled seductively through a nearby meadow.

"That water looks so good I might have some myself-- if only we could get to it. I don't think we can drive to it in the buggy. Somehow I have to get you out of those harnesses and walk down there."

The interlaced trappings of Bo's harness were a complete perplexity to Cheryl. After yanking, stretching, and even throwing in a few unladylike comments, she sat panting on the running board of her buggy. Then she started going through the rig looking for some sort of tool that might be used on the harness. In the end, she even looked to her large, silver sequined purse that she remembered she had packed special before the jump.

"Let's see here. Here's my girl scout compass—don't know why I'd ever need that. Sun tan lotion. Sewing kit. Aspirin. Money—the realistic-looking stuff Carson had copied on his printer. Nail file. A Holiday Inn complimentary cosmetics travel packet. Deodorant. Hmm, a few things in the pocket on the side – what's this—a cell phone!"

It was momentary glimmer of hope, but even Cheryl Thayer remembered the cell phone would not work here. She had this discussion with Lydia before, but it still did not make perfect sense but she was sure her daughter was right. Cheryl began to dig deeper into the side pockets. There she dug out a map she had brought along, "A Tourist's Guide to the Gettysburg Area".

"That's no good for anything," she snapped and tossed it back into the bag.

"What's this?" Cheryl asked herself as she drew out a small pocket knife, stamped with the word EVERSHARP. This was one item she had inadvertently left there—a piece of equipment with which Kronos had equipped all its time travelers when they had been sent to rescue the original mission members in Pompeii. Norton Higby told them this was a space-age knife that would be able to cut through virtually anything

"Don't see where any of this stuff would help me," complained Cheryl as she nearly pitched the knife back into the bag with the other stuff. "Oh wait a second. Maybe I could use this knife to cut off Bo's harness."

Cheryl's assumption was correct. The heavy-duty leather harnessing was no match for the Kronos steel she wielded. How she managed to work so efficiently without impaling Bo or cutting off any number of her fingers was the biggest mystery, but in very short order she had successfully severed all the main leather straps and freed her horse from its constraints.

Whistling happily, she led Bo to the stream where he drank insatiably for several minutes. Cheryl then decided to take her turn, but unfortunately became schooled on the hidden perils of muddy creek banks, sliding less than gracefully, both legs flailing in the air with an ungainly show of ruffles and muddy linens, into the water. For the longest time, all she could do was sit awkwardly in the murky shallows of the brook with a look of disgust as the mocking waters swirled around her.

Her reaction likely surprised even herself. Cheryl suddenly began laughing hysterically as Bo turned, looking at her inquisitively. While squealing like a kid at a water park and scooping cupped handfuls of the cool water into her mouth and on her face, Cheryl suddenly flipped back and splashed into the puddle gathering behind her.

"Oh Bo, I've wanted to do this for a long time," Cheryl giggled. "But now I think I have to get serious and get us back home."

With the word "home" Bo's ears perked. The word obviously invoked a trained response. Slowly the horse made its way up the bank and onto the road where he waited patiently for Cheryl.

"Guess we can't hook you back up to this," she said as she emerged onto the road near the buggy. "We're going to need some new harness things first. There's a farm house about a mile up the road. Let's go, Bo."

At that command Bo turned immediately south toward town, walked for about twenty yards, stopped, and turned back to Cheryl, his ears again twitching inquisitively.

"No, Bo, not that way. Let's go home this way."

The familiar repeated command of "Go home" was all Bo needed. Likely he had been waiting all day for it and, as one would have it, was always the only order Cheryl would have needed to get back to the inn. Bo wheeled and trotted resolutely in the direction to which he had been commanded, leaving Cheryl standing alone on the road.

"What a dumb horse," complained Cheryl as she watched Bo trot resolutely south.

With that Cheryl headed north toward the farmhouse she could see in the distance. Several ominous rumblings to the south near Gettysburg caused her to stop and look back.

"Sounds like a storm coming. I hope Bo gets out of the rain."

27

W HEN LYDIA RETURNED to 1863 Hartsfield Inn, Hardwick was waiting in her room.

"It's all my fault, Lydia," he said wringing his hands. "I should never have insisted on making this journey and particularly having your mom come along. It was a bit selfish, I admit. I so much wanted to see Civil War era Gettysburg."

"No, Dr. Hardwick. It's not your fault. I could have avoided the whole fiasco by refusing to let you come along on what should have been a personal time trip. I wanted to find out more about the mysterious Hunter Mathews, and this is what it got me. I knew, too, about my mother's propensity to find trouble, and she's done it again. No, Dr. Hardwick, it's not your fault."

"In any event, I want to go with you on your search. I overheard the lieutenant directing you to the south. I think I can be of help since I have a map and do understand the battlefield area fairly well."

Lydia knew the best thing Hardwick could do was to remain active and feel useful. His thoughts about the map and knowledge of the region would actually be helpful as well.

"All right then, you can come. But as for me, I'm ridding myself of this darned dress and putting on pants. I've had my fill of this frilly stuff."

Lydia rooted through the costume trunk and dragged out a worn-looking pair of soldier's uniform pants that surprisingly fit her fairly well. Her own leather boots looked authentic enough for this expedition, and she commandeered an abandoned blue shirt and field cap from a coat rack in the restaurant that she felt successfully completed her outfit. Hardwick ordered two horses saddled and brought up. Within half an hour of the meeting with Mathews, Lydia Thayer and Carson Hardwick were galloping south on the Taneytown Road.

"We'll ride along some of these side roads, Lydia," Hardwick shouted over the din of the hooves. "Then we'll spread westward a little. If she's not here, we'll head back to the inn. Mathews' cavalry will likely have Cheryl back by then."

Lydia nodded assent as the two riders turned right and left off the main road, combing the side roads. It was not long before they dismounted in the valley where Little Round Top towered above them to the east and the shadowy granite rocks of Devil's Den to the west. From the crest of the rocks, came a quick flash, a reflection that had gone unnoticed to the untrained eyes of the two time travelers.

"It's a Yank, Cap'n--an important officer of some sort too." A soldier dressed in butternut brown, his rifle respectfully balanced in his arms, had been watching the progress of the Professor Hardwick in his general's uniform and another soldier or two who were mostly veiled by the thick foliage for several minutes.

"You're sure, lad?" grimaced the Confederate Officer. "Don't want to give up our position over some minor soldier."

The two men had been perched in a crevice between two massive granite boulders. These rocks were part of a line of similar boulders that ran roughly parallel to the ridge where their army was beginning to slowly form along Seminary Ridge, coming in from the northwest along Cashtown Road, and across from the potential Yankee positions on the hill to the east. Their standing orders, right from Longstreet himself, were to set up a sharpshooter post in the rocks and do whatever damage possible and to take out important personnel at any opportunity presented.

The officer raised his glass and verified the high-rank of the officer in the valley. "Probably reconnoitering our positions. Arrogant SOB. Why doesn't he leave that menial task to some underling rather than risk his own hide?"

"Don't know 'bout that, sir," said the soldier toting the rifle. "I think he's a goin' to pay for it anyway."

"Think you can pick him off, soldier?"

"Long as he doesn't high-tail it 'fore I gets my chance," he smiled, securely resting the stock of his rifle on a natural v in the stones. The sharpshooter licked his fingers, touched his sight, and checked the wind.

The map Hardwick carried indicated the stream that they crossed was named Plum Run.

"Professor, are you positive it's safe here?" Lydia Thayer was nervous. She remembered the feeling she had that morning, and that sense had never failed her yet. They had both heard gunfire earlier, but Hardwick assured her they were all right.

"The sound of cannons and battle carries long distances, dear," he said calmly. "Everything will be fine. This is the last place this far south your mother may have accidentally turned off the road. If she's not here, we'll widen our search to the north and then go back."

Lydia had been on a number of battlefields before, in various times and places through history courtesy of her time travel abilities. It seems, though, once a part of combat, people soon develop a certain animal sense--an intuition-- when imminent danger is afoot. Lydia had that feeling right now.

"This is the thirtieth of June, right? Or is it the thirty-first?" returned Hardwick a bit uncertainly, removing his coat and stepping casually in toward Lydia who had taken cover in a grove of oak saplings. "The battle doesn't begin until tomorrow--and then it's up further north--at least until the second of July. We should be fine, Lydia …"

"Professor, there are only thirty days in June …"

Neither of them heard the whine of the sniper's bullet, but Hardwick felt the splintering as the projectile violently shattering the spindly trunk of one of the small trees near him, showering his face with a spray of stinging oak shards.

"Down, Lydia!" yelled Hardwick as he dove to the ground. "That, I believe, was a shot from over near Devil's Den! Keep your head down now."

Hardwick was crouching low as his eyes searched the edge of the cliffs from which he had expected the rifle fire had come. He had been aware, through various readings of personal accounts that prior to the battle, that there had indeed been a handful of soldiers from both the North and South who had been around before the battle had commenced, either scouting or foraging, but he certainly did not expect to become their target.

"Lydia, dear, I think it's time we got out of here," said Hardwick sheepishly. "Guess I was wrong about trouble … " The professor expected a sarcastic reply since Lydia had just moments earlier suggested imminent danger, but, remarkably, there was no caustic response from her.

"Lydia, you're awful quiet …"

As Dr. Hardwick's gaze came around to Lydia, his heart nearly stopped! There in the shadows, lay Lydia Thayer, with what seemed a terrible wound oozing blood from the side of her head!

Carson Hardwick was on his knees scrambling before the unconscious and profusely bleeding Lydia Thayer.

"My God, Lydia, I'm so sorry, don't die, please," begged the professor desperately. Tears were now glistening on the old man's face. Not only was Carson Hardwick concerned for the girl who had somewhat grudgingly granted him the dream journey he had begged for, but he had become acutely aware of the impending danger that now confronted him from the Confederate lines. At any time, another shot could ring out, ending his own life. Even if that did not happen, he feared he would likely never return to the twenty first century without Lydia's unique powers.

Hardwick bent low over Lydia and thankfully found she was still breathing. The bullet intended for Hardwick luckily had struck one of the thicker oak saplings near them, but the shattered remnants of the tree had struck Lydia, opening a bloody but superficial wound on the left side of her head. Instinctively, Hardwick dropped to both knees and propped up her head on his lap. Lydia's eyelids wavered as Hardwick mopped blood and compressed the wound with his shirt.

"What … what happened?" she said trembling.

"You're shot, Lydia. Can you get us out of here? You need a hospital."

Lydia was blinking, still stunned. "Shot? What ... what do you mean?" It took several minutes before she could make any sensible assessment of her circumstances. Lydia raised herself, glanced around at the situation and placed her trembling hand on Hardwick's arm. "OK Professor, put your head against my temple."

Despite the blood, Carson Hardwick did as directed, experiencing the tackiness of Lydia's oozing head wound.

"I feel real shaky, professor--let's try to go."

As Lydia concentrated her full efforts to making the time jump, she was vaguely aware of another presence—a hovering manifestation— perhaps a fabrication of her own mind. All she could think of was the stories she had heard of near death occurrences.

In an instant, with a warm embrace of angel arms, the burden on Lydia's mind was freed.

28

THE NEXT MISSION Thelma chose for Jones and Rashid would be to witness the miracle of loaves and fishes. Once again, the fear of the other avatars she had created from past jumps would necessarily prevent her overt presence.

"Jones, listen carefully to my instructions," said Thelma firmly. "I am sending you and Mr. Rashid to a spot along the coast where there will be thousands of people listening to Jesus preach."

"Could I inquire," said Jones, arising from a squatting positon beside the cook fire, "just when you plan to take us back to our own time and civilization. Both of us are getting bit tired of this dismal food and the rustic camping trip you have subjected us to, Mrs. Thayer."

"It's not so bad, Mr. Jones," piped in Verma Rashid. "Kinda reminds me of when I was a kid …"

"Rashid—you are out of order!" hissed Manning Jones.

"Yes sir. Sorry sir."

Thelma turned to Jones and calmly and succinctly replied. "Neither of you is in much of a position to negotiate, gentlemen. It seems, as I have mentioned previously, that you are in a considerably better position than before when you were at the mercy of an untold number of Jurassic nightmares. In an instant I could pluck you from the relative safety of this era and have you dropped back to that time if you wish."

While Jones showed little obvious emotion as to Thelma's terse response beyond a few quick blinks, the expression of complete terror on Rashid's countenance needed no explanation.

"Ah Mrs. Thayer, you misunderstand me," laughed Jones. "It is not for my own benefit, of course, but rather for my companion's. You see Rashid has a rather large family that is likely worried about him …"

"Oh they never would miss me …" said Verma weakly, still rattled by Thelma's implied threat.

"Rashid! "growled Jones.

Verma lowered his head apologetically and stared into the smoldering cook fire.

"In any event," continued Thelma, "I would have you take the burros I have procured for your use and travel along the Sea until you come to the place I have indicated on the map I have had drawn up. I assume, Mr. Jones, that at least you are qualified enough to read a map?"

"Of course," answered the billionaire. "Cartography was one of my main interests in school."

"You should have no trouble with these directions then," said Thelma, handing him a folded document. "It is produced on paper common to this time."

"So what is it you want from us when we see your Jesus?"

"Basically, listen, and observe. I will tell you now I want you to witness what many in Christian churches have referred to as the miracle of loaves and fishes. I want you to report back to me what you think. Also, just in case you see … me … there, do not be surprised. Do not speak to me or act any different than rest of the crowd. In other words, keep a low profile."

"I understand then," returned Jones. "Watch, keep a low profile, and do not acknowledge your presence. Is that correct?"

"Yes, you've got it, Mr. Jones."

"So when do we go then?"

"No time like the present, gentlemen. I've packed up a third burro with a few things not to make your experience so trying—a few coins, a bit of food, water, and some bedding. You will be spending an overnighter."

"Isn't there an inn or something where we can sleep?" whined Rashid. "We've been sleeping on the floor of this cave for a couple weeks."

"No, sorry. This place is in the middle of nowhere. I'm afraid you will be sleeping under the stars tonight."

Jones looked over the map Thelma had given to him with Rashid looking over his shoulder with a quizzical look at the document.

Fifteen minutes later, the two had clumsily mounted their burros and made their way down to the gravelly seaside heading east along its outskirts. Thelma watched as the two specks finally disappeared into the ever-present morning mists that hung there along the coast.

Thelma wanted very much to be there when the two arrived, but the fear of accidentally meeting up with avatars made her hesitate for a bit.

I need to be there. I have a feeling that something important is going to happen, but I have to avoid the other Thelma's. I've been there twice before in the past and each time I've avoided any contact, but this will be more difficult—more difficult each instance I go to the same time.

It would be a much easier trip for Thelma than for Jones and Rashid. She simply returned to the time where her Ford van awaited, drove along the coastal highway for about two hours, parked in the lot of a local restaurant, applied sufficient sunscreen for her needs, and, with a skin flask of water, walked about a mile and a half to the location she had previously identified. With a few glances left and right, Thelma, unobserved, dissolved into the past.

The hillside upon which she had arrived was already crowded with more than a thousand people so attentive to the awaited spectacle that none noticed Thelma materialize in the scrubby underbrush nearby. The position she had chosen was as far removed from her previous jumps there that she could remember. Thelma strained her memory about any movement she may have previously made on the hillside.

It had been important for her to disguise herself as best as possible, and she had been careful to obtain an appropriate dark dress and black cowl as required by Hebrew law. A small group of women was making its way toward her along the rocky path.

Bending slightly and leaning on the withered cane she had brought, she called out to them in a practiced voice. "Unclean! Unclean! Stand away."

The women stopped abruptly and climbed a short distance up along the hillside and bypassed what for all appearance was one of the many lepers who had been drawn to the presence of Jesus the Healer. Thelma knew the role of leper would likely prove to be an effective disguise because it would give her more legitimacy in getting closer to the man who was delivering his sermon along the hillside that morning. On this particular jump, she planned on getting closer to Jesus than she had ever done before. The disguise she had chosen would, she hoped, also serve as some semblance of protection from meeting one of the other Thelma avatars she knew were present that day who would likely avoid the company of one so diseased.

Thelma used her cover to great advantage; a fearful segment of the crowd parted several yards in front of her as she moved closer to where Jesus was now speaking. At the same time she watched for the other avatars and also the arrival of her hand-picked witnesses, Manning Jones and Verma Rashid.

Nearly an hour after her initial arrival, the duo finally appeared, weaving its way through the assembled multitude. Manning Jones, as instructed by Thelma, maintained a calm composure doing nothing that might attract the attention of anyone, but Rashid, straggling several yards behind Jones, was waving and smiling at people in the audience as if he were some sort of celebrity. Eventually Jones stopped and pointed emphatically to a grassy spot upon which Rashid grudgingly took a seat noticeably pouting.

In her travels, Thelma had heard Jesus speak to the crowds, and, as usual, was duly impressed. This was in fact the third time she had witnessed this particular appearance of Jesus and knew exactly what would be happening next. There was a signal given by some of the men who accompanied Jesus. Originally Thelma had been surprised that these tough-looking men turned out to be the Disciples but then came to realize they had all been recruited from the brawny fishermen of Galilee area. When these burly men issued a visual command for the throng to be seated, there was an immediate response by the people. It was then a few fish and some loaves were presented.

"There is but enough here for you and your men," a young man apologized.

Jesus stepped up and spoke to the lad for a moment, looked into the tattered basket he had offered him.

"The people here are hungry," he announced to his disciples. "Feed them what we have."

Two larger baskets were brought up and the fish were placed in one and the loaves into another.

Thelma, who, since the two had left her had decided to travel back and watch from a short but safe distance, looked out into the gathering and picked up Jones and Rashid who intently watched what was going on in front of them. When assistants began drawing fish after fish and loaf after loaf from the original basket, and placed into additional baskets being brought down to them, a great hush at once fell over the masses. Some stood and watched in awe while others spoke quietly as the food was distributed among them by the Teacher's followers. As they ate, the volume of the crowd's voice increased and many more began to stand. Here and there a cheer or chant broke out. A few of them prayed.

It was here that Thelma took the chance she might get a bit closer to Jesus as she edged along the perimeter of the path near the bottom of the hill. In her mind, with all the security, she hardly expected to get very close, but she felt a need to attempt it.

"You there! Leper, keep your distance!" shouted a muscular man. "Stay back."

"I'm no leper," screamed Thelma throwing back the hood of her cowl. "I've got to see your Master."

The man moved toward her, stretching his arms wide, effectively hindering her advance. She knew at once she would have no chance to get through the security surrounding her Messiah. It was at that moment that she looked up through the blinding glare of the noon sun in her face. From that light came a soft-spoken voice—a voice she immediately recognized as that of Jesus.

"Thelma Thayer, what is it you wish from me?" Jesus placed his hand on Thelma's trembling shoulder.

"You remember me?" gasped Thelma.

"How could I forget you. You have been with me in many facets of my life."

"But ... you've never formally recognized me ... until now, that is. I mean, I figured I was hidden. I never meant to be intrusive ... you know—to interfere with things. You mean you knew I was there all the time and never let me or Cecil know?"

"Was that not the way you wished it, Thelma Thayer? You and your husband Cecil?"

"What do you know of me? Do you know from where it is that I come?"

"It seems your origin is not so important is it? We are all in this together, no matter who we are or the place from which we have come."

Thelma Thayer was in a state of shock. For years she and her husband had stealthily moved through time, often in the disguise of people of the era, and she was proud of the fact that no one ever seemed to think they were anything except the people they portrayed. She was in for a greater shock when Jesus spoke again.

"Thelma Thayer, your family is in great need of your gift. Your husband has asked me to speak on his behalf. I believe you should make haste to assist them and abandon the project you have on hand."

In that moment, Thelma Thayer was seated alone on the hillside above the Sea of Galilee, visibly shaken and in tears.

2 9

LYDIA FOUND HERSELF slipping through in the vagueness of the time between consciousness and awake. How long she remained in this state was not certain, but the dreamy periods of awake were now becoming longer in duration. With these periods she was becoming more aware of what had happened to her, and now Lydia was beginning to remember more details of what had happened to her on the battlefield with Hardwick. Here and there she sensed someone with her in a brightly-lighted room. Angels perhaps?

I've been shot. Somewhere on the Gettysburg battlefield. I must be dead. My God, how will my mother and Hardwick get back to their own time without me?

Lydia's eyes fluttered open.

"Hello young lady. I'm glad to see you're back with us," whispered a middle-aged gentleman in white. "I'm Doctor Milton Thomas."

"Where … when am I?" gasped Lydia.

"You're still here in the Gettysburg area, but we are presently in the year 1903. Away from any danger from the battle."

"Yes, I'm remembering things. I have to go back there and get my mother and Professor Hardwick. I feel weak."

"Much too weak to attempt a time jump, young lady," agreed Dr. Thomas. "You'll find you are sedated to the point where your time transfer powers are not presently available."

"You know about my abilities?"

Dr. Thomas stared at Lydia. "You don't believe you are the only one with these powers do you? There are quite a few of us, actually.

That's how we recognized you near Devil's Den. In fact, we recognize a number of visitors from the future. It seems the battle is a very popular destination for time travelers. You aren't the first you know. We're glad to be able to help you because sometimes there are those who are not so lucky."

"You mean killed?" gasped Lydia.

"That and other unfortunate accidents. Some of them have simply disappeared. They said it might be caused by a person accidentally meeting one of his or her own selves in time," said Dr. Thomas. "By the way, do you mind introducing yourself?"

"My name's Lydia—Lydia Thayer,"

There was at once a stunned look on the doctor's face. "Thayer! You wouldn't happen to be a relationship to a *Thelma* Thayer by any chance?"

Lydia smiled weakly at the idea that someone actually knew her grandmother. "She's my grandma. How do you know her, doctor?"

"My dear, Miss Thayer. Your grandmother is quite legendary around here. She has visited us several times here before. It seems, we have pleasantly discovered, she is the single jumper we have ever found that is adept in multiple transfers. I mean she has shown the innate ability to actually move other individuals without powers through the time-space continuum with her. This had been virtually unknown and she has worked with some of us to help us in developing this special ability for them. To a limited degree it has been successful. Case in point was how one of our people named Jack Brenner was able to pull you from the battlefield after your unfortunate meeting with a Rebel bullet."

Lydia looked a little confused. "Doctor Thomas, I've been taking people with me on time jumps for some time. I've taken my mother a couple of times and this time I brought two people with me to Gettysburg. Oh! Couldn't you bring Professor Hardwick off the battlefield too?"

Dr. Thomas' eyebrows rose in curved arcs at Lydia's astounding revelation about her abilities similar to Thelma Thayer's.

"Sorry, Miss Thayer, but it was a real strain on Jack to even bring you. He's been resting—in sort of a recovery period since rescuing you."

"I've got to get back to them. I'm responsible for their well-being. My mother's lost somewhere near the battle, and who knows what's happened to the professor by now."

"We'll make a special effort to send people out to locate them, but I doubt either of them can be transferred. Not only is a transfer a strain on the jumpers, but they wouldn't be able to jump ahead to any more than this year, 1903."

"I could do it if you find them."

"Not at this time, Miss Thayer. You are still sedated from your injury and you need time to recover. Your teleporting skills are on hold as long as you are feeling the effects of the injection." Doctor Thomas sat in the chair near Lydia's head, knitted his fingers together clumsily, and sported a slight crooked smile. "In the meantime, though, we can perhaps tap your expertise in how you developed multiple transfers."

"Most likely it's inherited, I would suppose," answered Lydia. "I've been able to do it without even trying like when I took my mother to the Renaissance. I have to admit though that Grandma Thelma was really good at it. She saved three of us from Pompeii and Mount Vesuvius all at once. I think that someday I might be as adept as she is. I actually feel more powerful in that propensity every time I do it."

"Impressive. Any time travelers I know would pay a king's ransom to be able to move just one person, let only several. How many, do you suppose is your limit?"

Lydia nodded. "I have no real idea. Grandma was quite good at it, but I only know of those instances I mentioned. I suppose she helped you a lot then when you met her here in the past."

"She sure did. But again, the success was limited to only a few of our special, stronger people, and it is always a big strain even on them."

"I'll bet she was able to tell you a few things about the future too," said Lydia, changing the topic a bit.

"Right. She came from the 1970's at the time and gave us some sketchy information of two very terrible wars that were to come, and she warned us about something she called the Spanish flu that she hoped we all would avoid. I believe she said it was during the first of what she called world wars. I had found it a bit difficult to fathom our involvement in those wars because of our present nation's isolationist views about the country, but I have no doubt your grandmother is right about those things. She reminded us we have had to be careful not to influence history with our special foreknowledge though, so we are bound to hold her secrets and only use them for our own benefit."

Despite the deluge of vital information pressed on her, Lydia could feel the familiar wave of unconsciousness from which she had recently awakened approaching her.

The doctor reached up and adjusted Lydia's pillow. "Just lie back and rest, Miss Thayer. In a few days or so, you should be as good as new."

"But Dr. Thomas … I, I, can't … take time to … rest … Mom and Hardwick …"

Lydia futilely attempted resisting the fluttering of her eyelids as her voice trailed off.

30

ARDWICK FOUND HIMSELF kneeling in the open. By now after experiencing time travel with Lydia, he easily recognized the familiar feeling of being projected from one time to another. Yet, there was something wrong in this instance. The sounds of warfare Hardwick had previously heard as distant and innocuous were closer and more thunderous than ever. Instead of being transferred safely away from the imminent danger of small arms fire, it appeared, Hardwick had simply been relocated—it seems he was now in both another day and as well as another part of the battlefield! A bullet without warning screamed past him and ricocheted off a massive granite boulder a few feet from him. A thundering exchange of cannon fire began to erupt on both sides, forcing Hardwick to dive, panic-stricken over the grassy ledge of a small embankment where the waters of the run trickled by in a shallow stream bed. Several balls hit with dull thuds near him, thoroughly pelting him with pebbles, clods of dirt, and debris of some sort. Carson Hardwick might, under more normal circumstances, have avoided getting himself soaked in the tiny brook in which he had taken cover, but at this time, he could not bury himself deep enough in the protection of the tiny stream. Breathing heavily, the Metro University professor dove low, drenched and completely covered with slimy, black muck.

Just as quickly as it had begun, the cannonade ceased, and Hardwick raised himself from the quagmire from which he had chosen to save himself. "We've got to get out of here, Lydia," he gurgled, sputtering out a mouthful of rancid water. It was then that Hardwick noticed the coppery tint the stream had taken. "It's blood! Blood in the water," he gagged.

Despite the potential danger from a cross fire of bullets, Hardwick managed to deliriously crawl onto the bank, lying there panting and violently retching. In the next moment, he raised his eyes weakly, only to witness a scene that later lived on in recurrent nightmares. Face-to-face, less than a couple of feet from him was a man, whose gaze, locked with his own, appeared frozen, a languid smile still lingering on his lips. Hardwick, in horror realized the man's mouth had continued to twitch gruesomely as if trying to form some secret warning. The terrified professor, hoping to flee, rose up on his knees only to realize the horrendous head that faced him was completely disembodied! In the next few moments, Hardwick became dreadfully conscious that the little meadow, in which he had taken cover, appearing like the aftermath of some crazy rock concert, was littered with the awful carnage and destruction of the recent artillery bombardment. Contorted bodies lay in every twisted position imaginable, and a bizarre tangle of discombobulated body parts were strewn everywhere with no apparent order. Terrified, Hardwick, tried to desperately scuttle crablike away from this horrible scene he had been dropped into, but to his utter dismay, found the ground so soaked with the gore of battle, all he could do was lie there slithering helplessly in the grotesque quagmire.

"My God, Lydia, where are you? Get me out of here. How could I ever have gotten us into this mess?" he rasped as loudly as he could manage.

Now, the high whining of bullets began to once again sing threateningly around him, and constantly threw face-stinging wood splinters and fragments of all sorts of rubble at him as he covered his head and cowered in a fetal position among the dead on the field.

From the heights to the east, Union observers were able to begin making out through the diminished smoke more of what was happening.

"Sir, there's someone down there still alive. One of ours, I believe. He's making some kind of wild gesturing, but I can't figure it out."

"Orderly! My glass!" squalled the lieutenant.

The corporal snapped open a chrome telescope about a foot long and handed it sharply to the officer. The lieutenant, with a short scan, focused on the excitedly gesturing man in the opening near the creek, struggling weakly to make his way in their direction.

"He's an officer, Corporal, I believe--an elderly man." There was a protracted pause. "I've seen the gentleman before--but dressed more formally then. Yes, Corporal Gridley, just a few days ago in the town. If I'm not mistaken, it's that Inspector General. I recognize that fancy sword and scabbard he carried with him. What in God's name is he doing down there not more than a thousand yards from the Rebs?"

"Looks like he's calling us to come on down, sir," Corporal Gridley commented. "Do you suppose he needs help or something?"

Lieutenant Dixon continued scanning the woods beyond the man as Gridley spoke.

"In the woods there--about halfway up that rise. There's movement! It looks like the whole Johnny Reb army is advancing toward us."

"Lieutenant, sir," shrieked a man as the Confederate artillery barrage started to diminish. "Sir, I think I can make my way down there through that little ravine on the left."

"Sergeant Taylor, it's a terrible risk, but go for it if you can. That man is a general, and his life surely holds a great deal of importance. Probably just as vital, we don't want him captured by the advancing enemy. You understand your responsibility if you cannot bring him back? We'll give you supporting fire to hold them off!"

Before the lieutenant had finished his orders, Sergeant Robert Taylor had dropped into the ravine that ran toward the creek and was sprinting low toward the trapped officer. From the low ridge to the west a great din now arose—the sound of Rebel cheers as they advanced. To the petrified Carson Hardwick, it sounded very much like the horrific, amplified screams of hundreds of wild hyenas and monkeys he had witnessed at the primate house at the Chicago Zoo.

"They're making a charge—right now Sir," shouted the Corporal.

"Signal to the artillery. Open up and give them some cover. It's their only chance!"

The battery attached to the forward unit opened up with canister and grape shot. The tops of trees in the valley suddenly lost their foliage as the shot screamed over the head of Carson Hardwick who had by now lost all semblance of sanity.

"Sir, sir, are you alive? I'm coming for you," shouted Taylor as he came within twenty yards of the groveling Hardwick. Sergeant Taylor began weaving expertly among the aspen saplings along the creek bank, crouching low, toward the pitiful professor. When he finally reached Hardwick, he seized him by his jacket and rolled the delirious man toward him, face up.

"Sir, where are you hit? Let me get you out of this hellhole. I think you're the only survivor in this whole unit." Though Hardwick could hardly care at the time, he was able to recognize the soldier's sergeant's stripes on his right sleeve.

"Sergeant, thank God." Looking around, he came to the realization that Lydia was not anywhere around them. "Do you see a young lady here, Sergeant? Her name's Lydia—Lydia Thayer. You have to find her too. It's imperative!"

"Sir, you're imagining things. You're on a collapsed skirmish line near Gettysburg. There is no Lydia—whatever. There are no women on the battlefield, Sir. Just let me get you out of here. I hear we've lost John Reynolds. We can't afford to lose another officer today."

Keeping a low profile, the two men, Hardwick greatly assisted by the heroic Sergeant Taylor, zigzagged up a low grade and into the cover of a cluster of oak trees.

"I don't know whether I can make it, Sergeant," said Hardwick and they reached the base of the grade. "It's my legs. They won't carry me another foot. I'll never make it up this hill."

"Sir, climb on my back," ordered Sergeant Taylor, slipping Hardwick's arms over his shoulders and dragging him higher on his hip.

For nearly one hundred yards, the man with his burden, looking much like some deformed hunch-backed monster, continued his evasive route along the hill, staggering from one ravine to another, tree to tree, and then with one quick, desperate leap reached the copse of trees where they were met by the helpful outstretched grasps of several wide-eyed Union soldiers.

"Good work, Sergeant Taylor," shouted Lieutenant Dixon as several minie balls screamed above them snapping through the branches of the sheltering grove of trees. "Get this general to safety. Take a couple of men with you. I'm sure Ol' Snapping Turtle will be elated over this man's rescue. Might even get a compliment or two!"

31

"I HAVE TO admit. I was rather impressed with the whole show," announced Manning Jones. "I watched everything and everyone around the whole production. I couldn't figure it out and I can usually come up with something to explain away any magician's act. Your Jesus has either one hell of an act or else he really works magic."

"You wouldn't want to consider any other possibility, would you, Mr. Jones?" asked Thelma calmly.

"You're referring to that religious mumbo jumbo, I guess."

"Yes, I suppose I am, but that would be more difficult for you to accept, I think, than *real* magic."

"The fish was great," joined in Verma Rashid. "Bread wasn't bad either."

"What is it you would have me believe, Mrs. Thayer? I think I could agree to anything if it would end our so-called mission here and get us home," said Jones.

Thelma shook her head and looked up a while as she mulled over Jones' pretentious words and considered her upcoming response. By this time Thelma accepted that Jones was much too hardened in his ways to be swayed by something so simple as a couple of unexplainable miracles. The sorry part was she really did not have the time right now to work with him—not if she were to respond to the message she had recently received concerning her family.

"Mr. Jones, Mr. Rashid," started Thelma resigning, "perhaps you fail to recall the original mission. My plan was to have you meet Jesus of Nazareth and let him talk with you. Many people have indicated to me that you, especially you Mr. Jones, have no redemptive societal value. That, in my estimation, is a bit harsh. Some say you are even the embodiment of Satan himself! Personally I have not given up on you. Maybe I'm stupid. The unfortunate thing is that this whole project has to be put on hold."

"You mean we get to go back home?" squealed Rashid.

"No, Verma, not yet. You see I have an important situation that I must address. It is a bit complicated, and I fear, I may be the only solution. In the meantime, the two of you will remain here."

"Mrs. Thayer! How can you do this?" protested Jones. "How do you expect us to take care of ourselves in this time? In this wilderness?"

"I've given it considerable thought. First of all, I can't take you back with me right now. The responsibility of watching you two, hoping you don't try to escape, or whatever else your warped minds might devise, is just too great. I feel I must apply all of my energies to the vital task at hand. I will be leaving you with sufficient supplies for several weeks. In addition, I will leave my coin purse that contains much more value than you might imagine. I doubt you will need it since there are not many places around here where you can spend it. Just consider it an emergency fund in case something would happen to me and I could not return."

"Not return, Madam!" protested Rashid. "That would leave us here alone with no chance to ever get back."

"Well then, gentlemen, you might try something new and pray that nothing happens to me," smiled Thelma.

"You've made up your mind then, Madam?" said Jones softly, a bit resigned.

"Yes, yes I have."

"Well then, I wish you well and only hope your success brings you back quickly."

"You actually sound somewhat civilized about my plan, Jones. Perhaps there is some chance to rehabilitate you after all."

"One never knows." Jones was smiling. "And might I suggest that I handle that purse you are having us keep. I fear Verma has little knowledge of those sorts of things."

It was not long before Thelma had packed a few of her personal items and was ready to jump back.

"Oh, guys, here is a care package for you. Ba'arta' Hardware store was a bit limited in choices but here are some things to pass the time. A couple souvenir decks of cards replete with pictures of palm trees, a Monopoly game, printed in Arabic (sorry, nothing in English), and finally, a Yahtzee game. I hope these will keep your minds busy till I get back."

"Thank you, Mam," said Jones. "Can't think of much else I'd rather be doing than playing board games with Verma."

"Yeah, right," added Verma Rashid happily.

A moment later, Thelma had vanished and reappeared about fifty yards from her dust-covered Ford Econoline van. Within twenty-four hours, she had arrived in Tel Aviv and procured airfare to Rome.

32

CARSON HARDWICK WAS still in a state of shock. Two blue-uniformed men, one of them Sergeant Robert Taylor who had been instrumental in his rescue, supported him along the muddy ruts of the stone and rail fence-lined Taneytown Road leading up to the Leister farmhouse. The house was situated just over the ridge that seemed to disconnect this part of the world from the battlefield Hardwick had just traumatically experienced. The white picket-fenced cottage sat peacefully amid a flourishing peach and apple orchard with a small herd of grazing horses roaming carefree in an adjoining enclosure. As they approached, an aide rushed out to them from the house from the walkway leading from the building, bending his ear and speaking to one of Hardwick's assistants as he was handed the professor's bogus credentials. The aide's eyes widened and he walked briskly to the front steps of the Leister House, standing stiffly at attention..

"General Meade, Sir ..." stuttered the orderly, managing a textbook salute.

The officer he addressed sat by himself on the open porch of the small farmhouse, a man who had quickly established a cantankerous reputation for himself, even among fellow officers. Many who had come to know him often referred to him as a nasty tempered "goggle-eyed snapping turtle".

"What is it, Corporal? Spit it out man." The officer, one elbow planted firmly on the chart on the table before him, was intensely scowling at a dog-eared, smudged, and randomly marked up map. It is doubtful whether George Meade could ever have later recognized the young man standing nervously before him.

"From the battlefield, Sir. There's a man they've brought up—an officer, Sir. I believe he's wearing the uniform of the subordinate to the Inspector-General. His papers bear the signature of Inspector-General Randolph Macy. It is reported these men accompanying him have rescued him from a skirmish near the town."

"Macy, you say? Of course. Someone to check me out—from Washington. Bring him in, Corporal. Who is he?"

"Sir, his papers identify him as Major General Carson Hardwick."

"Hardwick, you say? Can't say I've met him," said Meade pausing in thought. "All these damned meddlers. Probably just one of Macy's lackeys. Maybe I could get a handle on Lee if they'd let me alone—give me some time to think."

Sergeant Taylor was still steadying a mud and blood-spattered Carson Hardwick. The Metro University history professor, still a bit pale and shaken from his bewildering experience with Lydia Thayer, combined with the intensity and horrendous carnage he had witnessed in his short foray, was just coming to the realization he was now in the presence of one of the major historic personalities of the battle of Gettysburg. General George Meade, the newly-appointed commander of the Army of the Potomac, had risen from his wicker rocking chair as Hardwick was assisted up the step onto the front porch; the general stood facing the man he suspected was almost certainly there to critically evaluate his performance in the key days of his first battle. However, George Meade could readily see that Hardwick had been in the midst of a fight. He had seen many gallant men emerge from intense conflict like the one presenting itself on this battlefield, bloodied and dazed. Meade respected officers like this Hardwick fellow who apparently risked himself in the forefront of battle along with his men.

Meade snapped the dazed officer a crisp salute, but Hardwick could only return a feeble brush of his right eyebrow.

"Major General Hardwick, what is it I can help you with? You realize I've only had a short time here to get everything in place. And now this—this great battle is thrust on me—no time for preparation. Hope you don't mind the absence of formality …"

"Oh no, Sir," Hardwick gulped. "I mean, I'm honored to meet you. Someone of your stature."

"Please don't humor me, Major General. We all know I'm here because Hooker wanted out. I am perfectly confident I'm a capable leader, but I also am aware that, at least in the eyes of Washington, I'm untested in anything beyond corps commander." Meade slammed his palm on the map on the table and glowered at Hardwick. "And now here I am, thrown into the cauldron so to speak."

"Ah, General Meade, I'm quite certain you'll do just fine," replied Hardwick, who was now beginning to emerge from the daze of his battle shock. "In fact, I'm *very* certain of it. You *will* win this battle!" smirked Hardwick who was now more rapidly regaining his composure. The assurance of the Monday Night Quarterback did a great deal to considerably inflate the professor's confidence.

"The casualties, Major General, they are horrendous," replied Meade. "Somehow the boys're holding Lee back at Culp's Hill. We've suffered a great loss west of the town with the death of John Reynolds. Too bad he wasn't given this appointment. I think he would have been more qualified than I. Anyway, we need to hold that position on Culp's. Without it the whole right side will fold up." Meade was glassy-eyed now, a stunned composure overcoming him. "I hope the left side holds too. I can't afford any more insubordination from Sickles. All the man wants is personal glory. I'm worried he might do something stupid to jeopardize our whole position. I've sent my son over there to report on him and we've found he is sending skirmishers out without any orders from me. I'm afraid a bad situation is developing over there."

Carson Hardwick motioned to an open chair. "Do you mind, Sir? I'm a bit fatigued."

"Sorry Hardwick, guess I'm a little wrapped up in my own situation."

"No problem, General," Hardwick smiled as he sat. "And you're right about Sickles. I can see him trying something like advancing ahead and exposing our flank—or something like that," Hardwick countered quickly. "I would also suggest you utilize Hancock to straighten out that gentleman"

"We agree on that Mr. Hardwick!"

Carson Hardwick figured he was on a roll now. "Well General, I'm positive the men on Little Round Top can hold back the Rebs ..."

"Little Round Top? What are you saying?"

Hardwick slipped over to the map and pointed to the high knoll on the southern flank of the Union lines. "There—that high rise of land. It commands the whole area. Perfect for surveillance, I'd say. Besides, if the enemy gets up there, your whole position on this ridge will be compromised."

"Hmm. Yes, I believe you're right about that. I'll have a unit of Strong Vincent's men ordered over there as soon as possible."

"I'd suggest you use the Twentieth Maine under Joshua Chamberlain to defend it," said Hardwick smugly as he coincidentally remembered some of the historical details of that particular unit's courageous stand. Carson Hardwick had gleaned that bit of remembrance from the movie, *Gettysburg*, he had rented back home about the ill-fated assault by the Southerners on Little Round Top.

"Major General, I see you know a bit about my command." General Meade gritted his teeth a bit when he spoke. "You're apparently more acquainted with some of my units than I?"

Hardwick smiled defensively. "I've spent my life studying battles of this sort."

"I wonder why they did not appoint you to this command, Sir," growled Meade. "Do you have any other of your illuminating suggestions?"

"Oh nothing much, General—nothing I'm certain you have not already formulated yourself."

Carson Hardwick moved confidently to the map, sharply tapping each location he had seen in dozens of books on the Battle of Gettysburg. "Here is where Lee will come—the center. I suggest you establish the bulk of your artillery right here."

"But Mr. Hardwick, "snapped Meade, "all of Lee's assaults so far have been on the right and left—never in the center. It seems this falls perfectly in line with his strategies in past battles, Bull Run, Fredericksburg, Antietam—to roll up the ends of our lines and attack from both sides trapping us in the middle."

"This is Robert E. Lee, General. Look for the unexpected. I'm certain he will try to convince you he's going to continue attacking the ends of your line in the morning, but believe me, this …" Hardwick tapped the center of the map again, "here, is where the main attack will come. If you hold your reserves behind the ridge, they will be in place to rush in to fill any gaps that might develop during the fray."

"How can you be so sure, man?" asked Meade. "You've seen a lot of action I assume?"

"Yes, most assuredly, General—Mexico, the Indian wars, and a few smaller scrimmages this past fall … But mostly, I have to say that much of what I know comes from studying this and many other battles like it." Hardwick looked askance at Meade, mentally calculating whether the general would accept the cover story he had meticulously improvised.

Meade looked a bit puzzled. "You speak as if you have already been through this battle."

"That couldn't be possible now could it, General?" returned Hardwick quickly.

"I don't know. There are so many unknowns. What if you're wrong, Sir? Should I weaken my flanks in favor of strengthening the center? And what about Stuart? No one knows where that devil is and why he hasn't yet shown his face in this battle."

Hardwick had once again swollen to full command of his pedantic ego, dwelling on the vast store of battle trivia he had memorized over many years of teaching about Gettysburg. He had always secretly dreamt of himself in this improbable position, and now he was envisioning himself fulfilling his heretofore unreachable visions.

"General," he said pausing and then speaking with an air of assurance, "the left will hold. Little Round Top, you will discover, can be defended by a relatively small band of brave men—like the ones I've suggested. On the right, Culp's and Cemetery Hill should be fortified as strongly as possible with earthworks and log battlements, but placing the men there to be able to shift efficiently into a position of support for the charge that will undoubtedly take place in the middle is vital. I doubt the Southerners can break through your defensive line there if you do that. It is also my guess—my educated guess of course—that JEB Stuart will not be a great factor in this engagement. Knowing his personality, I feel it's highly likely he's off harmlessly joyriding somewhere. I sincerely believe your own cavalry under Stockton and Custer presently scouting the outskirts of the field to the north east, if given the chance, will hold him off if he should attempt to enter the fray."

"I wish I had all the confidence you have, my good man." Meade looked sideways at Hardwick. "But I guess someone must agree with you—someone higher up who maybe sent you here? Perhaps the President himself?"

"General! Not at all! You are to have full control of the actions of the army under your command. It would be foolish to undermine the authority of the general appointed by the President. As for me, even though I have never communicated with President Lincoln about your abilities, I understand he has full confidence in you."

General Meade leaned against the porch railing, calmly mulling over the information he had just received from this unexpected source.

"Much of what you say rings of the truth, Hardwick. If what you say is accurate, you could be a valuable resource around my headquarters. Would you consider hanging around for a while. I have my generals coming up for war council in a half hour. Or would you rather go with your unit in the field, Sir?"

The Metro Chicago history professor had no more desire witness any more of the violence and destruction of history being made, especially after his latest brutal and unnerving experiences. Having no unit might raise questions as well. Without hesitation, Hardwick had made up his mind. *What could be safer than the headquarters of the Commander of the Army of the Potomac,* he thought .

"General, I would be honored to be a part of your war council," Hardwick decided resolutely. "And as for my unit, I am presently unattached and would feel I would be serving our country better right here, at least for now."

33

"HELLO! HELLO! ANYONE in there!"

Cheryl Thayer rapped desperately on the front door of the farmhouse she had finally reached after nearly an hour's trudge in the afternoon heat. The house had looked much closer to her when she had made her decision "to take a short walk" to the building she had noticed in the distance. Now, in her estimation, she looked something like one of the filthy ragamuffins from Oliver Twist. Besides the fatiguing walk, Cheryl was caked with mud from the creek into which she had fallen, encrusted with the fine dust from the road, and drenched in her own perspiration from temperatures nearly reaching ninety that day.

"Hello in there!" she called again frantically thudding the palms of her hands on the door. "Isn't anyone home around here?"

After a few minutes, Cheryl plopped down onto the porch and pouted. "If you don't come to the door, I'm going to cry," she threatened the unseen residents.

At first, there was a hand that briefly parted the blue gingham curtains. Then the door handle rattled slightly and momentarily opened just a crack. Almost in the same instant the entry way swished open to reveal a slightly-built woman standing over Cheryl and wielding a long, rusted rifle.

"Who in God's name are you, woman?" she snarled. "You look like you came through a bramble patch."

"Oh thank goodness. I thought no one was home."

"Is there anyone with you? You didn't bring any soldiers?"

"Oh no, Ma'am. Just me. I had a breakdown and my horse sort of ran away. What a dumb horse he was anyway."

Saying nothing, the woman leaned out and looked up and down the road as if to verify what Cheryl had said to her.

"Get in here now, before someone comes along. There've been soldier boys—both blue and gray—making their rounds off and on for about a week. So far, I've had no trouble, but who knows how long that'll last."

"Are you here alone then?"

"Yes. I've been a widow for about two years now. Sam was shot at Bull Run. He later passed in the hospital with some sort of infection. Been here alone with the farm since then."

"My name's Cheryl Thayer. What's yours?"

"Oh sorry for the poor manners. It's just that I have to be so careful. My name's Charlene Pickens. Glad to meet you Cheryl."

"Mutual," sighed the exhausted traveler.

It took a great effort for Cheryl to rise due to both her fatigue and the weight of her saturated dress, but was assisted inside by the wiry young lady from the doorway.

"You're going to have to clean up a bit if you want to sit on any of my furniture. I'm sure we can find something around here to fit you. Use the pump in the back springhouse so no one will see you. In the meantime, I'll rustle up something for you to eat. You look famished."

Charlene Pickens pointed Cheryl in the right direction to the springhouse. Even though the water from the pump was ice cold, Cheryl thought nothing ever felt so good. When she was washed up, she discovered the clothes chosen for her—a pair of denim overalls and light blue short-sleeved shirt. They fit almost perfectly.

"Didn't want to give you women's clothes, Cheryl," said her hostess appearing nearby, "I figured you might be making your way back along the road to town tomorrow and a woman on the road with all these men around … I suppose this might work better for you. It could prove be best if you might seem to be a working lass rather than someone significant. I couldn't help noticing your soiled dress—a bit fancy to be cavortin' around this countryside in, you know. Suppose you're someone important from society?"

"Oh, no," started Cheryl, then stopped herself. "I mean, not *that* important. I'm just a simple actress you see—from Pittsburgh. Just did a play there called *Our American* … something or other. I forget the name now. I came here with a Professor from college named Carson Hardwick. Well anyway, he's not really, not here anyway. Here he's a general. But he doesn't fight or anything. He's here to … Oh dear, I'm spilling the beans again, I fear. My daughter brought us both here just for a fun trip, but now she's interested in that handsome officer. Oh she's probably looking for me now. I hope she doesn't get lost. Maybe she has a horse smarter than Bo that knows the way back to town."

Charlene stared for a moment. "Well, anyway, you're here and, for the moment, safe."

"Right, and I'm sure no soldier in his right mind would show up here, not with you and that nasty-looking gun there."

"This thing?" smiled Charlene holding it in front of her. "I wouldn't know the first thing about it even if it still worked."

"You mean?"

"Hasn't fired for as long as I've known. I think it belonged to someone in Sam's family years ago. It's a flintlock, Sam used to say. We just hang it on the fireplace for a decoration or something."

"Well it sure scared the crap out of me, Charlene."

Charlene was still not sure how to make out her guest.

Perhaps she has escaped from the asylum in town she thought. *That's probably the answer. With all the confusion and all …*

"Maybe we should get some rest and see how things go in the morning, Cheryl," suggested Charlene. "You can sleep on the guest bed in the side room."

Cheryl had no memory after falling into that bed fully clothed, sleeping soundly till mid morning and being greeted by, what at first she thought it was a dream, .the friendly aroma of savory bacon and brewing coffee. Then she, all at once, remembered where she was, and her eyes flashed open. Rolling from the bed, Cheryl made her way to the kitchen.

"You're a savior, Charlene. I'm so hungry I could eat a horse!"

Charlene smiled. "I'm afraid you're going to have to settle for a pig right now. I need all our horses to pull the wagon."

"Oh silly girl! You know what I mean."

"Just sit down. Enjoy the bounty of my table. It seems you have a difficult journey ahead of you today."

Cheryl needed no further invitation and proceeded to completely enjoy a sumptuous feast of bacon, eggs, crusty homemade bread with butter, and most of all, the best coffee she could remember.

"I'm going to lend you my horse and wagon to get you back to town. Once there, merely leave them at the hotel livery. Fred Dillon will be coming this way by afternoon when he makes deliveries. It wouldn't be any problem for him to hitch Big Brown and the wagon onto his rig and bring them back."

"Great, that won't be any trouble for me. I'm getting to be a bit of an expert in handling these horse things, you know. Thanks for everything. Maybe I'll get a chance to come back for a visit before we go back ..."

The conversation between the two women was unexpectedly interrupted by the rhythmic beat of galloping horses approaching from the north. Charlene darted to the side window.

"It's soldiers approaching, Cheryl. Keep quiet and hope they don't try to come in."

"Oh! Soldiers! No problem, Charlene. I know these guys. Spent yesterday morning getting a tour of their camp and all their horses and stuff," shouted Cheryl, cutting off the warning she had been given. "They can help me get back and you won't have to lend me your things."

"No, no, Cheryl, they're not ..."

"I'll just go out on the porch and wave them down."

"But Cheryl, these cavalrymen aren't ..."

"Don't worry. They're all great guys."

Cheryl pushed open the door and ran out onto the porch and stood by the railing.

"Yoo hoo! Up here guys. I'm Cheryl Thayer. I know you're looking for me, but I'm not lost."

The three gray-clad horseman had passed by and likely had no particular interest in the Pickens farm until Cheryl's shout out. Now they had stopped and conducted an animated discussion about the blond woman's vociferous invitation.

"Cheryl!" rasped Charlene from inside the house. "I think these men are Rebs."

"Don't be silly. These guys are coming from town."

"Town? Cheryl, Gettysburg is to the south, not to the north where these two men have come. Look at their uniforms."

"Quite dashing aren't they? I've always loved cavalry guys in the movies."

"Movies?"

"Oops, sorry, Lydia. Did it again," whispered Cheryl to herself.

One of the men had wheeled his horse around and trotted his horse up the Pickens farm lane to the house. The man doffed his wide-brimmed hat and bowed low at the waist.

"Chawmed to meet you, Madam," he drawled. "Wouldn't have expected to find such a sweet flower in these here fields. Muh name's Corporal Trevor Sneed with Stuart's Mounted. Can I be of assistance?"

"Oh Corporal, you're so dashing. My name's Cheryl Thayer," gushed Cheryl. "And I was just hoping you might get me back to town."

"Which town might that be Ma'am?"

"Why Gettysburg of course, where else is there around here," laughed Cheryl.

Corporal Sneed leaned forward as if to hear better. "Do you live there, Miss Cheryl?"

"Oh no, of course not. I'm just visiting here with my daughter and my friend Carson. As I told my friend Charlene, Carson's a college professor from Chicago. Right now he's a general in the army ..."

"A *general* you say?" Even though he attempted an outward calmness, the cavalryman's eyebrows were arched high. "What unit, might I ask?"

"Oh no unit, just a general of some sort. I believe he mentioned Inspector. But he doesn't really inspect anything. All he does is hang around. You know—trying to impress all the other generals."

"Are there other officers in Gettysburg then?"

"Oh sure, lots of them! I can't even remember their names. I think Lydia told me one of them invented baseball, but I can't recall his name. Of course there's Lieutenant Mathews who's in charge of the cavalry guys there. You probably know him."

"That's raht, I'm sure I do." Corporal Sneed was gesturing with his raised gloved hand to the men on the road to come up.

"Cheryl!" came a hissing voice from inside. "Be careful what you say."

"Oh, right," Cheryl whispered to the secreted Charlene. "I'm being careful you know, Lydia made me promise not to be ana ... ana ... whatever that word was."

"This lovely creature needs our help men. Ahm sure we could accommodate her. I think we should take her right to Jeb."

"Jeb, that sounds familiar, Do I know him? Is he from Florida?"

"Everyone knows Jeb, Ma'am," grinned Sneed snidely. "especially the ladies."

"My buggy's down the road a couple of miles. Could you hook up one of your horses to it and bring it back with us?"

"Curtis! Go down the road a bit and see if you can bring up the lady's buggy," snapped the corporal. Then turning back to Cheryl, he smiled again. "I would bet you are veritable stream of information Miss Thayer. You could be rather useful to our campaign."

Suddenly, Cheryl was unceremoniously jerked back through the doorway.

"Oww, Charlene, that hurt. What's wrong."

"Be quiet! You're telling them everything," growled Charlene Pickens.

"Oh who's this? Another one? I suppose you're attached to the Army of the Potomac as well?" said Corporal Sneed pushing ahead.

"Oh no, she's just a farm girl, Mr. Sneed. She doesn't know much except about her farm, but she sure cooks a mean breakfast. There're a few pieces of bacon and some scrumptious homemade bread left over. I'll bet she wouldn't mind you finishing it up." Charlene was emphatically shaking her head at Cheryl.

"Thanks for the invite, Ma'am. Don't mind if I do." With that Corporal Sneed pushed open the door held by Charlene and strolled past her into the kitchen where he stuffed the few remaining pieces of bacon in his mouth and shoved the bread slices into his pockets and then stuck two still-warm loaves under his arm. "My squad will enjoy these a bit later."

"Corporal," said Charlene grabbing the cavalryman by the elbow, "don't listen to this woman. She came here last night, and all she could do was say weird things. I suspect she's escaped from the local asylum. Yes that's it. I think her husband was killed, she's gone out of her mind, and now she makes up things. I'm sure she doesn't know any general or lieutenant or anyone else for that matter."

"Perhaps you're right, Miss." Sneed looked suspiciously at Cheryl. "But I figger I'll let Stuart decide that. Thanks again for the bacon and bread."

"You're welcome," then she uttered under her breath. "Be careful you don't choke on it."

Shortly, Private Curtis returned with Cheryl's rig in tow.

"Might this be yours, Ma'am?" he shouted. "I found the harnessing but it was all cut up somehow."

"Oh I did that. I had to get Bo loose so he could get a drink. Don't worry. We can get more at the liver store."

"The livery?"

"Right, isn't that what I said?"

"Yes Ma'am, that's what you said," agreed Sneed. "Curtis, you take the responsibility of pulling that buggy and our special guest here, back to headquarters. Climb aboard, my dear."

"Oh good," said Cheryl, reaching behind the seat, "there's my bag."

"Did you check that bag, Curtis? There might be some important information you can get from it. Confiscate it."

"All right, Corporal," Curtis replied, grabbing the bag from Cheryl's grasp.

"Give me that back!" squealed Cheryl shrilly. "There's personal stuff in there—women's things you know!" Cheryl had now grabbed the strap of the bag and, catching him off balance, almost pulled an embarrassed Private Curtis from his mount.

"Let her keep it fer now," smirked Sneed. "She might pull your arm off if 'n you don't."

"Thank you!" Cheryl held the bag closely to her chest with both arms.

The corporal signaled them to move on back north, and the little troop of men advanced along the road with the clattering rig and its passenger unintelligibly chattering and gesturing above the noise and dust of the highway.

Just a little less than an hour later, the peculiar-looking troupe swung left off the roadway into a copse of walnut trees where perhaps a hundred horses stood tethered to lines stretched between some of the trees. Most of the men there were seated or standing around cook fires and either eating or talking.

"Hey!" squalled Cheryl, looking around at the scene. "When are we getting back to town? Did you guys get lost or something?"

"We're not lost, Ma'am. Peers you're our prisoner, Ma'am," responded one dark-bearded and superbly-dressed gentleman standing to the front near the buggy, holding his hat at his waist. The hat exhibited a large fluffy ostrich feather in its band.

"Prisoner! I've played that game before. Release, I think we called it."

"This is no game, my dear. We are the Confederate Cavalry, First Virginia, and I am Brigadier General Jeb Stuart, and if you don't mind a whole lot, we are going to ask you some questions."

"Oh, how nice. You have such nice manners for a soldier, you know."

"Thank you, Madam," replied Stuart, his eyes showing a quaint twinkle that he normally only reserved for the opposite sex. "But let's get down to business. It seems you have been residing in the village of Gettysburg, and my scouts say you have been associating with Union officers there. Is this true?"

"Oh, *associating* doesn't sound very nice," argued Cheryl. "I think *visiting with* would be a better way to describe it."

"Anyway, then, were you *visiting with* some generals of the Union Army?"

"Sure. Lydia and the professor and myself. We came from Pittsburgh to see the battlefield. But Lydia came to see the Lieutenant, you know.

But she met him in Chicago about ten years from now. He lost one of his arms, she told me, but it's back now. I know that sounds strange, but that's what happened."

"Orderly, come here. Bring some writing materials and write down some of this. Help me to make some sense out of it as well," protested Stuart.

"Yes sir!" said the orderly as he scrambled up and into a sitting position in the dirt.

"Are there many soldiers there?" asked Stuart.

"There's some in the inn and some out by the trees with their horses, about what you've got here I suppose. They've got some nice horses. The Lieutenant told me what he called them, but I can't remember things like that."

"Is there anything of value in the town that we might use?"

"Oh it's a neat place. Lots of stores and things. I love their clothes at the mall and the shoe outlets. Then there's the wax museum and the electric map. I love visiting the Eisenhower Farm. You know he was the president of the United States. I can't forget the ice cream store either. Oh, I think that's not there now, just in the future. Oh I get so confused about that. I mean what's here now and what's in the future. The hotel's always here I know both then and now. Lydia keeps going back to the future to get things and try to get a text message to Bill so he would know where we were. He gets so upset like when I met Leonardo Da Vinci. He said I told him too much, but who would believe that! Oh Mr. Stuart, I love that little red flower in your lapel. What is it?"

"It's a carnation."

"You look so debonair. I could see you with a cape wrapped around your shoulders ..."

"I already have a cape, Mrs. Thayer."

"Oh how dashing! It must be exciting to ride around with your cape and feathered hat!"

"Anyway, Ma'am, let's get back to the topic. Are there other soldiers around Gettysburg?"

"I think not much," continued Cheryl. "Unless you count those people hanging around in uniforms, mostly older. They call them re-actors or something like that. I met a couple of them at McDonald's. Nice guys, but a little weird. They sometimes have pretend battles and march around and shoot guns with no bullets and lots of smoke. The people love it. Bill always liked them but I liked to hang around in the shops and restaurants while he and Lydia watched the re-actors."

"Are you getting anything out of this, orderly?" said Stuart aside.

"I'm trying to decipher the information, Sir."

Turning back to Cheryl, he pointed at her bag. "Do you mind very much if I look through that?"

"Well since you've been so nice to me, I'll let you see it but you have to let me take things out and explain them."

"Of course."

The first item that tumbled out into the dirt was the Eversharp knife Cheryl had used to cut Bo's harnesses.

"That thing is really sharp," she said wide-eyed. "Kronos gave it to me and said it would cut through about anything. Said it was space-age metal, whatever that is. You can have it if you want because it sort of scares me. I cut up all of Bo's leather straps and harnesses and stuff in a few minutes."

Stuart flipped the knife open and tested it on a piece of rope that was cut through effortlessly in a short effortless motion.

"I've never seen anything of this quality," Stuart responded as he flipped the knife closed. "Thank you, Mrs. Thayer."

"We have lots more of those knives back home. Here're some other items—mostly things like deodorant and makeup. Here's my Girl Scout compass. Keeps me from getting lost you know. That's what they tell me, but I have no way in Heaven how it works! Oh here's my cell phone. You might be interested in that. You can't make any calls because I've been told there're no satellites right now, but they can still take pictures I think. Let's see."

Pressing the on button, Cheryl waited briefly.

"Darn, the battery's dead. Well I'll charge it up when I get back to the hotel. All I need is an outlet."

Jeb Stuart was becoming more mystified by the moment. "That thing looks strange. Do you mind if I look at it?"

"No, go ahead. It's dead though."

Turning it over several times, Stuart's expression remained unchanged. "Unusual material—looks sort of like ivory or perhaps mother-of-pearl. A little glass window? What is this thing?"

Cheryl shrugged. "An I-phone. I think that's just what they call it, I guess. Apple makes it. See the little apple with a bite out of it?"

She then casually pulled out the wad of counterfeit money she had brought with her. "It's the money Carson gave me. I counted it about five times and each time the amount was different. The last time I counted it, there was one hundred and sixty-two dollars. You can have that too because I can get lots more where that came from. Besides I can't spend it at home either. Don't know what good it is. I told Lydia we could use it in the Monopoly game if we got low there."

Cheryl fished around again in the bag and pulled out the tourist map of Gettysburg. "This is a map of the town," Cheryl announced. "Very informative, I think. Never made a lot of sense to me, but Bill and Lydia always carried one when they came here."

Stuart's expression had become more and more perplexed as he interviewed the strange woman his men had found at the Perkins farm, but now his face brightened.

"Map? Could I examine it please?"

Cheryl willingly passed the map to the cavalry general.

"Extremely fine quality," murmured Stuart as he opened the twenty-first century tourist map. "The printer obviously has an outstanding reputation, and someone even went to the trouble of colorizing the work. If I compare it to one of our maps, it has some familiar landmarks but has lots of symbols and places I've never seen."

The pleased expression Stuart had adopted slipped back once again into puzzlement. Most of the names of places were those which he had never heard, even though he had possession of several quality charts of the region.

"What is this?" he asked.

Words and places such as Cyclorama, National Military Park, Battlefield Map, Jenny Wade House, Visitor Center, and other modern references confounded him enough, but allusions to items such as

Pickett's Charge, High Point of the Confederacy and lists of the names of monuments dedicated to the hundreds of well-known units that were to achieve fame or battlefield glory on that field of combat. There were several items like Gettysburg Regional Airport, Gettysburg Outlet Shoppes, The Links at Gettysburg Golf Course, and references that were completely outside his nineteenth century realm of his understanding.

"Is this some sort of code, Mrs. Thayer? Could you explain them to me?" he asked, indicating some of the more bewildering entries.

"I can try, but I'm not that good with maps. But here goes." Cheryl looked over the map, her eyebrows knitted in deep thought as Stuart pointed at items on the chart. The Cyclorama is a huge picture of the battlefield that goes around and around sort of. People go there and watch a movie first, just to tell them what they're going to see, but they probably don't remember anyway! You stand up high and see all the stuff down below. Kinda makes me dizzy and I just close my eyes. I can't believe those things really happened. They're just so horrible you know. The National Park, well that's just what it says. It's a park and it's national. It kind of covers everything there. I understand you can't cut down trees and stuff like that. Does that make sense? People go there and see all the battle scenes, something like they were when they happened. Or maybe they're going to happen. Oh this is making me confused. The Gettysburg Outlet is what I told you about before. A great place to buy things—shoes, clothes, jewelry, all sorts of things. There's a Food Court too. Arby's, Chick Fil-A, some pizza places—lots of good things to eat! Oh, and Jenny Wade's House is so sad. The poor girl is killed, shot I think by a bullet that just whizzes in and gets her while she's baking bread or cakes. Lydia introduced her to me—oh that was before she was dead of course, but now she isn't dead yet. I think that has to happen. Oh confusing. Don't worry, I think you would need Lydia to go to those places because they're in the future."

Jeb Stuart was coming down with a severe migraine.

"Do you want to know about the airport and the golf courses?" Cheryl inquired. "Are you all right?"

"Yes, tell me about the airport and the golf courses," Stuart answered. "I can hardly wait to hear about them."

"Airports. That's easy. That's where the planes land and take off. The ones around here are too small for the big 747's and that, but the little ones land here all the time. Got that?"

"Mmm, yeah, I got it. Airports. Planes, 747's."

"Then there are the golf courses. Bill loves to go to them, but he always is upset when he comes home. They have these little white balls with dots all over them—sometimes they're yellow or even pink if you're a lady. Well, all you do is hit it and hope that sometime the ball goes in the hole. Do you understand?"

"Perfectly!" said Stuart softly.

"Do you need anything else explained?"

"No, not right now. I've had as much as I can take of this gibberish."

"Oh General Stuart. It's not gibberish. It makes perfect sense to everyone I know."

"By chance, are any of the people you know doctors?"

"Only Carson Hardwick, he is a doctor. You know he teaches at a college in Chicago and he talked me into coming here with Lydia and him."

"That's what I suspected."

"Well then, would you see that I get back to town? I think they're all worried about me by now."

"Why don't you go freshen up a bit while I decide what to do?" said the general.

"All right, sounds like a plan."

Stuart watched wearily as some of the men took Cheryl away to a private tent. The orderly who had been busily writing as fast as he could, still sat in the dust with a stunned look on his face.

"Did you get anything out of that interrogation, Thomas?"

"Nothing that makes any sense. It seems to me there are two possibilities—either Gettysburg, with all its strangely coded places is part of an advanced and magical society, or else our guest, Miss Cheryl, is completely out of her mind."

"My thoughts precisely, Thomas. What do you think we should do with her?'

"We could take her in the woods and shoot her," suggested the orderly.

"Hmm, not really an option, my good man. That wouldn't be the gentlemanly thing to do, now would it?"

"I suppose not, but what do you have in mind?"

"Actually, I feel the most productive thing we could do would be to somehow sneak her back to the Yanks. If she does the same thing to their brains as she did to mine this afternoon, in a day or so, we could just walk into their lines and put them out of their misery!"

"Sounds like a wonderful idea, General."

34

JOHN DODSWORTH HAS become a terrific friend despite the first impressions I had of him. When I first came to Kronos, I saw John as a mysterious and solitary person bordering on being a recluse. One can usually pinpoint individuals like that. Just looking at his eyes, I felt I could detect that John felt he could trust no one, and his subsequent actions seemed to support that. He was obviously confused when it came to judging character. Scientists are seldom a good judge of character, and John tested the waters a bit in temporarily siding with the greedy billionaire, Manning Jones, and nearly manipulated the time-space continuum, if successful, in a way that would surely have negatively contorted history. John, fortunately, came to see through the deceitful devices of Jones, and he devised an ingenious scheme that utterly changed the complexion of Jones' evil plans.

One thing was certain. John Dodsworth is an established genius with computer programming. In recent times, without John's presence, Kronos had become almost completely inactive without his brilliance. Scientists there had been disappointingly unsuccessful in replicating John's work in artificial time travel in the two years after he had disappeared. Rumor had it at the time that John had mysteriously vanished somewhere into time and possibly could have been killed in some terrible technical glitch. That was almost true except for the action of my mother, Thelma.

In the past two years, John has become a good friend, revealing himself and his work in time travel to only a privileged few, including myself, my parents, Mel Currier, Kaye Spahr, and Trinia Williams.

There was still mistrust evident of most of the people at Kronos. I cannot blame him for being so vigilant after his mistake originally trusting Manning Jones, but now, gradually, I felt he had reexamined his feelings for them, but I felt it would still take something extraordinary to finally sway him over. My personal problems, I feel, rekindled his return to the Kronos fold.

Briefly after our return to the present at Ostia, John approached me about his take on the situation.

"It's your daughter, Lydia, isn't it?" asked John Dodsworth. "She's in some kind of trouble somewhere in time."

"Yes, both she and Cheryl," I replied. "Seems Cheryl is missing somewhere around the Battle of Gettysburg. I believe in 1863."

"The beginning of July in that year, if I recall."

"Anyway, it appears the only way to help them would be at the hands of my mother, and, according to Cecil, she's somewhere in the first century on a mission of her own. He has a plan to somehow involve Jesus in luring her back, but I'm not sure how that's working out. If Thelma doesn't return, I'm afraid the two of them are going to be in a lot of trouble."

"There is another option, Bill," answered Dodsworth. "What I mean to say is we still have the Kronos alternative. They have several time casings developed that we could use."

"But those casings are useless without the software to apply to them," I replied, knowing full well John controlled the key to that vital software.

"And who possesses that software, I might ask," smiled John.

"Why it's you, John, but you've effectively left Kronos behind. For the most part, they all believe you're dead, except, of course for the time jump team and a couple of others. I couldn't ask you to destroy the cover you've so expertly fashioned."

"Bill, I'm a bit disappointed in you. Is there any reason to assume I am unable to properly set my priorities when it comes to things so important to my friends?"

I was greatly impressed with John's newfound ethics, and for several minutes I was unable to respond to him, turning momentarily away and staring at nothing in particular, simply attempting to regain my composure.

"John, I greatly appreciate what you say, but what could you do?"

"Simple. I go back to our time, fly out to Pittsburgh, and drive to the Kronos facility in West Virginia. I would have to call Norton to let me past security into the complex. From there I would have the time travel casings we had fabricated taken from mothballs and loaded on a truck destined for Gettysburg, and from there, back in time to July 2, 1863, right in the middle of the battle area."

"But you would expose your concealment to those at Kronos. How else could you get their cooperation?"

"Bill! Priorities, priorities. Remember? I think it's time to return to my calling. And if you're worried about their cooperation, don't forget I have the ace card—the key to the software and the passwords that run their program. They won't have a real choice."

"OK, but you're not going alone are you? I'm the logical one to go along."

"Of course. You and the others—Mel, Kaye, Trinia, and a few other strong arms who've been trained for rescue teams. Remember the guys who saved you out of Pompeii? We'll have to pull out some period costumes so we'll fit in, but that shouldn't be difficult."

"Sounds like a plan," I slapped John on the back.. "Let me tell Cecil. Likely he'll stay here and wait for Mom. He still believes she'll show. He's likely right about her, but who knows when?"

35

MANNING JONES SAT awkwardly on the stone floor of the cave, several teetering towers of glittering coins piled in front of him. For most of the past hour he had sorted, counted, examined, and re-stacked the money he had carefully extracted from the leather pouch Thelma had left for Rashid and him before she had transported herself away into the future. Rashid occupied himself with rooting through the boxes that held the games left for them that Thelma suggested might keep them entertained until her return. Rashid was irritably leafing through the instructions for the Monopoly game, having little success deciphering the Arabic language in which it was written.

"Rashid, come over here," called Jones.

"Hey, Manning, could you help me with this game?" cried a frustrated Rashid.

"Forget the stupid game. Come here." Jones motioned for his partner to have a seat with him against the rock wall of the cave. Pointing at the money, he asked, "Do you know what this is?"

"It's money, Mr. Jones."

"Of course it is. But it's a lot more. It's part of a plan to get us out of here."

"Looks like a good bit of cash. Probably over a hundred bucks, I'd say."

"Rashid, you have no idea how much is here. In these three piles are forty-three silver shekels. Here in this pile is an assortment of gold Phoenician drevums. The third stack is an array of lesser bronze and copper coins. Together, they amount to more than most men in this time could see in three lifetimes."

Verma Rashid smiled but was obviously confused. "Where did Mrs. Thayer get all this money?"

"That old woman got it from Kronos. This is all Kronos money. It's counterfeit of course, but it doesn't matter. No one around here could ever tell the difference between Kronos coins and the real ones. It doesn't make any difference because both the silver in the shekels and the gold in the drevums are purer than anything made in this century, or for centuries beyond that I'm sure."

"Why do we need a plan, Mr. Jones? Can't we just wait for Mrs. Thayer to come back and get us?"

Jones just shook his head disgustedly.

"We need a backup plan, Rashid. We still have to be prepared to escape back to our time with the old woman if left with that alternative, but I strongly fear our so-called escape with the old woman's help might just lead us into another inescapable time travel prison."

"Don't you trust her, Manning? Remember she saved us from those awful creatures in that steamy nightmare jungle."

"Verma, Verma, who do you think put us there in the first place? And what about our friends who met their ghastly demise at the mercy of those same creatures that could have devoured us as well? Add to that, I never appreciated getting zapped with that stun gun of hers. If it weren't for the fact that she might be our only way out of this situation, I would have likely stuck a knife between her ribs a long time ago."

Rashid shrugged. "I was thinking it may have been that Dodsworth guy. He's the one who took us all back to that dreadful place, wasn't he?"

"I doubt it was Dodsworth's doings," answered Jones sourly. "John Dodsworth was one of those who himself likely met a dreadful end in one of those monster's stomach after we left him in that swamp. I would think he would never have sacrificed himself just to destroy us. Could you imagine anyone actually giving up his own life to help the good of other people? I categorically think not. The only one in my mind left capable of stranding us back in that horrible spot in the first place would be the old conniving woman, Thelma Thayer."

"So what now, Mr. Jones?" said Verma, now more confused than ever.

Jones gathered a handful of the coins into the leather pouch as he talked.

"First, we do what Thayer wanted. We find that Jesus fellow and talk with him. That was what she wanted from us to begin with. She said something to me about rehabilitation, I believe. When she comes back, we can tell her we took the initiative ourselves to fulfill her mission. We could tell her that Jesus the magician changed our lives and we swore never to do anything bad again. If our other part of the plan doesn't come through, we can still fall back on the original one."

"Mr. Jones, that sounds like a good plan, but, like you say, where does that leave us?"

Manning Jones had now folded his arms across his chest and glared intensely at Verma as he spoke.

"No one gets the best of Manning Jones. I've been going along with this old hag because I had no choice at the time. I've been waiting for this chance. Now that she's abandoned us, I can attempt implementing my own idea."

Manning Jones touched Verma Rashid's shoulder and stared intensely into his eyes, simulating as much an appearance of frankness as he was capable.

"This Jesus," rasped Jones, "what do you think of him? I mean-- these so-called miracles and such?"

"Didn't you say they were just magic tricks?"

"I'm not so sure now, Rashid. No matter how I looked at it, I couldn't explain away the trick with the wine or the strange appearance of thousands of fish and loaves to feed all those people—just almost instantly. It was like those loaves of bread and fish just kept coming. I mean, where did they come from? Even in modern times with all that technology I don't know how those stunts could have been replicated. In this time of antiquity, I think it's absolutely impossible. Perhaps this Jesus has some power that I could not foresee. Maybe that power, if it's real, could get us out of here. I believe we have to play that card if we don't want to rely on Old Lady Thayer.

"I have a bad feeling about this, Manning," said Rashid.

"Well then, Rashid, you can stay here and be crow bait. As for me, this man might be our ticket out of here!"

"So where do we start?" asked a wide-eyed Rashid.

"Let's gather up everything we can carry. We have the three donkeys to ride and carry our stuff. We just head on down along the sea until we find him or someone who can tell us where to look for him. It shouldn't be too hard, seeing that he's such a personality around here."

Verma hustled around the cave gathering everything he could pack onto the back of one of the donkeys while Jones steadied their rope bridles and affectionately caressed the bag of coins he had bound to the belt on his waist. In less than a half hour, the duo resolutely proceeded eastward along the same rocky beach they had once traveled recently at the direction of their captor, Thelma Thayer.

36

To Cecil Thayer, Thelma's appearance at John Dodsworth's camp near the ruins of ancient Ostia, was not much of a surprise to him, but it was certainly a relief.

"My dear," sighed Cecil after a strong embrace for his prodigal wife, "I hope you've resolved the personal questions you've sought on your recent quest."

"A very enlightening experience. I'm satisfied personally, but I never got a chance to finalize my rehabilitation plans for Manning Jones. I had to leave him there temporarily when I got the news I had to come back to help."

"That's all right. I doubt Jones can get away without your help, but I still hold out very little hope that he has any redeeming social value. Perhaps I'm wrong, but I've never felt there was much chance for optimism for him and was pretty much against your idea of rescuing him from a very deserving fate. I think John Dodsworth made his opinion well known when you and he originally devised the plan to dump him and his demented gang in Jurassic Italy. I don't think he would have agreed with your rescue mission."

"I disagree. It seems to me that Jones and his friend Rashid have made great strides in that area. They've been quite cooperative and rather friendly with me in the First Century situation in which I've placed them. I feel there's hope."

Cecil rolled his eyes and shrugged.

"By the way, that was rather clever how you got Jesus to inform me of the situation back here," interjected Thelma. "It took me a bit to realize you were responsible."

"I've learned a few tricks from you, my dear."

"So, fill me in as to what's going on"

"It's the same old thing—only this time it's a bit more serious, I fear. It seems Lydia has been exercising her time travel abilities …"

"Not particularly surprising," interrupted Thelma.

"Well this time she's taken her mother with her along with a history professor from Chicago-- back to Gettysburg at the time of the battle."

"A bit disappointing. I thought she had learned her lesson about our daughter-in-law, Cheryl, with those other two time travel fiascos. Lydia doesn't seem to be able to consider the understanding these people should have. It appears she can do all right for herself, but inevitably runs into problems when she has to be responsible for the others she takes with her."

"You're right of course. Bill got a text message from Lydia calling for help. This time it seems Cheryl has somehow gotten herself lost, and that has greatly complicated the issue. Who knows what else may have gone wrong since we last heard?"

Thelma was just shaking her head. "So you have a plan then?"

"I do. Plus we have invaluable help from John Dodsworth and the original time travel crew from Kronos. They've gone ahead to West Virginia to consolidate a rescue team. I think that will be a good idea since we have multiple individuals involved in this fiasco. It might be a complicated task for one person. I've arranged with John to have a meeting place to the south of the battlefield—a place where we can all meet once we've arrived. I'll show you the place we've selected just in case you need to go there."

"I take it John will have the cooperation of Kronos then?"

"Yes, I believe he will get it, but that's another story. When we have time, I'll tell you about it. As for now, we have to get a plane out of here and get to 1863 Gettysburg."

37

I T WAS CERTAINLY a shock—but a pleasant jolt to be sure—when John Dodsworth and I strolled through the doors of Kronos' phony ski resort. Everyone in the lobby, it seemed, froze and stood or sat with mouths dropped open for what seemed an interminable span of time.

"John! John Dodsworth! Is it really you?" squealed a wide-eyed Letty Blair as she emerged from the resort cafeteria. Letty's breakfast tray teetered precariously in her left hand as she gestured excitedly with her right. "I mean—we all thought you were ..." Letty's voice trailed off.

"Dead, you mean, Letty," laughed John. "Well that was as near to true as I would ever want it, I think, but here I am as alive as anyone could imagine."

In those few moments, the people in the lobby came back to life themselves, but aside from a few whispers, they all returned to become the sham characters to which they had been assigned by Kronos in order to keep up the ruse of the ski resort, mindlessly wandering about the facility or reading a newspaper that had been read and reread many times that day.

"Well, John, it is certainly good to see you again. I assume you've come back to the fold so to speak," grinned Joe Richards extending his hand in welcome as he darted across the room. Joe Richards was one of the computer programmers—he referred to himself as a "computer architect" when people asked him what he did at Kronos. He and the other architects had been at a loss and were almost desperate for a way to restart the Kronos time travel program that had remained stagnant since Dodsworth's disappearance.

John had become aware that he alone held the key to the computers that could revive the program, but he had been hesitant to do it. For some time, he held the belief that there were too many people who wanted to get hold of valuable secrets about traveling in time that only he could release. John had often reminded his technicians that he had no reservations about their personal honesty, but scientists like them were notoriously poor judges of character. He had witnessed this firsthand in the person of Manning Jones, the billionaire who had amassed much of his fortune using information he had gleaned from Kronos time travelers. After years of observation he became convinced that, even though not perfect, there were a number of trusted individuals, particularly Mom and Dad and our time travel team at Kronos with whom he could work with relative assurance of honest outcomes.

"Yes, Joe. I'm back and prepared to jumpstart our program." John raised his eyebrows a bit. "Of course I expect to have more control of our missions and the people who get involved with the time travel events."

"But John, I can't authorize that myself," protested Joe. "You know I have to take it back to the board."

"Don't take too long, Joe. You know how I never had much patience with red tape. I suggest you see them ASAP. I have a project of great importance that needs a priority rating that can't wait."

"John, John, these things take time."

"Time! Time is what it's all about my good man. And time is running out for this program without my input. I know that and so do you. I can disappear just as fast as I did before, Joe. I suggest you see that board today."

"Now don't be hasty, John," gasped Joe Richards. "I'll do my best."

As it turned out, most of the board had fortunately been available and were meeting that day deep in the bowels of the Kronos facility. Anton Lueehuik and Marge Paladin were with some of the newer panel members and together had seriously been considering the dissolution of the time travel program that seemed to be going nowhere.

"John's here?" smiled Marge. "Well that changes everything, of course."

After hearing of John's requirements for his return, some of the newer members shook their heads. "I don't feel we can hand over that much power to one man," protested Kenneth Dean. "I thought we were losing control before. Some of us still have no idea how we are financed. I say no."

A few assembled there at the table nodded assent.

"I for one feel we have no choice, ladies and gentlemen." Marge had leaned forward and looked in Mr. Dean's face. "It's John's way, or—as they say in the common vernacular—the highway. I'm not sure if you realize John is the only one qualified to run the program that controls the Kronos computers."

"Are we to be terrorized, Miss Paladin—to be held ransom by this John Dodsworth?" growled Anthony Perry sitting by Mr. Dean.

"Let's be serious, my fellow directors," sighed Anton Leeuenhuik. "If we wish to go forward, we have no choice. Besides, I, for one, can vouch for John Dodsworth. He was an important cog before and he is more important now. If he wishes to have more control running this thing, I see no reason why we can't go along with him. What would it hurt? Without him we would have nothing. With him, we have a new start. And, I might add, a dynamic start."

A few directors still mumbled a bit, but when the voting took place, it was nearly unanimous. Only two dissenting votes of twelve.

"Joe," announced Paladin succinctly, "tell John we agree to his terms, and ask him when we can get started."

38

A PLATOON OF Jeb Stuart's men had been given the task of returning Cheryl Thayer safely to the Union ranks as quickly and secretly as possible and had concluded that the best route to take would be a circular route from the northeast. They had seen Cheryl's strange tourist map and chose a road named Hanover Road. It was marked with the number 30 which made no sense to them.

"Obviously some Yank code," suggested one man. "But one thing I figure is that we can sneak in about evenin'. No one should be expecting us to come in from that direction with such a small force as we have. Anyway, we'll bring her in that way leadin' her buggy. If they see us comin' we can slap her horse on the rump and turn tail and ride outta there as fast as we can."

It's a great wonder the Reb platoon got as far as it did. No one should have been able to keep Cheryl quiet unless indeed they would have shot her. Some of the cavalrymen seriously thought about it but knew they had direct orders from Stuart to keep Cheryl safe to the Union lines. "I've got to thank you boys," Cheryl hollered aloud to the wincing men in front of the column. "I can't say I've been treated so well for a couple days now."

"Ma'am, your voice—could you please keep it down? We're near Yank lines."

"Why do you need me to be quiet, sir?"

"Oh, Ma'am, I don't know why. I guess I don't want to spook the horses …"

"You don't have to tell me about that!" shouted Cheryl, not heeding the soldier's request to be quiet. "My horse, Bo, took off running for town as soon as I raised my voice I suppose. Anyway he left me and that's why you have to take care of me."

One lad tried offering Cheryl something to eat, in the hope that loading her mouth would keep her voice muffled.

"Oh no you don't!" protested Cheryl. batting away the offered soldier's rations. "One of your other buddies tried to poison me with that stuff, and then he gave me a drink of whiskey that was about the worst stuff I ever tasted! It almost made me throw up."

Perhaps Cheryl's usual uproar actually assisted in the success of the mission to get her through Northern lines. No one trying to sneak up on enemy lines would have made such a clamor as that created by Cheryl's incessant boisterous chatter. Nor was it very likely any sane enemy would ever consider boldly transporting a loud and overexcited woman like this one perched in the seat of a doctor's buggy through their lines. Even when Confederates spotted a contingent of three or four men posted along a low ridge, the men in the Yankee lookout cheerfully waved at the loquacious woman and her gray-clad guard as they passed by in the dimming twilight.

The soldier who seemed in charge called softly to Cheryl when he noticed a large barn ahead, around which was considerable activity. He quickly made his decision. "There over on that hillside, Ma'am, that's where a bunch of your people are stayin' We can leave you off there."

"You actually want me to go sleep in a barn tonight?" moaned Cheryl. "Just take me back to that Jeb fellow. I liked his place better."

Three men simultaneously slapped the rump of Cheryl's harness horse, and her rig lurched forward and bounced recklessly along the roadway toward the Union lines despite the loud protesting squalls of its driver. The horse and buggy unceremoniously skidded to a sliding stop when a blue-clad soldier desperately latched onto the horse's rigging and dug his feet into the turf like a rodeo bulldogger, heroically controlling the runaway rig.

"Halt, who are you?" demanded the breathless soldier.

"Why I'm Cheryl Thayer. And who are you, young man?"

There was brief flicker of recognition in the lad's face.

"Why you're that lady everyone's been looking for, aren't you?"

"Oh I don't know about everyone, but I'll bet Lyd and the Professor—I mean the general—are certainly trying to find me I suppose. Probably that young handsome officer too. What's his name? You know, the Errol Flynn guy."

"How'd you get here? I mean in the middle of the battlefield, right here at this field hospital?"

"Hospital? This is a hospital? Why it looks like an old barn to me."

"Who were those men who were with you?" asked the soldier. "Why didn't they come over?"

"Oh those guys were part of Jeb's men. They were really nice to me and gave me another horse and all."

"Jeb's men? " The man looked confused and perhaps a bit excited. "You don't mean Jeb *Stuart* by chance?"

"Why yes, that's him. I heard them call him General Stuart. He's not too far away you know. You'll probably get to meet him sometime soon. He's just up there in that direction a short way," Cheryl indicated pointing to the north.

The young soldier's eyes widened at the information he got about the notorious cavalry commander who often raided a number of towns and impudently rode around Union lines almost unimpeded.

"Lieutenant, come here. Listen to this!" called the soldier.

"What is it Private?" said a man stumbling along a rock pathway by the barn.

"It's Stuart. They've finally located him and he's on his way here. This woman was in Stuart's camp if we are to believe her. Some of his men were just here too."

After a brief account of Cheryl's revelations as well as her notable identity connected to a Union general, the lieutenant wheeled around and shouted orders to another soldier who had been beckoned to him.

"There's not much time, Corporal. Get this information to Meade as quickly as you can. Stuart's making his way to our lines just off to the north. If we can rally our own cavalry and bring them to bear around Hanover Road, we might be able to stop him."

"Mrs. Thayer, my name is Lieutenant Cornell Edwards," the man rattled on, "you might stay in a tent over on the other side of the barn. I'm sorry we can't offer much comfort. The only beds in the hospital which are often no more than tables or rough-hewn planks are being utilized for the wounded."

"Wounded? Wounded from what?" asked a startled Cheryl.

"The battle of course, Mrs. Thayer. There's been considerable fighting for two days now. Surely you've heard the gunfire and cannons?"

"That wasn't thunder? Oh my, of course not. How silly. This is the Battle of Gettysburg. How could I have been so dumb?" Cheryl had both hands to her face as if all of a sudden the realization of what she was witnessing was a bit more than a personal adventure.

"Those wounded men in the barn," said Cheryl, "maybe I could help. I studied nursing in college you know."

"I didn't realize anyone, particularly women, actually studied nursing in college, Mrs. Thayer. We have a bunch of volunteer women who are helping, but they are a bit overwhelmed. I'm certain they could use your assistance."

"Show me the way, Lieutenant."

An icy shudder ran through Cheryl as she stood in the doorway of the barn. The low groans emanating from the make-shift hospital Cheryl had just before mistakenly identified as likely from the lowing of cattle, she grasped now as the moans and cries of the wounded soldiers being treated there. Row upon row of writhing, blood-stained men in various postures—some were lying, some sitting, and others attempting to stand, often leaning near the white-washed stone of the barn's basement. About a half-dozen women tended to or comforted the men who appeared in diverse stages of pain or discomfort. The only pronounced lights other than some isolated candles flickering diffusely in a few dim corners of the barn were some dusky kerosene lanterns hanging on vertical beams in place near tables at the far end of the converted hospital, reminding Cheryl of empty shells of locust husks she had seen in the shrubbery near her house.

"What are they doing over there, Lieutenant?" asked Cheryl, feeling warm tears beginning to well up in her eyes.

"The doctors, Mrs. Thayer. They're doing amputations. The doctors sometimes do over a hundred in a day."

"Amputations! That many? Can't some of them be saved?"

"Likely not. It's the only way, I fear. It's better an arm or leg than to live with a mutilated appendage or die from loss of blood. If we had regular hospitals perhaps a few might be saved—but the regular hospitals are so far away."

"Well then, let me do what I can. I know some things I've learned." Cheryl fought the urge to say what she learned in the future but all she could see in her mind was Lydia scowling at her." It might help some if I can see to them."

"I'll introduce you to the head nurse and she can put you to work then."

The two walked through the murky light to one of the women who was carefully bandaging the wound on a man's thigh.

"Ma'am, this is Mrs. Cheryl Thayer. She says she is trained as a nurse and wants to assist here."

"Hello Mrs. Thayer, I'm glad you're here. Any help is appreciated, especially someone who has training. My name is Nellie--Nellie Leith. Many of us have been trained by Clara Barton, you know."

"Clara Barton! Why she's the founder of ..." Cheryl once again fought to suppress her knowledge about Clara Barton and the American Red Cross. "I mean some people have heard of her and what you are all doing in the field of medicine," In nursing school, Cheryl had researched Clara Barton and her recruitment of women for wartime hospitals during the war. Clara and her innovative techniques had been one of her devoted interests.

"News travels fast on a battlefield I suppose. At this point, Clara cannot be here herself. She's in Virginia now attending to the boys from some of the recent action down there."

"Anyway, how can I help?"

"You could start by cutting material into strips from these shirts and dresses into bandages. We're pretty well caught up for today, but I fear tomorrow's action will bring a dramatic need for plenty more."

"Sounds good to me. Where do you sterilize these bandages once they're cut into strips?" asked Cheryl.

"Sterilize? What do you mean?"

Cheryl had a blank look, once again realizing she was about to inadvertently reveal futuristic medical ideas to Nellie.

"In my training," Cheryl went on, fabricating a tale as she went. "We find there is much better success with infection in wounds if the bandages are boiled in hot water before use."

"Where did you hear anything like that?"

"Oh, in Pittsburgh. They have some good hospitals there you know."

"I guess in that sooty city, washing bandages is likely a good idea. Anyway, if it makes you feel better, go ahead and boil them as long as time permits. Maybe your idea could show some merit. It's worth a try."

Cheryl worked for several hours cutting the fabric into bandages and then soaking them in water dumped into a black kettle she found in an out building; then she set the kettle atop the coals of a nearby cook fire. After boiling, she fished them out with a metal andiron she found by the barn that she had sterilized over the fire. She asked a soldier to help run a rope along between two trees where she hung the bandages to dry for the next day's needs. Cheryl knew she could never come close to disinfecting every bandage in that field hospital, but she felt good with her efforts that somehow, she might save the limbs or even the lives of some of the soldiers who might be brought from battle to that particular place. Perhaps, too, she thought, maybe Clara Barton and her corps of nurses might eventually help realize the effectiveness her procedures.

After finishing her disinfection process, Cheryl realized the adrenalin was still pumping and along with the trauma of seeing and hearing the wounded men throughout the evening, she would need to calm herself before she would be able to fall asleep that night. Cheryl felt a walk through the hospital talking and reassuring the injured soldiers might help her work off the adrenalin high she had developed. The intensity of the cries had waned a bit, only occasionally hearing someone cry out as if having a bad dream. Slowly she made her way through the infirmary, occasionally stopping and speaking softly, comforting one lad or another along the way, sometimes with a drink of water, a wet rag on the forehead, or simply a few words..

As she made her way through the rows of makeshift beds, she came to the far end where some of the more seriously wounded were lying. Some of these men would be victims of more amputations in the upcoming days she thought. Is there any way she might help? She began to examine a few of the wounds of these more critical men. One man had a missing foot, likely the victim of cannon fire. Cheryl was surprised she was so calm about the tragedies of the battle as she approached one man after the other. She came to the final bed—it was likely adapted from the kitchen table from the farmhouse. This man, she thought to herself after a cursory examination, could easily have his arm saved if only we had access to modern medicine or hospital.

"Dear, be brave," she whispered to him, placing her hand on his fevered brow.

"Mrs. Thayer!" came a voice weakened by the pain he had endured that day.

"Oh my God, it's you Hunter Mathews!" choked Cheryl.

In horror, she spun and ran through a nearby doorway into the barnyard, then turned sharply and at once began to slip uncontrollably in a slimy, treacherous mud, falling headfirst into a pile of debris alongside the fencerow, unable to effectively extricate herself from the rubbish into which she had become entangled.

"What's wrong?" A woman's authoritarian voice emerged from just inside the darkened doorway of the hospital.

The dim light of Nellie Leith's locust husk lantern shone diffusely over a pallid Cheryl Thayer, awkwardly recovering from her flop into that day's ghastly mound of amputated limbs!

39

WHAT HAD SEEMED a relatively simple task had become much more problematic for Jones and Rashid. Jones had figured it would be an easy task to find the man, Jesus, whom he preferred to call "The Magician" even though he truly hoped for his own sake, that he was a bit more than some prodigious illusionist. Manning Jones was counting on it, in fact. He indicated to Rashid that all they had to do was to hike around the region near the Sea of Galilee and they would soon come upon the man they wanted, but it turned out not to be so simple. Jesus the Galilean apparently kept himself on the move, often straying off onto side trips in his travels.

Manning Jones had the advantage of the Kronos ULIT translator implanted in his ear and was able to proficiently communicate in any of the local dialects and even in Romanic Latin if needed. Everywhere he went, villagers and wanderers offered versions of stories they had heard of Jesus, or, in some cases, witnessed. There were plenty of rumors and stories floating around such as of Jesus purportedly healing a number of people of various ailments such as blindness, hearing loss, lameness, leprosy, and others.

"He has been known to cast out demons," another man offered.

"I have heard he has even brought someone back from death," added his wife.

When Rashid heard of these feats after Jones' brief translation to him, his eyes bugged out.

"Wow, Manning, you're right! If he can raise people from the dead, he can surely do a simple thing like send us back home. He sounds like one of the Super Heroes!"

Manning just shook his head in disbelief. "Only superstitious locals would ever believe tales like that. No one, not even me, could bring anyone back from the dead."

"I don't know," interrupted Rashid, "isn't that what Mrs. Thayer did for us?"

Manning Jones was in no mood to argue with Rashid's wacky revelations.

"Rashid," Jones cut in, "one of the things I would like to get hold of would be a weapon of some sort and arm ourselves. I've never felt safe as we travel about with all this money." Jones fondly tapped his change purse. "I've hidden the rest of the gold coins in the packs on the animals, but if bandits would strike, they'd likely find those too."

"But Manning, Mrs. Thayer told us not to have …"

"I don't give a damn what that old witch says! Forget her for now. We'll only use her if this present idea doesn't pan out. What I need now is someone who can get us what we need."

It's an odd thing, but evil seems to gravitate towards like elements. People, who are basically wicked, like Manning Jones, have an inner sense about people like them, and when he and Rashid browsed through the market place he found the contact for which he had yearned.

"Gentlemen, my name is Eban," chortled a bowing, scrawny man with a dark mouth of mostly-missing teeth. Both men were quick to notice the well-healed stub of a missing index finger on the man's right hand. "I feel there is something I have here you might find useful." Eban, greedily eyeing Jones' bulging purse, spread his arms wide in a generous offering of his pitiful array of wares-- blankets, pots, and other household items, spread on the ground in front of him.

"Not unless you have something I can find useful, like a sword or something?" grunted Jones waving him away with his hand.

"Oh, but how would I, a poor market vender, be able to do to legally satisfy such a request?" Eban squinted at the two men, surveying them carefully. "Weapons are forbidden by our Roman overseers, and I understand there are active troops in this very vicinity." The man's eyes were darting shiftily in all directions.

Manning Jones fumbled with casual detachment with the leather thongs of his purse as he shrewdly observed the shopkeeper begin to salivate a bit at his movements.

"There is a way we can talk more discreetly about this matter?" whispered Jones, aware of Eban's trembling hand. When Jones raised his eyes, he was greeted with the shopkeeper's toothless grin that he was sure presented the opening for which he had probed.

"You are a stranger, my friend. How do I know I can trust you?" quivered Eban without taking his eyes from Jones' purse. "Your accent is not of this region and is different, but it is certainly not Roman."

"The only thing about me that's Roman is my gold," he breathed in a low voice as he removed a shiny golden lugdunum from his remarkable leather pouch.

Eban could no longer maintain himself, as both his knees buckled at the sight of the valuable coin, and he went to a kneeling position. Eban's lips moved a bit as if he were attempting to talk or possibly kiss the venerable object presented before him.

"Yes, yes," he stuttered uncontrollably, never attempting to gain eye contact with his potential buyers. "I believe I might locate such an object for you."

Scrambling on all fours, Eban unwrapped a blanket from a small heap of brightly-dyed material near a small tower of precariously leaning pottery in the center of his household goods. The leather-handled knife, about ten inches in length, was shiny but a bit pocked. Eban hopped back on his knees awkwardly propelling himself with his free arm and dropped his precious bundle at Jones' feet.

"Is this the best you can do, Eban?" growled Jones taking the knife, examining it, and flipping it back onto the open cloth. "This coin I offer you alone would satisfy your abject existence for a year or more."

"Oh, sir, I can do much, much better, given a chance. I know of men nearby who have access to much better things of which you would most definitely like. Of course those men would require payment as well."

"Can you take us there, Eban?"

"Yes, of course, but I must secure my goods before we go."

"Forget this junk. No self-respecting thief would want any of it anyway. Here take the coin." Jones flipped it insolently at the scrambling man. "I'm certain it will cover any losses."

"Yes, yes, of course. Thank you, sir."

"And let me take the knife, Eban. I can use it until I get something better."

With a bit of sham ceremony, Eban presented the weapon to Manning Jones with both hands and with a slight genuflect."

"At your service, sir. Bring your pack animals and your belongings and follow me. It's about a half hour journey to the man's camp. Let me go ahead a bit," he suggested with a sideways glance. "These people know me."

The mini caravan wound through the narrow street leading out among the groves of trees to the south of town. Eban led the way about fifty yards or so ahead of the two men leading their three pack animals.

"Manning, do you really trust this guy?" asked Verma Rashid.

"Of course not!" hissed Jones. "But I think we've reached the point of desperation, and we have to be able to be flexible in our transactions with these people. Dealing with individuals in this century is not much different that in ours."

"I'd feel better if I had a knife or some weapon for myself."

"Well I'd feel better if you didn't," flashed Jones.

The first indication of the location of the mysterious encampment was their awareness of a slight rise in the land off to the right side of the road, a low hill topped by a dense copse of what Jones thought were likely olive trees. A rather persistent cloud of gray wood smoke broiled out from the heavy underbrush.

"This is the place, sir!" shouted Eban running up the slope with his arms up. "I'll go ahead and make sure they are aware it's all right to come up."

"Stay close together," suggested Jones to Rashid. "Keep near to the donkeys if there's trouble."

As Eban got to the thicket, several dark-bearded men were at once glaring down the slope and speaking with the shopkeeper in low tones. After a brief confab, Eban came down, returning to his recent benefactor.

"He says it's all right to come up," grinned Eban.

"Here's my plan, Eban," jumped in Jones. "I'm not sure we can trust your man. I'm going to have one of us come up and negotiate a bit; then we'll all join together after he hears our plan."

"Sounds all right to me."

"Give us a minute, Eban. I have to consult with my—partner."

Once aside, Jones outlined his idea to Rashid. He understood the criminal mind well, having been associated with them in various walks of his life. He most certainly did not trust Eban. He had easily recognized the unmistakable look of greed. He was rightfully suspicious with the situation and knew the men in the camp would just as likely cut their throats and take all their money and other stuff as give them what they wanted and let them leave.

"Rashid, I'm sending you up there."

"Me! Why me Mr. Jones?"

"Relax. Everything's going to be good. Listen. Go there and give them a note from me. It indicates we want some weapons. Oh if they have horses, we'll take them. The note says we have lots of money—but we've buried it somewhere along the road."

"Gosh, Manning, I didn't see you bury the money. That was smart of you."

"You aren't always aware of the things I do," Manning reminded him. Actually Jones never had buried the money at all and it was still hidden on the donkeys, but he could not imagine why it would be good for Rashid to know that.

"Rashid, the message says we have lots of gold and they will be greatly compensated for any help they give us."

"What if they don't believe us and they kill me!"

"Don't worry," Jones assured him. "And when it's safe for me to come up, just wave a white cloth. If you wave another color, I'll know it's a trick and I'll escape."

"Manning! You'd leave me there?"

"Of course not, Rashid. I'll just go and round up some help and come back and rescue you."

"Oh."

"Now go on up and do your job. Remember, it might be the only way we can get out of this situation."

By now, Rashid had come to believe that Manning Jones was the only one in the world who was his true friend. There was no hesitation as he turned and quick-stepped up the hillside to the camp in the grove. As he got to the top, a man came up and grabbed his arm and pulled a lengthy knife, holding it to Rashid's throat.

"Hold it, hold it there, sir," squealed Rashid in English. "You don't want to hurt me or you'll never see our gold and silver. It's hidden you know, and you will never find it without me and Manning."

"He's got a whole bag full of money," grunted Eban, who now stood erect with his arms crossed. "Look at this coin." He tossed it to one of the more prominent men who was obviously the accepted leader of a troop of about a dozen tough-looking men wielding a variety of nasty weapons.

"Hmm, it says here there's more of this buried somewhere? Lots of it—millions in fact—somewhere along the road."

"Where? I'll shove this sword through your guts if you don't tell me." grunted the leader to Rashid.

Verma Rashid fully understood the universal gesture of a threatening sword. "Oh, sir, I don't know." sputtered Rashid in his own language. "Manning is the only one who knows, sir,"

The bandit leader motioned for Rashid to have Jones come up. "Why did your friend send up such an idiot? Well then, have your man come up then. I'll talk it over with him then."

Rashid was relieved even though he did not perfectly comprehend his adversary. He grabbed the towel he had brought with him and went to the edge of the trees and waved it back and forth above his head.

A few moments later, accompanied by an escort from a few of Eban's companions, Jones was standing confidently in their midst.

"My name's Barabbas," snarled the man. "And you're …?"

"Manning Jones, my friend." He said extending his hand. But Barabbas ignored the gesture.

"Where are you from? What are you doing here?"

"I'm from a place you wouldn't likely know—from over the seas to the west. I'm a very wealthy man—who commands many men and ships."

"You're an ally of Rome then?"

"Not at all, Mr. Barabbas, just the opposite in fact." Manning Jones was quick on his feet when spinning fabrications. "It seems we are competing for markets all over the known world. I'm constantly looking for new allies, especially those who have a particular dislike for the Romans, and I project you as one of those potential partners. See, here is a small sample of what wealth I possess." Jones dramatically pitched his pouch of coins spilling out wildly on the ground.

Two of the men, one of them Eban, leapt hysterically at the treasure rattling in the dust before them. In one horrific lightning slash of his Spanish sword, Barabbas deftly chopped off one of the greedy shopkeeper's remaining fingers on his right hand, and with another swift back swing of his left arm sent the other man head-over-heels with a great burst of crimson spewing from a broken nose. Behind Jones, Rashid turned pale, swooned, and fell backwards onto the ground. If Jones had been affected by the violence, he did not indicate it, standing stoically, now with his handshake offered once again.

"Mr. Manning Jones, I feel we may have the basis of a lasting friendship," smiled Barabbas grasping Jones' hand firmly.

40

CARSON HARDWICK AS a boy had long dreamt of the excitement of imagining himself draped in the glory of battles, particularly in the Civil War arena. He could imagine the whine of bullets, the thunder of cannon, and the acrid smell of gunpowder on the battlefield. Sometimes he held a saber aloft, leading men in a valiant charge across a battlefield filled with explosions and cries of the men as they charged the enemy position, culminating in a final bayonet thrust over the Confederate ramparts while holding Old Glory in one arm and his bloodied saber in the other. As a professor of history at Metro University, he had nurtured these unfulfilled dreams by gathering an expansive and widely-envied collection of artifacts, weapons, uniforms, records, diaries, or whatever else might turn up in his research,

The hard reality of actually recently participating in one of these so-called glorious conflicts had mellowed his attitude considerably. The real thing was not much like his fancied visions at all. In the mundane life he experienced at the university in downtown Chicago, he was never quite prepared for what happened to him in 1863 Gettysburg. The fear, the sounds of battle, the horrific bloodshed, and all the other dangers of battle which he barely survived at Plum Run all combined to violently jolt him back to reality. It had been only through a miracle and the heroism of Sergeant Taylor that he made it through at all.

Carson had no desire, now as he relaxed on the rocking chair of the front porch of George Meade's headquarters a few hundred yards behind the center of Cemetery Ridge, to ever go back to that danger. The professor, even though he had never smoked before, had accepted one of the general's fine cigars which smoldered innocently on the wooden railing in front of him. Now and then, he sipped warm Kentucky bourbon from a tumbler he balanced on one knee.

I've made whatever contribution I could to this battle without interference with the Kronos directive he convinced himself as he watched with a detached interest at the ever-hectic machinery of war. Hundreds of men, like a busy anthill accidentally kicked over, scurried by in all directions seemingly with no bearing, along the ridge, into the rear, forward, or whatever. Tents were hurriedly erected not far from the house. Cannons and caissons groaned and creaked along the road, interrupted now and then by the clatter of cavalrymen and various nickering protests of straining horses as various equipment proceeded in disciplined lines on its way to the front line. It didn't matter much to Hardwick now, as long as no one expected him to move along with that nightmarish paraphernalia of war.

The Metro professor had certainly used his futuristic knowledge of the battle to "suggest" to General Meade what might best be practical in the upcoming conflict—coming as close as possible to violating the Kronos initiative not to interfere or change anything in history. Now Carson was satisfied to sit back and watch. The faraway sharp snaps of small arms like distant firecrackers, the occasional singing of an errant rifle ball overhead, the remote grunting of incessant enemy cannons from Seminary Ridge followed abruptly by the nearby deafening Union responses-- other than for a few fleeting reminders of his own battlefield experience this background litter hardly bothered him at all in his position behind the protection of the powerful Union lines and the high rise of land they defended. He discerned what was to be the final outcome on this battlefield and clearly understood the gray Rebel lines would never reach the spot he now peacefully occupied.

"General Hardwick, could you help us apprise the situation?" George Meade called from inside where a number of other officers had assembled in war council.

"Gentlemen, this is General Carson Hardwick recently here from Washington and the Inspector General's office. His advice seems solid and I ask him now to listen in and perhaps enhance some of our ideas about what is about to happen from both perspectives."

Hardwick, a bit bothered by the intrusion of his supposed duties, slipped through the doorway somewhat cautiously and stood near Meade's left side and listened a bit disinterestedly as several of the men spoke in droning tones that made him wish he could relax and nap in the rocking chair he had just left. Perhaps, too, the half empty whiskey bottle had some influence on his mood as well.

"And what is your opinion of that, General Hardwick?" one officer suddenly interjected.

Hardwick had no idea what had been said, so he chose instead to turn and half-intelligently and gaze out the window over the battlefield, just to collect his senses.

Pointing the half dead cigar, he muttered a few almost-unintelligible comments. "Over there---the enemy." There was a prolonged pause over this revealing information. "They're coming shortly after noon tomorrow with everything they have. Remember what I told you the other day—a feint to the north and south first, but the real attack comes right here in the middle. When they come, don't shoot till you see the whites of their eyes-- I mean—hold your fire. Save your best stuff till they are right there in front of you. Then you can't miss, can you?"

"General, do you mean the cannon too?" gasped another man.

"Absolutely, my good man. Do you think those cannon balls you've been wasting for a day and a half are actually hitting anything? I think they're just knocking over trees on Seminary Ridge."

"Hmm," thought Meade rubbing his chin. "Ollie, your artillery batteries have been complaining the guns are overheated and sometimes there are large gaps while waiting for the delivery of munitions, sometimes leaving the gunners short. Perhaps for that reason alone, it might be smart to hold them back just before Hardwick's predicted assault on our center can begin."

"But General Meade, sir, are you placing too much trust in this man? He's unknown." An officer who identified himself as Brigadier General John Sedgewick spoke up, somewhat upset his role at Gettysburg had been rather minor thus far.

"Well, John, he's been right so far. Everything he's said has been solid, and he seems to have a lot of dedicated knowledge of the field. Besides, what would it hurt? If we wait and no assault comes, we're no worse or better off than before. If it does come, we'll have the advantage of point-blank shooting, better-supplied batteries, and rested cannons."

There were a few shoulder shrugs, but there was general agreement among the generals sitting around the table. The generals were introduced to Hardwick as John Gibbon of II Corps, Abner Doubleday of I Corps and Oliver Howard of XI Corps, all of whom were to head the centralized defense along Cemetery Ridge where, Hardwick knew from history, the famed Pickett's Charge would be the fiercest.

"All right, Hardwick, we're ready with your idea. Would you like to be on the front lines when the fight begins? I could assign you to one of the regiments," asked Meade. "It's your right you know."

Carson Hardwick had previously taken a steadying place against the wall and had once again become a bit bleary, and his eyes had begun to flutter a bit. But in an instant he was awake, lost his balance, and slid sideways onto the floor. It was probably fortunate the professor hit his head against the doorjamb as he fell receiving a superficial cut resulting in a tiny rivulet of very convincing blood. That accident was the only possible excuse he could have had for not joining the glory of the front line.

"Carson! Are you all right? Someone help me with the general. He's been through a lot in the past few days. We found him on the battlefield, the sole survivor of a Reb attack, you know."

"I'm a bit woozy, I'm afraid," answered Hardwick groggily. "I think I'm going to have to pass on the battlefield offer, I fear, even though I can hardly stand the thought of not being a part of it."

"We understand, man. Orderly, help him somewhere comfortable."

"The rocking chair on the porch. That'll be fine. Just so I can hear the sweet sounds of the conflict out there. That's all I need right now. You guys go out there and enjoy yourselves. Oh, and do you have a clean glass? I think I got some cigar ashes in this one."

As the orderly helped Hardwick to the porch, the others watched him.

"Poor fellow," remarked John Gibbon as he filed by and out through the picket fence into the roadway. "I'll bet this battle was all he waited for his whole life. Now this."

"Yes," said Doubleday, "he's one of our nation's real heroes."

That day in the late afternoon, Meade stood on the porch, his left hand on Hardwick's shoulder. A rickety wagon drew up in front of the house and a middle-aged dark-haired, bespectacled man with a mustache and beard bounded out appearing very much out of place in Meade's military camp without a uniform.

"General, I'd like to get a photo of your headquarters, if you don't mind. For posterity."

"Your name, sir?" asked Meade gruffly. We don't have much time for this foolishness.

"It's Mathew—Mathew Brady, the photographer assigned by the War Department."

"Well then, take your damned picture if you must. Do we have to go inside?"

"No, of course not. People in the picture actually enhance it. Just don't move or you'll be a blur!"

"All right, Hardwick and I will just sit here while you take the photograph. Right, Carson?"

Even in his dull-witted state, Hardwick recognized the name of Mathew Brady, the famed Civil War photographer whose hundreds of pictures appeared in innumerable books he had read. His first instinct was to stand tall for the photo for all to see. It might be fun to see his face when he looked back in a book of Gettysburg photos if he were ever fortunate enough to get back home.

Then it hit him. This is exactly what Lydia had warned him against. He should not be identified for future historians. He had not always been completely on board with the mandated Kronos directive, but his thoughts of Lydia's disappearance came back and how he knew he was responsible for her being wounded on the battlefield. He certainly owed it to her to keep his word.

When Brady was just ready to hit the shutter on the camera, Hardwick grabbed a wide-brimmed officer's hat someone left hanging on a rail and pulled it down low over his forehead just as the flash powder ignited.

"You camera shy, Carson?" said Meade.

"Yeah, a bit. And that reminds me. When it comes down to mentioning me about anything that's happened, please don't."

"I don't understand."

"It's like this, Sir. You know Washington. I think they would be upset if they thought I came here to tell you how to run this battle and all—to give you instruction. I mean, I was supposed to be here secretly, you know, evaluating everyone and all. It's difficult for a military man like me not to get involved. They might not look so kindly on my extracurricular activities so to speak, so if you don't mind, please see to it my name is not mentioned—no credit or anything. You and the others can have all the acclaim. I don't want any of it."

"I see. I completely understand. You have my word. I'll be sure they all understand and I'll get word to the others. Your position is quite noble, indeed. It's been my pleasure to work with you."

"Appreciate it, General. Do you mind much if I relax a bit here in your chair? My back's bothering me some."

Later that night, Hardwick suddenly awoke sweating from one of his nightmares—ones that would come to haunt him for years—about his previous experiences on the front. Everything was still. An eerie silence pervaded everywhere after what seemed like never-ending gunfire. Carson knew he couldn't sleep for a while so he actually ventured over to the ridge and the front lines. There, several miles off, he was able to plainly see the thousands of Southern campfires strung along Seminary Ridge like strings of clear Christmas lights. Those lights represented men—many of whom were to die in the next day's battle. Somehow Carson Hardwick wanted to stop everything, but he knew that would not be possible even if he would want to resist the Kronos noninterference directive he had promised to honor.

His slumber that night was fitful, but by mid-morning he was aroused by the renewed sounds of Confederate shells screaming in like banshees as they whistled over the ridge and into the wooded area behind them to the east.

"So the attack begins," whispered Carson sitting on the edge of his bed. "May God help them all."

Without warning the Confederate bombardment that had previously been relatively harmless to the area around Meade's headquarters had somehow found the range and began to effectively rain in near the house. Fortunately for the Union forces along the ridge, the Southern artillery barrage was badly missing its mark, screaming above the ridge and their forward lines. Unfortunately for the support people, the assembling reinforcements to the rear, and Meade's headquarters on the back slope of the ridge, the shells were accurately training in on them instead. One apple tree in the yard blew apart in a shower of wood shards. All kinds of debris hit the side of the house. Horses corralled in the fences nearby whinnied and screamed as several shells fell in among them leaving one stallion sprawling and squealing in its horrifying death throes.

"I wasn't expecting this!" gasped Carson Hardwick as he desperately dove to the floor.

At that time another shell slammed violently into Meade's headquarters, showering splintery wreckage all over the hapless professor.

I'm getting out of this death trap thought Hardwick as he scrambled out the back door on all fours, hunched over, and sprinted for the line of boulders at the edge of the woods.

41

"**D**OPPELGANGERS."

Lydia's mind had been in a dreamlike state for-- who knows how long? Doctor Milton Thomas had given her a sedative, and now she felt things were becoming clearer, but then what did this vague comment mean? She knew what a doppelganger was—a ghost or spirit of some sort. But what did Dr. Thomas mean?

The doctor had obviously been studying Lydia's gradual emergence from the influence of the sedative he had given her with certain curiosity, his dark unmoving eyes peering intensely over the gold rims of his bifocals.

"Doppelgangers, Miss Thayer," grunted Dr. Thomas. "That's the problem around here. No matter where you go around the battlefield, there's someone you can find traveling around time who is curious about the big battle that happened here. Apparently it's quite popular as historians go. No matter where anyone might go, he could possibly experience one of the other time travelers. Unfortunately the problem gets much worse when jumpers decide to return on multiple visits. That's when they meet these doppelgangers—actually themselves, you know—and then there's big trouble."

"Oh you mean *avatars*, Doctor. We call them avatars in our time."

"It makes no difference what you call them, Miss Thayer, the result is the same. We are aware of nearly a half dozen known disappearances of time travelers who we feel have met their doppelgangers—or ava … however you identify them. There is great danger for you just to haphazardly hop around the area from one place and time to another! In effect you could land right on top of one of your …"

"Avatars," interjected Lydia.

"Yes, yes, whatever—but it is imperative for you to be extremely careful. We here at the clinic have instituted a required process for all our time jumpers to carefully log every time jump they make—the *exact* day and time—to the second if possible—to avoid any unpleasant surprise meetings with themselves." Doctor Thomas paused and took a deep breath. "I know your sense of duty motivates you to return to the scene of your mishap as soon as you can and evacuate your professor friend and your mother, but before you leave this room I strongly advise you to, as precisely as possible, ascertain the exact moments and places you have visited. I must remind you it is a matter of life and death, both for you and those you choose to take with you to avoid at all costs. Actually it would be extremely prudent of you to do this for every time jump in which you were ever involved."

"Wow, I can hardly imagine how many places and times to which my Grandmother and Grandfather have traveled! It seems they have been to the time of Christ and Jerusalem so many times. It's Grandma Thelma's favorite place to jump. Also I know they've both been to Pompeii at least twice. I hope they know to be careful."

"I'm sure she knows the dangers. We've actually sat here together in this building a number of times and pondered just those situations. Unfortunately one of the places that is most dangerous for her and Cecil is right here in Gettysburg. I would estimate she and Cecil came here fifteen to twenty times. She actually tells me of times she would come here, just out of curiosity while her family was touring the battlefield."

"Probably saw me as a kid with Mom and Dad."

"Almost certainly. And that's the problem. Neither of them could ever accidentally return to that particular time and place, or—they'd just cease to exist! And, I might add, you could never go back and contact or come in near proximity to yourself in those same or any other situations."

"That's a chilling thought," gulped Lydia.

"And that's why your grandmother Thelma limits her visits here as well," the doctor added.

A deafening whistle like a shrill tea kettle from outside the window caused Lydia to quickly spring to her feet at the squealing sound. There she witnessed some sort of hissing rattletrap vehicle clatter by, a goggled driver wearing a white lab coat-like smock mounted atop the a high leather seat, oblivious to his startled yet captivated audience.

"Don't mind him. That's just Jackson," Milton Thomas casually informed her. "It's one of those steam cars. Horseless carriages. They're the wave of the future you know."

"I wouldn't bet on them myself," smirked Lydia shrewdly. "Perhaps you might rely a bit more on the gasoline cars than the steam models."

"Oh I wouldn't think … oh, yes of course," the doctor brightened a bit at the realization of Lydia's unintended foreshadowing. "—the gasoline vehicles you say?"

"Have you ever heard of Henry Ford?"

"No, can't say I have."

"Well just remember him a bit if you're considering an investment in the near future," Lydia whispered.

The doctor had a pad of paper and was busily jotting down the name Lydia had revealed to him. These bits of information such as the one gleaned here as well as from other time travelers from upcoming events would be added to his growing cache of future-inspired data.

"In any event," the doctor continued, "it would be to everyone's advantage to formulate an extensive list of all the places and times you have visited recently."

"You don't have a laptop, do you?" joked Lydia.

"A lap top? Is this something else I need to know?" The doctor was reaching for his writing pad.

"No, no, it's something you'll never see I'm afraid. Sorry. Let's get going on my list so I can get going."

42

THE FIRST LEG of their journey was the simplest. Once again, the time-jumping couple took advantage of pre-911 travel and its complicated security at airports by using air reservations a few years before the New York terrorist attacks. Tickets into Baltimore International were easily purchased, and the flight was uneventful, just as was the renting of the Suburban and the drive up 95, 270 and 15 into Gettysburg. Once there, Thelma and Cecil spent some time rummaging through their favorite costume shops in town that specialized in nineteenth century accoutrements of all sorts. Thelma preferred Abraham's while Cecil found what he needed at Hilbert's.

"We are a bit limited as to where we can appear, my dear," Thelma reminded Cecil. "We've been here so many times I fear there are but a few places during the battle where we can land."

"You don't think I haven't given that a lot of thought on our flight? It's almost as bad as our jaunts into the time of Jesus! I'm sure it's worse for you there. I think we've been to the site of every major miracle at least once. We've had some close calls with our duplicates—avatars--as Kronos calls them."

"I know, Cecil. This last quest without you I had to stay back and send in Manning Jones and Rashid without me. I know we've previously been to the wedding at Canaan three times. I often wonder what happens to us if our avatars there have a chance meeting."

"The only thing we can do is be extremely careful and keep clear-cut records of our own comings and goings. This sounds a bit strange, but both we and our avatars should be made aware of the extreme dangers associated with any potential get-togethers."

"Agreed," said Cecil. "Now let's look at our options during the battle. It seems we've spent considerable time in the town itself. Both of us should avoid that area, even though it might be one of the safer places based on the history of the battlefield action. If you remember, despite a massive cannonade from both sides and incessant small arms fire, civilian fatalities and injuries were almost non-existent in the town."

"And you might as well forget about Little Round Top," Thelma reminded her husband. "You were all over that hilltop during some of the most horrible fighting, and I have no desire to go there myself."

"I think I provided some valuable insight in the Union victory by Chamberlain on the second day. Besides I was sufficiently protected by the Kronos komodo armor."

"Not your head, dear," Thelma readily pointed out.

"So where do you think we might find our granddaughter then? Places for women were limited since not many females actually participated in the battle."

"You're right, but, knowing Lydia, we might find her right in the middle of Pickett's charge," grimaced Thelma. "But odds are we will find her somewhere behind the lines, possibly in a field hospital or behind the lines helping to load supplies on wagons. I'm sure she's involved."

"And what about Cheryl? Who knows where that woman might end up?"

"My mother used to have a saying," Thelma reminisced, "that some people fall into the outhouse and then come up smelling like roses. Well that certainly describes our daughter-in-law."

"Anyway," smiled Cecil, "let's concentrate on some thoughts as to where we can go rather than where we cannot."

"What do you have in mind?"

"I for one might go over to Seminary Ridge among the Confederates to see if Lyd somehow got separated and ended up there. Except in modern times, I've never been behind the Confederate lines on Seminary."

"And isn't that a bit dangerous, my dear husband? That's right in the front lines as I recall."

"Front lines—yes, but there were never any Union assaults on that location. Everything was defensive for the North in this battle, and I have no plans to participate in that final charge. Defending defensive positions for the North rather than attacking is what made this particular conflict different from others. I think that was the big difference in the final result. Besides, I still have the komodo for protection."

"Except for …"

"I know—the head, right?"

"And what's your plan for me? I don't think they'd let a woman, especially an old lady like me, on the front lines."

"I was thinking you might take a look to the rear of the northern lines along Cemetery Ridge. We'd talked about that idea a bit. You know, check the hospitals and such."

Thelma stared momentarily without responding. "I hope we don't find either of them there, Cecil," she finally replied softly. "At least not as patients."

The two packed all their recently-rented paraphernalia into the Suburban and took 30 west past a sign outside a brick building indicating "Robert E. Lee's Headquarters" and then turned past the Lutheran Seminary and south on the oak-shaded park road lined with an army of statues, memorial plaques, and lifeless cannons arranged in their positions to challenge the long-gone ghosts of the battlefield. About a mile along, Cecil pulled through a copse of towering oaks and stopped there. There he got out and opened the back hatch, pulling out a plastic-wrapped uniform that Thelma, even in her countless trips here, did not recognize. When Cecil had laboriously ripped open and stripped the plastic off the suit, it revealed a dark blue uniform with a white braided epauleted jacket and matching blue slacks. From a round hat box, he pulled out a feathered bicorn similar to one worn by a naval admiral. The final addition to his accoutrements was a slightly curved, gleaming parade sword in an elaborate chromed scabbard.

"Now what is this costume? I thought I'd seen them all."

"I've done a bit of reading, dear. It seems there was a bit of interest in the Confederacy by some foreign powers, particularly Britain. This is the uniform of a British major. They actually had foreign officers as well as common soldiers in the Rebel ranks—observers—who sometimes actually offered advice. I like that part. Can you imagine me giving Lee advice not to send an assault on the Union center?"

"Cecil, you're not planning on changing history are you?" sputtered Thelma.

"Of course not, my dear, do you actually think Lee or any of his generals would take my advice anyway? Yet, it would be fun to offer my outlandish notions and later tell them 'I told you so!' after the battle," grinned Cecil devilishly. "Anyway I'm going to take a walk through the area and ask a few questions to see if I can get a lead on either of our girls. All you need to do is drop me off, so to speak."

Thelma shrugged and motioned for Cecil to come up. A slight touch at the temples and the two immediately found themselves unexpectedly greeted by the jarring impact of an exploding shell and splintering of a great tree trunk a dozen or so feet above them and then being unceremoniously driven to the ground by the concussion and a shower of small twigs.

"So much for safety," choked a stunned Thelma as she brushed debris from her face and hair.

"Just a random shot," returned Cecil, rising and dusting off his once-immaculate uniform. "Maybe you should take off and get over to the other side. Use your car finder app to get back to this same spot to pick me up. And be sure," he added, "to alter the time a bit to avoid our avatars."

Thelma needed little encouragement to return to the time from which she had come. In a moment, she was standing by the Suburban in the serene grove of oaks from which she had left. Just out of curiosity, she looked at the treeline, but found it difficult to detect any results of the 1863 bombardment. From there, she set her app as Cecil had suggested to her and retraced her route along Seminary Ridge Road, turned along 30 back into the town, and then at the traffic circle, headed south along 134. The GPS on her phone eventually took her down Sach's Road and appropriately to a lane called Hospital Road. Like her husband, Thelma had done her research as well. Her destination was to be the Spangler Farm beyond Cemetery Ridge, one of the main locations that had been utilized as a Union field hospital during the battle. She had read recent newspaper articles about the attempts to restore the site as much as possible employing a variety of reenactors. Thelma knew, too, that access to the area was restricted in more recent times and attainable now only as part of the Gettysburg National Battlefield tour program. That would be a very small problem since all she had to do was enter the park in a year she had chosen—1973-- long before the renovations at Spangler's Farm had even been planned, establish herself somewhere in a spot she could covertly appear during the battle, and walk from there to the makeshift hospital set up on Spangler's homestead.

The place Thelma chose was about a mile from the farm, a place where she felt she would not be noticed when she materialized. Likely battlefield hospital personnel would be much too distracted by their business at hand than to be watching for some spirit-like figure to appear up the road. She drove by the place slowly, hoping to glean any information about the barn that might be helpful in her foray into 1863, but the building appeared pretty much abandoned here in this time. Thelma pulled the Suburban into a graveled pull-off area she felt was sufficiently distant from her target where she could proceed to unload a few items and rearrange her selected costume.

Thelma had given some thought as to her attire. At first, she figured some sort of nurse's uniform would be the most appropriate, but after some consideration, she came to the conclusion that nurse's uniforms as we know them in our time were not in vogue—merely choosing the useful clothing a woman might employ in her daily work regimen would be best. With that consideration, she had adopted a plain long dark brown skirt and a white, long-sleeved blouse she had imitated from photos she had noticed of the local townsfolk.

After a last-minute adjustment and a deep breath, Thelma faded into the past.

43

"ROUGHLY FIVE MILES from Gettysburg," affirmed John Dodsworth. "This will be our operating base. It's secluded and no one would likely see our equipment unless he would actually fall into it."

The team, in a twelve passenger Ford Econoline, had followed the forty foot eighteen-wheeler driven by recent time travel veteran Marcus Firenza, across West Virginia route 68 from its secret Kronos location along the snow-covered route through the Alleghenies, finally turning north through Maryland before entering southern Pennsylvania near Breezewood. John Dodsworth, riding shotgun in the big rig, wore dark glasses and a stern face as the trailer, garishly camouflage-painted briefly dropped behind the van on a long grade.

"My God, why did John choose that ugly trailer?" Kate Spahr buried her head in her hands. "I feel like we're going on maneuvers with my old National Guard unit!"

"Probably living out his fantasies," I suggested. "He never got the chance to join the military—likely would've failed the physicals anyway, I think."

Before long the truck resumed the lead and after about a half hour, signaled a right turn, taking a wide left sweep, and slipped expertly onto a narrow, slushy back road. The location Dodsworth had chosen to employ as a base of operations was certainly isolated, tucked along a narrow graveled lane in a brushy ravine which I judged to be a few miles south of Big Round Top.

"Looks like a strange place to pull over," sneered Trinia. "Why so far from Gettysburg? Do you expect us to walk?"

"No problem, Miss Williams," smiled John turning and directing Firenza to open the trailer doors. As the doors yawned open, John held out his arm and bowed. "Your rides ..."

"Horses! John I love them," squealed Trinia delightfully at the sight of several horses, stamping restlessly in the straw and manure cluttering the bottom of the truck. Trinia had always proven to be an excellent horsewoman, and had recently used her equestrian skills to great advantage in enhancing her legend as "The Black Medusa" in ancient Pompeii and the Middle East. Horses as a mode of transportation could not have pleased her more.

"Wait a second, John," I pointed out. "How are we going to get these horses back to 1863? As I recall, those time capsules Kronos uses are just large enough to barely accommodate a human."

"Bill, you have no faith in me. Do you think I wasn't prepared to take care of those trivial matters? Take a closer look inside the trailer."

I carefully swung open the one side door. Other than the six horses and a few large boxes, I could see no capsules at all.

"Don't look so puzzled, Bill. You forget the maintenance garage in Ostia so easily?" John's eyes rose in arches reminding me of the Joker in Batman. "And you never got to see the fancy so-called capsule at Pompeii I used to trick Jones into his untimely demise either. The capsule I developed was actually an army surplus Sikorsky helicopter containing a two ton heavy troop carrier with a team of half dozen of Jones' hand-picked ruffians! This semi was easy. There is more space here than in the tiny scrunched garage at Salt Marsh."

"You mean the truck is the capsule, John?" I gasped. "Just about the time I think you've lost all your marbles, you come back looking like the genius you are."

John just shrugged as the wide-eyed team crowded around the truck, staring in disbelief.

"Of course, and we and the horses and all the stuff we need will be in 1863 Pennsylvania in short order. Just say when," offered Dodsworth.

"Before we make use of your wonderful device, John, I think we need an organizational meeting to review our plans we discussed earlier—just to make sure we're all together. We have a variety of uniforms and equipment, but we need to be as efficient as we can without putting ourselves into too much danger. As much as possible we should avoid the fighting."

The team of John Dodsworth, Mel Currier, Kaye Spahr, Marcus Firenza, and Trinia Williams nodded a simultaneous assent and gathered with me near the van. I took my place at the open side door of the Econoline while the others stood around me in a tight semicircle.

"The simplest thing would be for some of us, dressed as Northern soldiers, to infiltrate the lines at several points and ask questions about Lydia and Cheryl. I feel we shouldn't have much trouble locating them. I'm quite positive their presence in the area would be a bit well-known--if not even celebrated --especially knowing how my wife would likely make a spectacle of herself."

There was some soft laughter and a few amused expressions from our group. They all were aware of some of Cheryl's past adventures.

"Dodsworth," I continued, "as we agreed last week, you'll be staying with the equipment after the jump. If anything goes wrong, such as imminent discovery of this fabulous time travel apparatus—the trailer—you can jump back quickly. Also, Kaye, you will be staying here with John in case of a medical problem. We hopefully have enough equipment, medicine, antibiotics, or whatever to handle any sort of injury."

Kaye was a skilled doctor—adept in numerous fields of medicine. She had been selected as part of the original Kronos time travel team because of those skills. Upon her return, in a very short period, she had achieved international fame in a number of medical universities and hospitals, yet when she heard of our forthcoming adventures, she did not hesitate to drop those responsibilities and join us.

"Knowing how to manipulate the actual elapsed time," she had reasoned, "the interval I would be away would be minimal. I wouldn't even be missed at the university."

"Trinia, I know you're chomping at the bit so to speak, to jump on one of those horses in the trailer and go riding gloriously across the battlefield. But that wouldn't be prudent, of course. Chances of you being shot, with so much gunfire, would be high. Besides that, the logic of soldiers seeing a black woman riding horseback fearlessly between the lines seems a bit ludicrous."

"I understand, Bill," Trinia agreed. "Both Mel and I have essential roles in town."

"That's right, Trinia. You and Mel are to go into Gettysburg if possible and ask questions. Knowing the girls, they likely made arrangements in a nice hotel. Ask around and see what you can find."

"And we pose as simple black folk," added Mel Currier.

"Yes," I continued, "roles in which you can both use to move about with little fear of being stopped or questioned. You must pass behind Confederate lines—up behind Seminary Ridge. There you just play off as camp followers."

Trinia's eyes flashed. "You mean slaves?"

"After you get into town," I proceeded, ignoring Trinia's inferences, "if you find out anything, you can follow up on that information as you see fit. Remember, though; steer clear of the battle if at all possible. Our komodo armor is great stuff, but it doesn't make us invincible."

"You all right with this, Trinia?" asked Mel.

After a short awkward moment, Trinia growled, "Yeah."

"Marcus and I will dress as soldiers—cavalrymen to be exact. We will masquerade as two officers, Colonel William Thayer and Captain Marcus Firenza, who are apparently sole survivors of a fictitious unit supposedly in action the first day and were driven out of town to the east and are just now finding their way back to re-join the action. We're going to identify ourselves as remnants of the Second Pennsylvania Volunteers who had recently been sent here by Governor Curtin from Harrisburg. There really wasn't any such unit, but I feel if we avoid discussion with those individuals—who would be extremely few—who would be likely well-versed in the units fighting at Gettysburg, I doubt, with all the confusion of the battle, that anyone would question our status."

Marcus Firenza raised a finger. "We've researched a bit and found facts that support our fabrications. There were a number of units sent hastily and rather unexpectedly by some of the nearby states, particularly Pennsylvania who felt Harrisburg and Philadelphia were in danger of being taken."

"And another reminder," I reminded the team, "you are all provided with authentic costumes and props. Everyone has stun guns. Marcus and I have sidearms that are the newest Kronos technology. These pistols ..." I held up a holstered weapon that looked much like the Colts the Union officers utilized at the time. "They perform as well, or perhaps better than, the weapons Kronos had its rescue team use at the Pompeii rescue."

"They kind of looked like something from outer space," said Firenza. "These look like something from the time of the battle."

"And Mel and Trinia are equipped with the same firepower as ours but covertly incorporated within a walking stick for Mel and several tools—a hoe and a shovel—for Trinia. It'll be a very effective means of hiding the stun weapons."

"A bit more degrading, I think." Trinia had picked up the hoe and examined it with distaste.

"Degrading, perhaps," I said, "but necessary. You'll be able to perfectly maintain your pretense. Besides, there's no telling what would happen if anyone, particularly the Confederates, might do if they found a gun on a black person. They'd likely shoot you on the spot."

"Nice uniforms." Trinia held up my cavalry colonel's jacket. "Ours make us look like Aunt Jemima and Uncle Ben!"

"Trinia ..." snapped Mel.

"Oh I'm all right with it, Mel. It's just it gives me bad vibes about the social status of the black people at the time—in both the North and the South. I'd never put up with that crap if I could help it. It's like we're relapsing."

"As long as you remember, you can't change the future by meddling with the past," I added.

"Well," broke in a wild-eyed, high-voiced John Dodsworth suddenly appearing with a strange-looking headpiece he had likely constructed from an old metal funnel with coils of wires loosely dangling from it, "are we ready for the time jump?"

John's attempts at humor were always taken good-naturedly, but I could never quite be sure how serious he was, but the team's trepidations over the launch were sufficiently alleviated, which was obviously his goal. They all piled into the back of the trailer, smiling and in good humor, even when John persisted his zany antics.

"Hold on! We could be in for a rough landing!" called out John in a shrill voice as he pulled an oversized and obviously contrived lever. I knew from past expeditions that John was simply tapping the ENTER key on his laptop as he distracted everyone with his sham equipment.

There was the familiar whirling sensation associated with a jump, but all at once it seemed as if our equilibrium had changed. The floor of trailer had shifted a bit and there was a teetering feeling. The horses in the back had started shifting about and whinnying nervously as the movement of our trailer capsule became more pronounced.

"Out—everyone out," I yelled opening the side door.

Fortunately for us the trailer had slid front first onto the hillside and we had but a short hop to safety. The weight quickly shifted as we leapt from the open door and the truck gently tilted back to the rear.

"What'd I tell you?" smiled John sheepishly.

It took most of the morning to steady the trailer using the vehicle's stabilizing jacks and some flat rocks retrieved from a nearby streambed. It was then we led the horses out to an adjacent meadow where they grazed. Kaye's Kronos hospital was set up in the cleaned and thoroughly sterilized front compartment, and everyone concentrated on his or her own essentials for the mission.

"I see now why you decided to adopt the camouflage motif for the trailer," commented Mel.

"And when we get this netting over the whole rig," agreed John, "the cover-up of our base of operations will be even more complete. I doubt anyone would be strolling along here anyway, but this seals the deal."

"Are we ready to move out?" I called out. We were all anxious to retrieve the girls and get out of this time period.

44

MANNING JONES' BOND with the bandit, Barabbas, was, as he saw it, a natural one. There was a real connection there. Both seemed focused on their goals and would stop at nothing to gain them. In the few days after they had met, around an evening campfire, Barabbas explained to Jones what he was doing.

"It's the Romans," he snarled, "They've been so overbearing and hateful to our people since their armies came in and overpowered us. Our little band of rebels can do little other than harass them at every point—robbing small supply caravans or killing messengers and such-- and wait for the day when significant numbers join in and rise up against them."

Jones bobbed his head in animated agreement. In actuality, Manning would have been more likely to take the side of the Romans, but knew that his advantage at this time would lie with Barabbas.

"The money I gave you should help then, my good man," Jones reminded him. "And I have lots more where that came from."

"It will certainly help in recruitment, Mr. Jones. There aren't many who can just leave home and family and join up with me."

"As for me," continued the billionaire, "I am requesting your assistance in my simple quest—to find the man those around here refer to as the Nazarene. His name is Jesus."

"So why do you seek this man, my friend? It is rumored he is a performer of many miracles in this region—things like curing leprosy, blindness, casting out demons and such. I've never witnessed any of it myself, but have spoken with a considerable number who say it is true."

Jones pondered his response for some time, knowing full well he could not reveal his true reasons for employing the skill of the Nazarene.

"It's my mother," Jones lied. Manning's mother had died alone in a rundown nursing home in Newark twenty years ago. "She's dying of a disease—consumption I think they call it. Yes, that's it. I think this Jesus can help me. I'm hoping you can locate this healer for my dear old mother. It seems he's pretty slippery. Rashid and I have been searching for weeks and haven't come across him."

"Slippery is a good word for it, but I suppose that's certainly out of necessity. I understand the authorities are after him, including some of the religious hierarchy and Romans as well. Some Jews don't like his claims or what he is teaching, and the Romans treat him as a threat too. Many locals think he is the Messiah and is coming to lead the people out of captivity."

"Sounds like a recruit with all those credentials," sighed Jones.

Barabbas poked at the dying embers of his campfire with his short sword and casually tossed a piece of wood on it.

"I think I can help you meet Jesus of Nazareth. It might take some time, but I feel sure I can help you."

For a few weeks, Jones and Rashid kept low profiles, particularly during a sudden raid on a local military post or an attack on a Roman supply line. There was always some improvised problem with his horse or his weapons that prevented his joining the foray. No one ever questioned the reason for Rashid's non-participation. After his return from the failed 4 BC intervention mission, Jones had been made succinctly aware of the Kronos directive about killing people in the past during time travel and how that could possibly affect people from the future. The last thing he wanted was to unwittingly be responsible for the death of one of his own ancestors that could lead to his own disappearance as in the *Back to the Future* films.

It was at the inception of one raid that Jones and Rashid conveniently ducked out, making a hasty but *important* visit to the nearby village to gather vital information -- just when the word came to them that Barabbas was about to order an attack.

"Where's the information, Mr. Jones? Who are we meeting?" Rashid was absently gawking around the town square.

If Manning Jones weren't afraid of making a scene, he probably would have slapped his foolish companion in the face.

"Just wait," responded Jones through gritting teeth.

The turn of events in the ongoing saga of the two men quickly changed. There was an abrupt scream from a woman in the crowd, followed suddenly by the identifiable clatter of hooves and armor associated with the approach of the Roman cavalry unit that rumbled into the square, brandishing gleaming spears, scattering residents through the nearby alleyways, leaving only the surprised and fearful time travelers. Manning Jones' first reaction was to reach for his sword strapped beneath his outer robes, but his inborn survival instincts made him come to the speedy realization he would have little chance of survival.

"You two men there!" The officer of the unit, had ridden up, drawn his sword and placed its point sharply under Jones' chin. "We were just attacked by a band of thieves, but we drove them off. Some fled in this direction. Who are you? Identify yourself."

Manning Jones had raised both hands in an act of surrender. Speaking now in the Latin supported by the Kronos ULIT, Jones' voice was cracking a bit. "We're no one …," he started in stuttering protest.

"Centurion Regulus!" The shout came from the ranks of the Roman horse soldiers. "Centurion, what are you doing in this region? The last I saw you was years ago leading the unit pursuing the bunch of refugee people fleeing through the desert. Why are you dressed like this?"

Jones, being a quick thinker and possessing a magnificent memory of people he had once met, now had sufficient time to recover his wits, and without noticeable hesitation, was able to respond.

"Why Decanus Aquilo, it is good to meet you again. I see you still have maintained the leadership qualities with which I had endowed upon you."

Decanus Aquilo sharply saluted from the shoulder as the swordsman standing over Jones lowered his weapon in astonishment.

"Do you know this man, then Legionnaire?"

"I do, Tribune. This man is one of the great leaders posted by Herod the Great before his untimely death a few years back. His name is Centurion Mandela Regulus, assigned directly from Rome by Augustus himself and commanded a one hundred man force near Jerusalem."

"Centurion?" The tribune bowed slightly and offered a weak shoulder salute. "I then beg your forgiveness, Sir. Please understand our situation, what with all these bandits in the area …"

"You were just doing your duty, Tribune. You could not possibly have been aware. I will give a full report to your superiors—a glowing report, I might add. You could be in line for promotion, my good man."

"And this other man?" The officer gestured towards a stunned Verma Rashid, who neither understood any Latin nor was at all cognizant of the situation.

"The man is my aide," snapped Jones. "He is simply a half-wit who doesn't understand a word of our language. He speaks his own indistinguishable dialect that only I can decipher. I keep him because of his loyalty."

The Tribune sharply knitted his eyebrows. "I'm a bit curious about your situation, Centurion. I realize you owe me no explanation, but I am interested nevertheless."

Jones cast his eyes suspiciously from side to side. "You've heard of espionage I suppose? You see, I'm assigned by Rome as a spy. I can't even divulge who gave me the order. It's this Barabbas situation you understand. I was on the verge of getting all the information we would need to close the case. Anyway, now my cover's blown, so to speak. Every townsperson in the vicinity will soon be telling the rebel leader who I am."

"Once again, I apologize, Sir."

Jones waved his hand. "Don't worry, soldier. Just get me a good horse and some equipment and I'll join you."

"Yes Sir! And for your aide – a nice mount as well. I can fit you up with the armor from the men we lost in the recent skirmish, but I'm afraid you'll have to wait for the Centurion's mantle …"

As the tribune continued his attempted pacification of the mysterious Centurion, the remainder of the cavalry dismounted and made a half-hearted search of the town, knowing from past incidents that the chance of finding anyone in any of the buildings was practically zero. By the time they had completed their search, some of the bolder townspeople had emerged from hiding and were proceeding with their everyday undertakings in the streets.

"Assemble!" A trumpet sounded and then came the order again. "Assemble in two columns and prepare to move forward!"

As a single entity, the colorful column of bright reds and gold formed and moved snakelike through the town gates and south along the road. Two of the men at the rear of the column had pulled back a bit.

"Mica, this might not be a good time to bring it up, but there's something not right about this newly-discovered Centurion," whispered one soldier.

"What could be wrong?" rasped the other.

"I too was in Centurion Regulus' unit. I've been thinking about it. That was a while back. I was a new recruit, barely eighteen years old, and Mandela Regulus was, perhaps in his mid-twenties or even older. Sadly, I am nearing the end of my military career at age forty-three. I grant him he was in excellent condition then, but did you get a look at him now? I've noticed his physique as he removed his robes. The Centurion has hardly aged! If I would guess, he would be in his younger thirties. The gods have been quite kind to him."

"Are you positive it is the same person, Mica?"

"As certain as I can be, my friend. I worked close to the man in his legion, and—yes, I am certain. He even bears some of the same body scars he had then. Yes it is the same man without question, and this aide, the so-called half-wit he has with him, was his lieutenant."

"Indeed then, this man is truly favored by the gods!"

"Yet that is not all. Many forget things that have passed in time, but of this one, I have some strong remembrance. There was some controversy between him and Governor Herod. Regulus, in some sort of intrigue, was recalled to Rome, I believe. In any event, that was the last anyone saw or heard of him again. That is—until now."

"So what can you do about it, Mica?"

"When I get a chance, I'll talk privately with Aquilo. Perhaps I might jolt his memory about what happened. Besides Decanus, there are a few others, now officers, who served in the unit as well. Perhaps I could get some answers."

The two men spurred their horses and hastily re-joined the rear of the column.

From a crevice between two huge boulders on the knoll above the roadway, two men glowered hatefully at the passing troops.

"So, our friend Mr. Jones, was an ally of the Romans after all." Barabbas, for once, appeared fatigued. "It appears they were waiting for our ill-fated attack, and I have a strong suspicion Jones had something to do with it."

"Don't worry," growled his bearded compatriot, "one of our archers can easily put an arrow through his ugly face at the next turn of the road."

"Don't bother! It's not worth the chance one of our men could get hurt. We had enough casualties in that last attack. I have another one of my feelings that Manning Jones will get everything that's coming to him."

45

"WHY MISS LYDIA, you've returned," smiled David Hartsfield looking up from the lobby desk. "I wasn't sure when you would be back, given this unsettling set of circumstances. Everyone had feared the worst."

Once leaving Dr. Thomas' sanctuary for waylaid time travelers, Lydia had easily hitched a ride into town on a local farmer's produce wagon, briefly jumped back to the twenty-first century, slipped back into her room, changed into an appropriate period costume that featured a bonnet-like hat to cover her bandaged wound, and then arrived in her rented 1863 hotel room on the afternoon of July 2. Lydia was a bit disappointed in not finding her mother impatiently sitting there in the upper room waiting for her despite the fact the hotel was now in the hands of the Confederates.

"I was afraid you might let out my room to those Southern boys," laughed Lydia when she surprised David Hartsfield at the reservation desk.

"Oh, they wanted it, to be sure, but I insisted it was already occupied by a handsome young lady, whereas they merely bowed genteelly in that Southern way they have and told me they wouldn't think of taking a young lady's room. They took all the rest of them though—for the officers you understand. They've assured me the Confederate government would reimburse me in full once the war was finished. They offered to pay me in that Confederate currency they all carry with them, but I would suspect it will be as worthless as their promissory notes once the war is finished."

"My mother," interrupted Lydia, "did she ever come back to the hotel?"

"No, Miss Thayer, I'm afraid she did not. Her buggy horse, Bo, came back though—without the buggy or any of the harnessing. That was a bit strange, I think. I can't help but think she was waylaid by the Rebels."

"Perhaps some of these Confederate soldiers know something." Lydia looked hopefully around the dining room at a number of gray-clad officers at several of the tables.

"Let me introduce you," offered Hartsfield taking her by the elbow and leading her to a table occupied by three men, who all rose in one motion as they approached.

"This must be the lovely creature who resides in the upstairs apartment-- could I be correct in that assumption, Mr. Hartsfield?"

"General Ewell, this is Miss Lydia Thayer"

A thin, balding man with intense eyes bowed gracefully. "It is wonderful to see such a beautiful flower blooming here among the briars, Miss Thayer," he proceeded in a soft Virginian drawl while gently lifting her hand and lightly kissing her finger tips. "It would be our distinct pleasure if you might grace us with your presence at our table."

"Just for a bit, if you don't mind," said Lydia as she moved up to the table.

The man to the left deftly pulled a chair and gestured with a flashing smile. "Ma'am?"

"This is Major General Henry Heth ." Heth displayed a white turban-like dressing, wrapped fully around his head, likely from a recent wound. "The gentleman at attention at the far end of the table is Major General Jubal Early."

Each of the generals, in turn, cleverly deployed his own distinctive style of Southern gentility with a slight head bob or smile in Lydia's direction.

Without pause, Heth slid the chair under her as she sat. That signaled the others to be seated.

Jubal Early appeared as most of the other Confederates around the room—heavily bearded and serious-looking. "Do you realize, young lady that you are in the middle of an active battle zone? If you look around this town, you will notice that every other man, woman, or child has either run for the hills or hidden somewhere in a dark basement. Do you have no fear for yourself?"

"I'm not afraid at all." Lydia was confident, from her knowledge of history, that civilian casualties in the town had been virtually non-existent.

"You are spunky one, my dear," smiled Ewell. "I wish some of the irregulars from my Division had that much gumption. I would have had more confidence to attempt the assault on that miserable hill last evening"

"If Stonewall and his Division had been here, I think Cemetery Hill would be in Southern hands as we sit at this table," smirked General Early.

"Gentlemen, mind your manners now. We have a special guest, and it wouldn't do to show our unpleasant side," said Henry Heth calmly. "Let's talk of more pleasant things. I'm sure our fortunes on the field will be reversed today."

"You're right as always, Henry." Early dabbed his mouth gently with his napkin and then turning to Lydia, sighed forlornly, "So, if I might be so direct, Dear, what in Heaven's name brings you here to Gettysburg during this mighty conflagration, Miss Thayer?"

"Actually I'm searching for someone—someone who disappeared right before this battle began. I was hoping one of you may have heard something of her whereabouts."

"Her?" grinned Heth. "Another young lady like yourself?"

"Oh no, Sir, not a young lady. She's my mother. And I'm sure you would remember her if you met her."

"So what does she look like?" asked Ewell.

"And perhaps her name may have come up," added Jubal Early.

"Her name is Cheryl—Cheryl Thayer. And she's blond—very blond with long curls past her shoulders—in fact most people think her hair is almost yellow,"

"Buttercup yellow, I call it," interrupted Ewell while raising his eyes in pretended ecstasy.

"Yes, and she is rather slender, and most think she is a bit attractive."

"I'll bet she has curves in all the right places," said Ewell jumping back in.

Heth slapped his hand hard on the tabletop with a noise that at once drew the attention of the other tables. "That'll be enough of that Henry," he hissed through his closed teeth. "If nothing else, we are Southern gentlemen."

Lydia ignored the interplay of the generals and continued. "Likely the thing that is the most notable about my mother, I fear, is one that I find difficult to say. Unfortunately, it is likely important to reveal if I ever expect to find her. It seems she is a bit loud and talks incessantly …"

"Sounds like most women I know," cracked Ewell.

"Let me announce this to the rest of the officers present in the dining room. It's obvious none of us at the table have seen her," said Early. With that, he stood, and in a deep, booming voice obviously accustomed to command, announced:

"Gentlemen, this pretty young lady here at our table is asking us a favor. Have any of you seen or heard anything of a middle-aged woman—a rather becoming blonde lady, I understand, named Cheryl Thayer, who has been lost in this area for the last few days?"

The room was filled with low conversational mumble and a few shaking heads. Some officers ventured to call out.

"No, Ma'am"

"Sorry, haven't seen anything."

"We'll be a keepin' our eyes out though. You can rest assured," offered another.

"Thank you gentlemen." Jubal Early winced a bit as he turned to Lydia.

"Sorry we couldn't …"

There was a sudden raucous clatter of boots and a boisterous shout blared out. "My compatriots! I have returned. It is my sincere hope you have saved some Yankee wine and food for me!"

Standing in the doorway was another dark-bearded officer, who had now doffed his ostrich-plumed Stetson and held it above his head.

"Well I'll be," cried the gaudily clad man. "I haven't seen such a collection of old men since I visited the retirement home in Yellow Tavern!"

"Why Jeb, where've you been?" remarked one man.

"I've been out here scouting around, Ed Johnson. How about you?"

General Heth was disgusted by the man's cavalier attitude. "*Gallivanting* is more like it. Lee expected you to be here. Said you're the eyes and ears of the army. Anyway, we've been blinded while you've been absent."

"I've made amends with the Old Man," grinned Stuart. "My men and I are headed around to the rear of the Yanks. We're going to surprise them tomorrow morning and cut off their supply lines and generally wreak havoc around there. A few of my scouts, while on a special mission, were able to infiltrate behind Cemetery Ridge without anyone even knowing they were there. They were able to observe an almost completely unprotected supply line from the south."

"Oh, by the way, this young girl here is looking for her lost mother. No one here has seen her. Perhaps you, with all your wanderings might have noticed her somewhere."

Stuart at once noticed Lydia, walked up to her, placing his arm around her shoulder.

"Ah, yes. I wish, if it were possible, that we might have some time to go somewhere—somewhere private, perhaps over a julep or two-- and talk about it, my dear—what was your name?"

"It's Lydia, Sir—Lydia Thayer."

The officers in that room, through all their years of their association with Jeb Stuart, never before recalled any reaction like that in the cavalryman's countenance. Jeb Stuart's face had almost immediately crimsoned apple-red. The man's dark beard had begun to tremble a bit. For some time when the cavalry general attempted to speak, he could only make a few unintelligible gagging noises as though he had swallowed something he had not chewed properly. Some present that day were positive he was about to have a stroke!

"Thayer," gurgled Jeb Stuart, his eyes popping a bit, turned and exited in panicked desperation.

No one had ever seen Stuart leave any social gathering so quickly.

46

FROM THE OUTSET of his mission behind Southern lines, Cecil Thayer never felt he would have much success in the quest for Lydia or Cheryl in this locality, but he also knew he would have to cover all the bases just in case. His cover as a British adviser worked well. He had gone to great pain to provide himself with all the proper papers and letters of introduction. No one ever questioned his presence and did everything possible to provide him with anything they could possibly grant, and he was given free rein to wander anywhere he wanted.

"Major Thayer," a youthful orderly with light unkempt, straw-colored hair protruding from beneath his cap leisurely answered, "I am quite sure these young women you all seek are not here. By your request, I have sent couriers on horseback dashin' in both directions to ask about the two ladies in question, but there is no evidence available to support thar presence anywhere along this line. Undoubtedly, the men would have noticed the two women you all describe."

"Thank you Private, you have been rather helpful. At least I know I can eliminate this whole sector in my quest."

"Once we runs the Yanks off that hill over thar in the morning, we'll likely hear somethin' then," mused the orderly. "Maught be the Yanks are holding them for ransom or somethin' lak that."

"Well, Son," thought Cecil, "you just be real careful in tomorrow's fighting. I wouldn't want you getting hurt."

"Don't you be worryin' none 'bout me. Ah can take care of muhself jest fine." The lad tipped his cap and disappeared into the gathering darkness.

"No success, Major?" The voice came from a short distance near some of the thicker oaks. A man emerged like some shadowy spirit. "I'm Jim Longstreet, Major, and I've been following your search with some interest."

"Oh, you're General Longstreet?" Cecil easily recognized the uniform and actually remembered the man from the many photos he had seen in the museum shops.

"I didn't know I was such a celebrity." Longstreet drew hard on the pipe he held, and a screen of dense tobacco smoke temporarily swirled around his head. The general had paused and looked out over the field of the next day's action.

"I'm sure all of your advisers met with Bob not too long ago. I don't know what you talked about to Lee, but he has his heart set on a grand assault on the Northern center tomorrow."

Cecil thought for some time before he answered. He knew he'd like to speak on the futility of the charge, but he also was aware of the insignificance of his opinion when it came to Robert E. Lee. He had read extensively on Lee and was rightly impressed with his knowledge of battlefield tactics and the handling of his men, but he still had the urge to spill the beans, so to speak.

"I detect a note of disagreement," said Cecil as he approached the man.

"I just think it's a bad idea," Longstreet went on. "I mean, Bob has been extremely successful running a past campaign of brilliant defensive maneuvering and attacking only when he finds a weak spot in the enemy's armor. I know too, the General misses Stonewall, but there's no one who could ever take his place. He was like his right arm. I understand what is going on. He wants to convince the Union that this war is too expensive in lives, and the way to do that is to strike hard in their own territory. If we win here, Philadelphia will fall, and most of them here in the North won't have the heart for more conflict after that."

"A good concept, I think, but I agree with you, General. I don't think the South can afford a defeat here. It could be the beginning of the end."

"I've tried to get Bob to pull out and continue circling to the south until we get a better advantage, and perhaps cut off Washington, but all he says is 'The enemy is there, and I am going to attack him there.' He can be mighty stubborn when he wants."

"And I suppose he's got some support by the other officers then?" asked Cecil, who knew very well of the answers.

"Almost every man would follow Bobby Lee into the jaws of Hell if they asked him. They are all convinced they will assault those lines up there on the ridge tomorrow, overrun the Yankee positions, and crush the enemy into total submission. Men like George Pickett and Dick Garnett are some of the bravest and most patriotic men I have ever commanded, but I believe they whip themselves into a wild battle frenzy and completely lose their military sense."

"I'm sure you're not going to convince anyone else on the staff of your objections?"

"I wouldn't think of exposing the men to the idea that we're all not united in this endeavor. I don't like it, but if Lee says charge, I'll give the order. If we are not together in our efforts, we are nothing!"

Longstreet tapped the ashes from his pipe against the trunk of the nearest oak and once again stared long and hard at the hundreds of campfires beginning to appear like flickering sparks in the twilight high on the highlands to the east.

Cecil Thayer left James Longstreet with his heavy and conflicting ponderances while his own gloomy thoughts drifted to the unimaginable images of the upcoming chaos and carnage of the third day's action at Gettysburg. There was a disquieting, surreal calm on the battlefield as nightfall deepened along the ridge. The distant muted tones of Union Taps drifted along from somewhere to the east. Up and down the front, there was the occasional crackle of rifle fire like a schoolboy's firecrackers likely triggered by nervous sentries, but the cannons and serious noises of battle had all but evaporated into the night.

The sudden brilliant snap of blue light from among the nearby forest momentarily startled Cecil. Those nearby may have dismissed it as an unusual flash of lightning, but Cecil immediately knew *exactly* what it was.

47

"PERSONALLY, I'D LIKE to have been a bit more involved in the action," whined Trinia as she made her way along the dirt road leading from the line of low rugged hills from which they had come.

Trinia Williams and Mel Currier had hiked little more than a mile from the Kronos rendezvous point, looking more like two homeless vagabonds than elite time travelers specialized in combat and self-defense with which they had been trained. Mel carried his laser-enhanced staff while Trinia clutched a disguised hoe-like digging implement that potentially had more fire power than any small arms known at the time.

"You need to get over it, Trinia. You can't always be expecting to ride into an arena on a black charger with your dreadlocks flying in the wind and rescuing the oppressed like you did in Pompeii, though I have a feeling that, if you stick with this gig, you'll get your fair share of action."

"This whole get-up we're wearing is extremely distasteful and degrading, Mel. I'm aware we're considered free blacks, but I can't help feeling like one of the slaves. I can remember clearly my nightmares years ago where I imagined myself looking a lot like this. I woke up in a cold sweat then, and I don't feel much better about it now."

"I understand. I went through a period like that myself, but life goes on, and we have to make the best of what we have. And I must say we both were handed a wonderful, exciting, and meaningful alternative to what we had."

The dialog between the two was abruptly cut short. Trinia froze, bent slightly and pointed to a billow of white smoke curling lazily from the dense grove of trees ahead. The two instinctively crouched low, crossed the dirt road and dropped down to all fours and parted a few low-hanging bushes. There in a large clearing was what could best be described as a bustling refugee camp. That, as they soon discovered, was exactly what the place was—a refugee camp.

"Looks like you folks are heading in the wrong direction. That's the way back to town right through all the Rebs. You aren't runaways, are you? If you are, you better not get caught. If they find any of you black folks, they won't treat you very well even if they can't prove you're not Southern property. The Negroes in town—the free Negroes—are plenty scared too. A good number of them are here with us now. Some say they're accused of being runaways, and they were threatened they would get beaten and taken South." The man addressing them was named Charles Dawes, a shopkeeper from Gettysburg.

"We're free blacks," returned Trinia quickly remembering to maintain their masquerade. "If any of those crackers bother me, I'll …"

"She'll run like the wind," Mel interrupted her. "Sometimes Trinia gets excited over these things, but she's pretty much harmless."

"Yeah—harmless," seethed Trinia clenching her teeth.

"Some people opted to stay there," continued Dawes, "perhaps to hide in the basements and barns and guard their possessions they thought they could keep from the Rebs. As for us, we all grabbed what we could and headed down here. So far we've been lucky. There have been soldiers on both sides passing nearby, some not more than a hundred yards or so away, but none ever bothered us."

"You haven't seen two women around town? That's the real reason we're heading this way," said Mel.

Before they even had much time to give a detailed description of the Cheryl and Lydia, several in the camp volunteered information.

"That's the Thayer woman that disappeared the day before the Confederates arrived. She was out with some troops near Round Top when she apparently left the party and headed back to town on her own.

That's the last anyone saw her. A day later, her horse came back to town, but not Mrs. Thayer."

"Has anyone seen her daughter, Lydia?" asked Trinia.

"Now that's a strange one in itself," added another woman. "The girl was with the search party that was looking for her mom. She was with that general friend of hers, an older fellow. Anyway, both of them disappeared too, sort of evaporated, I guess. Several men were searching all over for them and Mrs. Thayer, especially the one young lieutenant—I can't recall his name. Well that's when all Hell broke loose over near Cashtown Road. The Rebs showed up with the whole damn Army of Northern Virginia, led by Robert E. Lee himself, and this battle got going in earnest, and all the Union soldiers in the area were recalled and started to concentrate in this area. There were skirmishes, bullets flying, cannons firing all over. That's when most of us decided to get out and find a temporary hiding place and ended up out here."

"I suggest the two of you just lie low a bit here with us," advised Dawes. "Doesn't sound so good for your women anyway—likely both dead with all this shooting and commotion."

"Charles!" scolded his wife Rose.

"Hey, my dear, let's face facts. If no one has found them by now, well …"

"And there's no reason to take chances with any of those slavers," added Laurie Freeman, one of the free Negroes from town. "If they're safe, they'll likely be all right when the Confederates leave. I suggest, as Mr. Dawes says, you just stay with us for a bit."

All the talk about nearby slavers and the supposed abuse churned up at their hands just brought Trinia's emotions to the boiling point.

"I'll just take a walk up there I think," growled Trinia, seeing their horrified looks. "I've got my papers, right here!" Trinia shook her counterfeit emancipation papers in the direction of the crowd.

Mel Currier stared hard at Trinia. "I think I might be convinced to travel with you—perhaps, but only if you settle yourself. We can't possibly get anything done if you go up there with a chip on your shoulder."

"I'll be all right; I'll be okay, Melvin. You know I'm always cool when the action starts. I'll be okay."

The two packed up and despite the warnings of the camp people, headed north toward the Confederate lines on Seminary Ridge. It wasn't long before they encountered their first sentries.

"Halt, who goes?" shouted a lad in a high-pitched voice as he stepped from his post near some massive boulders. The smooth-faced boy stood threateningly with a leveled rifle, facing Mel and Trinia.

"It's only a couple n_____s," barked another voice coming from above. A bewhiskered man appeared atop the rocks above them. "Check to see if they're runaways. No papers mean a trip back to the cotton fields, Uriah." The sentry let out a chortling, evil sort of laugh from his lofty perch.

Mel stepped ahead of Trinia, who was grasping her laser-hoe tightly in a clenched fist, casually drew his papers from his backpack, and slapped them in the young man's hands. "You'll find these in order, my good man."

"You'all sound almost civilized, boy," cracked the whiskered man as he clambered monkeylike down through the crevice between the rock. "That's what happens when we lets our n_____s read a few books. How 'bout yer woman here?"

Mel firmly squeezed Trinia's arm as she passed.

"Here you is," mocked Trinia, bowing and handing him her papers. "Oh Master, is there annuh thang ah can do fer you?" Trinia blinked her eyes seductively and smiled with as sincere a smile as any antagonistic woman could manage.

"Kinda like you, girl." A mostly-toothless tobacco-stained grin greeted Trinia. "Why not come on over here to the woods fer a while with me."

"Oh, ah think not, Master," drawled Trinia in her best fake darkie accent. "Ahm afeared you all muht not like me so much once yuh got to know me an' all."

"Aint seen many women fer a bit. I thinks you'all do jest fine," sighed the older man as he reached past Mel to grab Trinia.

In a sudden blast of blinding bright blue light that instantly illuminated nearly a hundred foot perimeter, accompanied simultaneously by a piercing crack like the sound of a giant bug zapper magnified about fifty times, the lecherous sentry was unceremoniously lifted off his feet and driven backwards like a rag doll into an disheveled heap near the base of his former rock outpost.

Uriah, his young friend, instantly dove, panic-stricken to the ground, his arms folded protectively over his head.

"What the *Hell* was that!" he squealed in high-pitched terror.

"Oops," quipped Trinia impishly, "Guess I forgot to turn down the power button."

Uriah, still stunned by Trinia's unexpected laser display, sat up rubbing his disbelieving eyes, fearfully staring over at his stupefied companion. "Is—is he dead?" he stammered.

"No, he'll be all right in a little while." Mel was stuck somewhere between holding back his laughter and condemning Trinia for her impulsive reaction. "Lightning, sir, I think—that's what hit him, I believe," he reassured the boy. "He's just a bit stunned by a random bolt, I believe."

Uriah looked up staring dumbfounded at the stars in the clear night sky.

"Melvin! Trinia! How did you two get here?" A loud shout burst from the dusky tree line. A faintly familiar man in a strange blue uniform—one Mel had never seen before-- emerged from the edge of darkness.

"Why Cecil Thayer, I wondered when you and Thelma would show up!" Mel called out promptly recognizing his recent fellow time traveler.

48

FIRENZA AND I rode east for a bit until we met up with a column of sweating soldiers trudging relentlessly north toward the battlefield, their faded blue uniforms covered with a heavy layer of fine, white dust. The men paid little attention to us and did not even offer a salute as we came up and rode alongside their unit.

"What unit is this sergeant?" shouted Marcus Firenza bending down toward one man

"Pennsylvania 155th Volunteers, Sir—what's left of us anyway. There're only about four hundred of us remaining out of a thousand or so in the beginning. We're under Pearson and we're moving to be attached with Chamberlain's Massachusetts somewhere called Little Round Top."

"That's just ahead a few more miles, Sergeant," said Firenza.

"I take it you've been to the fightin' then?"

"It's been touch and go there for a couple days," I added. "But our lines are getting pretty well established along the ridge to the south of town."

"Is the town very large?"

"Not so much. It's called Gettysburg, and it's simply been one of those crossroads towns one might often see in rural Pennsylvania. There are about four or five major roads that meet there. As for now, the Confederates control the town but we hold the heights. If my battle sense isn't about to fail me I believe there will be a large assault tomorrow."

"Ha!" snapped the sergeant. "Wouldn't dare be heavy fightin' without us. We've been in some tough ones, Colonel."

"Good luck then tomorrow, and tell your men to keep their heads down behind the rocks," I shouted as we spurred our horses to a moderate gallop ahead. I was well aware that the forces on Round Top would be spared from the most rigorous assaults on the third day, yet a solid common sense suggestion never hurts either.

The bustle and congestion of the ongoing preparation for conflict became more and more apparent as we moved toward the Northern lines. There was a seemingly endless gorge of creaking supply wagons, drawn mostly by mules, now and then pulled by heavy Clydesdale-like draught horses or grunting oxen, hundreds of orderly detachments of clattering artillery caissons, gruff officers shouting terse commands, and quick-stepping men doggedly advancing like an unwavering army of ants along the clogged byway.

As we came up, movement on the road became less pronounced with more smoky camps developing in the clearings and among the trees, each with its own standards hanging limply on flag poles. Men were in countless postures of relaxation, smoking pipes, preparing breakfast, or relaxing, playing card games or checkers.

"I suspect these men are the reserves that are to be called during the assault tomorrow," I suggested to Firenza. "Likely they made the difference in holding off the attack on the center."

Marcus Firenza nodded agreement and gestured to the ridge slanting upward away from us. "Here is the left flank of the Union Army. It begins at Little Round Top and extends for several miles northward and hooks around at Culp's Hill near Gettysburg."

"The famous fish hook."

"And a perfect defensive position," agreed Marcus. "It's no wonder, with the battlements on the ridge and the protected right flank at Culp's that the Confederate Army was unable to dislodge them."

Our disguises were perfect for our mission. The military status of Colonel for myself and Captain for Firenza kept ourselves low profile enough that we were able to go unimpeded without question among the men in the lines and camps asking about Cheryl and Lydia. Our ranks were high enough that the soldiers we spoke with felt obligated without being intimidated to help us. Unfortunately nearly all of the men had just recently arrived and were of little value in our pursuit. There was one man we finally came across late that afternoon, though, that offered us some hope.

"I saw them both—back before the Rebs got here. They and Lieutenant Mathews and some general who had just come in from Washington met at the Hardwick Inn. It seems both the women somehow left suddenly or were somehow lost, I'm not sure which. Anyway there was a search out for them, but I do not know if they ever turned up."

"That was before the battle, Corporal." I was a bit excited over this unexpected piece of information.

"Yes, yes—it was before the battle ever started," the man confirmed.

I turned and spoke low to Firenza. "That's good news, my friend. At least it seems less likely they weren't involved in any action and that they are probably still in the vicinity."

"There's the distinct possibility," suggested Firenza, "that with her unrivaled time travel abilities, Lydia could have jumped safely out of here to another time with her mother."

"And if that happened, we could arrive back home to both of them sitting in front of the TV watching soap operas." I smiled at that unlikely prospect since I knew Lydia would never leave us in such a position, likely figuring, correctly, everyone possible would be employed searching for her.

"Well, tomorrow is the day of the great assault," I said to Marcus. "If at all possible, I would like to get out of the line of fire before everything starts. We can spend the morning asking a few more people; then we should head for the safety of the rear. There's no sense unnecessarily endangering ourselves."

"Agreed. We're not going to be of much value wounded or even worse."

I suggested to my friend that it might be a good idea to find a place to spend the night in one of the camps around in the vicinity. I asked around among some of the non-commissioned officers.

"I suggest the substantial area set aside adjacent Meade's quarters. Many of the detached officers were being temporarily bivouacked there in tents," offered one man.

"We can't be too fussy," I returned. "Besides, the officers there are a likely trove of information that could help us in our search."

The soldier pointed us in the general direction of General Meade's camp and with a few simple added instructions, sent us on our way. In less than an hour, we had arrived at the bustling scene, once a local farm, that served as a general temporary camp for some newspaper writers, camp followers, and as mentioned previously, a few officers who temporarily were without command. I felt this was a great place to maintain our obscurity as detached officers. In short order without a word of command, a rather spacious tent supplied with two cots, was set up for us.

As evening approached the sounds of battle diminished almost to silence.

"The calm before the storm," I said to Marcus.

Some of the officers in the nearby tents and campfires had emerged around dusk and strolled mindlessly around the encampment complex. As it turned out many of them had already been acquainted from various participation in the long campaigns, but a few others engaged themselves in campfire introductions. Marcus and I figured this to be an opportune time to probe these men of their potential knowledge about the women.

"Colonel Bill Thayer—and this is Captain Mark Firenza," I said as I presented ourselves to a knot of men in front of one of the tents. "We're both from the one hundred tenth Pennsylvania Volunteers recently organized out of Pittsburgh."

"Hey, nice to meet you gentlemen," responded a middle-aged lieutenant. "I suppose you're here like most of us hoping to be reassigned. By the way, my name's Jordan Sensibaugh from Fort Wayne and this is Lieutenant Vince Gordon from Albany." He pulled the young lieutenant to the front where he nervously greeted us with a rather weak handshake. "And this other gruff-looking guy to my left is Captain Randall Nelson. He's from Philly. "Randy, meet Bill and Mark. They're from Pennsylvania too."

"How d'you do?" grunted the captain bowing slightly as he shook our hands.

"So where's your unit, men? Do you plan on entering the fray?" asked Lieutenant Sensibaugh a bit bluntly.

"Our unit's still assembling in Pittsburgh. I believe they were intentioned mainly for the defense of the armament factories out there just in case the Rebs raided, you know. There've been a few Confederate cavalry forays out in Ohio not more than fifty miles away."

"So what brings you and Mark here?" he went on.

"We weren't really expecting this," smiled Firenza. "We were heading to Harrisburg to complete our charter for the unit when we suddenly were kind of swept up in this whole thing."

"And now you're here and couldn't wait to get into the action!"

Marcus nodded sheepishly. "Yeah, that's about it, I suppose."

"Besides," I interjected, "it appears that my family—my wife and daughter--who had been traveling with us, somehow got separated, and we've spent most of the past few days searching for them. By some chance, you haven't heard anything?"

The men gave a few puzzled expressions and quickly admitted they hadn't heard a thing.

"Sorry, man."

"We'll keep a watch for them and ask around."

"Thank you, gentlemen," I said, shaking each of their hands again.

"You might check up at Meade's headquarters." Lieutenant Sensibaugh raised his right eyebrow and winked devilishly with his left eye. "That is if you don't mind being eaten alive by p____d off snapping turtle!"

The other two officers obviously considered this high humor, but for my part, I thought it might be a pretty good idea. Who would know more about the whole battlefield than the commander of the Army of the Potomac?

"Do you think it might not be a good idea to take a walk up there, Marcus?

"I agree, Bill, but it would probably be more advisable to wait for morning rather than attempt to barge in through their security in the dark."

273

"You're right, Marcus, but let's not forget tomorrow is the third day of the battle, and you know what that brings?"

"Yes, of course--the famous Pickett's charge—right here in the center of the line. We don't want to be in the middle of that mess."

"So—right after breakfast then."

That evening, the two weary time travelers sat quietly in deep thought around a small campfire and listened to the clear, mournful camp bugle tones playing taps, a sad reminder of what they knew was to come on the fateful third day at Gettysburg. Despite their dreams, both of them slept soundly that night.

Their deep slumber was rudely interrupted by a nearby blaring trumpet reveille followed immediately by the rhythmic rattle of assembly drums. The day was already getting warm. It seemed everyone was on the move. To the west, the dull thuds of Confederate cannons renewed their barrage. In an instant balls and shells began to whistle overhead, and with resounding snaps and cracks, several treetops were sheared, some falling in slow motion like giant feathers among the scrambling troops. At once the fast pace established in the area was double-timed, and men scattered like fleeing rats.

"Appears the Confederates are aiming a bit high," Marcus shouted as we both took cover behind one of the larger granite boulders scattered through the edge of the woods.

In the next moment, one of the wayward balls found the house on the rise and smashed through one wall.

"That's Meade's headquarters!" screamed a voice nearby.

Another ball screamed in after the other and unceremoniously blew off the rail of Meade's front porch. Another incoming shell erupted in a huge shower of dirt and debris in the pasture near the house.

As I made an effort to take better cover, I had a brief glimpse of dozens of soldiers scattering mindlessly in all directions amid the shrill sound of panicked and wounded horses in the nearby corral when I was suddenly and unceremoniously bowled over by the impact of one of the terrified blue-clad soldiers as his body hurtled over our protective boulder, landing squarely on my back.

49

CHERYL THAYER SPENT considerable time with Lieutenant Hunter Mathews who spent much of his time in fitful sleep in the hours after his surgery. She attempted to utilize as many of her modern nursing skills and knowledge of twenty-first century medicine as she could draw from her memory, but it was evident there was little more she could do than provide some of her clean, sterilized bandages for the benefit of the handsome young man she and her daughter had recently met at Hartsfield's Inn.

"There's not much more you can do for him, Cheryl," whispered Nellie Leith, the head nurse at Spangler's barn. "Captain Taggart, the head surgeon, hopes the young man can even survive at all. Already severe infection has set in. I'm afraid he will be fortunate to make it. You might be better served to work more with the other boys in the infirmary."

"But ... but ... you don't understand. Lieutenant Mathews ... he was with my daughter, Lydia. He might be my only link in finding her and the Professor."

"Well do what you can, Mrs. Thayer," Nellie answered with a troubled expression. She had seen this same condition in hundreds of soldiers in countless field hospitals after seemingly uncountable battles thus far in this terrible war. She knew the odds of survival for the young lieutenant were slim at best, but she had no desire to diminish Cheryl's hope for Mathews.

Cheryl looked sympathetically down at the slumbering soldier.

If only there were some antibiotics. That would likely do the trick she thought. *But that's ridiculous of course. There were no antibiotics during this wretched war.*

Cheryl decided to take Nellie's advice and see what she could do for the other men. She spent the next hour or so drifting around among the makeshift beds and tending to the needs of the patients as best she could, hoping to keep her mind off the needs of her recent acquaintance. Rising slowly from the care of another unconscious figure on a canvas cot, she turned to greet the figure of Nellie Leith accompanied by another older woman—a woman that she knew nut did not instantly comprehend.

"Cheryl!" The woman rushed over and bear-hugged Cheryl. "I kind of thought I might find you or Lydia in one of these hospitals."

"Oh my God, it's you Thelma," said Cheryl with a cracking voice. Tears, whether those of joy or relief, or whatever, streamed unashamedly down the cheeks of both women as they locked in embrace. Nellie Leith did not know why, but her eyes also filled with tears of shared emotion.

"I take it you women know each other?"

In her own rambling way, Cheryl, once alone with her mother-in-law, proceeded in relating to Thelma what had happened since they had arrived in town. Surprisingly, Thelma was able to follow her daughter-in-law's often incoherent story line with great understanding.

"This gentleman—this young lieutenant—you say Lydia has developed some sort of relationship with him? Not too serious I hope?"

"Oh no, she's just sort of met him. Well no, not really, she met him in Chicago in a few years. Oh you don't know ..."

"I understand completely. Don't forget, I've gotten mixed up in a *few* of these situations myself."

"Of course you have, Thelma," agreed Cheryl. "Sometimes it's easy to forget. You know I sometimes get confused when everyone starts throwing all these time travel things around. I sometimes forget what order things go in."

"So then," Thelma broke in before Cheryl started off on another of her renowned verbal journeys, "it appears we know this young man survives, at least until after Lydia sees him in Chicago. Perhaps it might not be too meddlesome on our part with the time-space continuum to make his convalescence a little more comfortable."

"And how could we do that? We don't have the proper medicines and all," sighed Cheryl, looking a bit helpless.

"Just wait here. I'll be back," said Thelma softly.

Cheryl turned to ask her what she had in mind, but when she looked up, Thelma was gone.

"Thelma?"

Almost before Cheryl had finished pronouncing her name, Thelma was standing at the other side of the cot from one of the unconscious men. This time she was accompanied by another woman—one that Cheryl was positive she had met before, but could not quite recall where. The woman wore a large bonnet that partially hid her face and wore period clothes and carried a black leather bag at her side.

Cheryl's blank expression obviously prompted Thelma's response.

"You remember Kaye, don't you, Cheryl? Kaye Spahr—one of those from the rescue team who helped you and the others escape volcanic Pompeii?"

"Yes, of course I do. Sorry, Kate. You know sometimes it's difficult to recognize people in a situation where you would never expect them."

"Hey no problem, Mrs. Thayer. It looks like you've been busy practicing medicine in my absence though."

"Anyway, Kaye has some things that might help Lydia's buddy, Hunter Mathews." Thelma gestured to the black bag.

"My problem," added Kaye Spahr, "is there are so many people I could likely help besides your friend. The situation is—we can't be changing history just because of my engrained healing passions and dedication to the Hippocratic Oath."

"How'd you get here so quickly?" gasped a stunned Cheryl Thayer.

"An instant here translated into several hours in another time. I simply went back to the future where I left my vehicle, drove to a spot John Dodsworth and Cecil had prearranged for a meeting, found Kaye there with all the medical equipment we would need, drove back with her to the parking area near here, and we both materialized, just as we are right now."

"Amazing!" gasped Cheryl. "Sounds complicated, but you did it."

"Could we see the patient then? Let's see what my magic medicine bag can do for him," smiled Kate.

In any other scenario, Kaye and her black bag might have been more obvious, but the few nurses on duty were so wrapped up in their own tasks, no one noticed the added personnel.

When Kaye was led to Hunter Mathews, her expression turned grim. "I think the doctors around here were correct in their prognosis. I doubt this man could possibly survive the night without our help. I'm not certain our help will be enough."

"Stand beside the bed, Cheryl and hide this plastic bag under your shawl and let the lines from it be hidden in the folds of your dress," said Kaye under her breath. "It's intravenous antibiotics and other medicines that should do the job. We can't let anyone around here see our apparatus since it isn't invented for a few decades. You'll have to stand here for an hour or so while the container drains."

"Here," suggested Thelma handing her daughter-in-law a Bible from one of the tables. "Hold this Bible open and pretend to be reading some prayers while you stand here."

"I won't be pretending," said Cheryl taking the Bible and holding it securely against the IV bag under her shawl.

Through the night Thelma and Kaye made checks on the patient and watched the plastic tubing carefully. Cheryl maintained her stoic position holding the IV bag until Kaye signaled it was empty.

"I feel like the Statue of Liberty," Cheryl said proudly.

When Nurse Nellie made her rounds she paused for a moment or two, intensely watching Cheryl. Nodding respectfully to Thelma and looking again at a statuesque Cheryl reading devoutly from the Bible, she whispered, "She's a very dedicated and religious woman. I hope her friend makes it."

Kaye Spahr made herself useful as well. She was able to spend what she described as *real quality time* with a number of the wounded men. In the times she was not with Lieutenant Mathews, she was circulating dutifully among the beds, offering water and solace to those lying there.

"I'm sorry you can't really help those guys as well," said Thelma when Kaye returned.

Kaye couldn't hide her guilty smile that Thelma easily discerned without difficulty.

"So what did you do Kaye?"

"Nothing big, just lightened my medical bag a bit by administering some of the extra Percodan I brought with me. A feel more assured those little pain pills will certainly make the boy's stay here a bit more restful."

Thelma looked slightly apprehensive at Kaye's light-hearted divulgement. "How many *extra* pills did you give out?"

Kaye raised her eyes thoughtfully as though making an actual count. "Hmm, about a hundred or so I'd make a guess."

It was no surprise to the three women the rest of the night that there was very little noise—virtually no wounded man called out in his sleep. It was likely one of the best nights of rest they had had in months. Even in the morning when great rumblings shook the foundations of Spangler's barn like a powerful earthquake, the men still slept blissfully. The nightmarish shrieks of artillery shells passed nearby like screaming airborne devils, followed by crashes and splintering sounds in the woods beyond the closest ridge.

"It's the start of another Confederate bombardment!" shouted Nellie Leith. "Keep your heads down and try to make some more room for more incoming wounded."

50

"Miss Thayer, I'm afraid we can't permit you to wander about the area, once we've come to the realization about your recent acquaintance with some enemy officers, right here in this hotel." Henry Heth looked somewhat apologetic as he spoke to Lydia as she sat at the table where she had just shared a delightful meal with several high-ranking Confederate generals. "It's come to light from Stuart that you and your mother were associating with some of the top Union brass, in particular, one she referred to as the Professor. You understand, it is to our advantage to keep you under guard until the conclusion of this battle, and then we will let you be on your way." Gesturing to a couple of men at the door, Heth called out as he turned away, "Corporal, come up here with a couple of your men and take custody of Miss Thayer."

Lydia smiled. She knew that in a blink of an eye, she could easily vanish right before their astonished faces and instantly reappear in virtually any time she wished. These proud and powerful generals and all their men could never hope to stop her or even comprehend what had happened to the friendly but mysterious vanishing girl. She smiled again. Perhaps they would think she was a ghost, or maybe even some sort of magician or even a witch. Even scarier, they might believe her to be some new secret Union weapon.

One of the men, a burly fellow with a serious look extracted a pair of heavy handcuffs from a knapsack as he approached Lydia.

I think not! thought Lydia. In an instant, she had vanished, and slickly reappeared about a foot to the left of the approaching men. One of them twisted and fell over his own feet, effectively entwining the other's leg in his own. Both ended up in a heap at General Heth's feet.

"What the f____!" shrieked the guard with the cuffs.

"If you don't mind, could you remove your butt from my face?"

Heth turned only to witness the confusion of his personal guard, now squirming on the floor and struggling to regain some sense of dignity.

"But—but, she just … I don't know what she did," gurgled the one guard.

"Get control of yourself gentlemen. I hope you can manage one young girl."

"I'm afraid you have me at a disadvantage, General," Lydia answered sweetly. "So what do you plan on doing with me, sir—throw me in a dungeon and feed me bread and water?"

"Oh no, my dear, nothing of the sort. Southern men are gentlemen. No harm will come to you. All we will expect is for you to accompany a couple of our men--that is, if they can handle you-- to an observation spot along the ridge to the west of town—a place where you can witness the victory of the Army of Northern Virginia over George Meade's great Army of the Potomac tomorrow. After that, we will employ a sufficient number of men to scour the area in search of your mother. If she is alive, we will find her."

"Well that's encouraging."

"Sorry for my directness, dear, but that's the reality of it all. With all these bullets and other armament flying around we often expect fringe casualties. Sometimes they cannot be avoided. After all, both you and your mother chose to be in a place where no woman should ever try to fit in."

"Well General, you have me at your mercy. What could little old me do to hurt your army?"

Lydia, possessing an advantage of undisputable historic knowledge of the battle's future, was fully aware of the shallowness of the general's vision of a Confederate victory on the final day and actually pitied Henry Heth and his misplaced hopes.

"So where are we going, General? I hope you don't plan on using those chains on me." Lydia had already decided to go along with Heth's plan. After all, being behind the Southern lines was as good a place as any to look for her mom.

"Look out on the ridge, Miss Thayer. Do you see that high building—the one with a high tower and cupola?"

"Yes, the Lutheran Seminary."

"That's correct, and I see you're fairly acquainted with the places around here. Perhaps you might be a little more dangerous than we first expected."

"I'm sure you'd never really know just what to expect from me, General," grinned Lydia impishly.

"Corporal, bring our guest along with us, and watch her closely. Forget the irons. Put her in the upper turret of the seminary and keep a guard on her."

"Oh you sound worried, sir. What do you think I'm going to do— just disappear and walk away?"

As the jittery corporal led Lydia away, Henry Heth attempted to light a cigar he had taken from his coat pocket, but, for some unnerving reason, his right hand had begun to tremble uncontrollably. Stuffing the cigar back into his pocket, he stared absently at the ceiling of the dining room.

"There's something strange about that girl—some really odd feeling I can't shake," mumbled Heth.

The upper room in the seminary tower was actually comfortable and afforded Lydia a grand view of most of the area south and east of town and along Cemetery Ridge. About an hour later, Heth had joined her in the white-fenced rooftop cupola.

"Tomorrow, Miss Thayer, I will take command of my corps near Culp's Hill, despite the fact I've been wounded.," Heth stated firmly. "General Lee has decided, that after a few feints on both Union flanks, to concentrate an overwhelming assault, there, on the Union center. When that happens, it will signal the end of the war. The way to Washington will lie open for our army to enter the city and force the Northern capitulation."

If you only knew thought Lydia. *Perhaps a taste of reality might be good for your ego.*

"General, could you help me? I think I dropped something around here," sighed Lydia looking around near the folds of her dress. "It's here somewhere."

"What is it, dear?" Heth bent to retrieve the imaginary object as Lydia bent and tipped her head lightly against the general. In a brief dizzying blur, Henry Heth came up, immediately aware of a dreadful change on the fields before him.

Out over the battlefield, a tremendous struggle was culminating. Union and Confederate forces were in the final brutal phases of what is commonly referred to as "Pickett's Charge." From the distance, Heth could easily see the utter failure of the Southern attack as well as the dreadful carnage on both sides of the line. Confederate soldiers, those who could still walk or even crawl, were streaming wildly back to the sanctuary of their own lines along Seminary Ridge. In the oaks below him, Ewell could see General Lee, mounted on his horse Traveler, his head bowed in defeat.

"My God, what is this? What is happening?" said Heth feeling weak in the knees and dropping to a kneeling position.

Lydia felt a tremendous pang of regret for what she had done, leaned in and bumped his head softly. *That's enough of that, I think.*

When the general finally regained his composure, he looked up, tears rolling down his tanned cheeks. Dusk was beginning to gently overtake the battlefield. There was no battle, no casualties, no retreat, and no General Lee.

"What the Hell just happened?" croaked the general.

With the assistance of his men, Henry Heth shakily made his way down the steps, eager to return to his command and get as far as he could from his recent nightmare.

That night from her observation point in the cupola of the Lutheran Seminary, Lydia thoughtfully observed the myriad of twinkling lights, drum beats, and bugle calls emanating from both lines along Cemetery and Seminary Ridges.

Richard G. Oswald

In the early dawn, the valley between the hills was filled with the fog of smoke and flashes of flame from the commencement of the relentless, thunderous pounding from opposing batteries. From her high perch she could see the various units assembling in the trees behind Confederate lines. From the north, a mounted squad of men clattered along Emmittsburg Road escorting a gray-haired gentleman dressed impeccably as a Southern gentleman. Lydia instantly recognized the man as Robert E. Lee.

The final day of the battle had arrived.

51

FOR A BRIEF period it appeared to Verma Rashid that his and his friend Manning Jones' original plans were completely crumbling. It seemed, first of all, that they were fading further and further from their most likely means of escape from this century. The rock cave near Galilee, the agreed on liaison point with Thelma Thayer, was a frighteningly distant memory for him with each step away from it becoming more petrifying to him. The backup plan Jones had devised seemed to lack any credibility. Jesus, sometimes referred to as the Nazorean or the Galilean, could not be found, a proverbial needle in the haystack. Jones had somehow come to expect the man he called "the magician" would have the ability to return them to their own time. All he had to do was find him and convince him to help them.

If that problem were not enough, some soldiers were now reporting to Jones that a few troublemakers were raising concerns about the validity of Centurion Mandela Regulus, the identity he had once assumed more than twenty years previously near Bethlehem. They were presently circulating harsh rumors of Jones questionable past, and that he had been unceremoniously recalled to Rome under some cloud of mystery. The actual fact was that Manning Jones and Rashid had been captured by Kronos and returned to the twenty-first century. What bothered many of the legionnaires was how Jones had now inexplicably reappeared, seemingly out of nowhere, looking impossibly as young as he had in his previous campaigns.

"Aren't you afraid, Manning? It seems you always remain cool, even in the hottest spots." Rashid's legs were trembling as he sat in their tent at Camp Julio XI about a mile outside Jerusalem.

"Relax, Verma," Jones reassured him. "Things are in motion now. Have faith in me. Rather, have faith in this ..." Jones held his leather coin bag aloft and jingled it.

"But those men—those stories they're telling. Aren't you afraid they're going to come here and arrest us or kill us—or both?"

Manning Jones never verbally answered Verma's concerns. That afternoon, a man named Velonius came to the tent of Mandela Regulus, and after a short meeting with Jones, left with a twisted sneer on his face. The damaging rumors stopped from that day forward. In fact, the two cavalrymen who had been investigating Centurion Regulus were never seen again. It might be added that Jones' purse was two gold pieces lighter.

"I don't know how you did it, Mr. Jones ..."

"*Mandela,* Rashid, don't forget."

"Sorry, sir. So what're your plans to get us back? Are we going back to the cave to meet Mrs. Thayer?"

"Only as a last resort, my good man. I'd rather not deal with that old witch if I can possibly help it. I still hold out hope that the Magician from Galilee will be our ticket home."

"But how, Mr. Jones?"

"The same way as always—money."

Verma Rashid had no idea how Manning Jones planned to implement his escape plan. From what he had seen from the Galilean, he strongly felt the man had little interest in the gold and silver in Jones' leather purse. But Jones plan did not necessarily revolve around paying off Jesus, rather than in using the money to get information on his whereabouts. The message was out on the street that there was a hefty reward to be had for valuable information about him. As a result of the feelers he put out, small snippets of information began to flow back to him, but for the most part were virtually useless. Jones did come to the realization, however, that he was not the only one looking for Jesus.

Many of the local religious leaders from a group called the Sadducees, along with many of the Pharisees, had similar interests.

"Someone in the inside," advised Jones to the dark-robed man with whom he spoke. The man named Talid, one of the upper elite of the Sadducee, was eager to hear of this Roman's plan to possibly overturn the power of the man they had unsuccessfully sought to discredit among the Jews for the last several years.

"All we need is someone who wants to make a little cash—someone in a trusted position," Jones continued.

"What sort of person might that be, Centurion?"

"Easy. Someone who deals with money, who knows the value of it and what it could do for him. Surely this little group of the Galilean that travels all over the countryside has some sort of treasurer or bookkeeper I would guess. Anyone dealing with money often grows to appreciate it."

The Sadducee were noted for cooperating with the Romans in the hope that the future of the region would include mutual leadership roles for members of their sect. This man, Centurion Regulus Mandela, was a strange one He didn't seem at all like most Romans who were basically altruistic, willing to sacrifice, as most soldiers are trained to do, for the good of their empire. This man had definite tendencies toward self enhancement.

"And where might we get this money—a significant amount that might tempt a man in this position. Our people keep tight restraints on monies of this sort."

Jones flipped his coin purse into the air, landing it with a resounding clank on the table between them.

"Silver. Last I counted them there were twenty or thirty coins in there. Would this be a strong consideration for temptation?"

Talid's fingers pulled open the drawstrings and dumped the coins in an impressive, clattering mound before him. Taking one of the coins, he held it in the light, carefully examining the image on it.

"High quality, high quality metal indeed. I can see the refiner took great pain to create purity in this metal, and the images of the Roman on them has a clarity I've never seen. Yes, Centurion, I believe these coins—there are more than enough—to influence most any man."

"And I'm sure any excess coins might find a warm spot in your own purse, Mr. Talid?"

Talid's eyes gleamed a bit at the prospect of the profit he would glean from this transaction as well as to promote his own credit among his sect.

"So, Centurion, what is it you want from me?"

Jones leaned over and stared strongly into Talid's face. "All I want is to have about fifteen minutes or so with this Jesus fellow—all alone mind you. After that, you can take him and interrogate him or whatever you think is necessary.

Talid drew back momentarily, but gazed dreamily back at Jones as he fleetingly mulled the idea over in his mind. "Yes, Centurion, I believe we have a deal."

Manning Jones hadn't expected such a rapid response from Talid, particularly now during some sort of huge religious festival being held in Jerusalem. It seemed everyone and his cousin was visiting relatives in the city. Two days after the meeting, Jones received a scrolled message in some sort of official wax seal, indicating where he would find the Galilean, likely alone. Jones was to meet in the olive gardens on the hill outside the city where he would be provided a guide through the orchards to speak with the man whom he wished to see.

Yes thought Manning Jones *I've saved the last ten gold drevums just for this situation. If Jesus of Nazareth is anything close to what he purports to be, I'm home. And if things go right I might even take my idiot friend Rashid with me.*

The following evening Manning Jones found himself being led by a shadowy figure who bore a tiny lantern lighted by a taper about the size of a birthday cake candle, barely enough light to see the gnarled hand that carried it.

"This way and be quiet. We don't want to alert his followers. I understand they are a rough bunch."

"I wouldn't want that, my good man," hissed Jones as he held loosely to the man's robes.

It was only about five minutes later when the two stopped.

"There, in the garden beyond the wells—there is the one they call the Master," whispered the shadow.

Sure enough, even in the low light, Jones could quite clearly make out the reclining shape of the man he recognized at once from the wedding feast in the town of Canaan. Jones bent low, approaching the man.

"Come on up, Mr. Jones. There's no need to slink like a thief in the night," said the man softly. "You've been wishing to speak with me for a long time."

"Oh, hello there." Jones stood up and proceeded cautiously to the man seated on a stone wall near the well. "Why, I didn't think you even noticed me, Mr. Jesus."

"I certainly have noticed you, Mr. Jones, and I have been expecting you. It seems you've waited until it's almost too late. I am afraid that you have placed yourself in a rather bad position."

"It's never too late, sir. You see I have a deal for you." Jones took out the gold coins from a small metal link purse. "These coins could purchase anything you could imagine, Mr. Jesus, and they're yours."

"Money is of no value to me, Mr. Jones. I am troubled that you make an attempt to tempt me with things of the world. What you wish from me is something to which I have no desire to commit myself since I have much more to dedicate to my flock."

"You're a shepherd?"

"Yes, of a sort. But your problem to which you seek safety must be solved by the person you have grown to hate and thus you must come to grips with that reality. Thelma Thayer, a gracious woman who has been rightly concerned for your dark soul, is the only one who would have helped you, but, for your part, I see you could never meet her expectations. I believe your fortunes are short-lived here in Jerusalem."

Manning Jones felt his blood pressure rising. How could anyone refuse such a generous offer? How could he possibly convince the Magician to help him? In his desperation, he felt he might have one more card to play.

"By the way, Mr. Jesus," grinned Jones trying to maintain his waning composure, "there's something else you should know. There are some people near here who are coming for you. I think they plan on doing you some real harm. Anyway, I can save you. Just say the word. And you know, when someone does something good for someone, they often respond in kind, right?"

"I'm afraid the die is already cast for me, Mr. Jones. I would like to have held out hope for you, but I fear there is little chance for your salvation. It seems everything you do is for yourself, and I believe you are truly an evil messenger of Satan."

Through the olive groves dozens of torches appeared bobbing through the trees in the distance, advancing slowly in their direction.

"This is your last chance. They're coming for you, my man."

Jesus of Nazareth rose quietly and moved down among the trees, seemingly defiant in the face of what was to come. A few minutes later, Jones became acutely aware of the sounds of shouting voices of a nearby scuffle and the torches briefly swung wildly during the ongoing confrontation.

More voices approached only this time closer.

"There, up on the hillside. Arrest that man! He's part of the conspiracy himself. Don't let him escape!" The man Jones knew as Talid stood a few feet from him, a nasty-looking stiletto style knife pointed dangerously close to his throat. "Arrest him. This man is a traitor and an enemy to Caesar."

Before Manning Jones could recover his senses, his arms were tightly locked behind his back by two men who had sprung from the bushes.

"And you won't be needing this Centurion, or whatever or whoever you are …" Talid deftly cut the leather thongs securing Jones' bulging coin purse.

"You can't take that. It's my only ticket home," shrieked Jones as grabbed for the purse.

Another man wielding a heavy club came up and knocked the terrified billionaire senseless.

52

Cecil Thayer had obtained a rather substantial tent about ten feet square pitched about a half mile north on Emmitsburg Road from where he had met Mel Currier and Trinia Williams, not far from the center of the line just about the spot where the planned attack on the Union center was to be launched in the morning. He, along with Trinia and Mel, spent the night in the midst of the busy preparations of the Confederate army. Considerable movement of men and materiel clattered back and forth in the dim light provided by hundreds of flickering kerosene lanterns strung along the split rail fences by the road and at other key points along the rebel encampment. The Southern soldiers were surprisingly upbeat, cheering and singing rousing choruses of *Dixie* and *Eatin' Goober Peas* and appeared unusually eager for the rumored morning assault to develop somewhere here where the troop buildup was presently assembling. A number of officers rode through on horseback, dismounted, and spent time rallying the men's spirits, supporting them of their military capabilities and past superiority demonstrated over the North in past action.

Bugle calls announced the morning awakening of the army although the three time travelers had risen much earlier.

"We had better move up now before the big attack is launched," suggested Cecil as he slipped on his officer's coat. "I doubt we'll be able to travel very well once the action commences and more so during the chaos resulting from the retreat. This could be our only chance to look for our lost people. I've obtained a few horses for us and they're ready to go."

"Finally, a bit of dignity!" smiled Trinia.

Mounting up they had traveled but several hundred yards from their camp, when they noticed James Longstreet huddled with several other men.

"That shorter, gray-haired man with Longstreet is Robert E. Lee," Cecil pronounced to his friends. "If memory serves me correctly, Lee was upset a bit that the attack did not proceed precisely at dawn as he had planned."

"Right," agreed Mel, "wasn't it because one of his generals—Ewell-- if I remember, didn't coordinate well and hesitated when he should have kept up the attack on the northern flank of Cemetery Hill."

"I believe you're correct," Cecil shrugged. "No one knows why he acted that way. It just seems he lost his nerve or something."

As they passed the officer's confab, General Longstreet, with whom Cecil had spoken the previous evening, walked over to him.

"Good morning, sir," James Longstreet called. "Looks like everything's going to get underway. I hope things go better than they did earlier. If this is going to be successful, all the parts have to move together."

"You couldn't talk Lee out of the frontal attack, then?" Cecil was fairly certain Longstreet wouldn't have any luck with that."

"Afraid not. But whatever happens, we're in this together. We all have to commit, even though I'm not too happy about it. I hope I'm wrong."

"Well, good luck then, General," sighed Cecil as we turned and proceeded up the road where soldiers were buzzing around like a nest of stirred up wasps.

"Hey there, man," called Cecil to one of them. "You haven't seen any lost women hereabouts? It seems this isn't going to be a good place for them to be hanging out once this assault begins."

"Hmm, the only woman I've seen is the one General Ewell had a few of us stash up in the tower of that seminary up there. The one you can see on the ridge. Seems he's afraid she's some sort of a spy."

"Her name isn't either Lydia or Cheryl is it?"

"Why I believe that one's name is Lydia. Yes that's her name I'm pretty sure." The man pointed at the seminary's cupola. "If you look real hard, you can see her standing up there in that balcony."

Before he could finish, Mel had slipped a small chrome telescope from its case and extended its focus, carefully scanning the rooftop of the Lutheran Seminary.

"It's Lydia, Cecil. She's up there watching out over the field."

Cecil looked a bit puzzled. "Mel, I can't understand why she hasn't gotten away from them. It would be a simple matter for her to just dematerialize and be gone."

"Maybe she's injured or something," suggested Trinia, taking the telescope from Mel. "Hey, look closer. Lydia has some sort of bandage on her head. Do you think a head injury might incapacitate her powers?"

Cecil took his turn with the telescope. "There's definitely a bandage on her head. You could be right."

"It's up to us to rescue her then," snapped Trinia holding up her fake hoe. "We each have these laser things that look like tools and we know how to use them."

In a single fluid motion like a circus bareback rider, Trinia was mounted on the nearest horse fiercely brandishing her Kronos laser-powered weapon. The two men swung onto their own mounts and the three horses broke into a steady gallop toward the seminary.

The outer door had no guard at all, but when they opened it, one man was there casually whittling on a piece of wood as he relaxed on the stairway that led upwards to the tower. He had little more time than to raise his eyes slightly before he was zapped into a limp heap by Trinia's flashing laser. Another soldier appearing at the top of the stairs with a rifle cradled in his right arm was met with a streaking another blue bolt of light and tumbled softly down the steps with his rifle clattering noisily behind him. Mel and Trinia, keeping low with lasers ready, lithely ascended the steep staircase and appeared at-the-ready on the top landing.

"Well, fancy meeting you guys here," Lydia said drolly as she faced them, her arms at her hips

"Are you okay?" Trinia was on one knee scanning the rooftop.

"Why sure," Lydia answered looking a bit mystified. "Why do you ask?"

"Your head," answered Cecil. "What happened?"

"Nothing much—a little incident near Devil's Den—I'm all right now."

"So what's with being locked up in this crow's nest? Why haven't you escaped?"

Lydia smiled a bit sheepishly. "I could get away any time I wanted, you know. I was just using this tower as a temporary observatory. I can see practically the whole battlefield, and what better place could I have to see if I could find Mom or Professor Hardwick than from this point?"

"Hardwick?"

This was the first time Cecil and the two rescuers had heard this name. In a few minutes, Lydia had updated them on what had occurred since she had arrived in town. Moments later, there was a commotion outside accompanied by the echoes of alarmed voices coming from the lower building as the alarm was sounded by one of the awakening guards.

"Up there! Surrender yourselves. You have no way to escape."

An earsplitting crash sounded followed by the ripping sound of a rifle bullet splintering into a post above the stairwell.

"I suppose this is the time to go," sighed Lydia softly. "Put your heads together with mine please."

There was a sudden rush of brisk spring air and the sharp chirping from the robins whose nest in the peaceful seminary cupola had been suddenly overrun by the four human intruders.

53

THE CONFEDERATE BOMBARDMENT continued unabated through most of the morning. Marcus Firenza and the Union general who had dived into the relative safety of our sanctuary behind a huge granite boulder and a heavy stand of towering oaks had little time to speak with each other, spending most of the time avoiding the constant fragments of splintered wood, rocks and other material emanating from erupting explosions from the Rebel salvos. Now and then a large oak bough crashed from the heights, scattering the men in the woods, but actually appeared to cause little harm to anyone other than for a few minor cuts and bruises. After a period of time, Marcus called out to me.

"Bill, it seems the worst of the impact of the barrage is back here to the rear where we are. A lot of the soldiers are actually moving up closer to the lines where no cannon ball hits appear to be falling."

Firenza was right in his observations. More and more men were finding themselves drawn in the general direction to the relative safety of the forward positions less than a few hundred yards from the Union defenses on the ridge. The barrage was actually doing little harm to the Northern defensive positions along the brow of the hill as well.

"Let's get out of here," I screamed above the continuing explosions around us. "If we stay here, we might be the only ones."

No more words needed said. The three of us jumped up and scrambled ahead, finally coming to a grassy knoll populated by about a hundred refugees like ourselves. There we sat for a while without speaking as the storm of balls raged over us, still crashing into the woods and open pastures to the rear.

"Say, General," I finally said, becoming aware of our friend's uniform, "I never really got the time to properly introduce myself." I decided it might be appropriate to offer a salute and I'm afraid I offered a rather sloppy substitute."

"I'm Carson Hardwick—from the Inspector General's office—presently unattached. I was staying at Meade's headquarters when my sleep was brazenly interrupted," declared the wayward general.

"This gentleman here with me is Captain Marcus Firenza," I gestured toward Marcus. "My name is Captain William Thayer, both of us with the 155th Pennsylvania."

"Thayer—you don't say. I know some people by that name."

I brightened at the prospect that this general had somehow come across our girls some at time during the conflict.

"Their names, by some chance, wouldn't be Cheryl or Lydia would they?"

Hardwick's face had suddenly shown a variety of emotions ranging from surprise, fear, and everything in between. His legs began to tremble, and he dropped to his knees.

"Yes, yes, that's their names," he gurgled. "Lydia—I hope she's all right. She was shot, out there by Devil's Den. Cheryl, her mom—she disappeared right before the battle began."

"Lydia was shot!" My heart was beating so hard I felt faint. "What happened to her? Where is she?"

Hardwick still appeared dazed as he tried to piece together what was happening. "Yes, I think she's all right," he whispered. "She was able to—you know—fade away—to some other time. Do you understand what I mean?"

"I certainly do, General. I am her father. We, and a significant number of people are presently scouring the area for their whereabouts. How do you fit into this situation?"

Carson Hardwick's eyes darted nervously from side to side, as though he expected someone to be eavesdropping on our conversation. "Mr. Thayer, I'm actually a professor of archaeology and history from Metro University in Chicago. Your daughter brought me and your wife to Gettysburg. And now things have gotten complicated. We've all been separated, and I suspect I may never get back to our own time."

"Well Mr.—professor—my concern is more for Cheryl and Lydia. Your getting back to the twenty-first century is of little consequence. That matter is simple to remedy. I need as many details as possible from you in order for us to possibly find the two of them."

Through the din of the mid-morning cannon salvo, which by now, we had grown somewhat accustomed to, the professor explained to us, in as much detail as he could, of what had happened since Lydia had brought them here and of his precarious experiences on the battlefield and how he had come to George Meade's headquarters. It appeared to me, after listening for some time, Hardwick might actually have enjoyed some of his experiences if he were not placed in so much danger as a result.

The sound of the battle had become much more intense and I was now becoming aware that we were now witnessing the famous and ill-fated assault on the Union center. Our position behind the line was still, we felt, one of the safer places to be as long as some stray bullet did not find its way to us. For the three of us, there was a bizarre interest in the scene being played out on the battlefield before our eyes. We had all heard and read of this action, but here, we were witnessing it. Our view was not perfect, mostly consisting of the action from behind the Union positions. We could see the Confederate battle flags waving defiantly through the smoke. We could hear the rattle of gunfire, the high shrill of the Rebel battle cry, and the crashing of Union artillery firing against the assault.

A shrill, desperate command rang out from the lines. "Canister men-switch to canister! Bring up the support from the rear! We could be overrun!"

The Southern battle flags had now reached the base of the stone wall near the copse of trees just down from us, and it did indeed appear the lines would likely be breached by the brave soldiers who had charged so valiantly over a half mile of ground overlooked by the Northern defenses. We were so intrigued with the action that we failed to realize a wave of men like an irresistible tsunami of human bodies had formed behind us and was rushing relentlessly toward the threatened breach. We had no choice. It was either get up and move with the wave, or be trampled to death! I could see the terror in Hardwick's face.

"Not again!" he rasped as he leapt desperately to his feet and began to run desperately with the groundswell.

As a single unit, a moving box, we advanced toward the fighting that had now become life or death for the men on both sides. I had never before witnessed such a display of bloodshed, violence, and brave fighting on both sides, and I never wish to ever be an eyewitness to it again. By the time we reached the scene, the clash was at its climax, with red flags and gray-clad warriors poised and leaping over the battlements into the press of defenders. Firenza, Hardwick and I had somehow stayed together, and I was resolved to do everything possible to keep ourselves safe from the ravages of the action.

"Keep low, Hardwick. Marcus and I have the komodo armor and possess some degree of protection."

The professor needed little encouragement to keep low. His recent experience had trained him well. In a single second, he was flat on the ground, both hands held tightly to his head. In that same instant, a trio of bayonet-wielding Rebs, who had scaled and swarmed the low stone wall screaming like banshees, rushed directly for us. Instinctively, both Firenza and I drew our laser pistols and dropped the three, who settled slowly to the ground at our feet with amazed, peaceful expressions on their faces just as they had reached us.

By the time we had recovered, the skirmish was done. Whichever men had succeeded in gaining the wall, were now either dead or being captured by the blue-clad men who had rushed in to reinforce the crumbling line. Some men still took shots of the retreating Confederates, but, for the most part, the assault was finished, and resounding victory cheers rolled along the Union line.

"Thank God for the komodo armor," laughed Firenza as he stuck his index finger through a hold in his shirt. "I figure I'd be a goner if it hadn't stopped this bullet." He shook a flattened bullet from his shirt as he talked.

Carson Hardwick, still stunned and shaken, sat up. Without any conscious effort, he drew the officer's sword from its chromed scabbard, just as George Meade astride his horse "Old Baldy" accompanied by a squad of personal guards and more reinforcing foot soldiers arrived.

"Hardwick! It's you, you old warhorse I should have known you couldn't keep out of this fight," he shouted clasping him on the shoulder. "You're due for a real citation, you know."

"No, no, General. It was nothing. I did nothing."

"You won't be able to hide now, not with your participation today, leading this reserve unit that likely saved the day."

"But, I didn't …"

"Hush up, Hardwick. I know your type. Can't get enough of this stuff."

George Meade looked out over the battlefield at the enemy army retreating toward Seminary Ridge. "We've been quite fortunate, Carson. Not only this, but our cavalry under Buford and Custer thwarted an attack on our rear—thanks to someone, a woman, who reported Jeb Stuart's advance out on the Hanover Road. Nearly seven thousand of them mind you. I think that's the beginning of our new dominance over the Southern cavalry.

And as for you, I'll get you back into command of a unit as soon as I ca so you can be on the front the rest of the war."

"No, no, General. Remember I don't want any publicity at all."

"You're not going to be able to avoid it now, my good man. Everyone here knows about you. I'll see you later."

"Get me out of here, Thayer," hissed Hardwick. "I don't think I ever want to hear another shot fired in anger again!"

"Don't be too worried, Professor. I think it would be to everyone's benefit if we got you out of this situation as quickly as we can. We'll find our horses and ride back to Dodsworth's camp and we can all meet there and get back to our time. Hopefully we won't have to wait too long to find our girls.

Once again, Hardwick needed little encouragement, and using all the influence he could, got a horse for himself, and along with

Marcus Firenza and me, we rode in a gallop, back to our time travel encampment to the south.

During the night a steady, drenching rain fell on war weary Gettysburg as the army of Robert E. Lee turned back south.

54

NELLIE LEITH WAS right. The previous two day's influx of wounded was light compared to the third day. The first casualties started arriving shortly after ten o'clock as the Confederate bombardment zeroed in on the rear encampments behind the ridge, catching many by surprise. Then the wounded and dying started turning up in larger numbers from Culp's and Cemetery Hill. That's when the orderlies and nurses began making some necessary judgments about many of the patients. Those who could walk or even limp away were removed from the hospital and loaded on ambulance wagons that moved them to secondary facilities that were being set up in towns not far away. There were also those men hurt so badly, in the eyes of the surgeons that they were never going to recover. Those men were set as carefully and respectfully as possible on bedrolls and blankets in shady areas near the woods. The real surge of wounded, though, began significantly as the final assaults on the center began to take place. Then, even some of the more seriously wounded were removed from the barn to make room for the ones with better odds of survival.

The nurses, many local women, all worked diligently among the soldiers, aiding the doctors and comforting as much as possible. Thelma, Cheryl and Kaye did more than their share of the workload. Cheryl's expertise as a modern nurse was invaluable, even though she was limited by lack of medicine and equipment. Kaye Spahr, a proven notable twenty-first century physician and head surgeon at Walter Reed stepped in much to the astonishment of the military doctors and performed surgical techniques they had never dreamt existed.

"Aren't you a bit afraid of interfering with history, Kaye?" whispered Thelma as Kaye proceeded to revive an abandoned young man most thought had already expired.

"My Hippocratic Oath doesn't specify in what time period I'm obligated to help people, does it?" returned Kaye wryly as she administered some modern-day pain capsules to the man she had saved.

"I suppose you're right," relented Thelma with a shrug.

By evening, the flow of injured and dying had become little more than a trickle and a dozen or so of the physically drained women volunteers including Cheryl, Kaye, and Thelma, were on a short break near the farmhouse.

"Ladies!" came a deep voice from a bewhiskered gentleman standing before what Cheryl understood to be some very ancient photography equipment.

"I realize you're all quite exhausted after your exemplary day's work, but, if you are willing, it will only take a few moments of your valuable time for me to immortalize you forever."

None of them were in the mood to resist, and lined up like ducks across the lawn as the man called out, "Don't move please. Any movement could blur the picture."

In a few minutes the man had removed and packed his equipment in his wagon.

"Mathew Brady," murmured Thelma groggily.

"Huh?" Cheryl was looking around, wondering to whom Thelma referred.

"On the wagon—it says *Mathew Brady, Photographer* right on the side."

"Oh yeah? Should I know the man from somewhere?" responded Cheryl.

"Mmm, I guess not," smiled Thelma weakly.

"I'm going to go make my rounds," said Kaye picking up her nearly-empty medical bag. "I think I'm going to check on Lydia's friend Hunter."

One by one the rest of the women dragged themselves up and returned to their duties.

"I feel we've done some good here," sighed Cheryl to her mother-in-law. "Now I only hope we can gather up Lydia and Professor Hardwick and get out of here. I don't know about you, but I can't ever remember being this tired."

"It's a good kind of tired," answered Thelma. "There's a real sense of accomplishment."

There was a sense of emergency on Kaye's face when she emerged from the infirmary. "Hunter's not there. He's not on the cot where we left him. I've looked all around and can't find any signs of him."

"Let's ask Nellie. She seems to have a grasp on what's going on," said Thelma. "I hope he wasn't one of those they gave up on."

Cheryl folded her arms on her chest and shook her head. "I don't think so. Remember Lydia saw him in Chicago after the war. He's around here somewhere. Let's ask."

When Kaye brought Nellie over, they found out Hunter Mathews had indeed been moved.

"Lieutenant Mathews was coming along very nicely around noon when all those injured guys were coming in. It was like a miracle. The doctors didn't hold out much hope for him you know. I think Cheryl's bedside prayers last night must have had a lot to do with it."

"So where'd he go?" snapped Cheryl impatiently.

"Oh, he'll be fine. He was looking strong and asking for Cheryl and someone named Lydia. They took him on one of the ambulances to Philadelphia. They have some of the better facilities there, you know"

Kaye wore an apprehensive look. "But he still needed some work on that arm. He could lose it if the tendons aren't cauterized properly and that has to be done soon before the lesions begin to heal."

Nellie looked a bit confused but was also aware of the fantastic displays of surgeries performed by this mysterious young woman. "Well I doubt that will be possible," she apologized. "He's somewhere between here and Philly. Who knows exactly where?"

All three of the women were depressed over Hunter's inopportune removal, even though they were fairly certain their actions had likely saved his life. In the end, they knew that history was, indeed, not changed at all with Hunter Mathews. The records say he survived serious wounds he had incurred at Gettysburg, but still ended up losing his left arm. Cheryl reminded Kaye and Thelma that Hunter had a missing arm when Lydia had found him.

"I feel bad he didn't find out what happened to Lydia," declared Thelma.

"Well what did happen to her?" Cheryl was starting to be more concerned as she realized no one seemed to have heard of her daughter's whereabouts.

"I'm not real sure, but one thing we can be assured of is she is around here somewhere and she finds her way back home. We know that because she told you she meets Hunter Mathews in the near future."

"But do we ever get back together? That's the question," replied Kaye.

"Ladies, not to worry! You have standing in front of you a veteran time jumper with the capabilities of taking you all back where you belong. I believe this w ill all come together, with John Dodsworth's and my own efforts. I have my SUV parked right over there in the trees."

Kaye and Cheryl both looked bug-eyed at the edge of the woods.

"Not in this time of course. A short trip by car to the other side of the battlefield—less any soldiers or warfare of course—quickly jump back to 1863, pick up my husband Cecil, and back to our own century. Simple."

"What about these people in the hospital? How can we leave them?" asked Cheryl sadly.

"I suppose we've done as much as we should, I suspect. Perhaps a bit more," smiled Kaye Spahr.

"I think it's time we depart before we relent and decide to stay," offered Thelma. "Both of you, over behind the barn. I don't think we want any of these people seeing us *magically* disappear into a mist, I suppose. It wouldn't help their mental disposition either, especially after the shock of the memory of modern technology we left them with."

Within an hour, Thelma had transported her fellow nurses back to 1973 and the deserted Spangler Farm where she picked up the Suburban she had left a short distance away and drove through the town to the spot along Seminary Ridge where she had originally planned to jump back to 1863 to retrieve her husband.

Thelma was a bit surprised to find Cecil already waiting there by the road, at the preassigned meeting spot, but when Lydia, Mel Currier, and Trinia Williams emerged unexpectedly from the tree line, Thelma understood immediately that Cecil had been transported from the past by her missing granddaughter. When Cheryl and Thelma saw Lydia sprinting toward them, they met her about halfway, lifting and nearly crushing her with suffocating bear hugs and kisses.

EPILOGUE

SHORTLY AFTER THELMA, along with Kaye and Cheryl, picked up Cecil, Lydia, Mel, and Trinia, she chauffeured them to the Dodsworth rendezvous point five miles south of Round Top where Marcus Firenza, Carson Hardwick, and I met them. Lydia and Professor Hardwick were reunited for the first time since the accident and their unfortunate separation near Devil's Den.

"Thank God," gasped Hardwick. "I thought I'd never see you again. I'm sorry I asked you to bring me here. Everything got so screwed up!"

"Don't blame yourself, Professor. I have to take full responsibility," apologized Lydia. "I'm the one who should necessarily be in control and no one else could have done this without my powers."

In the end, everyone was brought together. The full Kronos team, delighted that the rescue had been one hundred per cent, successful, headed back for debriefing to the Kronos facility in West Virginia soon after dropping Lydia, Cheryl, and Carson Hardwick at their hotel in Gettysburg. There they packed and returned home via the Turnpike first to the Thayer home in Beaver County, then a few days later, Hardwick was at his Metro University teaching post in Chicago.

Hardwick's *Advanced History of the Civil War* students noticed a significant difference in his attitude toward warfare. His previous bombastic and enthusiastic approach, often bordering on the theatric, intensely glorifying spirited infantry and cavalry attacks changed dramatically. Instead, his new posture took a dramatic turn in the other direction where he turned to condemn, through vivid and realistic descriptions, the evils and horrors of military combat.

"Your descriptions make it sound like you've actually experienced being in a battle," cracked one sarcastic student.

Carson Hardwick never quite responded to the statement, but a few other students noticed during that particular afternoon session that the Professor, after a prolonged and somewhat unnerving trancelike stare, where he secretly recalled his terrible, unnerving experience at Plum Run, a single tear rolled unashamedly down one cheek. Professor Hardwick's class was dismissed early that day.

Later on, the Professor wrote a letter to the board of the archaeology department briefly explaining that the incident at the MU201WP-144 dig in Ohioville concerning subculture SC835 at approximately 17.5 feet had been rectified after a prolonged personal and diligent research visit to the site, that the items thought to have been anachronistically unearthed that threatened to taint the important historic explorations there, were decidedly planted one night as a prank of some sort by a few unknown undergraduate students who had anonymously admitted to their tasteless misdemeanor. Hardwick then recommended to the board that the Western Pennsylvania site reopen without delay and have its invaluable work continue to be led by the brilliant Miss Lydia Thayer with full financial and academic support from the University.

Thelma and Cecil Thayer had once again resumed their reclusive life hidden away in a recent time period in the guise of a happy retired couple theoretically destined to living out the rest of its drab lives in a serene and uneventful existence. Cecil enjoyed the time he had chosen, one of the more glorious times in Pittsburgh sports history where the Steelers and Penguins both experienced considerable success. Cecil, though he agreed to never bet on games of which he already knew the results, became a bit of a local prognosticator, predicting the results of games and even calling some plays such as the Hines Ward flea-flicker in the Seahawk-Steelers Super Bowl and the James Harrison interception against Arizona in Tampa.

Of course being peaceful and uneventful was never the case at all, as Thelma and her husband constantly planned and staged a variety of special trips into various time periods throughout history. One of their first priorities was to return to the Holy Land to complete Thelma's most ambitious project to retrieve and possibly transform the selfish Manning Jones and his friend Verma Rashid.

"Extreme care has to be taken," Thelma reminded her husband. "If my tally serves me correctly, I have visited the ancient Middle East at the time of Jesus Christ about fifty times, a few more or less. You know what that means?"

"Avatars—as Kronos call them."

"Right. I like to refer to them as Shadows."

"Whatever you call them, it's getting extremely dangerous. I think we've visited Golgotha ten times already and have actually, if you recall, come face-to-face within twenty yards of one of your so-called Shadows along Via Dolorosa, Thelma!"

"I was scared to death, Cecil. I've heard stories about time travelers meeting their shadowy counterparts. No one really knows exactly how it happens or how close we need to be. We don't know if we just evaporate or explode or just what occurs, but I don't want to find out!

I keep reminding Lydia of the dangers involved, and how she has to keep a sharp vigilance on her time jumps too."

"It won't be long before it becomes a problem with Kronos jumps if they start getting serious about time travel," Cecil acknowledged to his wife.

"When we go this time, we have to watch," added Thelma. "I actually didn't go to Canaan this time back and Jones and Rashid actually saw one of my Shadows. I know too there was one around in the crowd at the time of the miracle of the loaves and fishes. I kept my distance from where I had jumped previously."

"I remember accompanying you to both of those places. You're right. We have to take more care each time," agreed Cecil.

Thelma and Cecil utilized the same techniques of travel as they had used previously to return to the Romanic Holy Land—air travel in the 70's, less the maximum security employed in more recent times, and then the rental of a decent vehicle, normally a van or SUV, and then jumping back from a pre-selected site. The first stop they made was the cave Thelma had once found as a base of operations along the Sea of Galilee where she had left her wayward friends. It was obvious Jones and Rashid were not there when they arrived. The pack animals, food, and any useful items, particularly the gold and silver coins Thelma had left, were gone as well.

"It shouldn't be that difficult to find them," said Thelma. "It'd be rather challenging to hide someone spending dozens of valuable gold and silver coins in a time like this. I can't imagine Jones lying low and not trying to gain influence for himself."

Cecil, momentarily tossing information back and forth in his head, waited for a bit before offering his theory. "Given the situation, I think Jones would be doing everything he could to get back to the future. He has to do that in one of two ways: either he has to find a place where you could find him easily, assuming he thinks you're coming back for him …"

"Why wouldn't I?"

"Who knows? Maybe he thinks you got killed or even just gave up on him? Anyway, if he thought that, he'd try to find an alternate way of getting back."

"Do you mean another time traveler?"

"That could be, but I doubt he figures there are very many around like yourself available. So, now, without much thought, if you were placed in that situation, where might you turn for help?

"Ha! I'd probably say prayers—or even talk to Jesus directly!" Thelma kidded.

"Exactly," snapped Cecil. "But Jones would likely not be praying. You explained to me that he was duly impressed with the water-to-wine and loaves and fishes miracles, right."

Thelma nodded solemnly. "I see what you're getting at."

"So if we find Jesus, we can likely find Jones and Rashid somewhere near, whether it's because they think Jesus can help them or whether Jones thinks that's where you'll show up."

As previously thought, it was not difficult to pick up Jones' trail. A few villagers and one filthy peddler with missing fingers were only too willing to speak about the strange man with a magnificent bag of gold and silver coins who later turned out to be a ruthless Roman Centurion and who reportedly had several of his own men murdered to protect some mysterious secret about his shady past. Thelma asked numerous of the newly-wealthy individuals they found in Jones' trace about the source of their inexplicable fortunes, only to be answered with vague and sheltered responses.

"I can't seem to find any more of the nouveau rich of the time, unless you'd like to consider someone like Judas Iscariot who came up with twenty pieces of silver …"

"Oh, it couldn't be. It wouldn't be possible, could it?"

The two tried to follow up their theory, but basically ended with a dead end. Then they accidentally discovered another of the newly-rich, a swarthy-looking gentleman named Talid whom they found flashing several silver coins in the marketplace. A few more silver pieces placed in his calloused palm loosened his tongue a bit.

"The man, this Mandela something or other," he continued, greedily eyeing their purse for a possible addition to the windfall money had already procured, "I believe he was arrested—up there in the olive orchards, in the place called Gethsemane." Talid's eyes shifted constantly as he talked. "They said he was a traitor, I believe. He was in some real trouble with the Romans. I heard he was pretending to be a Roman soldier, but apparently he wasn't."

That was about the limit of the information they could obtain from Talid. They weren't sure how much was truth or how much he withheld from us, but from there, no matter how hard they tried, they couldn't find any more information.

At a local inn while indulging in few cups of a rather ordinary local wine, Thelma and Cecil theorized on the fate of the billionaire. Several more cups later, the two joked about stranger and less likelihoods on the whereabouts of Jones and Rashid.

"It just hit me," chuckled a cheery-faced Cecil, "I can just see it in my mind—both of those two societal misfits being taken to the top of the hill outside Jerusalem and being executed—perhaps even crucified like Jesus …"

Thelma slapped her knee with her hand. "It'd serve him right!"

"Oh and what about this idea," grinned Cecil his face lighting up with a new thought. "Just what if—those two were actually the two criminals crucified with Christ!"

Both of them laughed hysterical belly laughs until it hurt.

"I can just see Jones begging Jesus to save him," cracked Thelma.

"And poor Rashid trying to shut him up!" shrieked Cecil in uncontrolled glee.

Another cup of what had now become a rather acceptable vintage for the duo and they happily wove their way a bit unsteadily back to the room they had rented in the inn. By morning, they had made the decision to, at least temporarily, abandon the search for Manning Jones and Verma Rashid and return to their own time-enhanced retirement refuge.

By the time the Thayer's had returned from the First Century the Kronos team had already met for its debriefing at the West Virginia complex. John Dodsworth reviewed his recent Gettysburg rescue plan, the assignments of all the Kronos personnel, and how he had developed the upgraded trailer-sized time transporter in the place of the antiquated and obsolete capsules he had originally created for the first Kronos time transmission.

"The software that runs the whole operation," Dodsworth explained, "is complicated particularly due to the fact that its original creators introduced a special 'smart' program that responded only to one operator. That operator was me. Any new commands or twists actually have to be keyed in using its ingrained advanced identification properties. At this point no one understands how to alter that initiative, which means that if I would disappear, or die, it would be many years before anyone could remedy the problem."

Those facts placed Dodsworth in a position of almost unlimited power at Kronos, and everyone there understood that fact. Fortunately there were many in the organization who had come to trust the eccentric software architect incontrovertibly and supported him one hundred percent even though they knew that Dodsworth would be unable to work without the experience and financial backing it had developed itself.. The other executives felt they had no choice in the matter. It was either accept John's terms or let the program fall apart.

Another matter that limited the progress of the program was the insistence by the Thayer's that Lydia's powers not be tapped without hers, Cheryl's, and my written permission. The original plan by Kronos was to use Thelma's brain transmissions during a laboratory time jump to develop a computer model that was capable of producing the same results. Computers just starting to grasp the potentials needed for that advanced work when Thelma and Cecil decided the Kronos scientists would hold much too much clout to satisfy her own high ethical principles. That's when both she and Cecil "retired", disappearing without a trace. Many felt certain she had somehow died in one of her time excursions. Even after the recent Gettysburg Mission, there were only a few trusted individuals who knew of Thelma's existence and they had sworn to never take it on their own recognizance to reveal that fact.

Lydia remained as active in everything in which she was involved as she could. At first she could not understand why she should not cooperate with Kronos, but she was convinced by Cheryl and me that it would be too everyone's advantage to hold back on this idea. Her extreme interests in history combined by her extraordinary time-jumping travel program greatly enhanced her knowledge of virtually any period of history in which she became interested. Every time she transmitted herself to one era or another she felt she learned something. Her transfer powers had become stronger as she grew older. Thelma recently related to Lydia she had even exceeded the limits of her own exceptionally extensive powers!

One area of Lydia's interest that many people could not understand was her attentiveness to the area of prosthetics. It seemed, for some time, she read everything she could find on the topic and even consulted with our surgeon-friend Kaye Spahr who had significant previous experience in the field herself. It wasn't until Cheryl casually explained to me about Hunter Mathews and his ill-fated accident in the loss of his arm, that I began to understand. Our suspicions were confirmed when several packages from Ace Prosthetic Dynamics began to arrive along with repeated regular visits and mysterious meetings with Kaye Spahr. Lydia never mentioned anything, and neither Cheryl nor I ever inquired, but I am quite positive she was visiting Hunter in 1860's Chicago and fitting him with a state-of-the-art artificial arm.

Originally, before our first experiences with Kronos, the idea of time travel had terrified me. I did it because I felt I had nothing else in life and felt it was the only thing I might contribute to society I was always uncertain, as I traveled through time episodes, as to whether my team and I would ever succeed in our missions, or at times, ever to be able to return to our own time. I considered every step to be a dangerous and unwarranted risk. Now, after five years of association with time jumps, I have come to the realization that these adrenaline-filled adventures have become a part of me. The innovative developments at Kronos such as advanced laser weapons, the ULIT language deciphering equipment and the extremely effective komodo skin armor has come to make our missions more operationally successful. I had once become to be subconsciously jealous of my mother, Thelma, and Lydia in having these powers. Now, with Kronos, I have begun to share, at least, in a minor sense, some of the same energies they possess. As indicated in the most recent of Lydia's briefings from the Gettysburg excursion, she discovered the common existence of male time jumpers even though our family had come to believe the genes from our family's time travel abilities, while passed through generations in both males and females, was only only active in the women. With further research it might be found that the men in our family may have the latent ability that only needs somehow awakened.

Recent adventures have sufficiently whetted my desire for more, and it is my hope there will be many more interesting and adventurous undertakings to come.